The Mermaid Chair

ALSO BY SUE MONK KIDD

The Secret Life of Bees
The Dance of the Dissident Daughter
When the Heart Waits

SUE MONK KIDD

The Mermaid Chair

Doubleday Large Print Home Library Edition

VIKING

VIKING
Published by the Penguin Group
Penguin Group (USA) Inc., 375 Hudson Street, New York, New York 10014, U.S.A.
Penguin Group (Canada), 10 Alcorn Avenue, Toronto, Ontario, Canada M4V 3B2 (a division of Pearson Penguin Canada Inc.)
Penguin Books Ltd, 80 Strand, London WC2R 0RL, England
Penguin Ireland, 25 St. Stephen's Green, Dublin 2, Ireland (a division of Penguin Books Ltd)
Penguin Books Australia Ltd, 250 Camberwell Road, Camberwell, Victoria 3124, Australia (a division of Pearson Australia Group Pty Ltd)
Penguin Books India Pvt Ltd, 11 Community Centre, Panchsheel Park, New Delhi–110 017, India
Penguin Group (NZ), Cnr Airborne and Rosedale Roads, Albany, Auckland 1310, New Zealand (a division of Pearson New Zealand Ltd)
Penguin Books (South Africa) (Pty) Ltd, 24 Sturdee Avenue, Rosebank, Johannesburg 2196, South Africa

Penguin Books Ltd, Registered Offices: 80 Strand, London WC2R 0RL, England

First published in 2005 by Viking Penguin, a member of Penguin Group (USA) Inc.

ISBN 0-7394-5205-3

Printed in the United States of America

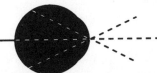

This Large Print Book carries the Seal of Approval of N.A.V.H.

*To Scott Taylor and Kellie Bayuzick Kidd
with much love*

Acknowledgments

It is a privilege to thank those who have made this book possible. I begin with my superb editor, Pamela Dorman. I cannot say enough about the importance of her magnificent editing or her ardent support of me and my work.

I am grateful to my literary agent, Jennifer Rudolph Walsh. A writer could not wish for a more brilliant guide or passionate advocate. My deep thanks also goes to Virginia Barber, a literary agent of extraordinary measure, who has been there for me from the beginning.

I am grateful to all the wonderful people at Viking Penguin: Susan Petersen Kennedy, Clare Ferraro, Kathryn Court, Francesca Belanger, Paul Buckley, Leigh Butler, Rakia Clark, Carolyn Coleburn, Tricia Conley, Maureen Donnelly, John Fagan, Hal Fessenden, Bruce Giffords, Victoria Klose, Judi Powers, Roseanne Serra, Nancy Sheppard, Julie Shiroishi, and Grace Veras. Thank you to the phenomenal sales department: Dick Heffernan, Norman Lidofsky, Mike Brennan, Phil Budnick, Mary Margaret Callahan, Hank Cochrane, Fred Huber, Tim McCall, Patrick Nolan, Don Redpath, Katya Shannon, Glenn Timony, and Trish Weyenberg.

I owe much to the following people for taking time to respond to my questions: Greg Reidinger, for sharing his expertise about boats and for his helpful ideas; Dr. Deborah Milling, for her generosity in assisting me with medical matters in the book; Tim Currie, for helping me grasp the intricacies of hand-tying cast nets; Trenholm Walker, for background on cases of environmental law; Dr. Frank Morris, who kindly provided me with Latin translations.

I cannot imagine having written this book without the loving community of friends who offered me much wisdom and encouragement: Terry Helwig, Susan Hull Walker, Carolyn Rivers, Trisha Sinnott, Curly Clark, Lynne Ravenel, Carol Graf, and Donna Farmer.

I'm grateful to Jim Helwig for friendship and laughter. Thanks to Patti Morrison for always being available with help and good coffee.

I would like to thank my family. My daughter, Ann Kidd Taylor, assisted me with research and also read each chapter as I finished it, offering excellent literary insights and story ideas. There is no doubt that *The Mermaid Chair* is a better novel because of Ann. Scott Taylor, my son-in-law, has been my ingenious computer and Web consultant, a strong promoter of my work who helped me find information about everything from baseball to the true color of shrimp. My son, Bob Kidd, and my daughter-in-law, Kellie Kidd, have cheered me on with avid enthusiasm and support. Roxie Kidd and Ben Taylor both came into my life as I wrote this novel and remind me every day of what really matters. My parents, Leah and Ridley Monk, have been true champions of my work and filled my life with love and goodness.

My deepest love and gratitude go to my husband, Sandy. During the writing of this book, he bestowed on me an abundance of love, humor, perspective, sound advice, patience, and the best of his culinary skills, threatening *only once* to join a support group for Spouses of Writers.

I don't love you as if you were a rose of salt, topaz
or arrow of carnations that propagate fire:
I love you as one loves certain dark things,
secretly, between the shadow and the soul.

—*Pablo Neruda*

Lovers don't finally meet somewhere.
They're in each other all along.

—*Rumi*

The Mermaid Chair

Prologue

In the middle of my marriage, when I was above all Hugh's wife and Dee's mother, one of those unambiguous women with no desire to disturb the universe, I fell in love with a Benedictine monk.

It happened during the winter and spring of 1988, though I'm only now, a year later, ready to speak of it. They say you can bear anything if you can tell a story about it.

My name is Jessie Sullivan. I stand at the bow of a ferry, looking across Bull's Bay toward Egret Island, a tiny barrier island off the coast of South Carolina where I grew up. I see it almost a mile out in the water, a small curve of russet and green. The wind is spiked with the smell of my childhood, and the water is ultramarine blue, shining like taffeta. Looking toward the northwest tip of the island, I can't yet see the spire from the monastery church, but I know it's there, pricking the white afternoon.

I marvel at how good I was before I met him, how I lived molded to the smallest space possible, my days the size of little beads that passed without passion through my fingers. So few people know what they're capable of. At forty-two I'd never done anything that took my own breath away, and I suppose now that was part of the problem—my chronic inability to astonish myself.

I promise you, no one judges me more harshly than I do myself; I caused a brilliant wreckage. Some say I fell from grace; they're being kind. I didn't fall—I dove.

Long ago, when my brother and I used to row his small bateau through the tangle of salt creeks on the island, back when I was still wild and went around with Spanish moss braided into my hair, creating those long and alarming coiffures, my father used to tell me that mermaids lived in the waters around the island. He claimed he'd seen them once from his boat—in the pink hours of the morning when the sun sat like a bobbing raspberry out on the water. The mermaids swam to his boat like dolphins, he said, leaping through the waves and diving.

I believed any and every outlandish thing he said. "Do they sit on rocks and comb their hair?" I asked him. Never mind that we didn't have rocks around the island, just the marsh grass turning with the wheel of the year—green to brown to yellow back to green—the everlasting cycle of the island, the one that also turned inside my body.

"Yes, mermaids sit around on rocks and primp," my father answered. "But their main job is saving humans. That's why they came to my boat—to be there in case I fell over."

In the end the mermaids did not save him. But I wonder if perhaps they saved *me*. I know this much: The mermaids came to me finally, in the pink hours of my life.

They are my consolation. For them I dove with arms outstretched, my life streaming out behind me, a leap against all proprieties and expectations, but a leap that was somehow saving and necessary. How can I ever explain or account for that? I dove, and a pair of invisible arms simply appeared, unstinting arms, like the musculature of grace suddenly revealing itself. They caught me after I hit the water, bearing me not to the surface but to the bottom, and only then pulling me up.

As the ferry approaches the island dock, the air hits me, laden with so many things: the smell of fish, the disturbance of birds, the green breath of palmetto palms, and already I feel the story loom like some strange creature surfacing from the water below. Perhaps I will be finished with it now. Perhaps I will forgive myself, and the story will hold me like a pair of arms for as long as I live.

The captain blows his horn, announcing our arrival, and I think, *Yes, here I am returning, the woman who bore herself to the bottom and back. Who wanted to swim like dolphins, leaping waves and diving. Who wanted only to belong to herself.*

CHAPTER
One

February 17, 1988, I opened my eyes and heard a procession of sounds: first the phone going off on the opposite side of the bed, rousing us at 5:04 a.m. to what could only be a calamity, then rain pummeling the roof of our old Victorian house, sluicing its sneaky way to the basement, and finally small puffs of air coming from Hugh's lower lip, each one perfectly timed, like a metronome.

Twenty years of this puffing. I'd heard it when he wasn't even asleep, when he sat in his leather wing chair after dinner, reading through the column of psychiatric journals rising from the floor, and it would seem like the cadence against which my entire life was set.

The phone rang again, and I lay there, waiting for Hugh to pick up, certain it was one of his patients, probably the paranoid schizophrenic who'd phoned last night convinced the CIA had him cornered in a federal building in downtown Atlanta.

A third ring, and Hugh fumbled for the receiver. "Yes, hello," he said, and his voice came out coarse, a hangover from sleep.

I rolled away from him then and stared across the room at the faint, watery light on the window, remembering that today was Ash Wednesday, feeling the inevitable rush of guilt.

My father had died on Ash Wednesday when I was nine years old, and in a convoluted way, a way that made no sense to anyone but me, it had been at least partially my fault.

There had been a fire on his boat, a fuel-tank explosion, they'd said. Pieces of the boat had washed up weeks later, including a portion of the stern with *Jes-Sea* printed on it. He'd named the boat for me, not for my brother, Mike, or even for my mother, whom he'd adored, but for me, Jessie.

I closed my eyes and saw oily flames and roaring orange light. An article in the Charleston newspaper had referred to the explosion as suspicious, and there had been some kind of investigation, though nothing had ever come of it—things Mike and I'd discovered only because we'd sneaked the clipping from Mother's dresser drawer, a strange, secret place filled with fractured rosaries, discarded saint medals, holy cards, and a small statue of Jesus missing his left arm. She had not imagined we would venture into all that broken-down holiness.

I went into that terrible sanctum almost every day for over a year and read the article obsessively, that one particular line: *"Police speculate that a spark from his pipe may have ignited a leak in the fuel line."*

I'd given him the pipe for Father's Day. Up until then he had never even smoked.

I still could not think of him apart from the word "suspicious," apart from this day, how he'd become ash the very day people everywhere—me, Mike, and my mother—got our foreheads smudged with it at church. Yet another irony in a whole black ensemble of them.

"Yes, of course I remember you," I heard

Hugh say into the phone, yanking me back to the call, the bleary morning. He said, "Yes, we're all fine here. And how are things there?"

This didn't sound like a patient. And it wasn't our daughter, Dee, I was sure of that. I could tell by the formality in his voice. I wondered if it was one of Hugh's colleagues. Or a resident at the hospital. They called sometimes to consult about a case, though generally *not* at five in the morning.

I slipped out from the covers and moved with bare feet to the window across the room, wanting to see how likely it was that rain would flood the basement again and wash out the pilot light on the hot-water heater. I stared out at the cold, granular deluge, the bluish fog, the street already swollen with water, and I shivered, wishing the house were easier to warm.

I'd nearly driven Hugh crazy to buy this big, impractical house, and even though we'd been in it seven years now, I still refused to criticize it. I loved the sixteen-foot ceilings and stained-glass transoms. And the turret—God, I loved the turret. How many houses had one of those? You had to climb the spiral stairs inside it to get to my art studio, a transformed third-floor attic space with a sharply slanted ceiling and a skylight—so remote and enchanting that Dee had dubbed it the "Rapunzel tower." She was always teasing me about it. "Hey, Mom, when are you gonna let your hair down?"

That was Dee being playful, being Dee, but we both knew what she meant—that I'd become too stuffy and self-protected. Too conventional. This past Christmas, while she was home, I'd posted a Gary Larson cartoon on the refrigerator with a magnet that proclaimed me WORLD'S GREATEST MOM. In it, two cows stood in their idyllic pasture. One announced to the other, "I don't care what they say, I'm not content." I'd meant it as a little joke, for Dee.

I remembered now how Hugh had laughed at it. Hugh, who read people as if they were human Rorschachs, yet he'd seen nothing suggestive in it. It was Dee who'd stood before it an inordinate amount of time, then given me a funny look. She hadn't laughed at all.

To be honest, I *had* been restless. It had started back in the fall—this feeling of time passing, of being postponed, pent up, not wanting to go up to my studio. The sensation would rise suddenly like freight from the ocean floor—the unexpected discontent of cows in their pasture. The constant chewing of all that cud.

With winter the feeling had deepened. I would see a neighbor running along the sidewalk in front of the house, training, I imagined, for a climb up Kilimanjaro. Or a friend at my book club giving a blow-by-blow of her bungee jump from a bridge in Australia. Or—and this was the worst of all—a TV show about some intrepid woman traveling alone in the blueness of Greece, and I'd be overcome by the little river of sparks that seemed to run beneath all that, the blood/sap/wine, aliveness, whatever it was. It had made me feel bereft over the immensity of the world, the extraordinary things people did with their lives—though, really, I didn't want to do any of those particular things. I didn't know then what I wanted, but the ache for it was palpable.

I felt it that morning standing beside the window, the quick, furtive way it insinuated itself, and I had no idea what to say to myself about it. Hugh seemed to think my little collapse of spirit, or whatever it was I was having, was about Dee's being away at college, the clichéd empty nest and all that.

Last fall, after we'd gotten her settled at Vanderbilt, Hugh and I'd rushed home so he could play in the Waverly Harris Cancer Classic, a tennis tournament he'd been worked up about all summer. He'd gone out in the Georgia heat for three months and practiced twice a week with a fancy Prince graphite racket. Then I'd ended up crying all the way home from Nashville. I kept picturing Dee standing in front of her dorm waving good-bye as we pulled away. She touched her eye, her chest, then pointed at us—a thing she'd done since she was a little girl. Eye. Heart. You. It did me in. When we got home, despite my protests, Hugh called his doubles partner, Scott, to take his place in the tournament, and stayed home and watched a movie with me. *An Officer and a Gentleman*. He pretended very hard to like it.

The deep sadness I felt in the car that day had lingered for a couple of weeks, but it had finally lifted. I *did* miss Dee—of course I did—but I couldn't believe that was the real heart of the matter.

Lately Hugh had pushed me to see Dr. Ilg,

one of the psychiatrists in his practice. I'd refused on the grounds that she had a parrot in her office.

I knew that would drive him crazy. This wasn't the real reason, of course—I have nothing against people's having parrots, except that they keep them in little cages. But I used it as a way of letting him know I wasn't taking the suggestion seriously. It was one of the rare times I didn't acquiesce to him.

"So she's got a parrot, so what?" he'd said. "You'd like her." Probably I would, but I couldn't quite bring myself to go that far—all that paddling around in the alphabet soup of one's childhood, scooping up letters, hoping to arrange them into enlightening sentences that would explain why things had turned out the way they had. It evoked a certain mutiny in me.

I did occasionally, though, play out imaginary sessions with Dr. Ilg in my head. I would tell her about my father, and, grunting, she would write it down on a little pad—which is all she ever seemed to do. I pictured her bird as a dazzling white cockatoo perched on the back of her chair, belting out all sorts of flagrant opinions, repeating itself like a Greek chorus: "You blame yourself, you blame your-self, you blame yourself."

Not long ago—I don't know what pos-sessed me to do it—I'd told Hugh about these make-believe sessions with Dr. Ilg, even about the bird, and he'd smiled. "Maybe you should just see the bird," he said. "Your Dr. Ilg sounds like an idiot."

Now, across the room, Hugh was listening to the person on the phone, muttering, "Uh-huh, uh-huh." His face had clamped down into what Dee called "the Big Frown," that pinched expression of grave and intense lis-tening in which you could almost see the various pistons in his brain—Freud, Jung, Adler, Horney, Winnicott—bobbing up and down.

Wind lapped over the roof, and I heard the house begin to sing—as it routinely did—with an operatic voice that was very Beverly "Shrill," as we liked to say. There were also doors that refused to close, ancient toilets that would suddenly decline to flush ("The toilets have gone anal-retentive again!" Dee would shout), and I had to keep constant vigilance to prevent Hugh from exterminat-ing the flying squirrels that lived in the fireplace in his study. If we ever got a divorce, he loved to joke, it would be about squirrels.

But I loved all of this; I truly did. It was only the basement floods and the winter drafts that I hated. And now, with Dee in her first year at Vanderbilt, the emptiness—I hated that.

Hugh was hunched on his side of the bed, his elbows balanced on his knees and the top two knobs of his spine visible through his pajamas. He said, "You realize this is a serious situation, don't you? She needs to see someone—I mean, an actual psychiatrist."

I felt sure then it was a resident at the hospital, though it did seem Hugh was talking down to him, and that was not like Hugh.

Through the window the neighborhood looked drowned, as if the houses—some as big as arks—might lift off their foundations and float down the street. I hated the thought of slogging out into this mess, but of course I would. I would drive to Sacred Heart of Mary over on Peachtree and get my forehead swiped with ashes. When Dee was small, she'd mistakenly called the church the "*Scared* Heart of Mary." The two of us still referred to it that way sometimes, and it occurred to me now how apt the name really was. I mean, if Mary was still around, like so many people thought, including my insatiably Catholic mother, maybe her heart *was* scared. Maybe it was because she was on such a high and impossible pedestal—Consummate Mother, Good Wife, All-Around Paragon of Perfect Womanhood. She was probably up there peering over the side, wishing for a ladder, a parachute, something to get her down from there.

I hadn't missed going to church on Ash Wednesday since my father had died—not once. Not even when Dee was a baby and I had to take her with me, stuffing her into a thick papoose of blankets, armored with pacifiers and bottles of pumped breast milk. I wondered why I'd kept subjecting myself to it—year after year at the Scared Heart of Mary. The priest with his dreary incantation: "Remember you are dust, to dust you shall return." The blotch of ash on my forehead.

I only knew I had carried my father this way my whole life.

Hugh was standing now. He said, "Do you want me to tell her?" He looked at me, and I felt the gathering of dread. I imagined a bright wave of water coming down the street, rounding the corner where old Mrs. Vandiver had erected a gazebo too close to her driveway; the wave, not mountainous like a tsunami but a shimmering hillside sweeping toward me, carrying off the ridiculous gazebo, mailboxes, doghouses, utility poles, azalea bushes. A clean, ruinous sweep.

"It's for you," Hugh said. I didn't move at first, and he called my name. "*Jessie*. The call—it's for you."

He held the receiver out to me, sitting there with his thick hair sticking up on the back of his head like a child's, looking grave and uneasy, and the window copious with water, a trillion pewter droplets coming down on the roof.

CHAPTER
Two

I reached for the robe draped on the bed-post. Pulling it around my shoulders, I took the phone while Hugh stood there, hovering, unsure whether to leave. I covered the mouthpiece. "No one died, did they?"

He shook his head.

"Go get dressed. Or go back to bed," I told him.

"No, wait—" he said, but I was already saying hello into the phone, and he turned then and walked into the bathroom.

"You poor thing, I've gotten you up at day-break," a woman's voice said. "But so you know, it wasn't deliberate. I've been up so long, I simply forgot how early it is."

"I'm sorry," I said. "Who is this?"

"Lord, I'm such a blooming optimist, I thought you'd recognize me. It's Kat. Egret Island Kat. Your godmother Kat. The Kat who changed your damn diapers."

My eyes closed automatically. She'd been my mother's best friend since forever—a petite woman in her sixties who wore folded-down, lace-trimmed socks with her high heels, suggesting a dainty, eccentric old lady whose formidability had thinned along with her bones. It was a great and dangerous deception.

I lowered myself to the bed, knowing there was only one reason she would call. It would have to do with my mother, the famously crazy Nelle Dubois, and judging from Hugh's reaction, it would not be good.

Mother lived on Egret Island, where once we'd all been a family—I would say an "ordinary" family, except we'd lived next door to a Benedictine monastery. You cannot have thirty or forty monks for next-door neighbors and claim it's ordinary.

The debris from my father's exploded boat had washed up onto their property. Several monks had brought the board with *Jes-Sea* on it and presented it to Mother like a military flag. She'd quietly made a fire in the fireplace, then called Kat and Hepzibah, the other member of their trinity. They'd come and stood there along with the monks, while Mother had ceremoniously tossed the board onto the flames. I'd watched as the letters blackened, as the board was consumed. I remembered it sometimes when I woke in the night, had even thought about it in the middle of my wedding ceremony. There had been no funeral, no memorial, only that moment to call back.

It was after that that Mother began going over to cook the monks' midday meal, something she'd now done for the last thirty-three years. She was more or less obsessed with them.

"I do believe our little island could sink into the sea, and it wouldn't faze you," Kat said. "What's it been? Five years, six months, and one week since you set foot here?"

"That sounds right," I said. My last visit, on the occasion of my mother's seventieth birthday, had been a disaster of biblical proportions.

I'd taken Dee, who was twelve, and we'd

presented Mother with a pair of gorgeous red silk pajamas from Saks, very Oriental, with a Chinese dragon embroidered on the top. She'd refused to accept them. And for the dumbest reason. It was because of the dragon, which she referred to alternately as "a beast," "a demon," and "a figure of moral turpitude." St. Margaret of Antioch had been swallowed by Satan in the shape of a dragon, she said. Did I really expect her to sleep in such a thing?

When she got like that, no one could reason with her. She'd hurled the pajamas into the trash can, and I'd packed our bags.

The last time I'd seen my mother, she was standing on the porch, shouting, "If you leave, don't come back!" And Dee, poor Dee, who only wanted a seminormal grandmother, crying.

Kat had driven us to the ferry that day in her golf cart—the one she drove maniacally around the island's dirt roads. She'd blown the air horn on it incessantly during the ride to distract Dee from crying.

Now, on the other end of the phone, Kat went on playfully scolding me about my absence from the island, an absence I'd come to love and protect.

I heard the shower in the bathroom come on. Heard it over the rain driving hard against the windows.

"How's Benne?" I asked. I was stalling, trying to ignore the feeling that something was perched over my head, about to fall.

"Fine," Kat said. "Still translating Max's every thought."

In spite of my growing anxiety, I laughed. Kat's daughter, who had to be forty by now, had been "not quite right" since birth, as Kat put it. The correct expression was "mentally challenged," but Benne was also peculiarly gifted, given to premonitions of uncanny exactitude. She simply knew things, extracting them out of the air through mysterious antennae the rest of us didn't possess. She was said to be particularly adept at deciphering the thoughts of Max, the island dog who belonged to no one and everyone.

"So what's Max saying these days?"

"The usual things—'My ears need scratching. My balls need licking. Why do you assume I want to fetch your idiotic stick?' "

I pictured Kat in her house perched high on stilts as all the island houses were. It was the color of lemons. I could see her sitting at the long oak table in the kitchen where over the years she, Hepzibah, and my mother had cracked and picked ten thousand blue crabs. "The Three Egreteers," my father had called them.

"Look, I called about your mother." She cleared her throat. "You need to come home and see about her, Jessie. No excuses."

I lay back on the bed; I felt like a tent collapsing, the center pole yanked out, followed by the billowy floating.

"My excuse," I said, "is that she doesn't want me there. She's—"

"*Impossible.* I know. But you can't pretend you don't have a mother."

I almost laughed. I could no more pretend I didn't have a mother than the sea could pretend it had no salt. My mother existed for me with a vengeance. Sometimes her voice would come piping through my bones and practically lift me off my feet.

I said, "I invited Mother here this past Christmas. Did she come? Of course she didn't. I send her things for her birthday, for Mother's Day—things without dragons on them, I hasten to say—and I never hear a word back."

I was glad Hugh was still in the shower so he couldn't hear. I was sure I'd just shouted.

"She doesn't need your gifts and your phone calls—she needs you."

Me.

Why did it always come to this, to *me,* to the daughter? Why didn't she call Mike out in California and harangue him? The last time I'd spoken to him, he said he'd become a Buddhist. Surely as a Buddhist he would have more patience for her.

Silence fell between us. I heard the shower go off, the pipes bang.

"Jessie," she said. "The reason I called . . . Yesterday your mother cut off her finger with a meat cleaver. Her right index finger."

Bad news registers belatedly with me; the words come, but not the meaning. They hover in the corner of the room for a while, up near the ceiling, while my body makes the necessary preparation. I said, "Is she okay?"

"She's going to be fine, but they had to operate on her hand at the hospital over in Mount Pleasant. Of course she pitched one of her famous fits and refused to spend the night there, so I brought her home with me last night. Right now she's in Benne's bed, sleeping off the painkillers, but the minute she wakes up, she's gonna want to go home."

Hugh opened the bathroom door, and a

gust of steam surged into the bedroom. "You okay?" he mouthed, and I nodded. He closed the door, and I heard him tap his razor on the sink. Three times like always.

"The thing is—" Kat stopped and took a breath. "Look, I'm just going to say it straight out. It wasn't an accident. Your mother went over to the monastery kitchen and cut off her finger. On purpose."

It hit me then—the full weight, the gruesomeness. I realized that part of me had been waiting for her to go and do something crazy for years. But not this.

"But why? Why would she do that?" I felt the beginnings of nausea.

"It's complicated, I guess, but the doctor who operated on her said it might be related to sleep deprivation. Nelle hadn't slept much for days, maybe weeks."

My abdomen contracted violently, and I dropped the phone onto the bed, rushing past Hugh, who was standing at the sink with a towel around his waist. Sweat ran down my ribs, and, throwing off the robe, I leaned over the toilet. After I emptied myself of what little there was to throw up, I went on retching plain air.

Hugh handed me a cold washcloth. "I'm sorry," he said. "I wanted to tell you myself, but she insisted on doing it. I shouldn't have let her."

I pointed through the doorway to the bed. "I need a moment, that's all. I left her on the phone."

He went over and picked up the receiver while I dabbed the cloth to the back of my neck. I sank onto the cane-bottomed chair in the bedroom, waiting for the cascading in my abdomen to stop.

"It's a hard thing for her to take in," I heard him say.

Mother had always been what you'd call fervent, making me and Mike drop pennies into empty milk jars for "pagan babies" and every Friday lighting the Sacred Heart of Jesus candles in the tall glasses and going to her knees on the floor in her bedroom, where she said all five decades of the rosary, kissing the crucifix on which Jesus had been rubbed down to a stick man from all the devotion. But people did that. It didn't mean they were crazy.

It was after the boat fire that Mother had turned into Joan of Arc—but without an army or a war, just the queer religious compulsions. Even then, though, I'd thought of her as normal-crazy, just a couple of degrees beyond fervent. When she wore so many saints' medals pinned to her bra that she clinked, when she started cooking at the monastery, behaving as if she owned the place, I'd told myself she was just an overextended Catholic obsessed with her salvation.

I walked over and held out my hand for the phone, and Hugh gave it to me. "This is hardly a bad case of insomnia," I said to Kat, interrupting whatever she'd been saying to Hugh. "She has finally gone insane."

"Don't you ever say that again!" Kat snapped. "Your mother is *not* insane. She's tormented. There's a difference. Vincent van Gogh cut off his ear—do you think *he* was insane?"

"Yes, as a matter of fact, I do."

"Well, a lot of very informed people think he was *tormented,*" she said.

Hugh was still standing there. I waved him away, unable to concentrate with him hovering over me like that. Shaking his head, he wandered into the walk-in closet across the room.

"And what is Mother tormented about?" I

demanded. "Please don't tell me it's my father's death. That was thirty-three years ago."

I'd always felt that Kat harbored some knowledge about Mother that was off-limits to me, a wall with a concealed room behind it. Kat didn't answer immediately, and I wondered if this time she might really tell me.

"You're looking for a reason," she said. "And that doesn't help. It doesn't change the present."

I sighed at the same moment Hugh stepped out of the closet wearing a long-sleeved blue oxford shirt buttoned all the way to his neck, a pair of white boxer shorts, and navy socks. He stood there fastening his watch onto his wrist, making the sound—the puffing sound with his mouth.

The scene felt almost circadian to me—methodical, daily, abiding—one I'd witnessed a thousand times without a trace of insurrection, yet now, in this most unlikely moment, just as this crisis with Mother had been dropped into my lap like a wailing infant, I felt the familiar discontent that had been growing in me all winter. It rose with such force it felt as if someone had physically struck me.

"So," Kat said. "Are you coming or not?"

"Yes, I'm coming. Of course I'm coming."

As I said the words, I was filled with relief. Not that I would be going home to Egret Island and dealing with this grotesque situation—there was no relief in that, only a great amount of trepidation. No, this remarkable sense of relief was coming, I realized, from the fact I would be going away *period.*

I sat on the bed holding the phone, surprised at myself, and ashamed. Because as awful as this situation with Mother was, I was almost glad for it. It was affording me something I hadn't known until this moment that I desperately wanted: a reason to leave. A good, proper, even noble reason to leave my beautiful pasture.

CHAPTER
Three

When I came downstairs, Hugh was making breakfast. I heard the hiss of Jimmy Dean sausage before I got to the kitchen.

"I'm not hungry," I told him.

"But you need to eat," he said. "You're not going to throw up again. Trust me."

Whenever a crisis of any kind appeared, Hugh made these great big breakfasts. He seemed to believe in their power to revive us.

Before coming downstairs, he'd booked me a one-way ticket to Charleston and arranged to cancel his early-afternoon patients so he could drive me to the airport.

I sat down at the breakfast bar, pushing

certain images out of my head: the meat cleaver, my mother's finger.

The refrigerator opened with a soft sucking noise, then closed. I watched Hugh crack four eggs. He stood at the stove with a spatula and shuffled them around in a pan. A row of damp brown curls skimmed the top of his collar. I started to say something about his needing a haircut, that he looked like an aging hippie, but I checked myself, or rather the impulse simply died on my tongue.

Instead I found myself staring at him. People were always staring at Hugh—in restaurants, theater lines, bookstore aisles. I would catch them stealing glimpses, mostly women. His hair and eyes had that rich autumn coloring that reminds you of cornucopias and Indian corn, and he had a beautiful cleft in the center of his chin.

Once I'd teased him that when we walked into a room together, no one noticed me because he was so much prettier, and he'd felt compelled to tell me that I was beautiful. But the truth was, I couldn't hold a candle to Hugh. Lately the skin on either side of my eyes had become etched with a fine weave of crisscrossing lines, and I sometimes found myself at the mirror pulling my temples back with my fingers. My hair had been an incredible nutmeg color for as long as I could remember, but it was twined now with a few strands of gray. For the first time, I could feel a hand at the small of my back nudging me toward the mysterious dwelling place of menopausal women. Already my friend Rae had disappeared in there, and she was just forty-five.

Hugh's aging seemed more benign, his handsomeness turning ripe, but it wasn't that so much as the combination of intelligence and kindness in his face that drew people. It had captured me back in the beginning.

I leaned forward onto the bar, the speckled granite cold on the bones of my elbows, remembering how we'd met, *needing* to remember how it once was. How *we* were.

He had showed up at my first so-called art exhibit, which had taken place in a ratty booth I'd rented at the Decatur Flea Market. I'd just graduated from Agnes Scott with a degree in art and inflated ideas about selling my work, becoming a bona fide artist. No one, however, had really looked at my art boxes all day, except for a woman who kept referring to them as "shadowboxes."

Hugh, in the second year of his psychiatric residency at Emory, came to the flea market that day for vegetables. As he wandered by my booth, his eyes lit on my "Kissing Geese" box. It was an odd creation, but in a way it was my favorite.

I'd painted the inside with a Victorian living-room scene—English rose wallpaper and fringed floor lamps—then placed a velvet dollhouse sofa in the box with two plastic geese glued onto the cushions, positioned so they appeared to be in the midst of a beak-to-beak kiss.

I'd been inspired by a newspaper story about a wild goose that had dropped out of the flock during migration to stay with his mate, who'd been injured in a mall parking lot. A store clerk had taken the hurt bird to a refuge, but her mate had wandered around the parking lot for over a week, honking forlornly, until the clerk took him to the refuge, too. The article said they'd been given a "room" together.

The news clipping was decoupaged around the outside of the box, and I'd attached a bicycle horn to the top, the kind with the red ball that sounds like a honking goose. Only about half the people who'd seen the box had actually squeezed the horn. I'd imagined that this said something about them. That they were more playful than the average person, less reserved.

Hugh bent over the box and read the article while I waited to see what he would do. He honked the horn twice.

"How much do you want for it?" he asked.

I paused, working up the courage to say twenty-five dollars.

"Would forty be enough?" he said, reaching for his wallet.

I hesitated again, bowled over that anyone would pay that much for kissing geese.

"Fifty?" he said.

I kept my face straight. "Okay, fifty."

We went out that same night. Four months later we were married. For years he kept the "Kissing Geese" box on his dresser, then moved it to a bookshelf in his study. A couple of years ago, I found him at his desk meticulously regluing all the pieces.

He confessed once that he paid all that money just to get me to go out with him, but the truth was, he loved the box, and his honking the horn really *had* said something about him, hinting at a side of Hugh few people saw. They always thought about his prodigious intellect, the ability he had to dissect and anatomize, but he loved to have fun and often instigated the most unexpected things: *We could go out and celebrate Mexican Independence Day, or would you prefer to go to the Mattress Races?* We'd spent a Saturday afternoon at a contest in which people attached wheels onto beds and raced through downtown Atlanta.

People also rarely noticed how deeply and thoroughly he felt things. He still cried whenever a patient took his own life, and he grew sad at times over the dark, excruciating corners people backed themselves into.

Last fall, while putting away the laundry, I came upon Hugh's jewelry case in the back of his underwear drawer. Maybe I shouldn't have, but I sat on the bed and went through it. It held all of Dee's baby teeth, tiny and yellowed like popcorn kernels, and several drawings she'd done on his prescription pad. There was his father's Pearl Harbor pin, his grandfather's pocketwatch, the four pairs of cuff links I'd bought him for various anniversaries. I slipped the rubber band off a small bundle of papers and found a creased photograph of me on our honeymoon in the Blue Ridge Mountains, posing in front of the cabin we'd rented. The rest were cards and little love notes I'd sent him over the years. He'd kept them all.

He was the first one of us to say I love you. Two weeks after we met, before we'd even made love. We were in a diner near the Emory campus, eating breakfast in a booth by the window. He said, "I hardly know anything about you, but I love you," and from that moment his commitment had been unyielding. Even now he rarely went a day without telling me.

In the beginning I'd felt so hungry for him, a ravenous kind of wanting that remained until Dee was born. Only then did it start to subside and grow domesticated. Like animals taken from the wild and put in nice, simulated habitats where they turned complacent, knowing exactly where their next meal would come from. All the hunt and surprise drained out of it.

Hugh set the plate of eggs and sausage in front of me. "There you go," he said.

We ate, side by side, the windows still varnished with early-morning dark. Rain rattled down the gutters, and I heard what sounded like a shutter banging in the distance.

I put down my fork and listened.

"On the island when the storms came, our

hurricane shutters used to slam against the house like that," I said, and my eyes began to fill.

Hugh stopped chewing and looked at me.

"Mother would drape a sheet over the kitchen table and crawl under it with me and Mike and read to us by flashlight. She nailed a crucifix to the underside of the table, and we would lie on the floor and stare up at it while she read. We called it the 'storm tent.' We thought nothing could harm us under there."

Hugh reached out his arm, and my shoulder slipped into the groove beneath his collarbone while my head glided into the nape of his neck, an oiled, automatic movement as old as our marriage.

We sat like that, pressed into each other, while the eggs went cold and the odd banging came and went, until I began to feel the ponderous meshing of our lives—unable to tell where his shoulder ended and my head began. It was the same sensation I'd had as a child when my father pressed the length of his finger against mine. As they rubbed together, they'd felt like a single digit.

I pulled away, straightening myself on the bar chair. "I can't believe what she's done," I said. "My God, Hugh, do you think she needs to be committed?"

"I couldn't say without talking to her. It sounds like an obsessional disorder."

I saw Hugh look down at my lap. I'd twisted the napkin around my finger as if I were trying to stop a hemorrhage. I unwound it, embarrassed at how talkative my body was when I didn't mean for it to be.

"Why her *finger?*" I said. "Of all things."

"There's not necessarily any rhyme or reason to it. That's the thing about obsessions—they're generally irrational." He stood up. "Look, why don't I come with you? I'll clear my calendar. We'll both go."

"No," I said. A little too emphatically. "She'll never talk to you about this, you know that. And you have all your patients here to take care of."

"Okay, but I don't want you handling this by yourself." He kissed me on the forehead. "Call Dee. Let her know where you'll be."

After he'd left for the office, I packed a suitcase, set it by the door, then climbed the stairs to my studio, wanting to make sure the roof hadn't leaked again.

I switched on a lamp, and a swatch of waxy yellow light fanned across my worktable—a big oak treasure I'd found in a secondhand store. A partially assembled art box was spread across it, covered in dust. I'd stopped working on it last December when Dee was home for Christmas break, and somehow I'd never gotten back up here.

I was inspecting the floor for puddles when the phone rang. Picking up the portable, I heard Dee's voice. "Guess what?" she said.

"What?"

"Dad sent me extra money, and I bought a navy pea coat."

I imagined her sitting cross-legged on her dorm bed, her long hair grazing her shoulders. People said she looked like Hugh. They had that same burnished look.

"A pea coat, huh? Please tell me this means you've given up the Harley-Davidson jacket."

"What about *you?* You had that red suede jacket with all the cowboy fringe."

I smiled, the lightness I always felt around Dee fading, though, as I thought of Mother. "Listen, honey, I was going to call you this morning. I'm leaving for the island today to see your grandmother. She's not well." It occurred to me Dee might think she was on her deathbed, so I told her the truth.

The first words out of Dee's mouth were, "Oh, *fuck.*"

"Dee!" I said. A little too indignantly, I suppose, but she'd genuinely shocked me. "That word is beneath you."

"I know," she said. "And I bet *you've* never said it once in your whole life."

I let out a long breath. "Look, I didn't mean to preach."

She was silent a moment. "Okay, I shouldn't have said it, but what Gran did is so twisted. Why would she do something like that?"

Dee, sharp-eyed in every other way, had always had a blind spot about her grandmother, re-creating her as a wonderfully doting eccentric. I imagined this would shatter her illusions once and for all.

"I have no idea," I said. "I wish I did."

"You'll take care of her, right?"

I closed my eyes and saw my mother in the storm tent, the time I'd found her there right after Dad died. It had been a perfect, sunny day.

"I'm going to try," I told Dee.

After I hung up, I sat down at the work-table and stared at the bits of mirror and eggshell I'd been gluing into the discarded box before abandoning it.

I *had* said the word. This past December, while Dee was home. I was standing in the shower, and Hugh had slipped into the bath-room, taken off his clothes, and stepped be-hind me, startling me so badly I'd jerked forward and knocked the shampoo bottle off the shelf that hung from the nozzle.

"Fuck," I'd said. Which wasn't like me. The word was not in my lexicon, and I don't know who'd been more astounded, me or Hugh.

After a pause Hugh had laughed. "Exactly. Fuck is exactly what I was thinking."

I didn't say anything, didn't turn around. His fingers moved along my ribs and brushed the edges of my breasts. I heard him make a tiny groaning sound in his throat. I tried to want him but couldn't help feeling intruded upon. Standing stiffly in the spray, I must've appeared like the trunk of a tree, a petrifying tree quietly going to stone.

After a few moments, the shower door opened and closed. He was gone.

For days after that, I went about in a state of severe and earnest trying. I stepped into the shower with Hugh not once but twice, contorting myself into extraordinary yogic positions. The second time I'd emerged with the red mark of the faucet handle on my back. A tattoo that looked remarkably like a crumpled bird.

One day while Dee was out hitting the after-Christmas sales with her friends, I'd showed up at Hugh's office after his last patient, suggesting we have sex on his sofa, and I suppose we would have, except his beeper went off. Someone had tried to kill herself. I'd driven home with all the trying knocked out of me.

The next day Dee had gone back to college.

I watched her car roll out of the driveway, down the street. After it had turned the corner, I'd gone inside to a stillness that was bewildering in its intensity.

The same stillness rose now in the studio. I looked up at the skylight. It was papered with elm leaves and a thick, putty-colored light. The rain and wind had stopped, and I heard the quietness for the first time, the way it clotted around my head.

Outside, the tires of Hugh's Volvo turned into the driveway. His car door slammed, and

I felt the vibration move through the walls. As I descended the stairs, the years between us seemed accumulated everywhere, filling the house, and it seemed strange to me, how love and habit blurred so thoroughly to make a life.

CHAPTER
Four

I hesitated as I stepped onto the ferry, one foot on the floating dock and one on the boat, caught momentarily by the rush of light across Bull's Bay. A half-dozen great white egrets flew up from the marsh grass nearby with their low-pitched throat calls. I moved on board and watched them through the plastic windows, the familiar ribbon they made crossing the bay, how they turned in unison toward Egret Island.

The ferry was actually an old pontoon boat named *Tidal Run.* I propped my suit-case beside a dirty-white cooler, beneath two red cardboard tide clocks nailed onto the wall. I sat down on a bench. Hugh had arranged for a driver to take me from the airport to the ferry landing in Awendaw. I'd made it just in time for the last run of the day. It was four o'clock.

There were only five other passengers, perhaps because it was winter and the tourists had not descended in full force. They usually came in the spring and summer to see the marsh brimming with egrets, how they teemed into the trees along the creeks, sitting in heaps of brightness. A few tourists—the hard-core history crowd that trickled over from Charleston—came to take Hepzibah's Grand Gullah Tour, which included a visit to the slave cemetery. Hepzibah was the culture keeper on the island or, as she liked to say, the African griot. She knew a thousand folktales and could speak perfect Gullah, a language the slaves had fashioned out of English and their native African tongues.

I studied the passengers, wondering if any were islanders I might recognize. Fewer than a hundred people, besides the monks, still lived on the island, and most had been there since I was a girl. I decided that everyone on the boat was a tourist.

One wore a Hard Rock Cafe T-shirt from Cancún and a red bandanna tied around his head. I imagined he must be freezing. He saw me looking at him and asked, "Have you ever stayed at the Island Dog?"

"No, but it's nice. You'll like it," I said, having to raise my voice over the boat engine.

A two-story, pale blue house with white hurricane shutters, it was the only B&B on the island. I wondered if Bonnie Langston still owned it. She was what Hepzibah called a *comya,* Gullah for somebody who comes from another place. If your ancestry was on the island, then you were a *binya. Comyas* were rare on Egret, but they did exist. My sole purpose after the age of ten had been to leave the island. "I want to be a *goya,*" I'd told Hepzibah once, and at first she'd laughed but then stopped and looked at me, down into the heartsick place that made me want to leave. "You can't leave home," she said with her gentlest voice. "You can go other places, all right—you can live on the other side of the world, but you can't ever leave home."

I felt now I'd proved her wrong.

"Be sure to eat at Max's Café," I told the tourist. "Order the shrimp and grits."

Actually, if he wanted to eat, the café was his only choice. Like the B&B, it'd been named for Max, the black Lab whose mind Benne could supposedly read. He met the ferry twice a day without fail and was something of a local celebrity. In warm weather, when the tables spilled out onto the sidewalk, he would trot around with an acquired sense of canine entitlement, giving mere human beings the opportunity to adore him. They would scramble for their cameras as if Lassie had come onto the set. He was famous not only for meeting the ferry with uncanny accuracy but for his immortality. Purportedly he was twenty-seven years old. Bonnie swore to it, but the truth was, the current Max was the fourth in a string of them. I'd been loving various Maxes since I was a kid.

There was a sand beach on the front of the island called Bone Yard, so named because driftwood formed huge, contorted sculptures along it. Hardly anyone ventured there, though, because the currents made it too dangerous for swimming and it was full of sand gnats. You only had to stand there to know that the ocean would take the island back one day.

Most of the tourists came for the guided tour of the monastery, St. Senara's abbey. It was named for a Celtic saint who'd been a mermaid before her conversion, and it had started as a simple outpost—or, as the monks said, "a daughter house"—of an abbey in Cornwall, England. The monks had built it themselves in the thirties on land donated by a Catholic family from Baltimore, who'd used it for a summer fishing camp. In the beginning the place was so unpopular that Egret Islanders—all of them Protestants—called it "St. Sin." Now Protestants were more or less extinct here.

The local guidebooks played up the monastery as a minor Low Country attraction, mostly because of the mermaid chair that sat in a side chapel in the church. A "beguiling chair," the books always said, and it was, actually. It was a replica of a very old, somewhat famous chair in the abbey's mother house. The arms had been carved into two winged mermaids painted with jeweled colors—vermilion fish tails, white wings, golden orange hair.

As children Mike and I used to slip into the church when no one was about, lured, of course, by the titillation of the nipples on the mermaids' exposed breasts, four shining in-laid garnet stones. I used to give Mike a hard time about sitting with his hands cupped around them. The memory of this caused me to laugh, and I looked up to see if the other passengers had noticed.

If the tourists were lucky and the chapel wasn't roped off, they could sit in the mermaid chair themselves and say a prayer to Senara, the mermaid saint. For some reason sitting in it was supposed to guarantee you an answer. At least that was the tradition. Mostly the whole thing came off like throwing pennies into a fountain and making wishes, but now and then you would see a real pilgrim, someone in a wheelchair rolling off the ferry, or someone with a small oxygen tank.

The ferry moved slowly through the salt creeks, past tiny marsh islands waving with yellowed spartina grass. The tide had ebbed, laying bare miles of oyster rakes. Everything looked undressed, exposed.

As the creeks widened out into the bay, we picked up speed. V's of brown pelicans lapped alongside us, outpacing the boat. I focused on them and, when they'd vanished, on the lifelines hanging in sloppy coils inside the ferry. I didn't want to think about my mother. On the plane I'd been saturated with dread, but out here that lifted some, maybe because of all the wind and freedom.

I tilted my head back against the window and breathed the marsh's sulfurous smell. The boat captain, in his faded red cap and wraparound metallic sunglasses, began to speak into a microphone. His voice coasted through the little speaker over my head in a memorized oration designed for tourists. He told them where to rent the golf carts that would take them around the island, gave them a little spiel about the egret rookery and fishing charters.

He closed with the same joke I'd heard the last time I'd come: "Folks, just remember there are alligators on the island. I doubt you'll see one this time of year, but if you do, keep in mind that you can't outrun an alligator. Just be sure you can outrun whoever you're with."

The tourists chuckled and nodded at one another, the whole business of venturing onto a Carolina barrier island suddenly thrust into a new and slightly dangerous light.

As the ferry slipped into the narrow waterways interlacing the marsh on the island's back side, I got up and walked out onto the deck. Swells of water glided past, the color of darkly steeped tea. Looking back at the wake, at the distance we'd covered, I realized how isolated I'd been growing up on an island without a bridge. I'd been thoroughly caged in by water, and yet I'd never felt lonely until I started high school on the mainland. I remembered Shem Watkins taking all of us kids, probably fewer than half a dozen of us, across Bull's Bay each morning in his shrimp boat, then picking us up in the afternoon. We'd called it the "shrimp bus."

Mike and I had imagined ourselves like the Swiss Family Robinson, he rowing his bateau through the creeks, stopping to bog for fiddler crabs, which we'd sold for bait at fifty cents a pound on the ferry dock. We'd known every channel and sandbar, exactly where the shell rakes might snag the boat's bottom during low tide. The summer I was nine, before everything collapsed, we'd been dauntless, scavenging for turkey tracks and alligator drags. At night, with the palmettos rattling wildly around the house, we'd slipped out through the window and gone to the slave cemetery, where we'd double- and triple-dog-dared the ghosts to come out.

Where had that girl gone? Staring into the tannic-looking waters, I felt a terrible craving for her.

I was surprised by the weight of memory, the awful contagion of family, of place. I remembered my father steering his twenty-foot Chris-Craft, the meerschaum pipe I'd bought him clamped between his teeth, and me tucked between his chest and the wheel. I could almost hear him calling, "Jessie, the dolphins are here," see myself racing for the rail, listening for their breath to spew, the slit of darkness as they broke the surface.

When the northwest side of the island came into view, I was already thinking about his boat exploding. About the clipping in Mother's drawer. *"Police speculate that a spark from his pipe may have ignited a leak in the fuel line."* I let my eyes sweep over the the water, remembering where it happened, then looked away.

I walked the length of the ferry rail and watched the island draw closer. It was only five miles long and two and half across, but it seemed even smaller from the boat. The rooftops of the shops behind the ferry dock came into view, laughing gulls looping over them, and beyond that the live oak, palm, and myrtle thickets that filled the green heart of the island.

The engine throttled down as the pontoon approached the dock. Someone threw a rope, and I heard the creaking of old wood as we were hitched tightly against the pilings.

On the pier a few people in beach chairs dangled rods over the side, fishing for channel bass. But no Kat and Benne. Kat had promised they would meet me. I went back inside the boat, collected my suitcase, then stood at the window as the other passengers debarked.

A few moments later, they came hurrying up with Max trotting behind them. They were holding hands, and Benne appeared to be half dragging Kat, who was wearing her high heels with the thin socks. Her hair was pulled up into a dark red topknot, a color my mother referred to as "port wine." Pieces of it were starting to unravel around her face.

They stopped at the edge of the dock and looked up at the boat. Max sat between them, wagging half of his tail as if it were jointed.

When Kat spotted me at the window, her chest rose visibly. "Well, don't just stand up there! Come on down here!" she yelled.

Benne sprang into a funny jig, lifting her feet and marching in place. "Jes-sie, Jessie," she chanted, and Max started to bark, which created an eruption of gulls along the edge of the dock. The other passengers paused to stare, then glanced at one another, embarrassed.

Home. There was nothing to do but collect my suitcase and wade into it.

There were half-moons, like pale, yellowish shadows, under Kat's eyes. She embraced me at the same moment the aroma of the island penetrated, a powerful brew of silt, old crab pots, salted air, and black, gooey mudflats alive and crawling with pungent creatures.

"You made it," Kat said, and I smiled at her.

Benne laid her round face against the sleeve of my coat and clung to me like a barnacle. I put my arm around her and gave her a squeeze.

"You didn't want to come," she said. "You hate coming here."

Kat cleared her throat. "All right, Benne, that's enough."

Benne was not finished, however. "Mama is standing on the bloodstain," she said.

I looked down. We all did. The dark, spattered edge of it was visible beneath Kat's shoe. I pictured the frenzied dash they must have made to the ferry dock, the ride across the water, Mother's hand wrapped in a JC Penney bath towel.

Kat slid back her foot, and we stood in the late afternoon, in a moment of perfect stillness, and stared at my mother's blood.

CHAPTER
Five

We piled onto Kat's golf cart, parked at the end of the pier. Benne sat on the back with my suitcase, and I climbed into the front seat, glancing warily at the air horn, thinking of the last harrowing ride in her cart.

"Don't worry," Kat said. "I won't use the horn unless someone is crazy enough to step out in front of me."

"I hate that odious thing," I said.

"Yes, well, hate it all you want, but it has saved the lives of countless tourists."

"Mama used to aim for tourists," Benne said.

"Oh, I did *not*."

"I believe it's impossible for Benne to tell a lie," I said, and Kat huffed as she pulled onto the narrow pavement.

Overhead the sky was turning orange. I had the sense of darkness pressing in, pooling behind the brightness. As we swept past the island shops, no one spoke, not even Benne.

The storefronts all had window boxes gorged with lavender pansies, even the tiny post office. Shem's Bait & Tackle had been painted the color of persimmons, and the carved wooden pelican outside Caw Caw General Store now wore a pony saddle, I imagined so that children could sit on it. We passed a handful of tourists in front of Egret Expeditions, signing up for boat tours and bird walks. Even at the nadir of winter, the place seemed alive.

I pointed to a small store wedged between Max's Café and the Island Dog B&B. It had a blue-and-white-striped awning and a sign in the window that read THE MERMAID'S TALE. "Didn't that used to be a fish market?"

"It went out of business," Kat said.

"That's Mama's store now," said Benne.

"No kidding? You own it? That gift shop?" I was surprised. I'd known Kat my whole life, and she'd never shown the least interest in shopkeeping. After her husband died—which had to be twenty years ago at least—she and Benne had lived contentedly off his pension and a little Social Security.

"I opened it last spring," Kat said.

"Who's minding the store right now?"

"When I'm there, it's open; when I'm not, it's closed," she said.

"I like the name," I told her.

"I wanted to call it 'Fin Fatale,' but your mother nixed that. The woman has no sense of humor."

"She never did."

"That's not true. Once upon a time, she had a *great* sense of humor," Kat said.

She lit out down the road, heading into the tinted light. I watched her lean forward as if she were willing the cart to surpass the eighteen-mile-per-hour speed limit, and so many things swam up to me—scraps of my mother's laughter, times when we were still normal and happy. Kat was right—Mother *had* possessed a great sense of humor once. I thought of the time she made co-conut shrimp and served it wearing a hula skirt. That time Mike was eight and got his poor penis stuck in a Coke bottle while urinating into it—for reasons none of us ever understood. His penis had, shall we say, expanded somewhat after entry. Mother had tried to act concerned but broke down laughing. She told him, "Mike, go sit in your room and picture Mother Teresa, and your penis will come right out."

"The biggest sellers in the shop are yellow signs that say 'Mermaid Xing,' " Kat was telling me. "Plus our mermaid booklets. You remember Father Dominic? He wrote up the story of St. Senara for us, and we got it printed in a little booklet titled *The Mermaid's Tale,* same name as the store. We can't keep them in stock. Dominic is always coming in wearing that damn fool hat of his, wanting to autograph copies. I tell him, 'For God's sake, Dominic, it's not like you're *Pat Conroy.*' "

I laughed. As a child I'd often bumped into Father Dominic as I played on the monastery grounds, waiting for Mother to finish in the kitchen; he'd always told me knock-knock jokes. But there had been another side to him, something somber I couldn't quite put my finger on. He had been one of the monks who'd come to the house that day bearing the remains of my father's boat, who'd stood there as Mother burned the boards in the fireplace.

"He still wears the straw hat?"

"Same one. The straw is starting to rot," she said.

We lapsed into silence as we skirted the back edge of the island, most of it an undeveloped tangle of wind-pruned trees. We came around a curve where the trees opened onto a prairie of caramel grasses and, beyond it, the ocean. The water was inking into purple, and something about this brought everything back, the reason I was here, what Mother had done with the cleaver. Her life had gotten so twisted and confused.

I wondered, if I'd been a better daughter, whether any of this would've happened. Shouldn't I have seen it coming? As far as I knew, she could be home at this very moment lopping off the rest of her fingers.

Why her finger? I thought. *Why that?*

Benne was singing to herself on the back-seat. I leaned over to Kat. "What happened to her finger? The one she cut off?"

"It's in a mayonnaise jar by her bed," she answered matter-of-factly.

The spire of the abbey church came into

view just as the paved road ran out. Kat didn't bother to slow down, and we bounced a foot in the air as we came onto the hard-caked dirt. Clouds of dust roiled up. "Hold on!" she shouted to Benne.

Kat's hair flew completely out of its bobby pins and fluttered behind her as we sailed by the monastery gate. Just past it sat the Star of the Sea Chapel, the white clapboard parish church where the monks said mass for the islanders and where all Egret Island children, including me, had attended grammar school. Every grade had been simultaneously taught by Anna Legare, who'd told me point-blank when I was ten that I was a born artist. She'd hung my endless sketches of boat wrecks on the chapel wall when I was eleven and invited the whole island to the "show." Kat had bought one for a quarter.

"Whatever happened to that picture of mine you bought and hung in your kitchen?"

"I still have it. It's hanging in the Mermaid's Tale now."

As we passed her driveway, I noticed the mermaid xing sign nailed to a post beside the mailbox.

A few seconds later, we slowed in front of

Mother's house, built in the style of an 1820s tidewater cottage, like most of the island homes. It stood on stilts in a forest of palmetto palms, with dormers and black shutters and a wide veranda that stretched across the front.

The house had always been some lush shade of green, but at the moment it was washed-out aqua. The yard was infested with yucca bristle and dollar weed, and standing in the middle of it was Mother's appalling bathtub grotto.

Over a decade ago, she'd enlisted Shem to bury an upright bathtub halfway into the ground, and, being slow to grasp the point, he'd left the end of the tub with the faucets on it exposed. Mother had gone ahead anyway and placed a concrete statue of Mary inside the porcelain arch. Now the tub had splotches of rust and some sort of plastic flower wired to the spigot.

The first time I saw the tub, I told Mother that all those tears Mary's statues reportedly cried were because of the extreme tackiness of her devotees. Dee, naturally, had thought the Bathtub Madonna was *awesome.*

As we rolled to a stop and Benne leaped

off the back, I saw Hepzibah standing on the porch. She wore one of her African outfits, a batik shift in scarlet and saffron colors that came to her ankles and a matching cloth coiled around her head. She looked tall and resplendent standing there.

"Well, if it isn't our Hottentot queen," said Kat, waving to her. She laid her hand on my arm. "Jessie, if your mother says fish fly, just nod and say, 'Yes, ma'am, fish fly.' Don't argue with her about anything, all right?"

"Some fish *can* fly," said Benne. "I saw a picture in a book."

Kat ignored her. She kept her eyes on my face. "Don't upset her."

I pulled away. "I'm not planning on upsetting anybody."

Hepzibah met me halfway on the porch steps, trailing the aroma of okra gumbo, and I knew she'd made us dinner. "We glad fa see oona," she said, lapsing into Gullah the way she used to whenever she greeted me.

I smiled, looked past her at the window lit from within. I stared at the wooden frame, how it was splintering a little, at a little smear glowing on the pane, and tears came, just enough so I couldn't hide them.

"Now, what's this about?" said Hepzibah,

and she pulled me into the dizzying designs on her dress.

I stepped back from her. It struck me as a ludicrous question. I might've said, *Well, for starters, there's a mayonnaise jar in the house with my mother's finger inside it,* but that would have been rude and undeserved, and besides, it wasn't my mother I was thinking about. It was my father.

The last time I'd seen Joseph Dubois, he'd been sitting at that window peeling an apple without breaking the skin—a minor stunt in his renowned repertoire of tricks. He was making a whirly girl. I'd sat on the floor that night in a puddle of lamplight and watched the irresistible way the peel had spun off the blade of his knife, nervous over whether he would make it all the way to the end without breaking it. I'd risen up on my knees as he'd come to the last turn. If he made it, I would get to hang the red spiral in my bedroom window with the other whirly girls he'd created, all of them suspended by sewing thread, bobbing at the glass pane in various stages of puckered decay.

"A whirly girl for my Whirly Girl," he'd said, calling me by his pet name and dropping it into my open palms.

Those were his last words to me.

I'd dashed to my room without looking back, without letting him know that what I loved best about this ritual was the part where he called me his Whirly Girl, how I imagined myself one of his perfect creations, the apple skins in my window a strange still frame of self-portraits.

Seeing my tears, Kat clattered up the steps in her heels and hovered over me with her arms flapping around her sides. She reminded me of a clapper rail, one of the noisiest birds in the marsh, a big hen of a bird, and I felt my anger at her melt before she spoke. "Jessie, I talk too much and can't keep my damn foot out of my mouth. Of course you wouldn't go in there and upset your mother. I—"

"It's okay," I said. "It wasn't that. Really."

Benne plodded up the steps, lugging my suitcase. She set it at the door. I thanked them all and said they could go, that I would be fine. I said the tears were because I was tired, that's all.

They drove away in the golf cart, lumbering over a series of tree roots—"island speed bumps," Kat called them. I told myself I should go inside, but I stood on the porch for a few minutes in a breeze that had chilled and darkened and smelled of the marsh, finishing whatever had come over me earlier— that little baptism of sadness.

CHAPTER
Six

Brother Thomas

He lay prostrate on the floor of the church with his arms stretched out on either side in the shape of the cross, punishment for the things he'd written in a small, leather-bound notebook. Father Sebastian, the prior at the monastery, had found it on the counter inside the abbey gift shop, where he'd left it for a few moments while he pointed a tourist to the restrooms at the rear of the store, then answered questions from another about the cast nets that were for sale in the shop. How long had the monks been making them? Had they learned the art from the islanders or had they brought it with them from Cornwall? Did they really sell enough of them to support the monastery? He wished now he hadn't taken so much time with the man.

It was February, Ash Wednesday, and the floor felt cold, even a little damp, through his black robe. He lay in the aisle between the choir stalls, which stood on either side of the nave facing each other, and listened as the monks sang evening prayer. Brother Timothy was crooning like a lounge singer, "O loving, O sweet Virgin Mary."

When they finished the Salve Regina, he heard the hinged seats built into each stall squeak as they were lifted, then a tired shuffling of feet as the monks lined up to be sprinkled with holy water by the abbot. Finally the lights went out, except for the one near the abbot's stall, and Brother Thomas was left in the near dark, in a luxuriant silence.

He was the youngest monk at forty-four, and also the newest, a so-called junior monk with temporary vows. His solemn vows— *usque ad mortem,* until death—were only four months away. What had he been thinking—giving a lecture to the man in the gift shop as if he'd been here half his life? He'd gone on and on about the cast nets.

He lay there and cursed himself. It had given Father Sebastian, who really should have been a marine and not a monk, an opportunity to thumb through his notebook and grow alarmed for the state of his soul. He'd taken it to the abbot, who was very old school about things and thoroughly Irish. Thomas had been summoned to his office, into the dreaded papal enclosure, as he sometimes thought of it. Now here he was on the floor.

He'd been lectured by the abbot a dozen times at least, but this was the first time he'd been punished, and it didn't seem so bad really, lying here. He would stay until the abbot felt he'd meditated long enough on the perils of doubt and sent someone to release him. He'd been here like this an hour, perhaps longer.

The floor of the church smelled of Murphy's oil soap and something else sour and slightly manure-ish that he realized was a mixture of pluff mud from the marsh and fertilizer from the garden. It was clogged and hardened into microscopic crevices in the wooden boards, having been tracked in on the monks' shoes for the last fifty years.

Here in this rarefied place—where they all imagined themselves marinating in holiness through their ceaseless rounds of chanting and prayer—was all this hidden mud and cow shit. It was hard to overestimate how much this pleased him. Brother Thomas had dreamed once about Christ's feet—not his crucifixion or his resurrection or his sacred heart but his *feet.*

The scent emanating from the church floor, even God's feet in his dream, made him think more highly of religion somehow. The other monks, Sebastian for instance, would have impugned the buildup in the floor crevices as profane, but Thomas lay there knowing suddenly that what he smelled was a fine patina of the most inviolate beauty, and shockingly holy. He was smelling the earth.

He'd been at St. Senara abbey on the small South Carolina island for nearly five years, each one of those years a bone of darkness that he'd gnawed. *And still no marrow of light,* he thought, though now and then he felt an occasional beam of it dart out of nowhere and hit him. Just as it had a moment ago when he'd caught that scent.

After his other life had ended, the one with his wife and his unborn child, he'd been incurably driven. Sometimes his quest seemed impossible, like an eye trying to look back and see its own self. All he'd discerned so far was that God seemed surreptitiously about and wrenchingly ordinary. That was all.

His real name was Whit O'Conner. Before, in that other life, he'd been an attorney in Raleigh thwarting developers and industrial polluters on behalf of various conservation and environmental groups. There had been a brick house with a landscaped yard, and his wife, Linda, seven and a half months pregnant. She'd worked as an office manager in an orthodontist's practice, but she'd wanted to stay home and raise their child, even though that wasn't fashionable. He'd liked that about her—that she wasn't fashionable. They'd met at Duke, gotten married the Sunday afternoon following her graduation in her family's tiny Methodist church near Flat Rock, North Carolina, and they'd never been apart until the tire came off the truck in front of her car on I-77. The medic who'd responded to the accident told him over and over that she had gone quickly, as if her leaving sooner would console him.

His sense of abandonment had been bottomless—not just by Linda and the promise of family but by God, whom he'd actually believed in. The kind of believing one does before immense suffering.

Linda had called him from work the day she died to tell him she was sure they were having a girl. Up until then she'd had no feeling either way, though he personally had believed all along it was a boy. The impression had come over her while standing in the shower that morning. She'd touched her abdomen and simply known. He smiled now, remembering this, and his lips brushed against the floor. After the funeral he'd learned from the coroner that she'd been right.

He couldn't remember precisely when it had first occurred to him to come here, but it had been around a year after her death. He'd sent his baptism and confirmation records, recommendations from two priests, and a long, carefully constructed letter. And still everyone, including the abbot, had said he was running away from his grief. They'd had no idea what they were talking about. He'd cradled his grief almost to the point of loving it. For so long he'd refused to give it up, because leaving it behind was like leaving her.

Sometimes he couldn't fathom why he'd thrown in his lot with these aging men. Some were grumpy to the point he went out of his way to avoid them, and at least four inched about with walkers and lived permanently in the infirmary. There was one monk, Brother Fabian, who was always writing letters of complaint to the pope about things the rest of them did, and posting copies in the corridors. Brother Basil had a bizarre tic, shouting out "Meep!" during choir or other odd, sacrosanct moments. *Meep.* What did it mean? It had driven Thomas nuts at first. But Basil was at least kind, unlike Sebastian.

Thomas had not been one of those people who romanticized monasteries, and if he had, that illusion would have evaporated the first week.

Simply, his grieving had opened into a larger abyss.

"I have come here not to find answers," he'd written in his notebook that first year,

"but to find a way to live in a world without any."

To be honest, he'd been turned away three times over the course of three years before the abbot, Dom Anthony, finally accepted him. Thomas was sure it was not because the abbot had changed his mind, but because he'd finally worn him down. Because, too, they'd needed a younger man, someone who could climb the ladder into the timber buttresses of the church and change the lightbulbs, who knew about computers— that the word "reboot" did not necessarily mean putting on your shoes again, as several monks seemed to think. Mostly they'd needed someone who could take their small boat into the creeks and measure egret eggs, count hatchlings, and test the water for salinity—work the monastery had been contracted to do for the South Carolina Department of Natural Resources to bring in extra income. Thomas was happy to do it. He loved disappearing into the rookery.

His arms had begun to ache a little around the elbows. He changed position and turned his head in the other direction. He saw the church as a mouse would see it. As a beetle. He rolled his eyes toward the ceiling without moving his head and felt he was lying at the bottom of the world, looking up. The place where all ladders start—wasn't that what Yeats had said? He had spent a lot of his time here reading—especially the poets, systematically going through the volumes in the library. He loved Yeats best.

He felt less consequential down here on the floor, and it struck him that all self-important people—the ones in Congress, in the Vatican, at AT&T perhaps—should lie down here for a while. They should lie here and look up, and see how different everything seemed.

He'd had an overly important sense of himself before coming here, he admitted it. The cases he'd tried—so many of them high profile—had often put him on the front page of state newspapers, and sometimes he still thought about that life with nostalgia. He remembered the time he'd prevented a big landfill company from trucking in sewage sludge from New York City, how it'd landed him in the *New York Times*, and then all the television interviews he'd given. He'd basked in that.

On the boat, the day he'd come here to

stay, he'd thought of the river Styx, of the ferryman ushering him across the last threshold. He'd imagined he was dying to his old life and coming ashore to a new one, one hidden out here in the water, hidden from the world. It was silly and overly dramatic, but he'd liked the analogy. Then it had turned out that it wasn't so much the water but the trees that had impressed him, how the branches were warped and curled in extravagant spirals from the ocean winds. The moment he'd seen them, he'd known that it was a place of harshness. Of enduring.

Of course he'd taken the name Brother Thomas because he was the resident doubter, and it was practically a cliché, but he took it anyway. He doubted God. Perhaps he would find there had never been a God. Or he would lose one God and find another. He didn't know. Despite this, he felt God the same way the arthritic monks felt rain coming in their joints. He felt only the hint of him.

On the first page of the notebook, he'd written "Disputed Questions" in honor of Thomas Merton, the monk who'd written a book by that title. He'd pointed this out to Dom Anthony as some sort of defense, but it had not saved him. If you were going to be heretical and get away with it, you needed to be dead long enough for people to get over the heresy and rediscover you.

He tried to recall the most damning parts of the notebook. Probably the questions that woke him in the night. He'd sat with his window open, listening to the buoys out on Bull's Bay make their sonorous music, and he'd written them all down. Questions about evil and whether it could exist without God's collusion, about Nietzsche's claim that God is dead, even theories that God is not a being in heaven but merely some guiding aspect in the human personality.

He felt a rush of dismay at the thought of the abbot's reading this. He wanted to get up and find him, to explain. But what would he say?

The wind rose outside, sweeping in from the bay, flapping over the roof. He imagined it tearing the surface of the water. The monastery bell clanged, calling the monks to sleep, telling them the Great Silence was beginning, and he wondered if the abbot had forgotten about him.

The church had filled up with shadows, the long slits of pale glass in the windows completely dark. He thought of the chapel behind the chancel, where the mermaid chair sat on a carpeted dais. He liked to go and sit in the chair sometimes, when no tourists were around. He always wondered why Senara, their famous little saint, had been carved on the chair in her mermaid form, a *half-nude* mermaid at that. He didn't object to the portrayal; he rather appreciated it. It was just so unlike the Benedictines to highlight her breasts.

From the moment he'd seen the mermaid chair, he'd loved Senara, not just for her mythic life in the sea but for how supposedly she'd heard the prayers of Egret Islanders and saved them, not only from hurricanes but from golf courses.

In the beginning he'd sat in the mermaid chair and thought of his wife, of making love to her. Now he could go weeks and not think of her. Sometimes when he thought of making love, it was simply with a woman, a generic woman, not Linda at all.

Back when he'd arrived as a postulant, it had not been hard to give up sex. He did not see then how he could make love to anyone but Linda. Her hair spread across the pillow, the smell of her—that was gone. Sex was gone. He'd let it go.

He felt a tightening at his groin. How ridiculous to think sex would stay away. Things would hide out in an underground place for a while, they would sink like the little weights the monks tied on their cast nets, but they wouldn't stay down there forever. Everything that goes down comes up. And then he almost laughed at the pun he'd made without intending to.

The past few months, he'd thought of sex too much. Doing without had become an actual sacrifice, but it didn't make him feel holy, only denied, more of a normal monk chafing at celibacy. In June he would take his last vows. And that would be that.

When the footsteps came at last, he closed his eyes, then opened them again when the sound stopped. He saw the toes of a pair of shoes, Reeboks, and the hem of a robe brushing against them.

The abbot spoke in his Irish brogue, not one bit of it flaked away after all these years. "I hope it was productive time."

"Yes, Reverend Father."

"Not too harsh, then?"

"No, Reverend Father."

Thomas didn't know how old Dom Anthony was, but he looked ancient gazing down, the skin of his face drooping from his chin and cheeks almost like ruffles. Sometimes the things he said sprang from such a timeless old world. Once, during a Sunday-morning chapter meeting, sitting on his thronelike chair holding his crosier, he'd said, "The same time St. Patrick drove the snakes from Ireland, he changed all the old pagan women into mermaids." Thomas had thought that quaint—and a little bizarre. Could the abbot really believe that?

"Go to bed now," Dom Anthony said.

Thomas lifted himself from the floor and walked out of the church into a night that was heaving about in the wind. He flipped his cowl over his head and crossed the central cloister, headed toward the duplex cottages scattered under the whorled oaks near the marsh.

He followed the path toward the cottage he shared with Father Dominic. Dominic was the abbey librarian and also the monastery prankster ("Every court has its jester," Dominic liked to say). He had aspirations of being a writer and kept Thomas up nights with his typing. Thomas had no idea what Dominic was working on, on the other side of the cottage, but he had a feeling it might be a murder mystery—an Irish abbot who turns up dead in the refectory, strangled with his own rosary. Something like that.

The path was lined with cement plaques announcing the stations of the cross, and Thomas moved past them through spiky bits of fog that had blown in from the ocean, thinking now of Dominic, who'd once drawn smiley faces on several of them. Of course Dom Anthony had made him scrub the plaques and then the choir stalls, while the rest of them got to watch *The Sound of Music* on television. Why couldn't *he* get into trouble the way Dominic did, for something droll and comic? Why did it have to be for the existential bullshit he wrote in his notebook?

He'd thought for a while he might get into trouble over the baseball card that he used to mark pages in his prayer book, but apparently no one, including the abbot, seemed to care. It surprised Thomas how much he missed simple things like baseball. Once in a while he got to watch a game on television, but it wasn't the same. Dale Murphy had hit forty-four home runs last year, and he'd seen only one of them.

Linda had given him the baseball card their last Christmas together. Eddie Matthews,

1953—there was no telling what she'd paid for it.

He envied Dominic, who had to be eighty at least and went about in a tattered straw hat everywhere except choir. He'd been the one who'd convinced the abbot to put a television in the music-listening room. Once Dominic had tapped on Thomas's door after the Great Silence and tried to convince him to sneak over and watch a special program about shooting the *Sports Illustrated* swimsuit issue. Thomas had not gone. He regretted it to this day.

He was nearly at his cottage when he stopped abruptly, thinking he heard a voice, a woman's voice calling in the distance. He looked east toward the rookery, his robe beating around his legs.

A whip-poor-will sang out. The Gullah woman on the island, Hepzibah Postell, the one who kept up the slave cemetery, had told him once that whip-poor-wills were the departed spirits of loved ones. Of course he didn't believe this, and he was pretty sure she didn't either, but he liked to think it was Linda out there singing. That it was her voice calling in the distance.

Thomas pictured his wife—or was it

merely the generic woman?—posing in a swimsuit. He imagined the place inside her thigh, just above her knees, the softness there. He thought about kissing that place.

He stood beneath a bent tree in the Great Silence, and he thought about falling into life and then about flying far above it. Then he heard it again—a woman's voice calling out. Not a bird singing or the wind moaning but a woman.

CHAPTER
Seven

The smell of gumbo hung inside the house in thick green ropes, like something you could swing on to get across the kitchen. I set my suitcase on the beige rug and walked down the hallway to Mother's bedroom. I called out, "Mother? It's me, Jessie," and my voice sounded grainy and tired.

She was not in her bed. The blanket was thrown back, and the white sheets were wadded up in a mess, as if children had gone berserk jumping up and down on them.

The bathroom door was shut, and fluorescent light leaked out from the bottom edge. As I waited for her to come out, I stretched

my achy shoulders and neck. A pair of worn-
out terry-cloth slippers had been tossed upside down on the rug, which was beige like
its sibling in the living room. Mother did not
believe in unbeige rugs. Or in walls or curtains in any color other than white, cream,
and ivory. She *did* believe in green paint outside, but inside, things had to be more or
less the color of tap water. The color of a life
bled completely out.

I regarded the old-fashioned dressing
table with the gathered skirt—was it beige or
was it white with a case of old age? In the
center of the dresser, Mother's ceramic
Madonna had a chubby Jesus hoisted onto
her hip and a look of postpartum depression
about her. Beside it was a photograph of my
father on his boat. The water was navy blue
and traveled behind him forever.

I was not thinking about how noiseless
Mother was behind the bathroom door; I was
preoccupied with the sense of wading back
into her life, into this room, swimming in
the contradictions she always stirred in me,
the tangle of love and loathing. I scanned the
bedside table: her old red-beaded rosary,
two prescription bottles, a roll of gauze, tape,
scissors, a digital clock. I realized I was look-

ing for the mayonnaise jar. It was nowhere in the room.

"Mother?"

I tapped on the bathroom door. Silence loomed back, and then a thin, sticky anxiety seeped from behind the door. I turned the knob and stepped inside. There was nothing but the minuscule bathroom. Empty.

I walked into the kitchen—a room so changeless it seemed magically frozen in place; entering it was like strolling back into the 1950s. The same can opener attached to the wall, the canisters with the rooster motif, copper teakettle, tin bread box, dingy teaspoons mounted on a wooden rack. The wall clock beside the refrigerator was a black cat with a swinging tail pendulum. The immortal Felix. I expected to see Mother sitting at the Formica table eating gumbo, but this room, too, was empty.

I hurried through the dining room, checked the two extra bedrooms—Mike's and my old rooms. She had to have been here while Hepzibah was in the house—what, ten minutes ago? I returned to the kitchen and looked up Hepzibah's number, but as I reached for the phone, I noticed the back door ajar.

Grabbing a flashlight, I stepped onto the back stairs, swinging the beam across the yard. The sash to Mother's blue bathrobe lay in a coil on the bottom step. I went down and retrieved it. The wind had picked up. It took the sash right out of my hand. I watched it jerk and flail into the darkness.

Where would she go?

I remembered the time Dee, five years old, had slipped away from me in North Lake Mall, the seizure of panic I'd felt, followed by an almost preternatural calm, by some voice inside telling me the only way to find Dee was to think like her. I'd sat on a bench and thought like Dee, then walked straight to the children's shoe store, where I'd found her among the Sesame Street tennis shoes, trying to lace Bert and Ernie onto her small feet. I knew only one thing Mother loved the way Dee had loved Bert and Ernie.

I found the path that led to the monastery at the back of the yard. It wasn't a long path, but it twisted through overarching wax myrtle and sweet bay and snags of dewberry vines. The monks had cut a crude opening for Mother in the monastery wall so she wouldn't have to go all the way around to the entrance when she came to cook for them.

They called it "Nelle's Gate." Mother, of course, ate that up. She'd told me about it at least fifty times.

As I stepped through it, I shouted her name. I heard an animal of some sort rustle in the brush, then a whip-poor-will, and when the wind died momentarily, the distant pitch and tumble of the ocean, that endless percussion it makes.

Mother had worn a foot trail to the main path that ran between the cloister and the monks' cottages. I followed it, pausing once or twice to call out to her, but the wind seemed to bat my voice right back at me. The moon had risen. It hung low out over the marsh, a startling orb of glassy light.

When I saw the back of the cloister en-clave, I cut off the flashlight and began to run. Everything flowed past me—the little markers with the stations of the cross, the plumes of mist, the sea wind, and the knotty ground. I swept past the stucco house where the monks made their nets, the sign over its door reading FORTUNA, MARIA, RETIA NOSTRA— Bless, Mary, Our Nets.

The statue of St. Senara was in an en-closed garden beside the church. I stepped through the gate into a dense haven of rosebushes, their limbs bare and reaching, forming candelabra shadows against the far wall. The monks had designed the garden with St. Senara's statue in the center and six evenly spaced paths leading in to her. She looked like the hub of a magnificent floral wheel.

I'd played here as a child. While Mother slaved in the monastery kitchen, I would come out here and pull dozens of rose heads off their stems, filling a sweetgrass basket with petals—a whole mishmash of colors—which I disposed of in secret ceremonies, tossing them into the marsh behind the church, around the trunks of certain venerable bearded oaks, and onto the seat of the mermaid chair, for some reason that being the most honored spot. It was my funeral game, a solemn play I'd indulged in after my father died. The petals were his ashes, and I'd thought what I was doing was saying good-bye, but it may have been just the opposite—that I was trying to hold on to him, tuck him in private places only I knew. I would find the petals weeks later, lumps of brown, dried rose chips.

The night seemed paler now, as if the wind had blown some of the darkness out of it. I stood still, letting my eyes roam across the tops of the rosebushes, along the paths plowed with moonlight. There was no sign of my mother.

I wished then I'd called Hepzibah and Kat instead of dashing over here, wasting all this time. I'd just been so sure she would be here, much surer than I'd been about Dee and the shoe store. Mother had made herself the Keeper of the Statue about the same time she'd started to work in the kitchen. She often trudged out here with a bucket of soapy water to wash the bird shit off it, and four times a year she waxed it with a paste that smelled like orange peel and limes. She came here to pour out the various and sundry torments of her life instead of going into the church and telling them to God. Senara was practically a nobody in the hierarchical world of saints, but Mother believed in her.

She loved to recount the story of my birth as proof of Senara's potency, how I was turned backward in her womb and became stuck during the delivery. She'd prayed to Senara, who'd promptly flipped me upside down, and I'd wriggled headfirst into the world.

Out here in the middle of the garden, the statue appeared like a stamen protruding from the center of a huge, winter-blighted flower. It occurred to me that the saint had presided the same way over my childhood, her shadow hovering above the emptiness that had come when I was nine.

The worst punishment Mike and I had ever received had come because we'd dressed the statue in a two-piece swimsuit, sunglasses, and a blond wig. We'd cut the bottom of the suit in half and pinned it together around Senara's hips. Some monks had thought the getup was funny, but Mother had cried over our disrespect and sentenced us to write the Agnus Dei five hundred times a day for a solid week: *Lamb of God, who takest away the sins of the world, have mercy on us.* Instead of being contrite, I'd merely felt confused about it all, as if I'd betrayed Senara and liberated her at the same time.

As I stood near the back of the garden, trying to think what to do now that Mother plainly wasn't here, I heard a thin scratching sound drift from the general vicinity of Senara's statue, like a small bird raking the ground for grubs and insects. I came up behind the statue, and there was Mother sitting on the ground with the mayonnaise jar, her white hair a neon splotch in the dark.

She wore her practical navy coat over a long chenille bathrobe and sat with her legs splayed out in front her, the way a child might sit in a sandbox. She was digging in the dirt with her left hand, using what looked like a stainless-steel soup ladle. The bandage on her right hand appeared the size of a child's baseball glove and was speckled with dirt.

She didn't see me; she was utterly absorbed in what she was doing. I stared at her silhouette for several seconds, my relief at finding her shifting into some fresh new dread. I said, "Mother, it's me, Jessie."

She reared back with a sudden jerk, and the ladle fell into her lap. *"Jesus, Mary, and Joseph!"* she cried. "You scared me to death! What are you doing here?"

I sank down beside her. "I'm out here looking for you," I replied, trying to sound natural and unalarmed. I even tried to smile.

"Well, you found me," she said, then picked up the ladle and resumed work on the mouse hole she'd made at the base of the statue.

"All right, we've established what *I'm* doing here. Now, what are *you* doing here?" I asked.

"It doesn't really concern you."

When I'd found Dee that day in the shoe store I'd grabbed her by the shoulders, wanting to scream at her for scaring me, and the same irrational anger flared in me now. I wanted to shake my mother till her teeth tumbled out.

"How can you say that?" I demanded. "Hepzibah must've told you I was here, and you took off before I could even get into the house. *You* scared *me* to death, too."

"Oh, for heaven's sake, I didn't mean to scare you. I just needed to take care of this."

This. What was *this?* I turned on the flashlight and directed a beam of light onto the mayonnaise jar. Her dismembered finger lay inside it. It looked very clean, and the nail appeared to have been filed. Lifting the jar level with my nose, I could see the shriveled edge of skin at the severed end with a piece of white bone protruding.

A sick feeling passed through me, similar to my nausea that morning. I closed my eyes and didn't speak, and Mother went on scraping at the cold ground. At last I said, "I don't know what you're doing out here, but you're not well, and you need to get up and come back to the house with me."

I felt suddenly bleary with exhaustion.

"What do you mean, I'm not well?" she said. "I'm perfectly well."

"*Really?* Since when is purposely cutting off your finger considered perfectly well?" I sighed. *"Jesus Christ!"*

She whirled toward me then. "Why don't you call on someone you *know?*" she said in a scalding tone. "Nobody asked you to come back."

"Kat asked me."

"Kat needs to mind her own business."

I snorted. "Well, fat chance of that."

I heard the beginnings of a laugh down in her throat, a rare melting sound I hadn't heard in so long, and for some reason it knocked my little wall of anger flat.

Sliding over so that our shoulders touched, I laid my hand on top of hers, the one still coiled around the spoon, and I thought maybe she would jerk it away, but she didn't. I felt the tiny stick bones in her hand, the soft lattice of veins. "I'm sorry. For everything," I said. "I really am."

She turned and looked at me, and I saw

that her eyes were brimming, reflecting like mirrors. She was the daughter, and I was the mother. We had reversed the natural order of things, and I couldn't fix it, couldn't reverse it. The thought was like a stab.

I said, "Tell me. Okay? Tell me why you did this to yourself."

She said, "Joe—your father," and then her jaw slumped down as if his name bore too much weight for her mouth. She looked at me and tried again. "Father Dominic . . ." she said, but her voice trailed off.

"What? What about Father Dominic?"

"Nothing," she said, and refused to go on. I couldn't imagine what sort of anguish was stoppered inside her, or what Father Dominic had to do with anything.

"I didn't get my ashes today," she said, and I realized I hadn't either. It was the first Ash Wednesday service I had missed since my father died.

Picking up the ladle, she scooped at the ground. "The dirt is too hard."

"Are you trying to bury your finger?" I asked.

"I just want to put it in a hole and cover it up."

If your mother says fish fly, just say, Yes, ma'am, fish fly.

I took the digging tool from her. "All right, then."

I gouged out the opening she'd made at the base of the statue until the hole was about six inches deep. She unscrewed the jar and pulled out her finger. She held it up, and both of us stared at it, Mother with a kind of dark reverence on her face and me subdued, almost numb.

We are burying my mother's finger, I told myself. *We are out here in a garden burying a finger, and it has something to do with my father. And with Father Dominic.* I think we could have lit the tip of her finger and let it burn like a taper and the moment wouldn't have seemed any stranger to me.

As Mother laid her finger in the hole, she turned it knuckle up and brushed the fingers on her good hand along the length of it before covering it with the spooned-out dirt. I watched it disappear, an image in my head of a small mouth opening and closing in the earth, swallowing a part of my mother that she could no longer endure.

The ground was spattered with dried rose petals, as if all the red flames had fallen off their candles. I raked up a papery handful. "Remember that you are dust and to dust you shall return," I said, and pressed a petal onto Mother's forehead, then one onto mine. "So now you have your ashes."

Mother smiled at me.

The garden became absolutely still and quiet, yet neither of us heard him approaching until he was almost beside us. Mother and I both looked up at the same moment and saw him step from behind the statue, materializing out of the shadows in his long robe, very tall, his face shining in the bright-lit night.

CHAPTER
Eight

I scrambled to my feet, while Mother continued to sit on the ground. The monk looked down at her. He had to be at least six-one or -two and had the lean, possessed look of an athlete, a swimmer perhaps, or a long-distance runner.

"Nelle?" he said. "Are you all right?"

He didn't ask what we were doing sitting on the ground in the dark with a soup ladle, an empty Hellmann's jar, and a fresh mound of dirt.

"I'm fine," Mother told him. "I came to see the saint, that's all."

He pushed back the cowl from his head, smiling at her, such an easy, infectious smile, and I saw that his hair was dark and impeccably short.

He glanced at Mother's bandaged hand. "I'm sorry about your injury. We prayed for you at mass."

He turned toward me, and we stared at each other for several seconds. In the sharp light of the moon, I noticed that his eyes were pale blue and his face deeply tanned. There was an irresistible look of boyishness about him, but something else, too, that struck me as serious, intense.

"Brother Thomas," he said, smiling again, and I felt an odd catch in my chest.

"I'm Nelle's daughter," I replied. "Jessie Sullivan."

Later I would revisit that encounter again and again. I would tell myself that when I met him, all the dark little wicks in the cells of my body lifted up in the knowledge that here he was—the one you wait for, but I don't know if that was really true, or if I only came to believe that it was. I'm sure I've burdened our first meeting with too much imagining. But I *did* feel that catch in

my chest; I saw him, and something happened.

Mother struggled to get to her feet, and he
offered her his hand, tugging her up, and
didn't let go until she had her balance.

"Who's cooking your meals?" she asked
him.

"Brother Timothy."

"Oh, not him!" she exclaimed. "I think he's
a very good refectorian—he does a good job
setting out the dishes and filling the milk
pitchers—but he can't cook."

"Of course he can't," said Thomas. "That's
why the abbot chose him. He made a very
mysterious casserole today. We've all been
forced into a Lenten fast."

Mother gave him a playful shove with her
good hand, and I caught a glimpse of the af-
fection the monks had for her. It surprised
me. I'd thought of her as the nettlesome
monastery mascot, but perhaps she was
more to them than that.

"Don't worry," she told him. "I'll be back in
the kitchen in a few days."

"No, you won't," I said, too abruptly. "It
could take weeks for your hand to heal." Her
eyes flared at me.

Thomas said, "Weeks! We'll all be starved by then. We'll be sanctified and purified from fasting, but we'll be completely emaciated."

"I'll bring Jessie with me," Mother said. "She'll help me do the cooking."

"No, no, you take your time getting well," he said to her. "I'm only teasing you."

"We need to get back," I muttered.

I followed them through the wrought-iron gate, down the path toward the house, Thomas holding Mother's elbow, guiding her along. She was chattering to him. I held the jar and ladle in one hand and aimed the flashlight with the other.

He walked with us all the way to Nelle's Gate. Mother paused before slipping through it. "Give me a blessing," she said.

He looked unnerved by the request, and I thought, *What an uncomfortable monk he is.* He raised his right hand over her head and traced a clumsy cross in the air. It seemed to satisfy her, and she strode off across her yard toward the house.

I stepped through the gate and looked at him from the other side of the wall. It was made of brick and came to my waist.

"Thanks for walking back with us," I said. "You didn't have to."

He smiled again, and the lines on either side of his mouth deepened. "It was no trouble. I was glad to."

"You must be wondering what Mother and I were doing out there." I set the jar and the dirt-crusted ladle on top of the wall, then put the flashlight down, too, pointing the stream of light off into the trees. I don't know why I suddenly felt compelled to explain things, probably out of embarrassment.

"She wasn't just visiting St. Senara. I found her on her knees beside the statue, trying to bury her finger in the dirt. She was so bent on doing it that I ended up digging the hole for her myself. I have no idea whether that was a good idea or not, whether I was helping her or making things worse."

He shook his head a little. "I probably would've done the same thing if I'd found her there," he said. "Do you think she was offering her finger to St. Senara?"

"To be honest, I don't know *anything* anymore when it comes to my mother."

He let his gaze settle on me, the same absorbing stare as before. "You know, a lot of us at the monastery feel like we should've seen what was coming. We're with Nelle every single day, and not one of us had a clue she was so . . ."

I thought he was going to say crazy. Or demented.

"Desperate," he said.

" 'Desperate' is putting it mildly," I told him.

"You're right, I suppose it is. At any rate, we feel bad about it."

There was a moment of silence when the chilled air rose up around us. I looked back for Mother. Yellow light poured out of the windows, drenching the air around the house. She had already climbed the back stairs and disappeared into the kitchen.

I realized I didn't want to go inside. Arching my neck, I looked up at the sky, at the milky smear of stars, feeling a momentary sensation of floating, of becoming unmoored from my life. When I looked back down, I saw his strong, browned hands resting on the bricks inches from my own and wondered what it would feel like to touch them.

"Look, if you need anything, if we can help somehow, call us," he said.

"You're only a wall away," I responded, and patted the bricks, trying to make a little joke, to ease how self-conscious I suddenly felt.

He laughed and pulled his cowl up over

his head. His face disappeared into the dark pocket.

I gathered up the objects on the wall, turned quickly, and crossed the lawn, hurrying. Not looking back.

CHAPTER
Nine

The next morning when I woke in my old room, I realized I'd dreamed about Brother Thomas.

I lay still while the room filled with light, and the whole thing came back to me, how we were floating on the ocean, lying side by side on an inflatable raft. I was wearing a swimsuit, something suspiciously like the two-piece suit Mike and I'd dressed St. Senara in all those years ago. Brother Thomas had on his black robe with the cowl pulled over his head. He rolled toward me, coming up on his elbow and gazing down at my face. The water moved under us with a

lulling rhythm, and there were pelicans diving, scooping up fish. He pushed his cowl
back and smiled in that same captivating
way he had in the garden, a smile I found in-
tensely sexual. Touching my cheek with his
hand, he said my name. *Jessie.* He said it in
his deep voice, and I felt the curve of my
back lift up. His fingers slid beneath me and
unhooked the top of my bathing suit. His
mouth was at my ear, the heat of his breath
rushing in and out. I turned to kiss him, but in
that unexpected way of dreams, I found myself suddenly sitting up on the raft in a panic,
with the sense of losing all track of time.
Around us there was nothing but vast, rolling
water as far as I could see.

I rarely remembered dreams. For me they
were frustrating mirages that hovered on the
edge of waking, then melted conspicuously
the moment I opened my eyes. But this one
had stayed with me in grand detail. In my
mind I could still see the pearls of seawater
beading up on the black wool of Brother
Thomas's robe from the splash of the pelicans. The burning, blue look in his eyes. His
fingers sliding beneath me.

I wondered for a second how Hugh, or
even Dr. Ilg, would analyze a dream like this,

but decided I didn't want to know. I sat up, letting my feet poke around at the edge of the bed for my slippers. I raked my fingers through my hair, pulling at several tangles, listening for sounds of Mother, but the house drifted in silence.

Mother and I both had fallen into bed last night, too tired to talk. The thought of instigating a conversation with her today made me want to slide back under the covers and make myself into a little curl. What would I say to her? *Do you have plans to sever any more body parts?* It sounded crass, horrible, but that's what I really wanted to know— whether she was a danger to herself, whether she needed committing to some place that could take care of her.

I shuffled to the kitchen and poked around in a cabinet until I found the bag of Maxwell House. I had to make the coffee in a twenty-year-old electric percolator with a fraying cord. I wondered if she'd even heard about Mr. Coffees. As the contraption *bloop-blooped,* I crept to Mother's door and listened. Her snores wafted through the room. Her insomnia, it seemed, had disappeared with her finger.

I went back to the kitchen. The room was dim with waking light, the air chilly. Striking a match, I lit the space heater, listening to the gas flames pop with the same little blue sounds as always. Loading two slices of bread into the toaster, I watched the coils down inside glow red and thought about Thomas the monk and how odd that whole encounter had been—how he'd appeared in the garden out of nowhere.

I thought of the two of us out there talking, the severe way his gaze had entered me. The flutter in my body. And then I'd had the kind of dream I'd heard Hugh speak of, in which some great, enigmatic plane flies through your sleep, opening its bombardier doors, dropping a small, ticking dream.

The toast popped up. I poured the coffee, drank it black while nibbling the bread. The heater had turned the room into a Carolina cypress swamp. I got up and snapped it off. I couldn't explain to myself why I was think-ing these things. Thinking about Brother Thomas—a *monk.* And in *that* way, that in-cendiary way.

I imagined Hugh back home, and a terrible vulnerability took over. It was as if the most carefully guarded place in me had been suddenly abandoned, left wide open and assailable—the place that told me who I was.

I got up and walked into the living room, that feeling from the dream returning, the awful sense of losing my moorings. On one of the walls, Mother had as many as fifteen or twenty photographs framed in a disorganized mess, some with that dingy, sepia look around the edges. Most were old school pictures of me and Mike. Hideous hairdos. Half-shut eyes. Wrinkled white blouses. Braces. Dee called it "the Wall of Embarrassment."

The only photo up there taken after the sixties was one of Hugh, Dee, and me in 1970, when Dee was a baby. I stared with resolve at the three of us, remembering how Hugh had rigged the delayed timer on the camera and we'd posed on the sofa, tucking Dee between us, her small, sleepy face wedged under our chins.

The same evening we'd taken the picture, we'd made love for the first time after Dee's birth. We were supposed to wait six weeks before having sex. It happened, though, two days early.

I'd passed by the nursery and seen Hugh leaning over Dee's crib. Even though she

was sound asleep, he was singing something to her very softly. An amber light was
spread across the ceiling from the night-
light, sifting down to sit on his shoulders like
a furring of dust.

Heat shot through my body, something
potent and sexual. It was the tenderness in
Hugh that hit me so forcibly—the sight of
him loving her without anyone knowing.

I felt suddenly possessed by the intimacy
we'd had creating her, the thought of her
flesh forming out of the things we'd done in
the next room. I went and slid my arms
around his waist. Pressing my cheek against
his back, I felt him turn to me. His hands
made slow circles over my body. He whispered, "We have two more days to wait," and
when I said I couldn't wait, he picked me up
and carried me to bed.

Loving him had seemed different—more
unbridled, deeper, more purely felt. It had
something to do with Dee, as if Hugh and I
belonged together in some new way, and the
thought seemed measureless and intoxicat-
ing to me.

Afterward, as we lay across the bed, Dee
woke up crying. While I fed her, Hugh set up
the camera. I was wearing a peach-colored

housecoat; I hadn't even gotten it buttoned up all the way, and Hugh—you should see his face in the photo, how content and amused and clandestine it looked. The picture always stirred a secretive feeling in me, followed by a little flourish of happiness spreading open like an exotic paper fan in the center of my chest. I stood there and waited for the feeling to come.

The event seemed so long ago. Like some glorious ship inside a bottle. I did not know how it got in there, or how to get it out.

I picked up the phone and started dialing.

"Hello," Hugh said, and his voice seemed to rise under me like solid ground.

"It's me," I said.

"I was just thinking about you. Are you all right? I tried to call last night. No one answered."

Oh, great, I was going to have to buy a Mr. Coffee *and* an answering machine.

"We were at the monastery," I said. "I found Mother over there burying her finger."

"As in digging a hole in the ground and covering it up?"

"That's what I mean."

There was a long pause. "I think that

might actually be a good sign, at least for the moment," he said. "It could mean she's settling down, that her obsession is going underground, so to speak."

I lifted my eyebrows, intrigued by this, almost hopeful. "You think so?"

"Could be," he said. "But, Jessie, she still needs professional help. She should've been admitted to the psychiatric unit. With time the pattern could start all over again."

I stretched the phone cord over to the table and sat down. "You mean she might cut off another finger?"

"Well, yes, or it could be something completely different. Obsessions like this are ego-dystonic, just random thoughts."

There was a little tapping noise, and I knew he was on the portable phone at the bathroom sink, shaving as we talked.

"But I don't think cutting off her finger was random. I really think it relates to something particular," I said.

"Oh, I doubt that," he said, dismissing the idea, dismissing me.

I sank back in the chair, letting out a sigh. "I'll talk to her today and see if—"

"I suppose that won't hurt, but I was

thinking. . . . I'm going to come to the island this weekend. You shouldn't handle this by yourself."

He'd interrupted me.

"No, I don't think it's a good idea for you to come," I said. "I think she would be more apt to—"

"It's too complicated for you to handle by yourself, Jessie."

It was, of course. It would be like my sitting down to solve a math equation that was two feet long; what was going on inside her was a conundrum so far beyond me it was pathetic. I was considering saying to him, *Yes, yes, you come fix things.* But it still felt wrong to me. Part of it was the feeling that I—the nonpsychiatrist in the family—really could help Mother better than he could. That I could figure things out better by myself.

And maybe, too, I didn't want Hugh here. I wanted this time for myself, to be on my own—was that so awful?

I told myself it had nothing to do with the monk and what had happened the night before. I mean, nothing *had* happened. No, this was about me for once, following my own idea about something. Later, though, I would wonder about that. Are motives ever that clear?

I stood up. "I *said* I will handle it. I don't want you to come." It came out angrier than I'd intended.

"*Jesus,*" he said. "You don't have to shout at me."

I looked back toward Mother's bedroom, hoping I hadn't awakened her. "Maybe I *feel* like shouting," I said. I didn't know why I was picking a fight.

"For God's sake, I was just trying to help. What's wrong with you?"

"Nothing," I snapped. "Nothing's wrong with me."

"Well, apparently there *is,*" he said, raising his voice.

"What you mean is, if I don't need your help, there's something wrong with me."

"Now you're being ridiculous," he said, and his tone was lacerating. "Did you hear me? You're being ridiculous."

And I hung up. I simply hung up. I refilled my coffee cup and sat with my hands wrapped around it. They were shaking a little.

I waited for the phone to ring, for him to call me back. When he didn't, I became anxious, filled with that strange turbulence that rises when you begin to wash up on the island of your own little self and you don't see how you could ever sustain yourself there.

After a while I bent down and peered under the table. The crucifix was still nailed beneath it. The storm-tent Jesus.

CHAPTER
Ten

That morning when I changed the bandage on Mother's hand, I had to look away from the wound more than once. Mother sat in the brown wicker chair at her dressing table while I cleaned the skin around the sutures with hydrogen peroxide and dabbed antibiotic ointment on a sterile pad. The cut was just below her knuckle on the "pointing finger," as she always referred to it. I kept thinking what a violent burst of energy it would've taken to bring the cleaver down with enough force to sever the bone. She winced when I placed the pad over the tender, swollen nub.

I glanced at the photograph of my father,

wondering what he would've thought of her now, the dreadful turn she'd taken after his death. What he would have thought of her slicing off her finger. Mother turned and looked at the photo, too. "I know what I did seems crazy to you."

Was she talking to him or to me? "I just wish you'd help me understand why you had to," I said.

She tapped the glass on the frame with her fingernail. It made a clicking sound in the room. "This picture was made the day he started his charter business."

I'd been five at the time. I didn't remember him as a shrimper, only as captain of the *Jes-Sea*. Before he'd bought the boat, he'd worked for Shem Watkins, "scrimping for shrimp," he said. He would take one of Shem's trawlers out for a week at a time and come back with four thousand pounds of shrimp in the hold. But all he'd wanted was to run his own business, be his own boss, with the freedom to be out on the water when he wanted and home with his family when he wanted. He'd come up with an in-shore fishing charter idea, saved and bought his Chris-Craft. Four years later it had exploded.

He said his religion was the sea. That it was his family. He'd told Mike and me stories about a sea kingdom ruled by a gang of ruthless mud snails and the brave keyhole limpets who tried to overthrow them. His imagination was ingenious. He told us we could make wands out of stingray barbs and, by waving them a certain way, cause the waves to sing "Dixie," something that had occupied us for fruitless hours. If we dreamed of a great egret, he said, we would find its feathers beneath our pillow the next morning. I woke more than once to white feathers in my bed, though I could never recall the egret dream that had brought them. And of course the ne plus ultra of all his stories— how he'd seen an entire pod of mermaids one dawn, swimming to his boat.

I could not remember a single time he'd attended mass, but he was the one who'd first taken me to the monastery to see the mermaid chair, who'd told me the story behind it. I think he'd only pretended to be a reprobate.

Though he refused to share Mother's religion, he seemed to admire it. Back then she was not pathological about it. Sometimes I think he married her because of her boundless capacity for faith, how she could swallow every preposterous doctrine, dogma, and story the church came up with. Maybe her faith in the church made up for his lack of it. My mother and father made a peculiar couple—Walt Whitman and Joan of Arc—but it'd worked. They had adored each other. I was sure of that.

Mother turned away from his photograph and waited as I finished winding the gauze bandage around her hand. She was wearing her blue chenille robe, minus the belt. She gathered the collar up around her neck, then let her hand drift down to the drawer, the one with all the religious bilge. She fingered the handle. I wondered if the clipping about his death was still in there.

Why had I given him the pipe?

Dad and I had seen it one day in Caw Caw General, and he'd admired it. He'd picked it up and pretended to take a puff. "I've always wanted to be the kind of man who smoked a pipe," he said. I'd taken every cent of my fiddler-crab money and bought it for him for Father's Day. Mother had told me not to, that she didn't want him smoking a pipe. I'd bought it anyway.

She'd never said a word to me about its being the cause of the fire.

I tore a piece of adhesive tape and fastened the end of the gauze to her wrist. She started to get up, but I knelt in front of her chair and placed my hands on her knees. I didn't know where to start. But I'd taken this on. I'd banished Hugh, and now it was all mine.

As I knelt there, my belief that I could handle it by myself was starting to break apart. Mother stared straight into my eyes. Her lower lids drooped down into deep curves, exposing their small pink linings. She looked timeless, older than her years.

I said, "Last night in the garden, you mentioned Father Dominic, remember?"

She shook her head. Her good hand lay in her lap, and I took it in mine, touching the tips of her fingers.

"I asked you why you did this to your finger, and you brought up Dad, and then you mentioned Father Dominic. Did he have something to do with your cutting off your finger?"

She gave me a blank look.

"Did he give you the idea that you should

do some kind of penance, something like that?"

The blankness turned to exasperation. "No, of course not."

"But cutting off your finger *was* penance, wasn't it?"

Her eyes darted away from my face.

"Please, Mother. We need to talk about it."

She pressed her teeth into her bottom lip and seemed to consider my question. I watched her touch a strand of her hair and thought how yellowish it looked.

"I can't talk about Dominic," she said finally.

"But why not?"

"I can't, that's all."

She picked up a prescription bottle and walked to the door. "I need to take my pain pill," she said, and vanished into the hall, leaving me on my knees beside her dresser.

CHAPTER
Eleven

I spent the morning on a cleaning campaign, determined to be helpful. I changed the sheets on Mother's bed, did the laundry, and scrubbed things that hadn't been touched in years: the bathroom grout, the venetian blinds, the coils on the back of the refrigerator. I went into the pantry and threw away everything that had expired—two huge bags of stuff. I dragged her rusting golf cart out of the garage and cranked it up to see if it worked, and, eyeing the grimy bathtub grotto, I hooked up the garden hose and gave it a good spray-cleaning.

Through all of this, I thought about Mother's

refusal to talk about my father's death, her strange mention of Father Dominic.

I thought on and off about Brother Thomas, too. I didn't mean to—he simply wormed his way in. At one point I'd found myself poised under the exposed lightbulb in the pantry, holding a twenty-eight-ounce can of tomatoes, and realized I'd been replaying some moment with him from the night before.

The day was warm, the sun bearing down with a throbbing winter brightness. Mother and I ate lunch on the front porch, balancing trays on our laps, eating the gumbo neither of us could face the night before. I tried to draw her out again about Dominic, but she sat there shuttered tightly.

Looking for some way, any way, to reach her, I asked if she'd like to call Dee at college, and she shook her head.

I gave up then. I listened to her spoon scratch the bottom of her bowl and knew I would have to find out about Dominic some other way. I doubted she would ever talk to me about anything, that we'd get to the "root of things," as Hugh had called it. I hated that he was probably right. It made me determined.

After lunch she lay down on her bed and

took a nap. It was as if she were making up now for all the lost sleep. While she dozed, I slipped into her room to get the name of her doctor from the prescription bottle, telling myself I should call him. But I never even copied it down.

I stood gazing at her dresser, the ceramic Mary with the plump Jesus planted on her hip. The drawer was right there. I pulled it out. The wood scraped, and I looked back at the bed. She didn't move.

The inside of the drawer brimmed with holy cards, rosaries, a prayer book, old photographs of Dee. I groped through all her cherished clutter as quietly as I could. Exactly the way I'd done when I was a child. *Was the clipping still here?* My heart was beating very fast.

Near the back my fingers bumped against something slender and hard. I knew what it was before I pulled it out. I froze for a second or two, the air bristling around me, bracing myself before I pulled it up.

It was the pipe I'd given my father.

I glanced again at Mother, then held it up to the light slanting through the window, and nothing made sense to me. My knees felt like sponges, wet and squishy—it was impossible to keep standing. I sat down on the chair.

How could the pipe be in the drawer? When had she put it here? It should have been at the bottom of the ocean along with the *Jes-Sea,* along with my father. I'd played it out in my mind so many times—the way it must have happened.

Joseph Dubois, standing on his boat in the last stain of darkness, looking east to where the sun has just lifted its shiny forehead over the water. He often took his boat out then to "greet the dawn"—that was his phrase for it. Mike and I would come to breakfast, and Dad would not be there, and we would say, "Is Dad still greeting the dawn?" We thought it was a common thing people did, like getting their hair cut. He would go alone on these excursions, smoke his pipe unperturbed, and watch the sea become a membrane of rolling light.

I'd pictured him on the last morning of his life tapping his pipe on the rail. Have you ever seen how sparks fly from the bowl of a pipe, how far they travel? He taps his pipe, and, unknown to him, the fuel line is leaking. One ember, a hundred times smaller than a moth, flies onto a drop of gas in the well near the engine. There is a pop, a puff of flame. The fire leaps from puddle to puddle like a stone skipping water. It lunges and crackles, and I always imagine that this is the moment he turns, just as the flames slam into the gas tank, the moment when everything blazes and bursts apart.

I'd envisioned it this way so often that I couldn't fathom it happening any other way. And everyone had said as much—the police, the newspaper, the entire island.

I closed my eyes. I felt that the center-piece of my history had been dug up and exposed as a complete and utter fiction. It left a gaping place I couldn't quite step over.

I was gripping the pipe almost painfully. I relaxed my hand. Bending over, I smelled the bowl of it, and it was like smelling him.

Everything began to rearrange itself then. *It wasn't the pipe that had caused the fire.* I sat at the dresser for several minutes while Mother slept across the room, and I let the knowledge pour over me: *I was not to blame.*

CHAPTER
Twelve

I took the pipe to my room. I doubted she would go through the drawer and miss it. As I tucked it inside my purse, the relief I felt became full-blooded anger. I began to pace. I had an overwhelming impulse to shake Mother awake and ask why she'd let me grow up believing that my pipe had been the cause of everything.

Mine had been a private blame, a heaviness no one sees, the kind that comes over you in dreams when you try to run but can barely move. I'd carried it like a weight in the shafts of my bones, and she'd let me. *She had let me.*

Wait. That wasn't completely fair. Maybe Mother had thought I didn't *know* about the pipe. She'd tried to protect me from knowing—never speaking about it, hiding the clipping—and yet it didn't excuse her. *It didn't.* She would have to think in some small corner of her head that Mike and I would find out. The whole island had known about the pipe, for Christ's sake. How could she think *we* didn't?

I could hear her breathing, an accordion rhythm that moved through the house. I didn't want to be there when she woke up. I scribbled a message and propped it on the kitchen table, saying I needed exercise, some air.

Hepzibah's house was less than a mile away, down a crook of road that wound past the slave cemetery, toward the egret rookery, and then around to the beach. I could see it as I came around a curve, surrounded by wild tufts of evening primrose and seaside spurge. I knocked on her iridescent blue front door and waited.

She didn't answer.

I followed the path to the back of the house. The little screen porch was unlocked, so I stepped inside and rapped on the door

to the kitchen, which was the same shiny in-
digo as the door in front. The blue was supposed to scare away the Booga Hag—a
haunting spirit said to suck the soul out of
you during the night. I doubted that Hepzibah believed in the Booga Hag, but she
loved the old Gullah ways. And just in case
the blue doors didn't deter the Hag, Hepzibah had planted a row of conch shells in her
garden.

On the side of the porch she had the so-
called show-and-tell table set up as always,
heaped with the ragged island treasures
she'd spent most of her life collecting.

I walked over to it, besieged by a sudden,
potent nostalgia. Mike and I had spent hours
huddled over this table. It was piled with stalks
of coral, crab claws, sea sponges, lightning
whelks, shark eyes, augers, jackknife clams.
Every lowly shell was remembered here, even
broken ones. I picked up several chipped
sand dollars, a starfish with two arms. Egret,
heron, and ibis feathers were wedged among
the objects, some standing straight up as if
they'd sprouted there.

In the center of the table, elevated on a
wooden box, was the elongated jawbone of
an alligator. Naturally this had been Mike's fa-

vorite object. Mine had been the chalk-white skull of a loggerhead turtle. In my imagination I'd swum with that turtle through boundless water, down to the floor of the ocean and back.

I poked around and discovered it stuffed among a pile of cockles.

The night Hepzibah had found the skull, we were having the All-Girls Picnic on the beach. At least that was how those occasions came to be known. I sat down now in an old rocker, holding the turtle skull in my hands, feeling the jolt of nostalgia again. I hadn't thought about the All-Girls Picnics in so long. Since I was a girl.

Kat had started them way back when both she and Mother were new brides, and Benne was only a toddler. Every May Day eve without fail, they'd gathered on Bone Yard Beach. If it was raining, they'd hold the picnic the first clear night after that, though I recall that one year Kat got tired of waiting and set up a tarp.

After Hepzibah hooked up with Mother and Kat, she joined the All-Girls Picnics, too, and then I got to come as soon as I could walk. They had stopped abruptly after Dad died.

I remembered the big feasts they made:

Kat's crab cakes, Hepzibah's fine hoppin' John, lots of wine. Mother usually brought her raisin-bread pudding and a bag of benne wafers in honor of Benne, who'd been named for the sesame cracker, because Kat had eaten so many of them when she was pregnant. Everyone got May Day presents— usually bubble bath and Revlon nail polish— only flaming red allowed. But that wasn't what made me love those times. It was because on that one night of the year, Mother, Kat, and Hepzibah metamorphosed into completely different creatures.

After we ate, they made a bonfire out of beach wood and danced while Benne and I sat on the sand over in the shadows and watched. Hepzibah beat her Gullah drum, making a sound so old that after a while it seemed to be swelling up out of the earth and rolling in from the ocean, and Kat shook an old tambourine, filling the air with silver vibrations. At a certain point, something took them over, and they moved faster and faster, their shadows making inky smears in the firelight.

The last year they held the picnic, the three of them waded into the water fully clothed, each holding a piece of thread that they'd yanked out of Mother's embroidered sweater. Benne and I stood with our toes touching the edge of the ocean and begged to come, too, and Kat said, "No, this is just for us. Y'all stay back there."

They walked out until the cold water creased their waists, and then they tied the three threads together. "Hurry up," they kept saying to one another, squealing when the waves lapped against them.

I'd believed then, and I still believed now, that it was some ritual of friendship they'd concocted on the spot, thanks to the wine and the dizziness brought on by their dancing. And Mother's conveniently unraveling sweater.

Kat flung their tied threads into the darkness, onto the waves, and they laughed. It was a voluptuous laughter, and mischievous, like children laughing.

As they scampered back, Hepzibah found the turtle skull. She practically tripped over it coming out of the water. She stood above it with the waves foaming around her feet, Mother and Kat still giggling and carrying on. "Tie yuh mout'," Hepzibah said, switching into Gullah, and everyone fell instantly silent.

"Look what the ocean has sent," she said,

and raised the skull out of the water, the ivory bone smooth and dripping, immaculate against the black night.

I believe they all thought it was a sign of some kind. They had bound their lives together out there in the water, and suddenly a turtle skull miraculously washed up at their feet.

For a long time after that—years and years—they'd passed the skull back and forth among them. I remembered it perched on our mantel for a while before it would resurface on Kat's bookshelf or here on Hepzibah's table. It must have reminded them of those nights, of the knots in their threads.

Now, sitting in the porch rocker, I rubbed the porous bone with my thumb and looked back at the blue door. Hepzibah obviously wasn't home.

I got up and put the skull back on the table, and for a moment the table seemed like more than a distant slab of childhood memory. It felt like a living part of me.

I'd known since I was ten that I would leave the island. On the first Ash Wednesday after Dad's death, the moment the priest touched my forehead, I'd felt myself rise up out of that little smudge of ash with the determination of a phoenix. *I will leave here,* I told myself. *I will fly away.* After college, I'd rarely come back, and when I had, it'd been with a dissociating arrogance. I hadn't even gotten married to Hugh here. The wedding had been in somebody's generic backyard garden in Atlanta, somebody we didn't even know that well. I thought about Kat teasing me, saying I'd forgotten the pluff mud whence I'd come, and she'd been right. I'd done everything in my power to erase this place.

The last thing I'd expected was to stand on Hepzibah's porch and feel a seizure of love for Egret Island. And not just for the island but for the woman my mother had been, dancing around a fire.

Something struck me then: I'd never done any of those things my mother had done. Never danced on a beach. Never made a bonfire. Never waded into the ocean at night with laughing women and tied my life to theirs.

CHAPTER Thirteen

The next morning I walked to the monastery. The sun, perky and yellow yesterday, had burrowed into a hole somewhere. Fog covered everything. It looked as if soup skim had formed over the entire island during the night. I wore my blue jeans and red coat and a clashing garnet baseball cap I'd found in the utility room with CAROLINA GAMECOCKS printed across the front. It was pulled low on my forehead, with my ponytail threaded through the hole in back.

I walked the same path I'd taken a couple of nights earlier when I'd gone searching for Mother. I could smell the dense, primal odor of the marsh carried in by the fog, and it made me think of Brother Thomas. His face formed in my mind, and my insides gave a funny lurch.

I was going to find Father Dominic. If I happened to run into Brother Thomas in the process, that was fine, but I told myself I wasn't going out of my way.

Naturally I had no idea what I would say to Dominic once I found him. I began to play with various strategies to learn what he knew about Mother's cutting off her finger.

What if I talk to Dominic, really level with him, and he goes and tells Mother? I hadn't considered this. Whatever progress I'd made with her would evaporate then and there. She would probably send me packing again.

I'd left her watching an old Julia Child cooking show on television. Mother loved Julia Child. I mean, *loved* her. She would say to me, "You think Julia Child is Catholic? She would have to be, wouldn't she?" Mother always copied down her recipes, especially anything with shrimp in it. If she wanted to cook one of Julia's shrimp dishes, she would simply send a monk out into the creek with a net.

The monks hand-tied the nets—six- and eight-footers—and sold them not only in the Low Country but in seaside boutiques and fishing stores all along the East Coast. I'd seen one once in a shop on Cape Cod when Hugh and I were vacationing. It'd been packaged with a fragment of Scripture printed on the label: "Cast your net." From the Gospel of John, I believe the label had said, so there was a kind of mandate from God to buy it. "Shrewd marketers, aren't they?" Hugh had commented. They were priced at seventy-five dollars.

Walking along, I remembered how the monks would sit on the shaved grass in the cloister square with strands of cotton twine and buckets of lead weights, their callused hands moving back and forth in a beautiful, mindless rhythm. I used to think that custom cast nets had to be the most exotic way on earth for monks to earn a living, but then a couple of years ago, Dee had told me about a "really cool monastery" out west that sold hay to movie stars for their llamas. We'd had this whole discussion about which monastery had the more unusual, or more auspicious, occupation. We'd decided it had to be llama feeding. But still, cast nets were a long way from making fudge or rhubarb jelly.

Mike had been a brilliant caster, holding the sides of the net in his hands, the top of it in his teeth, flinging it like a spinning Frisbee into the air. It would sail up into the light, then plunge into the creek with a huge *galump!* and a spray that rose like smoke rings off the surface. He would tug the net up and shake it, and the wiggling gray shrimp would spill around our feet.

As I came through the last clump of trees, I glanced toward the cottages where the monks lived, the red tile roofs glowing pink in the murky light. I was, I realized, wishing for a glimpse of Brother Thomas—hoping that a crack would appear in the viscous morning and he would step out in the same ghostly way he had in the garden.

Approaching the gate to the rose garden, I thought of Mother's finger in there and shuddered, remembering something I hadn't thought of in years. Mother and her *milagros.*

When I was a teenager, she'd ordered them routinely from a cheesy Catholic catalog. They'd looked like bracelet charms to me, except they were all severed body parts—feet, hearts, ears, torsos, heads, hands. Eventually I figured out that they were offerings, little prayers in the shape of the petitioners' afflictions. When Mother thought she had a cataract, she'd left an eye *milagro* at Senara's statue, and when her knee had flared with arthritis, she'd left a *milagro* in the shape of a leg.

I couldn't help but wonder if she'd intended her finger to be the ultimate *milagro.*

I skirted the back of the church and headed along a tree-lined avenue toward the Monastery Reception Center, near the abbey entrance. It looked like a small cottage. The porch had a sloping roof and was draped with browned honeysuckle. Inside was a monk with a bald head and uncivilized eyebrows that curled over a pair of black-framed glasses.

He nodded as I moved past him to a room the monks called the Gift Shop. I browsed through the display of cast nets, turned a squeaky rack of rosaries and saints' medals. Spotting a stack of teal green booklets, I picked one up, surprised to see it was the booklet Kat said she'd had printed. *The Mermaid's Tale.*

I flipped it open to the first page:

According to the legend recounted in Legenda Aurea: Readings on the Saints, in 1450 a beautiful Celtic mermaid named Asenora swam ashore on the coast of Cornwall where a Benedictine monastery had recently been established. After removing her fish tail and hiding it among the rocks, she explored the area on foot and discovered the community of men. She made many clandestine visits—

"It's the story behind our mermaid chair," a voice said, and I looked up from the passage to see the bald monk with his arms crossed tightly over his chest, as if he were battening himself down. He wore a large wooden cross around his neck, and there were droop lines at the corners of his mouth. "One of our monks wrote it. Pretty fanciful stuff, I'm afraid."

"Yes, I've always loved the story," I told him, realizing I hadn't heard it in ages. Most of it was fuzzy to me now.

"If you're here for the guided tour, I'm afraid you've just missed it, and there's not another one until three o'clock this afternoon, though quite honestly I don't see the big attraction. Just a lot of 'Here is the church where the monks pray, and here is the Net

House where the monks tie nets, and over there is the laundry where the monks wash their socks.' "

I thought he meant this to be funny, but when I laughed, he glowered at me a little. "No," I said, "I didn't come for the tour." I dug around in my jeans pocket for the ten-dollar bill I'd stuffed inside it and bought the book. "The author, Father Dominic—where could I find him?" I said. "I'd like to have him sign this for me."

"Sign the book?" He shook his head. "We won't be able to live with him if he starts autographing books. We can barely live with him now." Again, I wasn't sure whether he was being serious; he had that kind of sour way that made it hard to tell. "I imagine he's in the library somewhere," he said. "That would be the white stucco building next to the church. It's open to visitors, but some areas aren't. You'd be surprised where people end up. Yesterday a lady came wandering through the refectory while we were eating lunch. She took a picture of the salad bar!"

A woman roaming through prohibited areas struck me as amusing, as did his offense at it, but actually more amusing was the fact that the abbey had a salad bar. I wondered if Mother had come up with that. It was so implausibly *current* of her.

"I know the places that are off limits," I told him. "My mother is Nelle Dubois. I'm Jessie. I used to come here as a child." I don't know what made me tell him this; he wasn't the most welcoming person. I was even thinking how peculiar that he, of all the monks, would get assigned to the Reception Center. Perhaps it was part of a conspiracy to discourage visitors.

He said, "We're sorry about her troubles." It came out like an automated recording on an answering machine.

"And you are . . . ?"

"Oh, sorry. I'm Father Sebastian. I'm the prior here."

I tried to remember the monastic hierarchy. I was pretty sure the prior was the second in command, the one who, as Mother put it, kept the monastery on the straight and narrow.

Strolling to the library to find Father Dominic, I got a monumental case of cold feet. *What am I doing?* My steps slowed until I was just standing there, stymied with doubt. I considered going back to the house and calling Hugh. *On second thought,* you *come fix Mother,* I'd say. *I do not have the balls—or the ovaries, or whatever anatomical part is required.*

Glancing behind the church, I noticed the foot trail that led to the edge of the marsh. I followed it to a stone bench that sat beneath an oak.

Coward.

I didn't sit on the bench but instead plopped on the ground and sat there staring at the creek plaited with mist, the way it moved like a living vein, doglegging into the bay. I'd often come to this spot after my father died, the times I'd felt sad or lost. I'd shouted my name across the marsh, listening to the way it was magnified over the water, as if the spartina grasses were singing it, and how sometimes the wind would hoist it like a gull out toward the ocean. "Jessie," I would call, over and over and over.

I was holding the booklet I'd bought and opened it to the passage I'd been reading when Father Sebastian interrupted me.

. . . Suspicious that Asenora was no ordinary woman but a mermaid, and greatly alarmed by her presence, the abbot of the monastery hid himself by the water and waited. He witnessed Asenora swim ashore, remove her fish tail and hide it in a niche in the cliff.

When she wandered off in the direction of the abbey, the shrewd abbot retrieved the fish tail, bundling it into his robe. He tucked it inside a secret compartment hidden under the seat of his chair, in the church. Without her tail, the poor mermaid could never go back to the sea, and soon the wildness of it drained out of her. Asenora was converted, and eventually became St. Senara.

When my father used to tell me that part of the story, he talked about Asenora's "tragic fate"—losing her tail and getting stuck with a halo—and I got the impression, though it was only reading between the lines, that Dominic felt the same way. And, frankly, something about Father Dominic's writing this story at all caused an uneasiness in me.

An interesting footnote to the legend states that after her conversion Asenora sometimes missed the sea and her former life so strongly that she prowled the monastery at night in search of her tail. Conflicting stories exist about whether she ever found it. One story suggests she not only found her fish tail but donned it whenever she wanted to revisit her lost life, always returning, however, and replacing it inside the abbot's chair.

I thought of Mother and her crazy love for St. Senara, and I couldn't reconcile it with what I was reading. Senara was a saint who sneaked around looking for transportation back to her nefarious past. It had never really occurred to me how incongruous this was.

Some scholars suggest that the story of Saint Senara may have been created to help people choose the path of godly delight over that of sensual delight. But might it also be a way of emphasizing the importance of *both*?

Both? I hadn't expected him to write something like that—being a monk. I closed the booklet—sort of slapped it shut, to tell the truth. The tension was vibrating again in my chest.

Dampness from the grass had seeped through my jeans. I got to my feet, and when I turned around, I saw Father Dominic coming along the path toward me. He stopped on the other side of the stone bench. He was wearing the straw hat, and Kat had been right—whole sections of it had sprung loose. It was taking on the farcical appearance of a bird's nest.

"Knock, knock," he said, his eyes filled with amusement.

I hesitated. *So he remembers me.*

"Who's there?" I felt immensely awkward saying it, but I didn't see how I could *not* play along.

"Zoom."

"Zoom who?"

"Zoom did you expect?" he said, setting loose an opulent laugh that seemed oversize for the joke. "I don't think I've seen you since you were a girl. I hope you remember me?"

"Of course, Father Dominic," I said. "I . . . I was just—"

"You were just reading my little book, and from the way you closed it, I'm not sure you liked it very much." He laughed to let me know he was teasing, but it made me uncomfortable.

"No, no, I liked it." Neither of us spoke for a moment. I looked off at the marsh, embarrassed. The tide was receding, leaving plats of mud that looked tender and freshly peeled. I could see the holes of dozens of hibernating fiddler crabs, the tip ends of their claws barely protruding.

"Father Sebastian said you were looking for me. I believe you are in need of an autograph for your book."

"Oh. Yes, that's right. Would you mind?" I handed him the booklet, feeling caught in my little lie. "I'm sorry, I don't have a pen."

He produced one from inside his black scapular. He scrawled something on the inside cover, then handed it back.

He said, "This is a lovely spot, isn't it?"

"Yes . . . lovely."

The sea of grass behind us swayed with the breezes, and he shifted side to side beneath his robe as if he were one of them, a grass blade trying to get synchronized with the rest.

"So how's our Nelle?" he asked.

The question startled me. The curious way he'd said *"our Nelle,"* plus something in his voice, how her name came out softer than the other words.

Our Nelle. *Our.*

"Her hand is healing," I said. "The real problem is in here." I meant to touch my finger to my forehead but involuntarily tapped the flat bone over my heart, and I felt the rightness of that, as though my finger were trying to tell me something.

"Yes, I suppose the heart will cause us to do strange and wondrous things," Father Dominic said. He rapped his knuckles on his chest, and I had the feeling he was talking about impulses in his own heart.

He'd taken off his hat and was plucking at the wayward pieces on it. I had a memory of him that day the monks delivered the washed-up debris from my father's boat, how he'd stood at the fireplace in this very same posture, holding his hat, watching the board burn.

"Did you know she called the finger that she cut off her 'pointing finger'?" I asked.

He shook his head, and his face—such an old, kind face—changed a little, tightening and puckering in places.

I hesitated. Certain things were occurring to me in the moment—guesses, impressions—and I didn't know whether I should say them. "What if she cut it off to relieve a terrible sense of blame?"

He looked away from my face.

He knows.

A ravine of quiet opened between us. I remember a murmurous hum rising up like the swell of insects. It seemed to last a long time.

"Why did she do it?" I said.

He pretended I was being rhetorical. "Yes, why indeed?"

"No, I'm asking *you.* Why did she do it?"

"Has your mother said something to you to make you think I would know her motives?"

"She said she couldn't talk about her reasons."

He sighed, laced and unlaced his fingers. I was sure he was making a decision of some kind. "Jessie, I can only imagine how confusing this must be to you, but I can't tell you anything. I wish I could, but I can't."

"Did she tell you something during confession?"

This seemed to catch him off guard, as if such a thing hadn't occurred to him. He leaned toward me, wearing a gentle, knowing look, as if inviting a moment of intimacy between us. I thought for a second he might take my hand.

"All I'm saying is that maybe it wouldn't be good for your mother if we delved into it. I know that's just the opposite of what you might think—we've been brainwashed these days to believe we have to dig up every pitiable shred of our past and examine it half to death, but that doesn't always turn out best for a person. Nelle wants to keep whatever this is to herself. Maybe we should let her."

He pressed his lips together, and his face looked pained, pleading. "Jessie, I need you to trust me. Trust your mother."

I was about to argue with him when he reached out and, cupping my cheek with his hand, smiled in an austere, resigned way. I don't know why, but I didn't pull away, and we stayed like that a moment before he turned and walked back toward the church, arranging his ragged hat on his head.

CHAPTER
Fourteen

I sat on the bench with my back to the marsh and waited until Father Dominic was out of sight. *What just happened?*

He'd seemed so genuine. Earnest. *Jessie, I need you to trust me.* It seemed as if I should. He was, after all, an old monk who told knock-knock jokes. Everyone loved him. More to the point, Kat trusted him, and Kat Bowers was no fool. It would be impossible to dupe that woman.

Confused, I stretched my neck backward, watching two ospreys lap a wide circle through the fog. What if Father Dominic was right? Could I make things worse for Mother by trying to understand her reasons?

My eyes fell on *The Mermaid's Tale,* wedged next to me on the bench. I thumbed to the title page. *"Zoom did you expect?"* he'd written in peculiar slanted letters, then scrawled his name.

As I stared at it, it slowly dawned on me— I didn't trust him. I just didn't. I believed inside that I *should,* and there were Kat and Mother up to their earlobes in trust for Dominic, but I couldn't muster any of it for myself.

I glanced at my watch. It was just after eleven. I would have to get back soon and fix lunch for Mother, but I had a sudden impulse to slip inside the church and see the mermaid chair.

The last time I'd seen it had probably been twenty-five years ago, right before I'd left for college. Despite the considerable time Mike and I had spent horsing around on it as children, I always associated it with my father—I suppose because he was the one who'd first showed it to me, who'd told me the story behind it, who'd loved the chair nearly as much as his boat. Mother, on the other hand, had wanted nothing to do with it.

It hadn't always been that way. Up until Dad died, she hadn't minded the chair at all. Year after year he'd been one of the men who carried the mermaid chair on its two-mile procession from the church to the ferry dock for the Blessing of the Fleet, something she'd encouraged. Typically the monks chose the more pious men, and Joe Dubois had been an absolute pagan, but somehow he'd always wheedled himself into the job. He simply believed, he said, in blessing shrimp boats; he didn't care whether it was St. Senara, God, the monks, or Max the dog who performed the blessing. But I think it was more than that. While my mother loved Senara, the saint, my father loved her *other* nature—her life as Asenora, the mermaid.

The chair had round iron hooks on each arm for poles to slip through, and every April, early in the evening of St. Senara's feast day, four men lifted the rods onto their shoulders and paraded the chair from the church, through the abbey gate, past the island shops, as if it were Cleopatra's throne or the bier of a Greek god. I remember Mike and me marching beside our father the whole way, very brash and self-important—"peacocked," Mother had said—and the islanders flowing out behind us, undulating over the road in a long bridal train of color.

Walking now toward the church, I thought about those radiant processions, the prayer read by the abbot as he sat in the mermaid chair on the dock's edge, his hand lifted in blessing. And perhaps forty trawlers, not just from Egret Island but McClellanville and Mount Pleasant, too, moving past the dock, each one strung with colored lights, the water turning molten as darkness collected. After the boats were blessed, and the chair ceremoniously splashed with seawater, the islanders would toss Mermaid Tears—tiny pearl-colored pebbles—into the bay, as a way of honoring the mermaid saint's sadness at leaving the ocean. Then the entire island would gather around tables of fried and boiled shrimp at Max's Café.

Between the Net House and the church, there was a grassy area where the monks used to spread the cast nets on wooden racks and treat them with a coppery-smelling solution to keep them from rotting. The racks were gone now, but I could see a robed monk out there, tossing a bright yellow tennis ball to Max. His back was to me, but I noticed he was tall and that his hair was dark. When Max bounded back to him with the ball, the monk bent down and rubbed the dog's head. It was Brother Thomas.

As I walked toward him, he turned, and when he recognized me, his face filled with what looked exactly like pleasure. He came over to me, holding the tennis ball, Max trailing behind.

"I didn't mean to interrupt your game," I said, trying not to smile for some reason, but I couldn't restrain it. I felt a lavish sweep of happiness at the sight of him.

"I was just passing time with Max until day prayer and mass," he said.

There was a moment of silence in which I looked off at the trees, then back to find him watching me with the faintest accumulation of a smile. I thought of my dream, the two of us on the raft in the ocean. The images had come to me repeatedly over the last two days—his cowl falling back to reveal his face, his hand touching my cheek, sliding beneath my back. I felt self-conscious thinking about it in his presence. As if it might show through.

I abruptly dropped my gaze to the ground, where I saw his boots sticking out from beneath his robe, caked with dry mud from the marsh.

"My work shoes," he said. "I'm the rookery monk."

"The *what?*"

He laughed. "The rookery monk," he repeated.

"And what is that?"

"The state pays us to take care of the rookery—it's a protected refuge—so one of us is designated to go out every day and keep an eye on it."

"You don't make cast nets with the others?"

"No, thank God. I was terrible at it, plus I'm the youngest one here, so I got the outdoor job."

Max had been sitting patiently, waiting. "One more," Thomas told him, and sent the ball sailing into the air.

We watched Max for a second as he ran full speed through the haze.

"What does a rookery monk do, exactly?" I asked.

"He keeps track of the bird population—not just egrets but pelicans, herons, ospreys, most all of them. In the spring and summer, he counts and measures egret eggs, checks on the nests, the hatchlings, that kind of thing. This time of year is not so busy."

I could smell a fragrance coming from him. It was, I realized, grape jelly.

"So you watch birds."

He smiled. "That's the biggest part of it, but I do other things—inspect the oyster beds, collect water samples, whatever's needed. The Department of Natural Resources has a checklist for me." Max came bounding up with the ball in his mouth, and Thomas took it, tucking it inside his scapular. "Max usually goes out in the boat with me," he added, stroking the dog's back.

"I can tell you like the job," I said.

"To be honest, I think sometimes being out there on the creeks is what keeps me here."

"I know what you mean. I grew up on the creeks. My brother and I loved the birds. We used to go out in the rookery and watch the male egrets do their mating dance."

I'd blurted this without thinking. And it would've been nothing, *nothing,* just stupid conversation about birds, if, realizing what I'd said, I hadn't drawn in my breath, making that small, rasping sound of surprise. Redness washed up my neck into my cheeks, so of course he knew I was reading something sexual into what we were doing. I wanted to turn and run off, the way Max had done.

He was looking at me intently. I'm sure he knew what I was thinking, but he was kind, and he tried to smooth it over. He said, "Yes, I've seen it many times. It's beautiful the way they snap their bills and elongate their necks."

The truth was, I'd been snapping my bill and elongating my neck for the last five minutes.

"I've told you what *I* do," he was saying. "What is it *you* do?"

I stood there trying to make myself appear very straight and proper. I didn't know how to say who I was or what I did. What *did* I do? Keep house for Hugh? Paint scenes in little boxes and arrange a collage of objects inside them? No, I couldn't even claim that anymore. And Dee had grown up and gone away, so I couldn't say, "I'm a stay-at-home mom," in that cheerful way I used to.

I said, "You know, I was really on my way to see the mermaid chair. I shouldn't keep you."

"You're not keeping me at all. Come on, I'll walk you over there. Unless you want to be alone."

"All right," I said. I knew he'd detected the change in my demeanor, and I didn't know why he was being persistent. Did he want to be with me, or was he merely being hospitable?

He touched my elbow, guiding me onto the path that led around to the church, the same small, common gesture he'd used with Mother, but the pressure of his hand on my coat sent a current flying through me.

The church was deserted, filled with a throbbing silence. We eased along the nave between the choir stalls, moving past the altar into the narrow ambulatory behind the apse, where we paused at the arched entrance to a tiny chapel.

The mermaid chair sat on a raised platform that was carpeted in a dark wine color. The carpet, I noticed, had thinned down to patches of thread in several places. On the wall behind the chair, a narrow clerestory window let in a stripe of musty, sawdust light that fell across the seat.

I walked over and laid my hand on the back of the chair. It was carved with an intricate Celtic-knot design. The mermaids that made up the chair arms were still painted in green, gold, and red, though some of the brightness had faded since I'd seen them last.

I hadn't thought the sight of it would affect me, but my eyes welled up immediately. My father had sat on the chair and patted his knee for me to climb into his lap. Laying my cheek against the rough corduroy of his jacket, I'd whispered to him, "Are you praying?" Because that's what you did when you sat in the chair. You prayed for things, usually impossible things, and your prayers were supposed to be answered. Before Mother had acquired her odd aversion to the chair, she used to sing a verse to me, a rhyme every child on the island knew by heart.

> Sit in the chair,
> Say a prayer.
> An answer tomorrow
> From St. Senara.

My father had whispered back, "Yes, I'm praying, but don't you dare tell your mother. I'll never hear the end of it."

"What are you praying for?"

"For you."

I'd sat up, electrified by this. My father was saying a prayer for *me,* and whatever he asked—it would happen. "What are you asking?"

He'd touched the tip of his finger to my nose. "That you'll stay my Whirly Girl forever."

I noticed Brother Thomas still in the entranceway, looking uncertain about whether to stay or to leave me alone. I let my hand glide over the wooden locks of the mermaid's hair, then along her wings.

"I always wondered why she has wings," I said. "I never heard of mermaids having them. Do you know why?"

He took it as an invitation, which it was, and came to the other side of the chair, stepping into the dim, powdery light from the window. It made a streak on his robe. "The thinking around here is that she's part siren. Sirens have fish tails *and* wings."

Her wings reminded me suddenly of plumage. Of mating dances. "But I thought sirens were terrible creatures."

"You're probably thinking of the *Odyssey,* how they lured the sailors onto the rocks, but before that they were sea goddesses. They brought messages from the deep. Kind of like angels, but they didn't come down from heaven, they came up from the sea. Supposedly their messages would inspire or heal—so sirens weren't always bad."

I must have looked surprised that he knew so much about it, because he grinned slightly and said, "I fill in for Brother Bede sometimes; he's the one who leads the guided tours."

I heard a shuffling noise in the corridor, just outside the chapel, and looked around, expecting to see a monk step in, but no one did, and we went on talking a few more minutes about the mermaids on the chair. He told me he liked the idea of them having both wings and fish tails, because it meant they could carry on in two completely different worlds, that they belonged equally to the sky and sea, and he envied that. He talked at length about it, but I didn't find it high-minded, only intriguing, and, to be honest, it excited me that he possessed this kind of arcane knowledge.

I let my gaze travel to the chair arm again, pretending to be engrossed in the mermaid, the whole wing–fish tail conundrum, aware that he was still looking at me.

"Do you believe the story that anyone who sits in the chair and prays will be granted an answer?" I asked.

"Not in the magical sense, no."

"I take it you *don't* sit in the chair like the tourists and pray?"

"I suppose I pray in other ways."

"What ways?" I asked, realizing after I'd said it how intrusive it sounded. I was sure I'd never asked anyone about his prayer life before.

"Thomas Merton wrote that the birds were his prayers, and I guess I feel that way, too. I pray best by just being out in the marsh. It's the only praying my soul seems to really respond to."

Soul. The word rebounded to me, and I wondered, as I often had, what it was exactly. People talked about it all the time, but did anybody actually know? Sometimes I'd pictured it like a pilot light burning inside a person—a drop of fire from the invisible inferno people called God. Or a squashy substance, like a piece of clay or dental mold, which collected the sum of a person's experiences—a million indentations of happiness, desperation, fear, all the small piercings of beauty we've ever known. I might have asked him about it, but a bell began to ring in the belfry overhead. He stepped into the corridor, then turned back to me, and I could see the sharp blue in his eyes even from over there. "I don't pray in the mermaid chair, but, for the record, that doesn't mean it lacks power."

The bell clanged again. Smiling at me, he tucked his hands into his scapular with Max's tennis ball and walked away.

CHAPTER
Fifteen

When he'd gone, I sat down in the mermaid chair. It was hard and uncomfortable; some said it was made from a single piece of birch, though I imagine that was just more apocrypha. I pushed my spine to the back of the seat and felt my toes lift off the floor. At the other end of the church, the monks began to chant. I could not tell if it was in Latin. Their voices came in waves, flooding into the arched chapel.

My thoughts must have been spiraling up near the ceiling for a few minutes, soaring around with the chant, because all of a sudden I felt my concentration yanked downward into my body, which I realized was aroused and alive. I felt as if I were running, but I was perfectly still. Everything around me seemed to blaze up and breathe—colors, edges, the crumbs of light falling obliquely over my shoulders.

My hands were resting on the chair arms, the place where the curving backs of the mermaids blend into their fish tails. I moved my fingers around and underneath until I was gripping the nubby carving of the tails like a pair of reins. I had the sensation inside of wanting to stop myself and at the same time to let myself go.

My feelings about Thomas had been such a muddle. I'd let them slosh around in me like dirty water in the bottom of a boat, but now, sitting in the mermaid chair, I felt the sediment settle to the bottom, and everything was very clear to me. I wanted him with an almost ferocious desire.

Of course, the second I allowed myself the thought, I felt a reverberating shock, complete disgust, and yet my shame was inconsequential next to the force of my heart. It was as if something had come bursting through a wall. I thought of the Magritte painting, the locomotive thundering out of the fireplace.

The antiphons rocked back and forth in the air. I made myself take a long, slow breath, wanting the chair to live up to its reputation and do something, to work a miracle and make the overwhelming feelings evaporate. My desire, however, only seemed to grow. A desire for someone who, I reminded myself, was not Hugh. I didn't even know him, really. And yet I felt as if I did. As if I knew the deepest things inside him.

That's how it had been with Hugh all those years ago. Like meeting someone I already knew. Falling in love with Hugh had been like coming down with a terrible bout of insanity. I'd been consumed with him, almost sick with longing, unable to concentrate on anything else, and there had been no way to cure it, not that I'd wanted to then. There was no assertion of will when it came to falling in love. The heart did what it did. It had its own autonomy, like a country unto itself.

The air was poached with incense, vibrating with medieval singing. I pictured Thomas out there in one of the choir stalls and felt that same sense of being consumed, engulfed with wanting.

Worst of all, I could feel myself giving over to all of this, to whatever was coming. To a Great Ecstasy and a Great Catastrophe.

The realization frightened me, which is too mild a way of saying it. I'd not thought I was capable of falling in love again.

Earlier, when Thomas had asked me about myself, I'd not been able to speak, and I wondered now if that was because my sense of myself had been coming apart. I'd come to the island, and everything had disintegrated.

I closed my eyes. *Stop this. Stop.*

I hadn't meant it as a prayer, but when I opened my eyes, I was struck with the idea that maybe it had been, and I had a momentary surge of childish hope that now some power-that-be would be obligated to grant my request. Then it would all stop. The feelings, everything, and I would be absolved. Safe.

Of course, I didn't really believe that. *Sit in the chair. Say a prayer*—it was juvenile.

Yet even Thomas, who didn't believe it either, had said there was power in the chair. And there *was.* I felt it. I felt it as an unraveling of some kind.

What if *that* was the real power in the chair—its ability to undo you? What if it fished up the most forbidden feelings inside a person and splayed them open?

I stood up. Unable to face strolling back through the church in front of the monks, I blundered around in the ambulatory for a minute, opening the wrong doors before I located the sacristy's back door, leading out of the church.

I hurried across the quadrangle, the dense air hitting my face. Instead of the fog's lifting, as it had tried to do earlier when a lone curl of sunlight had appeared, the air had turned to soup.

When I stepped through the gate into Mother's backyard, I stopped, standing in the same spot where I'd lingered that night Thomas had walked us back to the house. I placed my palms on top of the brick wall and stared at the mortar, pocked with holes from the salt air. Across the yard the oleander bushes swayed, their greenness barely visible.

He's a monk, I thought.

Wanting to believe that this would save me.

CHAPTER
Sixteen

Brother Thomas

During the antiphonal chanting that preceded mass, Thomas noticed Father Sebastian looking at him, staring with his small eyes from behind the enormous black-framed glasses. Thomas wished he would stop. Once, Thomas stared pointedly back, and Sebastian had not even pretended to be embarrassed. Instead he'd nodded as if savoring a private thought or perhaps trying to say something.

Thomas was sweltering beneath his robe. He felt as if he were wrapped in pink insulation. Even in winter the wool was too hot, and the furnace continually blasted them with heat. The reason, as the abbot so thoughtfully put it, was that the older monks were "cold-blooded." Thomas had bitten down onto his back teeth to keep his face straight.

Three years ago he'd begun daily swims in the creek out in the rookery near the makeshift hermitage he'd built on one of the small marsh islands. He did it just to cool off. He swam more determinedly in the winter than in any other season, hurling himself into the frigid water. It reminded him of an illuminated scene in a medieval Book of Hours, called the Mouth of Hell, which pictured poor, scalded people bolting from an infernal opening toward a spoonful of cold water. His place was secluded, walled off by tall, abundant grasses. It had been formed by a tributary veering off from the creek and dead-ending in a hidden basin. His private swimming hole.

There were no such things as swim trunks in a monastery, so he swam naked. It was something he should probably confess during public *culpa* on Friday mornings, which was where they divulged such sins as "I was not paying attention and broke the ginger-jar lamp in the Reception Center" or "I snuck into the kitchen after night silence and ate the last of the cherry Jell-O," but he didn't really believe he was culpable. When he swam nude, he felt he was venturing out onto an exultant edge. Spiritual people had the habit of closing themselves off, numbing themselves down. He felt strongly about it—people needed to swim naked. Some more than others.

With sweat beading up over his lip, he closed his eyes and dreamed of the cold tide rushing over his bare skin.

The monks stood in choir in order of seniority, or *statio* as they called it: abbot, prior, subprior, novice master, then each monk by the longevity of his time there. Thomas stood in the last stall on the back row, left-hand side of the church.

As the prior, Father Sebastian was in the first row on the right-hand side, clutching his St. Andrew Daily Missal, which had been abolished back in the sixties. His stare had become obvious and glowering.

The reason for the staring became clear to Thomas suddenly. He tightened his fingers on his breviary. Father Sebastian had seen him talking to Jessie Sullivan. There had been that sound outside the chapel. He'd forgotten that Sebastian always came into the church through the sacristy. Undoubtedly he'd eavesdropped.

Certain things Thomas had said to her floated back to him. There had been nothing inappropriate. They'd talked about the mermaid chair. About *praying,* for heaven's sake. He had merely been friendly to the daughter of the woman who cooked their midday meal. What was wrong with that? Monks talked to visitors all the time.

He stood in his choir stall gorged with self-justification, his old attorney self risen like Lazarus. It was startling to feel that instinct alive in him, how easily he deliberated and defended his encounter with Jessie Sullivan, like it was evidence against him.

He stopped singing, and the abbot, noticing, glanced at him and frowned. Thomas began again, then stopped once more, his arms sagging. That he even needed to mount a defense was a revelation.

He let his eyes move slowly toward Sebastian and nodded when the older monk met his gaze. His nod was an admission to himself, a painful acquiescence that he could not defend himself, not truthfully, because he had thought of this woman since he first saw her in the rose garden sitting on the ground. He'd thought of the perfect oval of her face, how she'd looked at him before getting to her feet. Mostly he'd remembered the way her head had blotted out the moon when she'd stood erect. It had been rising behind her, and for one, maybe two seconds, she'd appeared like an eclipse, a thin corona around her head and her face cloaked behind a glowing shadow.

It had, frankly, taken his breath away. It had reminded him of something, though he couldn't say what. He'd walked them back to Nelle's house through the blackened stretch of trees, talking to her mother but in his mind picturing Jessie Sullivan's face behind that luminous darkness.

It had set off a longing in him that had not diminished as he'd hoped but had grown so acute he couldn't sleep some nights for thinking about her. He would get up then and read the poem by Yeats about going out to the hazel wood with a fire in one's head. Yeats had written it after he'd met Maude

Gonne, a woman he'd glimpsed one day standing by a window and fallen hopelessly in love with.

Thomas had felt increasingly foolish about it, at how enmeshed he was in wanting her. As if he'd been snared in one of the monastery's own cast nets. He'd been doing fine, for five years carried along on the rhythm of the abbey: *ora, labora, vita communis*—prayer, work, community. His life rested in this. Dom Anthony gave sermons sometimes on what he called acedia, the grueling sameness that could snare monks in tedium and boredom, but Thomas had never suffered from it. The cadence and measure of this place had consoled him through his terrible doubt, the profound anguish he'd felt at being left alive when those he'd loved were dead.

And then that one innocuous moment: this woman getting to her feet in a garden without flowers, her face dark and beautiful, and turning to him with light daubed around her head. It had shattered his deep contentment, the whole perfect order.

He felt her even now like something returning, flooding around him like the hidden waters where he swam.

He knew hardly anything about her, but he'd seen the ring on her finger, and that had been reassuring to him. She was married. He was grateful for that.

He thought of her deep blush when she'd talked about the egret mating dance. He'd foolishly gone with her to the mermaid chair, and now he would lie awake tonight with a vision of her standing in the chapel, her blue jeans tight across her hips.

The abbot led them into the mass, and at the moment when the host was raised, Thomas felt the onrush of longing, not for Jessie but for his home, his monastic home, this place he loved beyond all places. He looked at the wafer, asking God to satiate him with that little bite of Jesus, and resolved to put her out of his mind. He would shake himself free of this. He would.

As the monks filed from the church toward the refectory for lunch, he slipped away from them, following the path to his cottage, not wanting to eat.

Father Dominic was sitting on the porch in an Adirondack rocker that had once been painted green. He wore a brown-and-red-plaid afghan draped around his shoulders, not rocking the way he typically did but motionless, his gaze fixed on a clump of Spanish moss on the ground. Thomas realized he had not seen him at mass. For the first time, Dominic appeared old to him.

"Benedicite Dominus," Dominic said, looking up, using the old-fashioned greeting as he often did.

"Are you all right?" Thomas said. Except for the spring when Dominic had spent three weeks in the infirmary with pneumonia, Thomas couldn't remember the monk's ever missing mass.

Dominic smiled, his expression a little forced. "I'm fine. Just fine."

"You weren't at mass," Thomas said, stepping up onto the porch.

"Yes, God forgive me, I was taking my own communion here on the porch. Have you ever thought, Thomas, that if God could dwell in the host, he could just as easily dwell in other things, too, like that moss over there on the ground?"

Thomas regarded the ball of moss that had blown up beside the steps. It looked like a tumbleweed. "I think that sort of thing all the time. I just didn't know anyone else here did."

Dominic laughed. "And neither did I. So

we are two peas in a pod, then. Or maybe two heretics in a pod." He pushed against his feet, coaxing the chair into a gentle rock.

Thomas listened to the creaking wood. Impulsively he squatted down beside the chair. "Father Dominic, I know you're not my confessor, and the abbot wouldn't approve of this, but . . . would you hear my confession?"

Dominic stopped rocking. He leaned forward, giving Thomas a quizzical look. "Right here, you mean? Right now?"

Thomas nodded, his body tightened with urgency. He was racked with a sudden, powerful need to unburden himself.

"All right," Dominic said. "I've already missed mass, so I'm on a roll. Let's hear it."

Thomas situated himself on his knees beside the rocker. He said, "Bless me, Father, for I have sinned. It has been four days since my last confession."

Dominic stared off into the yard. From the angle of his eyes, Thomas guessed he was focused again on the moss.

Thomas said, "Father, something has happened. I seem to be falling in love. I met her in the rose garden."

The wind lifted around them, and they sat in the ruffling quietness, in the welcome, elegant cold. Simply saying the words—such unbridled, imperiling words—released a groundswell of feeling in Thomas. They ushered him to a place from which he could not return.

And there he was. Kneeling on the small porch beside Dominic. His head bowed. The day milk white. Loving a woman he hardly knew.

CHAPTER
Seventeen

In the strange days that followed my encounter with Brother Thomas in the abbey church, the rains began. Cold February monsoons. The island sloshed around in the Atlantic.

I remembered the winter rains from my childhood as grim, torrential episodes: Mike and I hurrying down the road to school huddled under an old boat tarp while the rain lashed at our legs and, when we were older, crossing the bay to meet the bus, the ferry bobbing around like a rubber duck.

For more than a week, I stood at the window in Mother's house watching the water fall through the oaks and spatter against the bathtub grotto out front. I cooked lackluster dinners out of the stockpile of food in the pantry, changed Mother's bandage, and methodically brought her cinnamon-colored pills and red-and-white capsules, but I always seemed to end up back at one of the windows, subdued and staring. I could feel myself receding to a place inside that was new to me. It was like slipping into a nautilus shell. I simply withdrew, winding down through the spiraling passageway to a small, dark hospice.

Some days Mother and I watched the Winter Olympics on her little television. It was a way to sit in a room together and carry on as if everything were normal. Mother would watch the screen while working her rosary, attacking the decades of red beads, and when she got through all five of them, twisting the Rubik's Cube Dee had sent her at least five Christmases ago, working it awkwardly with one hand. Eventually she would let the cube tumble out of her lap, then sit with her fingers still fidgeting.

We were both caught, I suppose, in our private distractions. Mother in her commonplace torments, her buried finger, her pastness. And me in growing thoughts of Brother Thomas, in a kind of incessant desiring I could not banish. And I tried, I *did* try.

I'd forgotten how that sort of craving felt, how it rose suddenly and loudly from the pit of my stomach like a flock of startled birds, then floated back down in the slow, beguiling way of feathers.

Where had all this sexual longing come from anyway? I used to imagine that women had a little tank of it lodged back behind their navels somewhere, a kind of erotic gas tank they'd come into the world with, and that I had used the entire contents of mine on Hugh those first years we were together. I'd recklessly emptied it out, and there was nothing I could do to refill it. I told Hugh once that I'd gotten the quart-size tank instead of the gallon-size, that it was like having a small bladder—some women had them and some didn't. He'd looked at me like I was crazy.

"Men don't have this situation," I'd explained to him. "You don't have to conserve the way we do. Your sexual appetite comes through a faucet you can turn on whenever you want. There's an unending supply; it's like getting water from a sink."

"Really?" he'd said. "Did you get all this in biology class?"

"There are things *not* recorded in books," I'd said.

"Apparently." He'd laughed as if I were kidding around.

I sort of was, and I sort of wasn't. I did believe that women had only so much libido, and when it was used up, it was used up.

Now I saw I'd had it wrong. There were no tanks, small or otherwise, just faucets. All of them connected to a bottomless erotic sea. Perhaps I'd let my faucet rust shut, or something had clogged it up. I didn't know.

Mother grew quiet during those days, too. She stopped talking about going back to the abbey to resume cooking for the monks. She consigned them to the miserable efforts of Brother Timothy. I kept thinking about what Hugh had said, how her need to rid herself of guilt could build up again. I worried. Every time I looked at her, I got the impression of something large and menacing locked in a cellar, wanting in.

For a day or so after she'd buried her finger, there had been a brief revival of her old self. She'd talked in her usual scattershot way about converting recipes for six into forty, about Julia Child, about the infallibility of the pope, about Mike. Thankfully she had not gotten wind of his Buddhism experiment. My mother did not typically have an unarticulated thought, and now she was all but silent. It was not a good sign.

I couldn't muster the energy, or the courage, to ask her again about Dominic or bring up the matter of my father's pipe.

Kat called almost every day. "Are you two still alive over there?" she'd ask. "Maybe I ought to come check on you." I would reassure her we were fine. I didn't want company, and she picked up on that.

Hugh called also. But only once. The phone rang two or three days after I'd sat in the mermaid chair and felt the floodgates open. Mother and I were watching a bobsled race.

The first words out of Hugh's mouth were, "Let's not fight." He wanted me to apologize for before. I could tell. He waited patiently.

"I don't want to fight either." That's all I could manage.

He waited some more. After a pointed sigh, he said, "I hope you've thought it over and changed your mind about my coming."

"I haven't changed my mind at all," I said.

"I still think I should do this by myself." It sounded harsh, so I tried to soften it up. "Try to understand it from my side, okay?"

He said automatically, "Okay," but I knew he wouldn't. That's one of the worst things about living with brilliant people—they're so used to being right they don't really have experience being anything else.

A blinding-white tiredness came over me as we talked. I didn't mention Dominic and how I suspected he was involved somehow because Hugh would have dissected it half to death. He would have told me how to proceed. I wanted to navigate by my own instincts.

"When are you coming home?" Hugh wanted to know.

Home. How could I tell him that at this moment I had an unbearable need to flee it. I had an urge to say, *Please, I want to be alone with my life right now, to go down into my nautilus shell and see what's there.* But I didn't say anything.

I was driven by a deep, sickening selfishness and that same discontent I'd felt back at home, but also by a kind of sorrowing love for myself. My life seemed sweet and dull and small and repellent. So much of it unused.

The last few days, I'd been thinking about

the life I'd meant to live, the one that had shone in my head a long time ago, full of art and sex and mesmerizing discussions about philosophy and politics and God. I'd owned my own gallery in that nonexistent life. I'd painted surrealistic works full of startling, dreamlike imagery.

There had been a moment a couple of years earlier when I might have reached for that life, at least for a little piece of it. Two days before Christmas, I'd crawled into a storage space beneath a dormer to retrieve my good china—a fine bone Lenox pattern that had been discontinued and was thus ir-replaceable. It was packed and stored in boxes, brought out for major holidays and the occasional wedding anniversary.

Dee saw me and knew instantly what I was doing. "Mom," she said, "why don't you use it more often? What are you saving it for?" Her voice was full of what I recognized instantly as pity.

Yes, what indeed? I didn't know, couldn't begin to say. My own funeral, perhaps. Dee would throw a wake, and people would stand around talking about how outstanding it was that I still had a complete twelve-piece set after all these years. What a tribute.

For days after that, I'd been deflated by my own shrunken world. When had my fear of broken plates gotten so grandiose? My desire for extravagant moments so small? After that, I'd made room for the china in one of the kitchen cabinets and used it indiscriminately. Because it was Wednesday. Because someone had purchased one of my art boxes. Because it appeared that on *Cheers* Sam was finally going to marry Diane. It hadn't gone much beyond the china, though, that good impulse toward largeness.

As I held the phone, I wanted to tell Hugh about it, the dormer and the china, but I wasn't sure it made any sense.

"Jessie," Hugh was saying, "did you hear me? When are you coming home?"

"I can't possibly know when I'll come home. Not yet. I could be here—I don't know—a long time."

"I see."

I think he did see, too. He saw that my being on the island was about more than taking care of Mother; it was about the disquiet I'd felt all winter. It was about me, about us.

But he didn't say that. He said, "Jessie, I love you."

This will come out sounding terrible, but I

felt he said it to test me, to see if I would say it back to him.

"I'll call you in a few days," I said.

When we hung up, I watched the window silver over with water, then walked back to the living room, to Mother and the TV and the bobsled race.

About four o'clock every afternoon, I would smell night coming. It would curl under the doors and windows—a wet, black smell. Wanting Thomas was worse at night.

I began to take long, involved baths at the first graying shade of darkness. I pilfered one of the emergency candles from Mother's old hurricane box and set it on the ledge of the tub. I lit it, then made the water as hot as I could stand, until the room swirled with steam. I often sprinkled cedar leaves from the backyard onto the water, or a handful of salt, or spoonfuls of Mother's lavender oil, as if I were creating a brew. The fragrance was sometimes overpowering.

I would slide down into it with only my nostrils sticking out. You would think I'd only now discovered water, its hot, silky feel.

Submerged, I would go off into a dreamy state. I had always loved Chagall's *Lovers in the Red Sky,* his painting of an entwined couple soaring above rooftops, above the moon. The image would come to me each time I sank into the water, the couple sometimes flying through a red sky but more often swimming in searing blue water.

Other times I would think of the mermaid Chagall had painted, suspended above the water, above the trees, a flying mermaid, but without wings, and I would think of Thomas saying he envied mermaids who belonged equally to the sea and to the sky.

One night I sat up in bed. Something was different. It was, I realized, the silence on the roof. I looked toward the window and saw that the clouds had parted. Moonlight was falling into the room like bits of mica.

I got up and went plundering through the house for something, anything, to draw with. I found a decrepit box of colored pencils in Mike's desk, where he must have left them two decades before. I stood at the kitchen table and sharpened them with a fish knife.

Unable to locate anything but notebook paper, I took down the large, framed picture of the Morris Island Lighthouse from over the mantel, wrestled out the print, and began to sketch impatiently on the back side of it, with a ravenous kind of movement that was commanding and completely foreign to me.

I covered the canvas with sweeping flows of blue water. In each corner I drew a nautilus shell with an orange light cracking out of it, and along the bottom turtle skulls, heaps of them rising in columns like a sunken civilization, the lost Atlantis. In the very center, I sketched the lovers. Their torsos were pressed together, their limbs braided. The woman's hair wound around them both like May ribbons. They were flying. Waterborne.

The work was exhilarating—and a little scary. Like driving a car and having a blowout. When I finished, I returned the lighthouse print to its frame and hung it back over the mantel, the lovers facing the wall.

It was impossible to go back to sleep. I was wildly keyed up. I went into the kitchen to make tea. I was sitting at the table, sipping chamomile from a chipped mug, when I heard scratching at the door, a pronounced, deliberate sound. Flipping on the porch light, I peered out the kitchen window. Max sat on the porch, his black coat bedraggled and sodden.

I opened the door. "Oh, Max, look at you."

He peered up at me with questioning eyes. "All right, come on in."

He was known to sleep at different homes on the island on a rotating basis, the schedule known only to him. Mother once said he showed up here every couple of months wanting a bed, but I doubted he arrived in the middle of the night. I wondered if his current landlord had turned him out. Had he seen the light on here?

I pulled out the old bedspread Mother kept for him in the pantry. As he curled up on it, I sat on the floor and dried him with a dish towel.

"What are you doing roaming around in the middle of the night?" I said. He pricked up his ears a little, then laid his head across my thigh.

I stroked his ears, remembering what Thomas had said about Max going out in the boat with him when he did his rookery duties.

"You like Brother Thomas?" I said. He thumped his tail, I imagine because of the syrup that had taken over my voice—the tone used for newborn babies, puppies, kittens. "I know, I like him, too."

Rubbing Max's head worked better than the tea. The wired feeling started to ebb.

"Max, what am I going to do?" I said. "I'm falling in love."

I'd come to this truth while sitting in the mermaid chair, but I hadn't said it aloud. It surprised me what a relief it was to make the confession, even to a dog.

Max let out a breath and closed his eyes. I didn't know how to stop feeling what I felt. To shake the idea that here was a person I was meant to find. It was not just the man who excited me—it was the sky in him, things in him that I did not know, had never tasted, might never taste perhaps. Right then it seemed almost easier to live with the devastation of my marriage than the regret of living my life without ever knowing him for sure, without flying through a red sky or a blue sea.

"My husband's name is Hugh," I said to Max, who was by now sound asleep. "Hugh," I said again, then went on saying it in my head as a way to rescue myself.

Hugh. Hugh. Hugh.

CHAPTER
Eighteen

On March 2, I rolled the golf cart out of the garage and drove over the muddy roads to the cluster of shops near the ferry. The sun had returned with the indifferent look of winter, a hard, small fire lodged high and bright. As I bumped along through the oaks, I felt like a creature emerging from underground.

I wanted to pick up a few groceries at Caw Caw General Store and see, too, if they sold paints—I needed something besides Mike's colored pencils. Mostly, though, I wanted to talk to Kat about Brother Dominic.

The ferry was docked, and a few tourists

meandered along the sidewalk with their windbreakers zipped to their necks. I parked in front of Kat's gift shop, where Max sat beneath the blue-and-white-striped awning.

Kat had nailed a small mirror beside the shop door, an old Gullah custom meant to scare away the Booga Hag.

As I opened the door, Max darted into the store ahead of me. Kat, Benne, and Hepzibah sat behind the counter, eating ice cream from plastic bowls. They were the only ones in the store.

"Jessie!" Benne cried.

Kat smiled at me. "Welcome to the world of living, breathing people. You want some ice cream?"

I shook my head.

Hepzibah was wearing an ebony shift with white lightning bolts on it and her signature matching head wrap. She looked like a beautiful thundercloud.

Max plopped at Benne's feet, and she patted him, cutting her eyes at me. "Mama said you've been acting rude."

"Oh, for Lord's sake, Benne, do you have to repeat every damn thing I say?"

"You think I've been rude?" I asked, wanting to tease her, but a little miffed, too.

She grinned. "Well, what do you call it when a person phones you every single day saying, 'Can I come visit? Can I bring you dinner? Can I come over and kiss your feet?' And all this person gets back is, 'We're fine, thank you. Go away now'?"

"I didn't say 'Go away now,' and I don't recall you asking to kiss my feet. If you'd like, though, you can do that now."

For some reason, whenever I got around Kat, I started behaving like her.

"Aren't we testy?" she said. "Of course, if *I'd* been cooped up with Nelle Dubois for two weeks, I'd be lobbing grenades at people."

I glanced around the shop for the first time. Tables and wall shelves brimmed with a bewildering array of items with mermaids on them: key chains, beach towels, greeting cards, embossed soaps, bottle openers, paperweights, night-lights. There were mermaid dolls, mermaid comb-and-mirror sets, even mermaids to hang on the Christmas tree. The MERMAID XING signs were stuck in an umbrella stand in the corner, and a dozen mermaid wind chimes dangled from the ceiling. In the center of the store was a table arranged with a pile of Father Dominic's booklets, *The Mermaid's Tale,* with a sign declaring them SPECIAL AUTOGRAPHED COPIES.

"Pick something out," said Kat. "A gift—some earrings or something."

"Thanks, but I couldn't."

"You're being rude again," she said.

I picked up a box of Mermaid Tears. "Okay, then, I'll take this."

Benne got a folding chair for me from a closet, and I sat.

"What brings you to town?" asked Hepzibah.

"Groceries. And I thought I'd see if I could find—" I stopped, hesitant to say it out loud. The old inclination, I suppose, to keep my art confined and safe, like a potentially fractious child restricted to her room. I looked down at my hands. My palms pushed together and held in the vise of my knees.

"Art supplies," I said with an effort I hoped no one noticed. "Watercolors, brushes, some cold-press paper . . ."

"Caw Caw sells electric hot-dog cookers and Chia Pets, but I doubt they have art supplies," Kat said. She reached for a pencil and paper on the counter. "Here, write down what you want, and I'll have Shem buy it for you next time he takes the ferry over."

I jotted down the basics while their spoons scraped around for the last of the ice cream.

"I take it you're planning to stay awhile, then?" said Hepzibah.

"Mother needs me, so yeah, I thought I would."

Kat lifted her eyebrows. "How long is 'awhile'?"

"I guess indefinitely," I said, wanting to get off the subject.

"What about Hugh?" she asked.

I thrust the list at her. "When you first called me, you accused me of neglecting Mother—I believe your exact words were, 'You can't go around like you don't have a mother.' And now you're accusing me of neglecting Hugh?" My voice hit a high, bleating note on the word "Hugh."

Kat acted like I'd smacked her in the face. "Good grief, Jessie, I don't care whether you're there taking care of Hugh. The man can take care of himself. Since when did I worry about men being taken care of by their wives? I was only wondering if everything's okay with you two."

"As if that's any of your business," Hepzibah said to her. I couldn't imagine what Kat was picking up on. "So tell us—how's Nelle?" Hepzibah asked.

I shrugged. "To be honest, I think Mother is depressed. All she does is sit in a chair, stare at the television, and work her Rubik's Cube."

"Lunch at Max's!" Kat blurted. The dog had been snoring gently with his head on Benne's shoe, but he slitted open his eyes at the mention of his name. "We'll all have lunch at the café this Saturday."

Over the years Mother had tried to tug her thread from the knot the three of them had made and thrown into the sea that night, the one that had held them together over the years. But Kat had refused to let her isolate herself. Her loyalty—and Hepzibah's, too—had never wavered, not once.

"That's a nice idea," I said, realizing I couldn't stay mad at Kat for more than three minutes. I don't know why that was—she was the most provoking woman I'd ever met. "But I doubt she'll come," I added.

"Tell her the pope will be having lunch at Max's this Saturday. That ought to do it."

Hepzibah turned to me. "Just tell her we've been missing her and need to see her face."

"I'll try," I said. "But don't expect much."

Glancing past them, I noticed the boat-wreck picture I'd painted when I was eleven, framed and hung over the cash register. "Oh, look, there's my picture."

A fiery white boat was lodged on the bottom of the ocean along with a smiling octopus, a giant clam with peeping eyes, and a herd of rocking sea horses. It looked like a happy page from a children's book—except for the boat burning in the middle of it all.

Fire beneath the water—was that how I'd seen his death as a child? An inferno nothing could extinguish? On the serrated surface of the water, gray ashes floated like plankton, but above it the sun smiled and the world was a becalmed, cloudless place. I'd never noticed how much ache was inside the picture until now—a child's wish for the world to return to its perfect self.

When I looked around, Hepzibah was studying me. "I remember when you made that picture. You were one sad little girl."

Kat scowled at her. "How festive of you to bring that up."

Hepzibah said, "Jessie *was* sad. She knows it, and we know it. So why not say it?" She'd never taken any kind of guff from Kat, which was probably why they got along so well.

"Why is it you never want to talk about that time?" I asked Kat. "I *want* to talk about it. I need to. I want to know, for instance, why everyone, including Mother, said it was a spark from my father's pipe that caused the fire."

"Because it *was* a spark from the pipe that caused the fire," Kat said, and I saw Hepzibah nod.

"Well, I found this in a drawer in Mother's bedroom," I said, digging the pipe from my purse. I cupped it in my palms like a communion wafer or a butterfly with a torn wing. A smell of tobacco mixed with licorice drifted from the pipe bowl.

They stared at it without speaking, their empty ice-cream bowls sitting crooked in their laps. Their faces were completely expressionless.

Finally Kat asked, "What did Nelle say about it?"

"I haven't mentioned the pipe to her yet. I'm afraid seeing it might send her over the edge again."

Kat held out her hand for the pipe, and I gave it to her. She turned it over several times, as if she might divine some answer from it. "The police were just speculating when they said it was the pipe that started the fire. So it was something else—what difference does it make now?" She handed the pipe back to me.

"But why would she let the police and everyone else believe that it was the pipe when she had it all along? Why would she lie about it?" I asked.

Sunlight poured through the storefront window from a little spout between the clouds, and all three of them turned their faces toward the dusty brightness.

"I went to see Father Dominic," I said. "I sort of accused him of knowing something about Mother cutting off her finger."

"You *didn't*," said Kat.

"I did. And you know what he told me? To leave matters alone. He said that if I didn't, it could hurt Mother."

"He said *that?*" Kat stood up and walked to the counter. "This doesn't make any sense." She glanced at Hepzibah, who seemed just as mystified as Kat was.

"He's hiding something," I insisted.

Kat walked behind my chair. Her hands floated down onto the tops of my shoulders and rested there. When she spoke, the acerbic edge that slipped so easily into her voice was gone. "We'll figure this out, Jessie, okay? I'll talk with Dominic."

I smiled up at her appreciatively. I could see the line along her jaw where her makeup ended. Her throat lifted as she swallowed, exposing a whole continent of tenderness in her.

The moment must have grown too dear for her, because she abruptly moved her hands and changed the subject. "In exchange, you're going to have to paint some mermaid pictures for me to sell in the store."

"What?"

She came around and stood in front of me. "You heard me. You said you were going to paint, so paint mermaids. They would sell like crazy in here. You can do it on consignment. We'll put a big price on them."

I stared at her, openmouthed. In my head I saw a canvas of lapis sky filled with winged mermaids flying around like angels and diving from great heights into the sea. I tried to remember what Thomas had said about mermaids with wings. Something about sea muses bringing messages from below. Living in two realms.

Kat said, "Well? What about it?"

"I might try it. We'll see."

The tourists I'd noticed earlier wandered in now, and Kat went to greet them while Hepzibah stood, saying she had to get home. I needed to go, too, but I went on sitting there with Benne, still thinking of Thomas.

During the last twelve days, caged up in Mother's house, I'd told myself so many contradictory things. That I was in love, and not only that, but it was a Great Love, and to walk away from it would be a denial of my life. And then alternately, that I was having an insane infatuation, that it was a heart-twisting moment in time that would eventually pass, and I had to be stoic.

I didn't see why loving someone had to have so much agony attached to it. It felt like a series of fresh cuts in the skin of my heart.

Benne straightened up and looked at me, squinting, the tip of her tongue resting on her bottom lip. "Jessie?" she said.

"What is it, Benne?"

She scooted her chair close to mine and pushed her lips against my ear the way children do when imparting secrets. "You love one of the monks," she whispered.

I reared back and blinked at her. "Where did you get such an idea?"

"I just know."

Refuting it to her would be pointless. Benne, of course, was never wrong.

I wanted to be angry with her, to swat her for snooping around in my heart, but she rose up on her seat smiling at me, a woman my age with the sweet mind of a child and a prodigious psychic ability. She didn't even know how dangerous truth could be, all the tiny, shattering seeds it carried.

"Benne," I said, taking her hand, "listen carefully. You mustn't say anything about this to anyone. Promise me."

"But I already did."

I turned loose her hand and closed my eyes for a moment before asking her. "Who?" I said. "Who did you tell?"

"Mama," she answered.

CHAPTER
Nineteen

A note had been slipped under the back door in the kitchen, folded inside a sealed, white envelope with a single word on the front: *Jessie.*

I found it after I got back from Kat's shop. Picking it up, I studied the writing—a bold, slanted script, but oddly filled with hesitation, as if the writer had stopped and started several times.

Some things you just know. Like Benne does.

I slid it into the pocket of my khakis at the same moment Mother walked into the room. "What's that?" she said.

"Nothing," I told her. "I dropped something."

I did not open it right away. I let it rest in the dark pouch along my thigh, pressing like a hand. I told myself, *First I will call my daughter. Then make tea. I will be sure Mother is situated, and then I will sit on the bed and sip the tea and open the envelope.*

I was an accomplished practitioner of delayed gratification. Hugh once said people who could delay gratification were highly mature. I could put off happiness for days, months, years. That's how "mature" I was. I learned it from eating Tootsie Roll Pops as a child. Mike would crunch through the candy shell immediately to get to the chocolate in the middle, while I licked and licked, wearing it down in an agonizingly slow process.

I dialed Dee's number in her dorm at Vanderbilt and listened to her chatter about her latest escapade. Her sorority had sponsored "the world's largest pillow fight," 312 people on a softball field, feathers everywhere. Apparently the event was witnessed by a so-called scrutineer from the *Guinness Book of World Records*.

"It was all my idea," she said proudly.

"I'm sure it was," I said. "My daughter—a world-record holder. I'm very proud."

"How's Gran?" she asked.

"She's okay," I said.

"Did you find out why she did it?"

"She won't talk to me yet, at least not about that. There's something she's hiding. The whole thing is complicated."

"Mom? I was remembering— I don't know, it's probably nothing."

"What? Tell me."

"It's just that one time when I visited her, a really long time ago, we were walking by that place where the slaves are buried, that cemetery, you know? And Gran totally freaked."

"What do you mean, 'freaked'?"

"She started crying and saying stuff."

"Do you remember what she was saying?"

"Not really. Just something about seeing a dead person's hand or fingers. I guess she was talking about the bodies in the cemetery, but she was real upset, and it kinda scared me."

"You never mentioned it."

"But she did crazy things like that. It was just Gran." Dee paused, and I could hear her U2 tape playing in the background. "I should have told you. Oh, Mom, you think if I'd said something, this wouldn't have happened?"

"Listen to me: It wouldn't have made a bit of difference in what she did. Believe me. Okay? Your Gran is sick, Dee."

"Okay," she said.

After we hung up, I made peppermint tea and took a cup to the living room. There was Mother, the television, the Rubik's Cube. The Russians had won an ice-skating medal, and their national anthem was like a funeral dirge weighing down the room. I set the cup on the table beside her and patted her shoulder. The episode Dee had described had only confused me more.

"Are you all right? How's your hand?"

"Fine. But I don't like peppermint tea," she said. "It tastes like toothpaste."

I closed the door to my room and turned the lock, then pulled the envelope out of my pocket. I placed it in the middle of the bed and sat down beside it. I sipped my tea and stared at it.

There was never any question I would open it. I was not trying to preserve those last moments of high and aggravated anticipation either—the slow, excruciating pleasure of wearing down to get to the chocolate. No, I was merely terrified. I was holding Pandora's envelope.

I tore it open and pulled out a lined white paper, ragged along one edge, as if it had been torn from a journal.

Jessie,
   I hope I'm not being too presumptuous in writing, but I wonder if you would like to go for a ride in the johnboat. The egrets aren't plentiful now, but I've spotted a colony of white pelicans, which is very rare. I'll be at the dock in the rookery tomorrow at 2:00 P.M., and I would be happy if you joined me.
                           Brother Thomas (Whit)

Whit. I touched the word with my finger, then said it out loud, sensing the intimacy that had gone into the act of disclosing his real name. It felt as though he'd offered a hidden part of himself to me, one the monastery did not own. And yet the note had a certain formality about it. *I would be happy if you joined me.*

I read it several times. I didn't realize that the teacup had turned over on the bed until I felt the wetness seep against my leg. I soaked up what I could with a towel, then lay down beside the dampness, breathing the smell of peppermint, the sweet cleanness of it drifting from the sheets like a fresh new beginning.

A half-dozen seagulls squatted behind me on the dock in the rookery in perfect formation, like a small squadron of planes waiting to take off. I had come early, too early. More out of caution than eagerness. I'd reasoned that if I arrived early and felt I couldn't go through with meeting him, I could simply leave. Unseen.

For almost an hour, I sat cross-legged at the edge of the dock beneath the gleaming, cloudless ceiling of light and studied the water. It looked tawny, the color of mangoes and cantaloupes, and the tide was flooding in, splashing against the pilings as if the creek had lost all patience.

A faded red canoe, almost pink now, lay upside down on one end of the dock, the bottom encrusted with barnacles. I recognized it as Hepzibah's. I'd been a passenger in it at least thirty years ago. On the other end, a spruce green johnboat, practically new, bobbed on the water, sunlight running in hypnotic wave patterns along the side.

I heard a board creak behind me, and the

gulls lifted. Turning, I saw him standing on the dock, gazing at me. He wore blue jeans and a denim shirt with the sleeves rolled to his elbows. His shoulders were broader, more muscular than I'd thought they would be, and his arms had the leathery look of someone who worked in the sun. A wooden pectoral cross hung around his neck, oddly discordant with the rest of him.

It was as if he'd been residing in an obscure place in my heart and suddenly stepped out of it. A real man, but not quite real either.

"You came," he said. "I didn't know if you would."

I got to my feet. "You promised white pelicans."

He laughed. "I said I'd *spotted* white pelicans. I can't promise we'll see them."

He climbed into the boat and, taking my hand, helped me step down into it. For a moment his face was close to mine. I could smell soap on his skin, starting to mingle with a slight muskiness from the warmth of the day.

I sat down on the front bench—Max's seat, I imagined—facing backward and watched as Thomas started the small outboard motor. He sat beside it as it churned the golden brown water, holding the rudder, easing us into the middle of the creek.

"Should I call you Thomas or Whit?" I asked.

"I haven't been called Whit in years. I wouldn't mind hearing it again."

"I assume your mother named you that. As opposed to the abbot."

"She named me John Whitney O'Conner and called me Whit."

"Okay, then, Whit," I said, trying it out.

We plied through the ebb-tide delta on the back side of the island at an idle. We threaded coils in the creek so narrow and lush in places I could almost stretch out my arms and touch the grasses on either side. We didn't try to converse anymore over the engine. I think we were both trying to get comfortable with the strangeness of what was happening, of being together in a little boat disappearing into the aloneness of the marsh.

He pointed to a flash of mullet, to several wood storks lifting out of the grass, to an osprey nest perched atop a dead pine.

We wound through the loops in the creek for a while before Whit sharply veered the boat into a tributary that eventually dead-ended in a circle of water surrounded by a wall of tall grass six or seven feet high. He cut the engine, and the silence and seclusion of the place welled up. I felt as though we'd passed through the eye of a tiny needle into a place that was out of time.

He slid the anchor over the side. "This is where I saw the white pelicans. I believe they're feeding near here, so if we're lucky, they'll fly over." He glanced at the sky, and I forced myself to do the same, to look away from his face. It was mottled with sunlight and a hint of beard stubble.

"What's that?" I asked, pointing to a wooden structure protruding above the brush on a tiny island some twenty or thirty yards behind him.

"Oh, that's my unofficial hermitage," he said. "It's basically nothing but a lean-to. I use it to read or just sit and meditate. I've been known to take naps in it, too. To be perfectly honest, I've probably napped in it more than I've meditated."

I clicked my tongue, teasingly. "Napping on the job." I felt ridiculously lighthearted.

"My napping wouldn't surprise the abbot,

but I'm afraid the lean-to would. He isn't aware it exists."

"Why?"

"I'm pretty sure he wouldn't allow me to have it."

I liked that there was a hidden part of him he kept separate from the monastery, a tiny bit of dissidence.

"Did you know white pelicans don't dive for food like the brown ones?" he said. "They work as a team. I've seen them sit on the water in a big circle and corral the fish to the center of it. It's ingenious, really."

"I think I must be a brown pelican," I said, and the moment it left my mouth, I thought how silly it sounded. Like one of those quizzes in women's magazines. If you were a color, what color would you be? If you were an animal . . .

"Why do you say that?" he asked.

"I don't know, I guess because I work alone."

"I don't even know what you do."

I was not good at saying, "I'm an artist." The words tended to get lodged in my throat. "I have an art studio," I said. "I fool around in it a little."

"So you're an artist," he said. I wasn't sure if anyone had ever called me that before. Even Hugh.

"What medium?" he asked.

"I do— I used to do a watercolor-tableau thing. I don't know how to describe it."

"Come on," he said. "Try."

I was surprised at how badly I wanted to tell him. I closed my eyes, trying to say it as eloquently as I could.

"I start with a wooden box, kind of like a shadowbox." I paused. I couldn't believe I'd said "shadowbox." *God.* I hated when people referred to it that way. "Wait, not a shadowbox; it's more like a Mexican *retablo.* And I paint a scene inside it. It could be a landscape, people, anything. Then I arrange things in front of the scene, like it's extending out of the painting—sort of a diorama effect."

I opened my eyes, and I remember how I was caught by the sight of him. How handsome he looked leaning forward with his elbows resting on his knees, listening so intently to me. In the strong light, his blue eyes were the exact color of his denim shirt.

"They sound wonderful," he said.

"Believe me, they're not that wonderful. I thought they were in the beginning. They started off being really satirical and quirky, but they became much more planned and . . ." I fumbled in my head for the word. "Unobjectionable," I heard myself say.

"That's an interesting way to put it."

I stared at him. Everything I was saying was coming out wrong. I didn't even know what I'd meant by "unobjectionable." "I guess I mean art should evoke some kind of reaction in a person, not just look beautiful. It should disturb people a little."

"Yeah, but look around." He threw out an arm, gesturing at the marsh grass, the water in quiet motion, the light floating on top of it like bits of froth. "Look at *this*. What about beauty for the sake of beauty? Sometimes I look at the trees out here, full of egrets, or a piece of art like Bernini's *The Ecstasy of Saint Teresa,* and I lose myself. Sometimes it explodes my notions of order and conduct, much more than if it were 'objectionable.' "

He spoke with passion and authority, gesturing with his hands so vigorously that the boat rocked at one point and I reached for the side to steady myself. It was almost as if I were experiencing the very thing he was trying to explain—this state of losing oneself.

He said, "I know what you're saying,

though—that you want your art to jolt people, to create an epiphany."

"Yes," I said.

"This is just my own opinion, but I think the real jolt doesn't come because the art is objectionable or because it evokes social critique but because the viewer becomes lost in the sheer beauty of it. It gives a person an experience of the eternal."

I couldn't speak. I was afraid, in fact, I might embarrass myself by crying, and I didn't even know why I felt the urge. It had been so long since I'd had a conversation like this.

The boat had drifted on the anchor line to the edge of the water, where a brown, parched, dormant scent hovered in the grasses. He leaned back on his elbows against the rail, and the boat dipped a little.

I said, "It sounds very mysterious."

"What's that?"

"This experience of the eternal you mentioned. You're going to think I'm dense, but what is it, exactly?"

He smiled. "No, I don't think you're dense. I hardly know what it is myself."

"But you're a monk."

"Yeah, but a weak, doubting one."

"But you've had a lot of these . . . eternal experiences, I can tell. And I don't have a clue what they are. I've spent most of my life being a mother and a wife, taking care of a house. When you said I was an artist . . . that's a stretch. I've only been puttering around with art."

He squinted, fixing his eyes on something just above my shoulder. "When I first came here," he said, "I had the impression that transcending the world was superior to simply being in it. I was always struggling to meditate, fast, detach, that kind of thing. One day in the rookery I realized that merely being out here, going about my work, was what made me the happiest. I finally figured out that what matters is just giving over to what you love."

He turned to me. "You've done that. I wouldn't worry too much about having eternal experiences. You can't manufacture them anyway. They're just little tastes of something timeless, a moment here and there when you're granted the bliss of stepping out of yourself. But I doubt they're more important than simply doing what you love."

He reached over the side and grazed the

water with his fingers. "You were fortunate to grow up here."

"Well, I didn't think so for a long time. I stopped loving the island when I was nine. To be honest, it was only when I came back this time that I started to love it again."

He leaned forward even farther. "What happened when you were nine? Do you mind my asking?"

"My father died in a boat fire. It was a fuel-tank explosion. They said a spark from his pipe caused it."

I closed my eyes, wanting to tell him how much of a daddy's girl I'd been, how when my father died, it was as if my whole child-hood collapsed. "The island changed for me after that. It turned into a kind of suffocating enclosure," I added.

Sitting in the boat, I reached up uncon-sciously and touched the place on my skin where the priest always drew the ash in the shape of a cross. It felt like a dead spot.

"And Mother," I went on, "she changed. She used to be fun-loving, normal, but after he died, she became obsessively religious. It was like she left us, too."

He didn't say, *Oh, I'm sorry, how terrible,* or any of those perfunctory things people said, but I glimpsed what struck me as sadness fill his eyes. As if a sorrowing place in him had recognized this same sorrowing place in me. I remember wondering what terrible thing might have happened to him.

A flash of blue overhead, and I looked up to see a heron with a fish wriggling in its beak. The bird's shadow slid over the boat, passing between us.

"The thing was, I gave him the pipe for Father's Day. So I always felt like—" I stopped.

"Like you'd caused it to happen," he said, finishing for me.

I nodded. "The funny thing is that I found the pipe in my mother's drawer the other day. She's had it all this time." I forced a laugh, and it made a thin, bitter sound in the air.

I didn't want to go into the questions about my father's death or the consequences of it—the gouged-out place inside me that I could not seem to fill up and Mother's long, dark slide. I wanted it to be the way it was a few moments before, when we'd talked about art, about the eternal.

I did have a fleeting impulse to ask him about Father Dominic, what he thought of him, but I dismissed that, too.

I shifted my position on the boat seat,

tucking one leg up under me. "So tell me," I said, "how long have you been here?"

He didn't answer right away. He seemed a little fazed by how abruptly I'd changed the subject. "Four years and seven months," he said eventually. "I'm to take my final vows in June."

"You mean, you haven't done that yet?"

"I'm what's called a 'simple professed' monk. You spend two years as a novice, three as a 'simple professed,' and then you decide whether you're going to stay forever."

And then you decide.

The words caused a commotion in me. I watched the wind lift the short ends of his hair. It shocked me how easy this was, how little conflict I felt inside, how enclosed we were in a world that seemed to have nothing to do with my life in Atlanta, with Hugh. I was actually sitting there imagining a future with this man.

"What did you do before?" I asked.

"I was a lawyer," he said, and for a split second all the self-possession and assurance I sensed in him flared in his voice, in the intense look that passed through his eyes, in the forceful way he sat up straighter on the seat. I had a sudden sense that his former life had been one of great import, yet that was all he said about it.

"What made you give that up and come here?"

"I'm not sure you want to know. It's a long, sad story."

"Well, I told you *my* long, sad story."

I'd wondered what terrible thing had happened to him, but I hadn't imagined it would be as awful as it was. He told me about a wife named Linda with fine blond hair and about their unborn baby whose nursery he'd painted the color of pumpkins because Linda craved pumpkin bread morning and night. They'd both died when a truck slammed into her car. Whit had been home at the time, putting the baby's crib together.

He talked about them in a voice that changed perceptibly, the volume sinking so low that I had to tilt my body forward to hear him. His eyes trailed off, too, traveling to the floor of the boat.

Finally, looking at me, he said, "She called me before getting in the car that day to say she was sure we were having a girl. That's the last thing she said to me."

"I'm sorry," I told him. "I can understand why you'd come here."

"Everyone thinks I came here out of grief, because I was running away. I'm not sure if I was or not. I don't think so. I think mostly I was running *toward* something."

"You mean God?"

"I think I wanted to know whether there actually was one."

"And is there?"

He laughed like I'd made the ultimate joke. "As if I would know."

"Even a weak, doubting monk must have some idea of that."

He was quiet a moment, watching a small egret fishing in the shallows at the edge of the water. "Sometimes I experience God like this Beautiful Nothing," he said. "And it seems then as though the whole point of life is just to rest in it. To contemplate it and love it and eventually disappear into it. And then other times it's just the opposite. God feels like a presence that engorges everything. I come out here, and it seems the divine is running rampant. That the marsh, the whole of Creation, is some dance God is doing, and we're meant to step into it, that's all. Do you know what I mean?"

I told him I did, but that was mostly a lie. Still, I sat there with a rush of desire for his

Beautiful Nothing, for his dance. But mostly for him.

A cloud bloused across the sun, and the air dimmed around us. As we sat in the changing light, the tide bulged under the boat and bumped it against the reeds. It rocked like Moses's basket on the waters of the Nile.

I became aware that he was staring straight at me. I could have turned away. I could have let it be another disposable moment in a whole lifetime of them, but I made a conscious decision to stare back, to let my gaze pierce the air like a blade and meet his. We stared a long time, perhaps a whole minute. Our eyes fastened like that. There was an unspoken intention in it. A kind of fierceness. I was aware of my breath coming faster, that something exhilarating but dangerous was happening, that we were *letting* it happen. He as much as I.

It became unbearable finally. I had to look away.

I think we could have been honest with each other right then and said what we were feeling. I believe we came very close. But the moment passed, the transparency of it hardened, and propriety set in.

"I'm sorry, it doesn't look as if the white pelicans are going to appear," he said. He glanced at his watch. "And I need to take you back so I can make my rounds through the rookery."

He began to pull on the anchor line. He nosed the boat through the little finger of water back into the creek, where he kicked the engine wide open. The noise from the motor filled my head. Looking back, I saw the white wake flow out behind us like the contrail of a jet, Whit sitting there in his blue shirt holding the rudder, big scallops of cloud overhead.

Then I saw them. The white pelicans were coming up behind us, flying low just above the water. I shouted, pointing up at them, and Whit turned the instant they rose sharply and sailed directly over us. They were drenched in light, the black tips of their wings gleaming. I counted eighteen of them moving in their synchronized way in one single, dazzling line. Then they were gone.

After Whit tied the boat up at the dock, he offered me his hand as I stepped from the boat, and I took it. He squeezed before he let go. I thanked him for the ride.

I left him standing on the dock. I could feel him watching me as I moved down the splintery planks of the walkway. When I reached the edge of the marsh, just before stepping into the silence of the trees, I looked back.

What matters is giving over to what you love.

CHAPTER
Twenty

When we arrived at Max's Café the following Saturday, Mother refused to go inside. She balked on the sidewalk like a spooked horse and wouldn't move. Kat, Benne, Hepzibah, and I tried to coax her to the door, but she was adamant. "Take me home," she said. "I mean it, take me home."

It had required all my tactics of persuasion, plus heavy-handed phone calls from Kat and Hepzibah both, to get her this far, and now it looked as if our well-meaning plan to reintroduce her into some kind of normal existence was going up in smoke. She didn't want to face the whispers and stares of people she'd known her whole life—and who could blame her? We'd finally convinced her that she'd have to face them sooner or later, and why not get it over with?

But that was before we stood on the sidewalk and saw the crowd through the café windows. It was only March 4, but there was a tinge of springtime in the breezes, and the place appeared jam-packed, not only with islanders but with tourists.

"If *you* were the village idiot instead of me, would *you* go in there, inviting everybody to make fun of you?" Mother demanded.

"You're damn right I would," said Kat. "And I'm not so sure I'm *not* the village idiot. You think people don't talk about me? About my big mouth or the air horn on my cart? Or about Benne—you don't think they talk about her? And what about Hepzibah—they have a field day with her, how she communicates with slave spirits at the cemetery, going around dressed up more African than the Africans?"

My hand went involuntarily to my mouth. I looked at Hepzibah, who had on a gorgeous caramel-and-black African print dress and turban and a necklace made from ostrich eggshell. She was the only person I knew more fearless than Kat, someone who could, if she wanted, clean Kat's clock, as they say.

She looked down at Kat's signature black heels and lacy socks and just stared. The socks were a light shade of *pink.*

"If you must know, I washed them with Benne's red nightshirt," Kat said.

Hepzibah turned to Mother. "If you aren't giving people around here something to talk about, Nelle, you've become too dull."

"But this is different," Mother said. "The people in there think I'm . . . insane. I would rather they think I'm dull."

"Bite . . . your . . . tongue," said Kat.

It killed Mother that the people she knew believed she'd lost her mind, but it bothered her much more that I might believe it. The day before, at breakfast, I'd screwed up my courage and asked her in the kindest voice I could, "Do you ever hear voices? Did a voice tell you to cut off your finger?"

She'd shot me a withering look. "I'm hearing a voice right now," she said, mocking me. "It's telling me you should pack your suitcase and go back to Atlanta. Go home, Jessie. I don't need you here. I don't want you here either."

I felt tears collecting. My bottom lids became bloated with them. It wasn't just her words but the look on her face, all the bright red bitterness in it.

I turned away, but she saw the tears, and the pressure that had been expanding around our heads broke. "Oh, Jessie," she said. She let her fingers brush against my arm and stay there with the tips resting near my elbow. It was about the tenderest gesture she'd made toward me since I'd left home for college.

"Don't mind me," she said. "I can't stand you thinking I've gone insane, that's all." She looked down at her bandage. "There weren't any voices, okay? I was feeling tired and distraught. I was holding the cleaver, and . . . it just seemed like it would be such a relief to bring it down on my finger."

For a moment she looked almost as bewildered by what she'd done as I was. Now, though, standing outside Max's Café, she just seemed scared.

Kat wore a scarf covered with yellow and red hibiscuses tucked around her neck. Whipping it off, she began winding it around Mother's hand, covering her old gauze bandage, which looked like a big white boxing glove. When Kat was finished, it looked like a big *floral* boxing glove.

"The best defense is a good offense," she said.

"I'm not wearing this scarf around my hand," Mother said.

Kat placed her fists on her hips. "Listen to me. Every single person on Egret Island knows you cut off your finger, and when you walk in there, every person with eyeballs is going to stare at you. So go in with a little pizzazz, why don't you? This will be like shoving it right back in their faces. You'll be saying, *Yes, this is the infamous hand with the missing finger. I've highlighted it for you with this colorful bandage. Take a good look.*"

Benne giggled.

Mother turned to Hepzibah for a second opinion.

"I hate to admit this, but I agree with Kat," Hepzibah said. "If you go into Max's and poke a little fun at yourself, you might defuse the whole thing."

I couldn't believe that Hepzibah had been sucked into Kat's screwball idea. "I don't know about this," I said.

"That's right, you don't," said Kat, and,

latching onto Mother's arm, she guided her to the door. More to the point, Mother *let* herself be guided, and that was the marvel to me, to see the power these women still had over her.

The door of the restaurant had one of those annoying tinkling bells attached. It jangled as we came through, and Bonnie Langston, who was plumper than I remembered her, rushed over, pressing her dimpled hand to her lips and suppressing a grin when she spotted the scarf tied around Mother's hand.

"I find white gauze boring," Mother told her.

Bonnie led us to a table in the exact middle of the room. And yes, every islander in there twisted around to stare at Mother's hibiscus-covered hand. Conversations died in midsentence.

And then, like Bonnie, people began to smile.

After we had studied our menus, Kat said, "Jessie, you've been here—what? Two weeks?"

"Two and a half."

"I was wondering if Hugh might be coming for a visit anytime soon."

"No," I said, remembering what Benne

had told her and feeling monumentally awkward. "He has his practice, you know. He can't just leave."

"Even for the weekend?"

"He's usually on call then."

I narrowed my eyes at Benne. For all I knew, she might clink her spoon on her water glass and announce to a hushed room that I was in love with a monk from the abbey. *St. Sin.*

Kat gestured at a mason jar that sat on the table beside the salt and pepper shakers. Half filled with quarters and dimes, it was labeled DOG FOOD DONATIONS. "Would you look at this? Bonnie is collecting money for Max's dog food."

Gazing around the room, I noticed a jar on every table.

"She probably uses it to buy all those damn Precious Moments figurines she has all over her B and B," Kat went on. "I mean, where *is* all this imaginary dog food she supposedly buys with it?" She put her hand on Mother's arm. "Nelle, you remember that time about a hundred years ago when we ordered six cases of dog food for the first Max? It was from some pet place in Charleston, and they sent all that *cat* food over on the ferry?"

Mother tilted her head, and you could see the memory break the surface of her thoughts and spill into her face. I watched the sheen in her eyes grow, beaming around the table like a sweep of brightness from a lighthouse. She laughed, and all of us stopped to admire the sound.

"Max ate every bit of it," she said. "He loved it, as I recall."

Kat leaned in close to her. "Yeah, he started acting very feline after that. All independent and condescending, chasing mice and spitting up hair balls."

Mother said, "Remember that time the first Max ate a piece of rope, and Kat and I ran down to the ferry and told Shem he had to take us across right then, because we had an emergency. You remember that, Kat?"

She was almost chirping. The floral bouquet of her hand waved in the air. I sat there in a state of confused wonder—we all did—as if we were witnessing the miracle of birth happening to someone we didn't know was pregnant.

She went on, "Shem said he couldn't make an unscheduled ferry run for a dog. I thought Kat was going to assault him. So he says, 'Okay, ladies, calm down, I'll take you,' and halfway across, Max threw up the rope and was perfectly fine."

Her face was aglitter. *Who is this woman?*

No one moved. Mother took a breath and picked up the story. "Well, we had made such a big deal about it, we hated to tell him, 'Oh, never mind,' so we pretended it was touch and go and spent a few hours walking Max around McClellanville before catching the ferry back."

Bonnie appeared then and took our lunch orders. After she left, Hepzibah said, "What about that time, Nelle, we went over to the abbey to help you wash and wax St. Senara's statue, and Max came along—I believe it was the Max before this one. You remember that?"

Mother tossed back her head and laughed with the most breathtaking hilarity, then said to me, "After we got St. Senara all cleaned, Max hiked his leg on her."

She seemed to have dropped through a crack in time, and it was the Nelle from thirty-four years ago. The one she'd lost or killed off.

I didn't want the reminiscing to stop. "Remember the All-Girls Picnics?" I said.

"The All-Girls Picnics!" Kat cried. "Now,

that was the most fun any three women ever had."

Hepzibah said, "This is the second time today I've agreed with you, Kat. I'm starting to worry about myself."

"And that time you found the turtle skull out in the water—remember that?" I said, looking at Hepzibah.

"Of course I do. I'm just surprised you do."

"I always loved that skull," I said, then slapped my hands together. "We should do it again—have an All-Girls Picnic."

"We *should,*" Kat said. "What a fine idea!"

Benne, who was sitting next to Mother, leaned over to her and, cupping her hand around her mouth, whispered loud enough for everyone at the table to hear, "You said you would never go to an All-Girls Picnic again."

Mother glanced around the table. The glint, I noticed, was beginning to leave her eyes.

"That was a long time ago, Benne," said Hepzibah. "People change their minds. Don't they, Nelle?"

"I can't," she said.

I reached for her hand as if I might pull her back to us. "But why?"

Benne piped up again. "She didn't want to have fun after your daddy died. Remember? She said, 'It's a travesty for me to be out there dancing and carrying on after what happened.' "

I shot Kat a look as if to say, Would you shut her up? Kat reached into the breadbasket and handed Benne a biscuit.

"Dad would've *wanted* you to keep having the picnics," I said.

Mother ran her hand up and down her glass of sweet tea.

"Come on, Nelle, do it for us. It'll be a hoot," said Kat.

"We'll invite Max," Hepzibah added.

Mother shrugged. I could see a sequin or two of light still floating in her eyes. "But no dancing," she said. "I don't want any dancing."

"We'll sit on the blanket and just talk, like we're doing now," said Kat. "If anybody dances, we'll shoot her."

Bonnie appeared with our lunches, plates of fried oysters and shrimp, crab cakes, red rice, and the black-eyed pea and grits cakes she was famous for. As we ate and talked, the old Nelle receded completely, but I knew that some remnant of my bygone mother still existed, and I felt for the first time that she might be fished up out of her madness, at least partially.

Across the room the door opened, and the little bell made a spangly sound that rippled across the room. I turned instinctively.

He stood just inside the door, his almond-brown head bowed toward the tiles on the floor as if he'd dropped a coin. He looked up with his eyes half closed and scanned the tables, and I felt my heart tumble and crash.

It was Hugh.

CHAPTER
Twenty-one

I watched him for several moments, thinking, *Wait, wait, that can't be Hugh. Hugh is in Atlanta.*

You know how it is when you see someone completely out of context, someone who isn't supposed to be there, how you're mildly disoriented, how it upends your sense of the moment? This was even a little worse than that for me. I sat at the table imagining that through some inexplicable amalgam of ESP, prescient insight, and suspicion, *he knew.*

He knew I'd sat in a boat with another man and wished I could float away with him to the other side of the world. He knew about the scene I had visualized a dozen or more times—the impossible, unbearable one—packing a suitcase and calmly walking out of the house, leaving him. He knew. And he had come, summoned all the way from Atlanta by the stench of my guilt.

When he spotted me, though, he smiled. His normal smile, the mouth ends pulled down, stretched with amusement as if he were resisting the moment his teeth would break through, this smile that had swept over me so many times.

As he walked to the table, I smiled back, an *abnormal* smile. Someone *trying* to smile, forcing herself to look normal and happy and carefree.

"Hugh, my goodness! What are you doing here? How did you know where to find us?" I said, folding my napkin, laying it neatly beside my plate. He looked thinner, slighter, different somehow.

He bent down and kissed my cheek. His own cheek was sandpapery, and I could tell he'd been sucking on one of his lemon lozenges. "I went into Caw Caw General to call the house and see if you could pick me up in the cart, and someone told me you were here." He put his hand on Mother's shoulder. "How are you, Nelle?"

"Perfectly fine," she said, and his eyes moved to examine her hand, the outlandish boxing-glove scarf-bandage.

He greeted Kat and Hepzibah.

"God, if you aren't the most handsome man I've ever seen," said Kat, and Hugh blushed, a thing you didn't see that much.

I was the one who suggested the two of us leave Max's Café and take a walk. I don't think I could've endured sitting there with him making small talk while Kat, Hepzibah, Benne, and Mother looked on.

We walked toward the center of the island along Slave Road, so named because it wound past the cemetery where the slaves had been buried. We talked with polite restraint, a kind of catch-up talk about what had been going on back home, how things were with Mother. My stomach felt alternately knotted and quivery.

When we came to the graveyard, we stopped automatically and stared at the cedar crosses Hepzibah had erected on each grave. They all faced east, so the dead could rise easier, or so she said. The island had been home to a small community of freed slaves after the Civil War. Eventually they all left or died off, but they'd been a presence here for a long time.

As we looked up at the massive live oak whose branches spread over the graves, I remembered what Dee had said on the phone about Mother's becoming upset here, carrying on about a dead person's finger.

Hugh sat on one of the limbs that had grown tired over the centuries of holding itself up and rested now on the earth. I followed, sitting beside him. We were quiet, Hugh looking at sky and air, at the twigs trembling on the ends of branches, while I studied tiny lime ferns and white, stubby mushrooms pushing through the dirt.

"This tree must be ancient," Hugh said.

"Eight hundred years old," I told him. A questionable "fact" everyone on the island loved to quote. "Or at least that's what people say. I guess there's really no way to verify it. Hepzibah says they can't take core samples, because apparently the tree has heart rot."

He let his eyes drift toward mine. They had that sudden look of psychiatric wisdom, the look he got when he was sure he'd seen through the camouflage of someone's words to an unintended meaning. I tried to read his face. What was he suggesting? That I'd said the poor tree had heart rot when really I was talking about myself?

"*What?*" I demanded, aggravated.

"What's going on, Jessie?"

"You know what's going on. I'm trying to deal with this situation with Mother. And I told you I wanted to handle it by myself, so of course here you are—Hugh to the rescue."

"Look, it's true that I don't think you should be trying to deal with this by yourself, but I didn't come all this way because of that."

"Why *are* you here, then? You snuck onto the island without even telling me you were coming."

He didn't respond. We sat for a minute with our shoulders taut and stared at the crosses. Little birds twitched in the moss over our heads.

I heard him sigh. He placed his hand on top of mine. "I didn't mean to start a fight. I came because . . . because I made reservations for us in Charleston, at the Omni. We'll take the afternoon ferry and check in at the hotel. We can have dinner at Magnolia's. It'll be an evening just for us, and I'll bring you back to the ferry in the morning."

I didn't look at him. I wanted to feel for him what I felt for Whit. I wanted to conjure it out of the air. I had a sudden panicked moment as I realized I could not get back to the place I'd been before.

"I can't," I said.

"What do you mean? Of course you can."

"How could you make all these plans without consulting me?"

"It's called a surprise."

"I don't want any surprises."

"What is wrong with you? You've been distant for months, Jessie. Then you come here and don't call, and when I call you, you start a fight. Now this."

I slid my hand away and felt my heart let go. Like fingers turning loose of the side of a boat. Dropping through layers of water.

I'd never felt more terrified.

"I want some time apart," I said. I hadn't known I was going to say this, and I looked at him, trying to see by his reaction if I really had.

His head jerked backward sharply. It reminded me of a flag snapping in the wind. I'd shocked him. I'd shocked myself.

He reddened, and I realized it was not shock coursing through him but anger. The most awful, hurt-drenched anger.

" 'Apart'? What the hell are you talking about?" he bellowed. I stood and took a step back from him. I thought he might shake me, and honest to God I almost wanted him to. "Apart from *me?* Is that what you mean? You want a goddamn separation?"

"A separation?" I stood there blinking, my heart gone eerily still. "I don't know. I . . . I just want to be on my own awhile."

"That's what a separation *is!*" he shouted.

He walked off into the gray shadows of the tree and stopped, his back to me. His shoulders moved up and down as though he was breathing hard. He was shaking his head as if bewildered. I took a step toward him at the same moment he began to walk away, along the road the way we'd come. He did not look back. He did not say good-bye. He walked with his hands in his pockets.

I watched with the feeling of life draining away, everything leaving, ending. An impulse to chase after him rose up. Part of me wanted to catch him in my arms, say, *I'm sorry, I'm sorry, I'm so horribly sorry,* but I didn't move. A strange, Novocained feeling was settling into my limbs.

He grew smaller and smaller, a moth fluttering away. When I could no longer see him, I went and sat back down on the tree.

The numbing weight filled me up. I stared at dimes of light moving on the ground and imagined Hugh at the ferry dock. I pictured him sitting on a bench waiting for the boat. Max was there, pushing his head onto Hugh's knee, trying to comfort him. I wanted Max to be there—someone to go and make things better.

Long ago, when I was nine, Mike and I had come pedaling by the cemetery and found Hepzibah pulling weeds between the graves. I thought of that now. It had been a day in winter, but warm like this day, and the sky had condensed into those brash purples that came so often here.

We'd stopped and laid our bikes on the ground. She looked at us and said, "Did I ever tell you about the two suns?"

Hepzibah was always telling me and Mike one of her folk-tales from Africa, which we devoured. We shook our heads and plopped down on the ground beside her, ready for another one.

"Over in Africa the Sonjo used to say one day two suns will rise," she told us. "One sun would come from the east, and one sun would come from the west. And when they met at the top of the sky, that would be the end."

I looked at Mike, and he looked at me. She didn't usually tell stories like this. I waited for more, for the rest of the tale, but, remarkably, she was finished.

"You mean the end of the *world?*" Mike said.

"I just mean that everything ends eventually. The two suns are always rising somewhere. That's part of life. Something ends, and then something else will begin. You understand?"

She was scaring me a little. I backed out of the cemetery without answering her and rode home as fast as I could. My father died a week later. I didn't go around Hepzibah for a long time. It was almost as if she'd known it was coming, though I realized later that was impossible.

As I sat here now, my body began to

shake, trembling like the air after a cannon-ade. I imagined the ferry pulling up to the dock, Hugh stepping onto it, seagulls circling his head. I saw the boat pull away and the stretch of water become wide. Overhead, the two suns were crashing.

CHAPTER
Twenty-two

I turned the golf cart into Kat's driveway the next morning, angling past the MERMAID XING sign, feeling unaccountably lighthearted, unclouded, emancipated, something bordering on frivolous. This after twisting around half the night in the sheets in guilt and alarm at what I'd done.

After Hugh had left yesterday, I'd sat beside the slave cemetery for an hour or more, until the paralysis wore off and the paroxysms of terror began. *What have I done?*

I'd called him last night, twice. He hadn't answered even though he'd had plenty of time to get back home. I hadn't known why I was calling, or what I would say if he answered. Probably I would have repeated a long litany of *I'm sorry, I'm sorry.* What I'd done seemed impossible to me, completely disorienting. Like I'd amputated something— not a mere digit on my hand but my marriage, the symbiosis that had sustained me. My life had been beautifully contained within Hugh's, like one of those Russian nesting dolls, encompassed in wifeness, in a cocoon of domesticity. And I'd demolished it. For what?

I'd sat on the edge of the bed remembering odd bits and pieces of things. The time when Dee was small and Hugh had sung the Humpty Dumpty song to her while balancing an egg on the edge of the table, how he'd let it go, demonstrating Humpty's great fall. She'd loved it so much that he'd killed off the entire carton, then afterward gotten down on the floor and cleaned up the whole mess. I'd thought of the silly game he played every Christmas—I Bet I Can Wear Every Present I Open. I don't mean sport shirts and slippers but fishing rods and steak knives. My part in this was to challenge him by buying one thing a human being seemingly could not wear. Last year it had been a cappuccino machine. Within two minutes he'd strapped it onto himself like a backpack using a couple of bungee cords. "Voilà," he'd said.

What if there were no more Hugh in my life? No more of these small antics, the moments we'd pieced together to form a history?

But were these habits of love—or love itself?

I forced myself to consider how irritating he could be: the way he dried the insides of his ears with the hem of his undershirt, that maddening puffing sound he made, the toothbrush tapping, the walking around in nothing but socks and oxford shirts buttoned to his neck, the pulling open of drawers and cabinets and never closing them. Worse, the tiresome overanalyzing, the incessant rightness, the entitlement he felt when it came to us—that tendency of his to be the benevolent puppeteer.

People move on, I'd told myself. They create new histories. Still, the panic had kept roiling until I'd fallen asleep.

This morning I'd wakened to a soft light folding in through the window, and my apprehension was gone, replaced by this strange buoyancy. I'd lain in bed, realizing I'd been dreaming. The dream had faded, except for one rapturous fragment still spinning at the edge of my awareness. A man and woman traveling beneath the ocean in a path of air bubbles and faint blue streams of light. They were breathing under the water. Holding hands.

The moment I'd opened my eyes, I'd felt their weightlessness in my arms and legs, the mysterious rush of the world below— opaque, free, dangerous, and utterly foreign. I'd wanted to go throw myself into its arms.

Standing at the window in my old bedroom, where the whirly girls used to hang, I'd watched the early-morning light creaming through the dark sky and twisted my wedding rings over my knuckle. I'd held them a little while before dropping them onto an embroidery needle stuck like a horseshoe nail in an old velvet pincushion on the dresser.

Now, pulling up in front of Kat's yellow house, I was a separated woman, and I didn't know if I was possessed by a state of extreme denial or extreme relief.

I parked the cart beside the steps. When Kat swung open the door, Hepzibah and Benne stood behind her in the hallway.

I'd come uninvited, leaving Mother riffling through a pile of recipe books. "I didn't know

if you'd be here or at the Mermaid's Tale," I
said to Kat.

"Today I open the shop after lunch," she
said, motioning me inside.

Hepzibah asked what they were all thinking. "How's Hugh this morning?"

"He left yesterday."

"I told you he did," said Benne, crossing
her arms over her chest.

Benne could be annoyingly smug and
sometimes, like now, downright irksome.

Kat ignored her. "What happened? The
man just got here yesterday."

"You know, you really ought to learn when
to shut up," Hepzibah told her. Taking my
hand, she led me to the kitchen, into a
warm, garlicky smell and the *hum-slosh* of
the dishwasher. The room was painted the
color of pluff mud—a rich, fermenting
brown—and there were mermaid doodads
everywhere. "I stopped by to have a cup of
coffee. We were just about to pour it," she
said.

She filled four mugs while we sat around
the long oak table. An earthenware bowl in the
center spilled over with plums, navel oranges,
green bell peppers, and gigantic lemons.

"Mother is like a new woman this morning," I said, wanting to steer the conversation away from Hugh. "I think the lunch did her a world of good. She's talking about going back to the monastery and cooking again. She's at home working on her menus."

"Well, make sure they hide the meat cleavers," Kat said.

"Kat!" cried Hepzibah.

I set down my cup. "You don't think she'd do it again?"

"No, actually I don't," Kat said. "But tell them to hide the cleavers anyway. You can't be too careful." She got up and placed a shopping bag beside my chair. "Shem dropped off your art supplies yesterday afternoon."

I rummaged through the bag, spreading the contents onto the table. There was a one-and-a-half-inch sable wash brush and a number four for small line work, a John Pike palette, and an eighteen-by-twenty-four tablet filled with 140-pound cold-press paper. The size of the paper unnerved me—it was much larger than I'd requested. And the paints were not student grade, as I'd asked for, but artist. *Artist.* I picked up each tube: Yellow Ocher, Indian Red, Cerulean Blue, Rose Madder, Burnt Sienna, Raw Umber, Thalo Green, Ultramarine.

I was only vaguely aware of the others watching me. A spot in my chest had flared up, creating a buzzing sensation like the sparklers Mike and I used to run around waving in the early dark of summer.

When I glanced up, Kat smiled at me. Pieces of her hair fell around her ears. Today it appeared to be ocher red. "So when can I expect to see mermaid paintings in my shop?"

"Art comes when it comes," I replied.

"Oh. Well. *Excuse* me," she said. "Let me rephrase that: When do you think your art might be *coming?*"

"As I recall, we had a deal. You were going to talk to Dominic and see what he might know about Mother's reasons for cutting off her finger—remember? And in exchange I was going to paint mermaids. So . . . did you?"

Kat's eyes drifted away toward the window over the sink, to the filigree of light on the counter. The moment stretched out. I could hear Benne fooling with the lid on the sugar bowl, clinking it up and down. Hepzibah rose from her chair and walked over to the coffeemaker where she poured herself another cup.

"I didn't talk with him, Jessie," Kat said, turning to me. "It just so happens I agree with Dominic. I don't think it does anybody any good, especially your mother, for us to go picking through whatever her reasons were. It's only going to upset Nelle. And it's pointless anyway. Look, I'm sorry. I know I told you I'd talk to him, but I don't think it's right. I wish you'd take my advice and drop it."

I felt a surge of anger at her, and yet I was half tempted to do what she'd said. Understanding my mother was exhausting, maybe even impossible.

"All right."

"You mean you'll drop it?" she asked.

"No, I mean, it's all right—I won't ask you to help me." I said it with resignation, with the anger bleeding out of me. Kat believed she was doing what was best, and I was never going to convince her otherwise.

She cocked her head and gave me a rueful smile, pretending to be contrite. "But you'll still paint the mermaids for me. Won't you?"

I sighed. "Oh, for God's sake, yes, I'll paint the mermaids." I wanted to be aggravated with her—I'd tried to sound that way—but when I looked down at the paints and brushes she'd gotten for me, I couldn't.

The phone rang, and Kat wandered off to answer it. Hepzibah stood at the sink rinsing out the coffeepot. The room filled with the sound of running water, and I had a momentary flash of my dream from the night before. I wondered what Whit was doing now—this very minute. I pictured him in his cottage, hunched over a desk covered with books, the cowl of his robe cradled between his shoulder blades. I saw him in the johnboat cutting through the creeks, saw that remarkable shade his eyes had turned in the sunlight—the color of denim.

It was adolescent to be thinking about him this way. But I was unable sometimes to think of anything else. I would imagine our bodies pressed together, me lifting out of myself into something timeless and large, where I could do anything, feel everything, where there would be no empty spaces inside to fill.

"Are you going to tell us why Hugh left?" asked Kat, slumped against the counter. I hadn't even heard her come back into the room.

"He hadn't really planned on staying," I answered.

"Not even one night?" She looked at my

left hand. "Yesterday you were wearing your wedding rings. Today you're not."

Benne stared at my hand from across the table, then at my face. It was that same look she'd given me in the Mermaid's Tale when she'd informed me that I was in love with one of the monks. The realization that she'd also informed her mother of this fact left me with an irrational need to confess everything.

As Hepzibah wandered over and stood next to Kat, it occurred to me that this was probably the reason I'd come here in the first place. Because I desperately needed confidantes. Because underneath I felt terrified. Because the weight of what I was carrying around was at least ten times heavier than I was, and I had come to the end of my ability to hold it. I wanted suddenly to kneel down in front of Kat and Hepzibah, lay my head in their respective laps, and feel their hands rest on my shoulders.

"Something awful has happened," I said, directing my attention to the bowl, then the tabletop. "Hugh and I have— I think we've separated." Shifting my eyes a little, I saw the hem of Hepzibah's dress, Kat's pointy shoes, a trellis of shadows falling from the window. The faucet was dripping over in the sink. Cof-

fee smells drifted around like ground fog. I
went on. "I've fallen in love with . . . with someone else."

I didn't look up. I wondered if their expres-
sions had flattened out with shock. I hadn't
felt ridiculous saying it to them, as I'd imagined I would. I *did* feel shame, but, I told myself, at least I was a woman having a real
experience, unwilling to pretend about it,
ready to take myself, my feelings, seriously.

Kat said, "Benne told us."

It was generally true that Benne was
never wrong, but it astonished me how easily they'd accepted her word on this.

"She told us this 'someone else' is one of
the monks," Kat added.

"Yes," I said. "Brother Thomas."

"He's the newest one, isn't he?" Hepzibah
asked.

I nodded. "His real name is Whit O'Conner."

"Did you tell Hugh?" Kat wanted to know.

"No, I . . . I couldn't."

"Good," said Kat, and she let out a breath.
"Sometimes being honest is really just being
stupid."

My hands, I noticed, rested in front of me
as if I were praying, my fingers laced so

tightly they were actually hurting. The tips of them were pulpy and red.

Kat sat on one side of me, while Hepzibah plopped down on the other and draped her brown hand over both of mine.

"When I think of Hugh, I feel terrible," I said. "But I can't get over the feeling that Whit is someone I'm supposed to be with. We went out in his boat a few days ago, to a place out in the rookery, and talked. He had a wife, who died." I stopped. "I'm not making sense."

"First of all, you don't *have* sense when you fall in love," said Kat. "And no one here's judging you. Not in this house anyway. Lord knows you won't see *me* throwing stones. I've been exactly where you are."

I looked at her and blinked. The arches of her eyebrows had traveled up on her forehead, and her mouth had taken on a bitter amusement. "Now, the man wasn't a monk. God—bless her heart—spared me that bit of humor. He was a harbor pilot in Charleston who used to come over here to fish and buy cast nets. God, I loved that man—despite the inconvenient fact I was married to Henry Bowers. I was just about your age, too, just old enough for the bottom to start falling out of things, you know? You look around and think, So this is *it?* I'd been married twenty years. *Twenty.* Which is about when the marriage glue gets so old it starts to harden and crack."

I felt my throat tighten a little. Hepzibah began to rub her thumb back and forth across mine. The friction, the rhythm of it, was soothing. My fingers unknotted, drooping toward my palms.

"I'm just saying I know what it's like to love somebody you think you shouldn't be loving," Kat went on. "There probably isn't a woman alive who doesn't know what that's like. Half of them fall for their gynecologists and the other half for their priests. You can't stop your heart from loving, really—it's like standing out there in the ocean yelling at the waves to stop.

"But you've got to hear this, too," Kat added. "I wish now I hadn't acted on those feelings. There was a lot of hurt caused, Jessie. To be honest, I'm not sure I could've done anything else but what I did, given how I felt and all, and how little I knew. I'm only saying I know what you're feeling and that you should think this through."

I sank back in my chair, hearing the croak and tick of wood in the seat. I turned and looked at Hepzibah. Her eyes were partly closed.

She said, "When I was forty, back before I started studying Gullah ways, I fell in love with a man in Beaufort who could quote you entire slave narratives passed down by word of mouth for a hundred years. I never knew anybody who cared so much about preserving their roots, and of course what I was loving was mostly my own hunger to do the same thing."

"What happened?" I asked.

"I was already divorced by then and wouldn't have minded remarrying, but he had a wife already. Kat is right, that didn't stop me from feeling what I was feeling. I decided, though, to love him without . . . you know, physically loving him, and it was hard, about the hardest thing I ever did, but I lived to be glad about it. The thing is, he got me exploring my roots, and so much came out of that."

Benne was leaning up on both elbows listening to these revelations with her lips parted and the bangs of her plain brown hair falling a half inch below her eyebrows. "I loved somebody," she announced with glowing eyes, and we all turned and stared at her.

"Well, do tell," said Kat. She seemed genuinely shocked by the declaration. "Who was this lucky man—your gynecologist or your priest?"

"Mike," she said. "And *I* couldn't get myself to stop feeling love either." She sat up straight and smiled, pleased to be one of us. "I told him the day he left for college. Everybody was on the dock, saying good-bye to him, remember? And I said, 'I love you,' and he said, 'I love you, too, Benne,' and then he got on the ferry." Kat patted her arm.

The room grew quiet. I realized what Kat and Hepzibah were doing, worrying about my getting hurt, trying to give me a big picture, some perspective I hadn't considered. I could understand in a way the point they were making, but I couldn't let it in. Maybe it's human nature to think one's own situation is the unique and incomparable one, the transcendent exception. Maybe the impulse I felt inside was wiser than all their opinions. I realized I was shaking my head and feeling slightly petulant.

"What if I'm really meant to be with him and I let this slip away?" I said.

"You *are* meant to be with him," said Benne.

A Benne truth? Or was it an outburst of romantic, wishful thinking by an adult who was mostly a child?

"Nobody can tell you what to do," Kat said. "This is your life. Your decision."

"E come a time when eby tub haffa res pon e won bottom," said Hepzibah, then translated: "At some point in life, you have to stand on your own two feet."

Kat stepped closer to me, her forehead rippled with little furrows. "Just be careful," she said.

I stood up. The paint tubes, the palette, the brushes were piled around the fruit bowl as if they'd fallen out of a cornucopia. I gathered them back into the shopping bag.

"I have been careful my whole life," I said.

I smiled at them, feeling like I *was* standing there on my own two feet.

"I saw your canoe on the dock in the rookery," I said to Hepzibah. "Do you mind if I borrow it?"

"Help yourself," she said.

She didn't ask why I wanted it. Neither did Kat. They knew already.

CHAPTER
Twenty-three

The day I paddled Hepzibah's once-red canoe through the winding creeks, I heard an alligator roar. It was mid-March, four days till spring, but warm enough that a few bulls had begun bellowing for mates out on the marsh banks. It sounded like distant thunder. By April there would be enough roaring to shake the creek water. Mike and I used to row the bateau through the hairpin turns when the ruckus was at full tilt, shouting at throngs of sunning turtles to head for the mud holes before they were all eaten.

Earlier, when I'd arrived on the rookery dock and flipped over the canoe, I'd discovered the turtle skull from the table on Hepzibah's porch propped beside the paddle. She'd obviously left it there for me. I remembered how she, Kat, and Mother had passed it back and forth all those years, a reminder of the way they'd knotted their lives together. The skull sat now on the fraying wicker seat at the bow, looking quite ancient, staring levelly ahead as if guiding the boat.

The mint green tint was climbing back into the blades of spartina grass, and around each curve an egret or heron stood like yard sculpture in the shallows. Their patience was unnerving. Just when I would give up on their ever moving again, they would spring to life, spearing a mud minnow.

I snaked along with the tail end of the ebb tide, making two wrong turns before I located the dead-end tributary where Whit had taken us the day we'd come out here together. When the corridor of grass opened into the cove of water where we'd sat in the johnboat and talked, I pulled the paddle across my lap and gave myself over to the breeze. It washed me up onto the tiny marsh island where Whit had built his hermitage on a hillock beneath a sole palmetto palm.

I wore the pair of old bogging boots

Mother used to wear to harvest oysters on the shell reefs, going out with Kat and Hepzibah, picking bushels for their New Year's Eve roast. Stepping out of the canoe, I sank over my ankles into mud. It was the exact consistency of cake batter, and it emitted a rotten stew of smells that I had grown up loving.

I dragged the canoe up into the grass. Sweltering, I peeled off my sweatshirt and tied it around my waist, then stood in my black T-shirt listening for the whir of Whit's johnboat. It had been at the dock when I'd left. I looked at my watch. I'd come at the same time we'd come before—when I thought he would be making his rookery rounds.

As I regarded the enclosure of water, the nearly perfect, hidden circle it made, I thought I heard the boat engine, and I froze a moment, watching the black skimmers swoop down and the surface churn silver with mullet, but the sound died and a moat of quiet surrounded me.

I'd brought a floppy basket filled with art supplies, thinking I would try to paint a little if Whit didn't show up. Honestly, I needed some actual reason for being out here, other than wanting to see him, something to fall back on. *I came out here to paint,* I could say.

As I retrieved the basket from the canoe, I impulsively picked up the turtle skull. It was silly to lug it around, but I didn't want to leave it behind. I picked my way through the needlegrass and palm scrub. When I arrived at Whit's lean-to, I laughed out loud. He'd stolen the design from depictions of the Bethlehem stable.

When I stepped under the sloping roof, I had to stoop slightly. A wire crab trap sat in the shadows near the back like a small table, with a cast net folded up beside it. He'd braided a cross out of palmetto leaf and nailed it up on a board, but other than that it could have been a hideout built by almost anyone.

Standing there, I knew why he loved this place. It was a different sort of cloister—secluded by water and marsh, a place untamed, without abbots and creeds, only instinct and the natural rhythms that had always existed here.

I placed the turtle skull on top of the crab trap, admiring the bleached-ivory look of it. I told myself it had belonged to a female, a three-hundred-pound loggerhead who'd dragged herself onto Bone Yard Beach year after year to fill the sand with eggs. Dad had taken Mike and me there one summer night when the beach was crawling with hatchlings. We'd watched them rushing toward the sea, toward a swatch of moonlight out on the water.

I laid my hand on the turtle skull and felt the backwash of Hepzibah's presence. Of Kat's. Even my mother's and Benne's.

I set up the tabletop easel I'd found at Caw Caw General, positioning it on the ground, arranging the watercolor tablet on it. I spread out my palette, charcoal sketching pencils, brushes, and a jar of water, and then, removing the boots, sat cross-legged in front of the paper and stared at the white space.

I'd already painted a dozen or more mermaids for Kat, staying up sometimes until after midnight to finish one. I'd started out doing the typical thing—mermaids on rocks, mermaids under the water, mermaids on top of the water—until I'd grown bored and begun to paint them in ordinary but unlikely places: driving a station wagon along I-85 in Atlanta with a baby mermaid strapped in a car seat in back; balancing on her tail fin before a stove, clad in a "Kiss the Cook" apron, frying fish in a skillet; and my favorite—sitting in a chair at a hair salon getting her long, silken tresses cut into a short, angular style with bangs.

"Now you're cooking," Kat had said. The paintings had sold immediately, and she'd begged me to bring her more.

Earlier I'd been struck with the idea of painting a mermaid paddling a canoe, wearing a life jacket, but now, as I held the pencil, I found myself making a line drawing of a woman's forehead and eyes, sketching it along the bottom edge of the paper as if she were peering over a wall. I drew her arms stretched over her head, her elbows pressed against her ears, giving the impression she was reaching with both hands for something over her head. I didn't know where the peculiar image was coming from.

I dampened the paper, laying on overlapping washes of blue, decreasing the pigment as I moved down the paper, creating lighter shades at the bottom around the woman's head. I painted in her head and arms, using sienna and umber. Her eyes were wide open, apprehensive, peering upward across the empty blue spaces that filled most of the paper. As a last touch, I shook the brush, gave it two quick snaps, creating a purposeful spatter along each of her arms.

When I put the brush down, the image appeared silly to me. But as I leaned back and looked again at what I'd done, the spatter beading her arms struck me as air bubbles and the variegated blues as levels of water. The painting, I decided, was upside down.

It was *not* a woman peering over a ledge with arms reaching up but a woman diving. I turned the picture 180 degrees and saw that it captured the moment when her arms and head first pierced the water, cutting cleanly into the emptiness below.

I kept staring at it. The moment I'd seen it reversed, I'd known—it was right *this* way.

I heard the droning of a boat engine far away, and my hand moved to my throat, lingering there as the sound grew closer. I pictured Whit approaching the island, catching sight of Hepzibah's canoe, wondering who was here. The noise dissolved as he cut the engine. A dog began to bark. Max.

Anticipation rose in my chest, the strange, euphoric energy that had made me increasingly unable to sleep or eat, filling me with endless renditions of the two of us together. It had made me bold and reckless. Had turned me into someone else. What would happen would happen.

I saw Max first. He loped up with his tongue dangling from the side of his mouth. I bent to pet him and, glancing up, saw Whit stepping over a rotting palmetto log. When he spotted me, he stopped.

I went on rubbing Max's head, my breath moving rapidly in and out of my nostrils. I said, "So this is the hermitage the abbot knows nothing about."

Still he didn't move, didn't speak. He wore the same denim shirt with the cross around his neck and held a tan canvas sack in one hand. I had the feeling it contained books. The light made brush marks on his face, obscuring it just enough that I couldn't read his expression. I didn't know if he was paralyzed with happiness or surprise. It could have been trepidation. He clearly knew what I was doing here. His entire body gave off the knowledge of it.

He slid one hand into his pocket and began walking toward me. I could see bits of gray shining in his black hair.

When he got to the easel, he dropped the sack and squatted beside my painting, relieved, I think, to have something to do.

"It's good," he said. "Very unusual."

I moved my thumb around the base of my finger, the place where my wedding rings had been. The skin felt bare and newly grown. Tender. He pretended to study the painting.

"I hope you don't mind me coming here to paint," I said. "I would've asked your permission, but . . . well, it's not like I could pick up the phone and call you."

"You don't have to ask my permission," he said. "This place belongs to everybody." He stood up but continued to look down at the picture with his back to me.

Around us the grasses rippled and swayed as though underwater. I wanted to go and slide my arms around him, press my face against his back, say, *It's okay, it is. We were meant for this,* but I couldn't be the one who said it. He had to hear it some other way, from inside himself. He had to believe in the rightness of it, as I did.

He looked painfully stiff standing there, and I wondered if he was struggling to hear the voice that would tell him what to do, the voice that would not be wrong, or if he was only barricading himself.

I told myself I would stand there in my bare feet one more minute, when it would be plain that the only dignified thing to do was put on my boots, gather up my art, and leave. I would paddle back and never speak of this again.

He turned around abruptly, almost as if he'd heard my thought. I stepped toward him, close enough to smell the saltiness coming from his chest, the damp circles under his arms. Light blazed up in the blue of his eyes. He reached out and pulled me to him, wrapping his arms around me. "Jessie," he whispered, pushing his face into my hair.

I closed my eyes and put my mouth at the opening of his shirt, let my lips open and close on his skin, tasting the flesh at the hollow of his throat, the taste of heat. I unfastened each small white button and kissed the skin beneath it. The wooden cross dangled over his breastbone, and I had to move it to one side in order to kiss the bone's small arch.

"Wait," he said, and pulled the leather cord over his head, letting the cross drop to the ground.

When I reached the button tucked inside his belt, I tugged his shirt out of his jeans and kept unbuttoning until he stood with his shirt wide open, a soft wind lifting the edges of it. He leaned over and kissed me. His mouth tasted like wine, left over from mass.

He led me into the flecked light of the hermitage, took off his shirt and spread it on the ground, then undressed me, lifting the T-shirt over my head, unsnapping my khakis, pulling them into a puddle around my ankles. I stepped out of them and stood in my light blue panties and matching bra and let him stare at me. He looked first at the indentation of my waist, that curve where it flares out to my hips, then glanced back at my face for a moment before letting his eyes wander to my breasts, then downward toward my thighs.

I stood unmoving, but there was an avalanche going on—an entire history sliding away.

He said, "I can't believe how beautiful you are."

I started to say, *No, no, I'm not,* but stopped myself. Instead I unhooked my bra and let it fall down next to his cross.

I watched him stoop and unlace his boots.

The skin on his shoulders was glazed with sunburn. He stood up, barefoot, bare-chested, his jeans low on his hips. "Come here," he said, and I went and leaned into the smoothness of his chest.

"I've wanted you from the beginning," he told me, and the way he said it—his eyes fixed on my face, a frown of purpose across his forehead—sent a tremor through me. He lowered me to the ground on top of his denim shirt and kissed the soft places on my throat, my breasts, my thighs.

We made love with the tide sweeping in around the island and Max asleep in the sun. There was a mystifying scent in the air, like burned sweetness. I decided later it was the smell of wisteria floating out from the island. As he moved above me, I heard the high-pitched call of an osprey coming from the height of clouds. I heard crab claws scurrying in the brush.

The ground was lumpy, gristly with vines and sprouting fan palms. One of them was jabbing into my shoulder, and my body had goose-pimpled over in the cool air, from the deep, cobalt shadows at the back of the lean-to. I began to tremble. Whit slid his hand under my shoulder, cradling it away from the pointy shoots on the palm. He said, "You all right?"

I nodded. I didn't mind any of it. I wanted to be here, lying on a tide-swept piece of earth, belonging to it, watched by the marsh, by the birds circling our heads.

He smiled at me, touching my face with his other hand, tracing the rim of my jaw, my lips and nose. He burrowed his face into my neck and breathed deeply, and I disappeared into the moment—Whit, the blood and bones in my body, the wildness of loving him.

I inhabited those moments in a way that was usually lost to me. They came through an amplifier that made the movement of our bodies and the pulsing world around us more vivid and radiant, more real. I could even feel how perishable *all* my moments really were, how all my life they had come to me begging to be lived, to be cherished even, and the impassive way I'd treated them.

Later I would think that if sex was really a conversation, a way of communicating something, what was it we had said to each other? Where had those desperate, eloquent voices come from?

Afterward I lay beside him, still nude,

warmed by his body, which gave off surprising waves of heat. There were smudges of mud on my hips, tiny green myrtle leaves pressed onto the backs of my legs. Max roused himself, wandered over, and curled up on the other side of me.

"I feel like that woman in the Gauguin painting," I said.

He tightened his arm around me. "Which one?"

"That exotic island woman he was always painting. You know. Usually she wore a red sarong."

He glanced at the turtle skull I'd placed on the crab trap, and smiled. Then he moved his finger along the gully between my breasts. I saw that his knuckle was bleeding from tiny punctures made by the sharp points of the fan palm.

I heard Max start to snore. Whit's eyes drifted closed. I could not understand drowsiness after sex. The cells in my own body were simmering in adrenaline.

When he began to breathe in the heavy way of sleep, I lay there and listened. The afternoon floated on the tide, pulled along like flotsam. Whit slept. I watched him. I watched everything with a kind of wonder. Once, a blur of white wings plummeted toward the creek—a diving osprey falling like an angel toward the water.

I felt evicted from my old life—no, not evicted, sprung. Free. I lay there—the Gauguin woman—held in the lushness of what had happened, feeling content, *alive.*

Only once did I think of Hugh and a spasm of shock swept through me, the rebound of my other life, the terrible moral wrongness of what I'd done. I cupped myself tightly against Whit's side until it passed.

When he woke, the sun was arching toward the west. From under the lean-to, I could see citron colors flooding along the horizon. He sat up. "It's late. I have to get back for vespers."

As I reached for my clothes, he said, "Are you sorry? About this?"

"I don't have any regrets," I told him. But it wasn't true. I regretted that I was married. That I would end up hurting Hugh, had already hurt him. That Dee could be hurt. That all the glue that had held us together for so long was coming apart. But I didn't regret what we'd done. I should have, I suppose, but I didn't. I knew I would do it again. Unless. Unless *he* was sorry.

I didn't ask him whether he was or not. I didn't want to know. I couldn't bear thinking he might go to vespers now and beg God to forgive him.

CHAPTER
Twenty-four

Whit

He did not go to vespers. He did not go to compline either. He crossed the cloister to his cottage, walking quickly. Inside, he sat at his desk without turning on the lamp and watched the darkness grow beyond the window, the quiet way it swallowed the trees.

He had not been touched for so long. *Years.* He'd had a kind of erotic jolt—at least that's how he would describe it in his notebook. When he could no longer distinguish the shape of the trees, he flipped on the lamp and wrote it all down, everything that had happened, what he felt inside.

He shouldn't have chanced putting it in writing, but he couldn't help it. Feelings had always been strange, inscrutable markings in his heart, like the ones he'd seen on the Rosetta stone once. He'd stared at the stone for a very long time while at least a hundred, maybe a thousand other museum tourists had come and gone. He'd felt he was looking at something deeply personal, and from then on he'd been trying to decipher the emotional scribbles inside himself by writing them down. Oddly, they became accessible that way, transposed into something deeply felt.

Like now. He could feel her hands on his back. See her body stretched across the ground, the goose flesh on her breasts. He could feel himself vanishing inside her again.

He put down his pen and stood up, needing to move. He paced from one side of his bed to the other, glancing at the crucifix nailed over the head. The bed was a simple mattress on a metal frame and took up most of the room. He wished he could lie down on the scratchy brown blanket and go instantly to sleep. He dreaded the long night to come.

He'd made love to a woman.

He didn't know how to go about his life in the abbey after that.

He lowered the venetian blinds on the casement windows and sat again at his desk. He tried to be practical, to dissect the situation. He wrote down logical-sounding premises for what had happened. That being with Jessie was a way to fill the loss of Linda. Or, now that he was on the brink of taking final vows, he was looking for a way out. Maybe his libido had been forced into such rigid denial that it had suddenly flipped to the other extreme. It even occurred to him that poets and monks had been using sexual imagery to write about their union with God for centuries. Could he have been looking for some consummation with God?

He read back over all the possible reasons he'd come up with, and they sounded ridiculous to him. They made him think of St. Thomas Aquinas and his *Summa Theologica,* which his novice master thought was sublime, and yet on his deathbed Aquinas himself had said that all of it was nothing but straw compared with the things he'd experienced, the things in his heart.

That's how Whit felt. As if his reasoning was a lot of straw. A lot of bullshit.

He'd done this unbelievable thing because he loved her, he wanted her—that's what he knew. He knew that life had erupted in him again, felt how much of a crater his heart had been before meeting her.

He closed the notebook and picked up his worn volume of Yeats, and it fell open to that passage he read and reread:

. . . Now that my ladder's gone,
I must lie down where all the ladders start,
In the foul rag-and-bone shop of the heart.

He got up and washed his face and hands in the sink. There were small cuts across his knuckles. He cleaned them with soap, then took off his shirt and held it to his nose and sniffed. He could smell her, could smell what they'd done. Instead of dropping it into the small laundry hamper, he hung it on the peg beside his extra shirts and robes.

Compline was over, and the Great Silence

had begun. The monks would be sealed in their rooms now. He'd heard Dominic come in half an hour earlier, heard the typewriter start up.

Whit slid a T-shirt over his head and put on his coat. He opened the door and closed it quietly behind him. He did not take a flashlight, only his rosary. It rattled in his pocket as he walked. The gilt edge of a new moon hung in the sky, and he knew there would be a spring tide in a few hours. It would spill out of the needlegrass like a broth overflowing its bowl. Out on the hummock where he'd made love to Jessie, the water would flood within twenty feet of his hermitage.

On the nights Whit couldn't sleep, he walked the stations of the cross. It took his mind off things; it calmed him. And he liked that the stations were not in the church, that they were simple cement plaques arranged like flagstones on the ground. He loved the serpentine path they made through the oaks behind the cottages. And the animals he sometimes glimpsed when he was walking, the sudden red glow of their eyes. He had seen striped skunks, red foxes, owls, and once a bobcat.

At the first station, he took out his rosary,

touched it to his forehead, and knelt beside the crude etching of Jesus standing before Pontius Pilate. JESUS IS CONDEMNED TO DIE. The abbot had said they must enter into the scenes when they walked the stations, become part of them, but he could barely keep his mind focused.

He closed his eyes and tried to remember the prayer he was supposed to say at the first station. He didn't know how he could *not* see her again. Right now he wanted to run the distance to her mother's house and knock on her window as if he were seventeen. He wanted to slide into her bed and wedge his knees behind her knees, twine his fingers with her fingers, mold his body against hers, and tell her what he felt.

He looked at the stone on the ground. He wanted to know if Jesus had struggled like this, had loved a woman this way. He wanted to think so.

At the second station—JESUS CARRIES HIS CROSS—Whit knelt again, more determined this time. He said the appointed prayer and contemplated the scene, shaking his head violently when the pictures of her came.

He was bent over the sixth station— VERONICA WIPES THE FACE OF JESUS—when he caught the beam of a penlight darting through the darkness, and a figure moving toward him. He rose to his feet. The figure was robed, he could tell that much, but with the deep shadows on the face, Whit didn't know that it was Father Sebastian until the father was practically standing in front of him.

The light cut across Whit's face. "So here you are," Sebastian said. "I just came from your cottage. I've been looking for you. You weren't at vespers, you weren't at dinner, and—mystery of mysteries—you weren't at compline. Now. Solve this great dilemma for me and explain where you were."

The tone in his voice made Whit uneasy, wary; it was almost as if he were being baited. As if Sebastian already knew. But how could he?

Whit looked up at the sprinkling of stars over his head, then at Sebastian, who had folded his arms over his scapular and was staring at Whit through the bottom of his massive glasses.

Sebastian had come from his cottage. Had he gone inside? Looked in Whit's notebook?

"So? I'm waiting," the older monk said. "Were you ill? If you were, you appear to have made a nice recovery."

"I wasn't ill, Father."

"What then?"

"I was in the rookery."

"You were in the rookery. Well, isn't that nice? Were you having fun out there while the rest of us were in choir doing our duty?"

"I'm sorry I missed choir."

"Look, Brother Thomas, I'm the prior. Responsible for the discipline of this monastery. I'm the one who's to make sure there's no wrong behavior. I'll not tolerate it, you understand?"

If he doesn't know, he surely suspects something.

Whit didn't respond. He stood still through a long silence, refusing to avoid Sebastian's eyes. He would not feel tawdry about this. It wasn't that he didn't feel blameworthy; he did. The moment he'd returned from the rookery, from loving her, the guilt had crashed down on him, incisive and powerful, the need to be forgiven stunning him with its severity, and yet some part of him felt impenitent, belonging only to her—an impervious piece of him that the abbey, even God, did not own and could not touch.

He looked away from Sebastian at the final eight stations dispersed through the

oaks, glowing faintly on the ground, and beyond them the enclosing wilderness of
marsh. He thought what a consolation this
place had been; his confinement had been a
freedom. A home. A dark and graceful
poverty. What would he do if the place he
most wanted to be was no longer the abbey
but a woman's heart?

"I don't know if I belong here," Whit said,
and his voice cracked on the last word.
Here.

Sebastian watched Whit wipe at the thin
film of tears that formed over his eyes, waiting as he cleared his throat and grasped for
composure. When the older monk spoke
again, his expression had changed, his face
disarmed. The ugliness was drained from his
voice. "I see." He shifted his feet, reached
beneath his glasses to rub his eyelids.

As his glasses settled again on his nose,
he said, "I want you to walk the rest of the
stations. If you like, you can do it on your
knees as a penance. But do it mainly as a
way of reflecting on your call. Ask yourself
why you came here, what it means to you to
be hidden here with God. Every one of us
has wondered if we belong here, Brother

Thomas. We've all had to give up something or someone." He looked at the ground. "You must carry your cross, you know. We all must."

Whit nodded at him. He wanted to say, *But I don't know what my cross is. Is it doing without her now that I've loved her? Or is it doing without the abbey? Or is it the peculiar agony of being spiritual and human at the same time?*

"When you've finished the stations, go to bed and get your rest," said Sebastian. "You wouldn't want to miss lauds in the morning. The word means 'return of the light.' May that be so for you."

"Yes, Father," he said.

He waited for Sebastian to leave, wondering if he would go to the abbot or keep all of this to himself. Sinking to his knees, he walked on them to the next station—JESUS FALLS THE SECOND TIME.

Whit repeated fragments of the laudate Psalms: " 'The Lord is gracious and merciful, slow to anger and abounding in steadfast love. . . . The Lord preserves all who love him. Praise the Lord, O my soul!' "

Then pieces of the Song of Zechariah:

" 'The day shall dawn upon us from on high to give light to those who sit in darkness. . . .' "

Whit wanted the light to come, the light Sebastian spoke of, but he wanted more to lie down in his own heart and hold the dark.

CHAPTER
Twenty-five

The morning after I made love to Whit O'Conner, I came into the kitchen and found Mother with the hibiscus scarf draped around the collar of her bathrobe, cooking Gullah rice perlo. Four giant aluminum stockpots of it. Enough for a monastery.

She lifted the lid on the largest pot, and tiers of white smoke wafted out, smelling like shrimp and andouille sausage.

"What are you *doing?*" I asked. "It's seven o'clock in the morning." I wanted coffee. I wanted to sit in the kitchen all by myself and sip it slowly.

"I'm cooking for the monks. We'll need to

get the perlo over there by eleven, before Brother Timothy starts fixing lunch. I'll need to warm it up. Set out some bread and make sweet tea."

Recipe books were spread across the kitchen table, mingled with onion skins, shrimp tails, and spatterings of Carolina Gold rice kernels. If she hadn't looked so *herself* standing there with an Our Lady of the Miraculous medal pinned to the scarf, waving a wooden spoon in the air as she talked, I might have protested at how crazy it was to cook the dish here and then have to haul it over there.

"How are we getting all this over to the abbey?" I asked.

"We'll drive it through the main gate in the golf cart." She seemed exasperated at having to point out the obvious to me.

I took my coffee mug to the front porch and sat in one of the wicker chairs with a quilt drawn around my shoulders. The clouds were light and spongy, floating high and soaked in a bronzy shade of gold. I slid my spine low in the chair so I could stare at them.

I'd slept without dreaming, waking once in an icy sweat, permeated by the same terror-struck feeling that had seized me momentarily as I lay beside Whit in the aftermath of what we'd done.

These paroxysms were, I realized later, a kind of aftershock. They would come and go for weeks, moments of violent disorientation in which I couldn't recognize myself, completely breaking apart how I understood my life, all the joints and couplings that held it together. It was the peculiar vertigo, the peculiar humility, that comes from realizing what you are really capable of. Those aftershocks would gradually taper off, but in the beginning they could almost paralyze me.

Last night the feeling had taken much longer to pass than it had on the island with Whit. Sitting on the side of the bed, trying to steady myself, I'd noticed the painting I'd done propped against the wall by the door, the underwater sheen on the woman's face glowing slightly, making her look half alive. The sight unnerved me, and I got up and stood in front of the dresser. The pincushion was there, my wedding rings pinned to it like insects, like specimens of a valuable but discarded life.

Gazing into the mirror, I saw myself as I was—a black silhouette in the room, a woman whose darkness had completely leaked through.

What if I lose Hugh and Whit both? What if I give up Hugh, only to have Whit turn away? I'll be alone, abandoned.

That was the deep, silent terror, wasn't it? The hole that would always need filling; standing there, I recognized how timeworn and venerable it was, stretching beyond Hugh, beyond Whit, going all the way back to my father.

This morning, though, there was none of that reverberating fear from the night before. I watched the clouds from the porch and thought of Whit, the bliss of our lovemaking, this new, other life waiting for me. I had the sense of being out on the furthest frontier of myself. It was, despite those intermittent convulsions, a surprisingly beautiful outpost.

I'd done something unthinkable, and yet I didn't regret it. I felt pulled unaccountably, almost forcibly to Whit, and yes, there was transgression and betrayal and wrongness in it, but also mystery and what felt like holiness, an actual holiness.

Driving to the abbey, we spotted Hepzibah in front of the Star of the Sea Chapel. She was holding her Gullah drum, standing on the porch of the little clapboard church talking to about a dozen people.

We'd come upon her Grand Gullah Tour.

I pulled up behind the group and stopped, wanting to hear a little bit of what she was saying, wondering if she actually beat the drum for them the way she used to do for us at the All-Girls Picnic. She was telling them the chapel was built on the ruins of a church for freed slaves.

She walked back and forth while she talked, tapping the drum softly with her fingers. I stared at her elaborate head wrap and caftan made from toffee-colored fabric covered with small zebras. She wore her famous hoop earrings. Kat had said once they were big enough for a cat to jump through, but I liked them on her.

"There's an old Gullah practice," she was saying. "Before our people can become church members, they go to a sacred place in the woods three times a day for a week and meditate on the state of their souls. We call it 'traveling,' because we're traveling inside."

She hit her drum with the flat of her hand and motioned the group into the chapel to look around.

When they were inside, she walked over and hugged Nelle first, then me.

As Mother got out to check the cord we'd used to anchor the pots on the backseat, Hepzibah leaned close to me.

"How are *you,* Jessie?" It was not simply a polite question; her eyes searched mine. I knew she wondered if I'd been with Whit in the rookery, if I'd found the turtle skull she'd left under the canoe.

"I'm fine, everything's fine," I said. "I wish I could hear the rest of the tour, but we're taking lunch to the monastery."

"Did you go for that canoe ride?" she asked.

I felt heat rise on the skin of my cheeks. "Yesterday," I said. "Thank you for the turtle skull," I added, thinking how I'd left it in Whit's hermitage as a talisman, hoping it would bring me back.

Mother was climbing into the cart.

"Hold on tight to it," Hepzibah whispered.

The monastery kitchen was a bright old room with long, beveled-pane windows and oak cabinets with small Celtic crosses burned into the bottom corners. It had not changed much since I was a child, playing sous-chef to

Mother. We'd stood at the worktable in the center of the room while she'd held out her hand and called out, "Potato masher. . . . Pastry cutter. . . . Apple corer. . . ." I'd snapped each item into her palm as if she were the surgeon and I the nurse. Our "cooking operation," as she called it, was serious business. We were feeding the holy.

The sight of the worktable filled my chest with a dull ache. I paused a moment, holding the perlo, staring at the scarred surface. The same dented copper pots dangled over it from the ceiling, catching light from the window. Was this where Mother had done it, where she'd stretched out her finger and brought down the meat cleaver, severing it right through the bone? Here, on our old operating table?

I set the pot on the stove and walked to the large stainless-steel sink, where I ran cold water over my hands. I was dabbing the back of my neck when Brother Timothy appeared, just in time to haul in the last stockpot. He seemed excessively excited by Mother's sudden, unexpected return, chattering to her about egg deliveries and the lack of decent tomatoes. He followed her around the kitchen as she opened and closed drawers,

rummaged inside the industrial-size refrigerator, and sniffed several clusters of oregano
drying on a counter. He walked with a shuffle, his body pitched forward like someone
barreling into a windstorm.

Mother took a clean but heavily stained
apron from a peg near the pantry door and
tied it around her. She flicked on the gas
burners and bent to peer at the blue fire that
licked the bottoms of the pots.

"I was told you two were in here," a voice
said behind us. "The entire abbey is in a jubi-
lant uproar over whatever it is you've got in
those pots." Father Dominic stood just inside
the doorway, looking flushed and a little anxious. He'd come so quickly he'd forgotten his
straw hat. An array of long white hairs were
spread carefully over his balding scalp.

I could not remember seeing my mother
and Dominic in a room together since the
day he'd come to our house bearing the remains of my father's drowned boat. Now I
watched them carefully, the way Mother took
an automatic step backward when she saw
him, her hand coming up to touch the side of
her neck.

Dominic looked at Brother Timothy. "Could

you go and fill the water pitchers in the refectory? And check the salt shakers."

Outranked, Timothy shrugged and crossed the kitchen, the scuff of his shoes sounding loud and sullen. When he was gone, Dominic lifted his hand to the top of his head, where he patted the web of hairs, assuring himself everything was still plastered in place. He scarcely looked at me, all his attention on Mother. I watched his eyes drift to her injured hand and take in the flesh-colored Ace bandage that had replaced the bulky gauze.

"I'm glad you feel well enough to cook for us again, Nelle. We've missed you."

It came back to me, how he'd said "our Nelle" the last time we'd talked, as if he possessed some part of her.

Mother wiped her hands back and forth on the front of her apron. "I'm glad to be back," she said, her words frosted, clipped off on the ends—that tone she got when she was repelled. I knew it well. She whirled around then and began savagely stirring the rice.

Dominic folded and unfolded his hands several times. His knuckles were enormous

and splotched with redness. Arthritis, I imagined. He offered me a strained smile. "Knock,
knock," he said.

I stood a moment wondering how to respond to this silly, relentless game of his.
The rice started to sputter over the heat. "I
don't think I want to play," I told him, borrow-
ing a little of Mother's tone.

It would've been absurd to go along, but I
also felt I was being loyal to her; clearly she
wanted no part of him. And yet she turned
around, embarrassed, I suppose, by my
rudeness, my refusal to humor him. "Who's
there?" she said, and cut her eyes at me.

After all her showy repugnance, it was the
last thing I expected. Now I felt she'd been
disloyal to me.

Dominic hesitated before going on, but I
realized later it was only because he was
discarding the joke he'd had in mind for me
and coming up with a fresh new one meant
only for her. Something daring and strangely
intimate.

"Orange," he said.

She pressed her lips tightly together and
lifted her chin a little. "Orange who?"

He walked within an arm's length of her,
positioning himself so I could not see his

face. He dropped his voice, hoping I would not hear him, but I *did* hear, barely: "Orange you ever going to forgive us?"

Mother's face was taut, giving nothing away. "And *orange* you ever going to leave so I can cook in peace?" she responded. She hustled into the pantry and returned with a bag of cornmeal. "Now, if you don't mind, I'm going to make hoecakes."

"Hoecakes!" Dominic exclaimed. "Saints preserve us! We don't deserve you." He sauntered toward the door but after a few paces paused and looked back at me. "Oh, Jessie, I almost forgot. There's someone in the library who would like a word with you."

I crossed the cloister quadrangle, forcing my limbs to move with unassuming casualness—the stroll of someone wandering over to the library to browse around, that was all.

I paused inside the door before a small statue of St. Benedict holding his rule and made myself read the wall plaque beside it the way I imagined a devout visitor would do. LISTEN, MY SON, TO YOUR MASTER'S PRECEPTS, AND INCLINE THE EAR OF YOUR HEART. My own heart was buffeting around in my chest, hammering wildly. Pellets of light from a window over the door bounced around on the pinewood floor. I took a long breath, trying to find my equilibrium.

I began to wander up and down the tunnels of books, pausing once in a while to crook my head sideways and read the titles: *On Contemplating God* by William of St. Thierry; Lucretius's *Nature of the Universe; The Collected Works of St. John of the Cross.* I listened for footsteps. Where was he?

By the time I arrived at the reading area in the back of the library, the charged feeling inside had only intensified. I sat down at one of three tables that faced an expansive window. The tabletop had been polished with such enterprise that I could see myself reflected in the buffed wood. My hair was a mess. I smoothed it down with my hands, then changed my mind and tried to fluff it up.

I gazed through the window, and the scene outside formed in my mind like a canvas—splotches of fuchsia azaleas tucked against the whitewashed house where the monks made nets. A Japanese maple, blue-tinged grass, a tiny knoll creased with shadow.

A door creaked behind me, and I turned to see Whit standing in the entrance of a small office that was situated just off the reading room. Father Dominic's office, it turned out.

He was wearing his robe and his rookery boots. My eyes went to the place on his neck I had kissed.

When I stepped into the office, he closed the door behind us, clicking the lock, and we stood for a moment in the cramped space with the smell of paraffin drifting from a candle on a wall sconce behind him. A fluorescent light hummed nosily over our heads. I noticed that the blinds were closed against the only window, and the artificial glare felt glowering and oppressive. Impulsively I reached over and flicked the switch, watching his face as the room plunged into a soft dimness.

A feeling of profound belonging, of intimacy, washed over me. I pictured him on the marsh island pressed against me, loving me, the breathing world around us again, the inviolate bond we'd made. I went and laid my face against his shoulder and felt his arms, the voluminous sleeves of his robe, come up slowly to enfold me.

"Jessie," he said after a moment. "The library is usually empty now, but we need to be careful." He glanced at the door, and I realized the enormous risk he was taking. "I only have fifteen minutes before choir, but I had to see you."

I lifted my head from his shoulder and looked up at him. Even in the half-light, I saw the tiny smudges of shadow beneath his eyes, and his posture seemed oddly stiff, as if his lungs had expanded and gotten stuck.

I was, I realized, terrified of what was going on inside him, his monkness, the power of what had brought him to the abbey. If we were going to be together—and I wanted this now with something close to desperation—he would have to want it, too, in that same way he'd wanted God, and I didn't know if I could compete with that. I didn't want to be one of those mythological sirens who lured sailors onto the rocks or, more to the point, like the mermaid Asenora who lured monks to their fall. I wanted to touch his face, to find the opening to his robe, but I made myself take a tiny step backward.

"Could you meet me tomorrow at two, at the dock in the rookery?" he was saying.

"Of course. I'll be there," I told him.

Silence again. He had left his hand resting loosely on my waist as we'd talked, but he withdrew it, and I watched him brush his finger across the front of his robe, at what I realized was one of my own long brown hairs.

"It's wonderful having your mother cooking for us again," he said. "I suppose that's a sign that she's mending."

So we were going to make common talk. We were going to stand in this little room—no longer suffused in wan, romantic hues but only in ordinary dimness—and use innocuous conversation as a defense.

"Her hand is nearly mended," I said, "but I worry that her mind may never be."

He glanced at a digital clock on the desk, sitting beside a little stack of Dominic's booklet, *The Mermaid's Tale.* There was a painfully conspicuous pause in which he cleared his throat. What *was* this heaviness in him? Caution? It could not be easy for him. Or was his demeanor, this tepidness, a reversal of some sort? Had he been so decimated by guilt that he was trying to return things to the way they were before? Was he simply scared?

"After Nelle did what she did," he said, "many of us couldn't help but think of the Scripture where Jesus talks about cutting off one's hand."

His words startled me. "There's a verse in Scripture about that?"

He scanned a wall shelf, retrieved a Bible, and began flipping the pages. "Here it is. It's part of Christ's Sermon on the Mount: 'If thy right hand offend thee, cut it off, and cast it from thee; for it is profitable for thee that one of thy members should perish, and not that thy whole body should be cast into hell.' "

I took the book out of his hands and read the words silently to myself, then snapped it shut. "That's it, isn't it? That's where she got the idea. Better to cut off her finger than have her whole body cast into hell." I shoved the Bible back onto the shelf. It was illogical, but I felt mildly indignant.

"Jesus was speaking symbolically. Obviously he didn't mean for anyone to take his words literally," Whit said.

"Well, don't you think he could've allowed for the possibility that a few crazy people might misinterpret his point? I mean, really, it's not the most responsible thing someone could say."

His lips twisted as if trying to hold back laughter, and his whole body seemed to release its grip and breathe again. Finally the laugh slipped out of him.

"What?" I said, starting to smile.

"I've heard Jesus referred to as a lot of things, but that's the first time I've ever heard anyone suggest he was irresponsible."

He reached over and touched my hair, let his knuckles brush the curve of my cheek. His eyes were lit up, but not only with amusement; they glistened in the way I remembered from our lovemaking. As I leaned up to kiss him a spark of static electricity leaped between us, and both of us jumped backward, laughing.

"See what happens when you call Jesus irresponsible?" I joked. "You get shocked."

"Seriously," he said, "there are some bizarre accounts of saints mutilating themselves. They seem to get the inspiration for it from this verse."

"I've been saying all along Mother was doing some kind of penance, even though Hugh thinks I'm wrong."

"Hugh?" he said.

And the room went still.

I'd said his name automatically, stupidly. Why had I brought him into it? I'd assumed then it was a thoughtless moment, but I wondered about that in the days that followed. Had I *wanted* to say Hugh's name? To throw the worst at Whit and see what he'd do? Was I lining up the hurdles, the secret realities that lay between us? He had brought up Jesus; I had brought up Hugh.

"Oh," I said. "Hugh is . . . he's my husband. He's a psychiatrist."

Whit looked away, back toward the day-blind window. He reached over and flipped the light back on, and we were plunged into a stinging brightness.

Desperate to smooth over the moment, to usher us around Hugh's name, I kept on talking. "It's just that he . . . well, he thinks Mother's impulse to cut off her finger was a meaningless, random obsession."

He tried to smile, looking at me as if to say, *All right, then, we'll go on as if nothing happened.* He said, "But *you* think it was penance for something particular?"

"Yes. I just don't know what for." The casualness I was forcing into my voice sounded desperate. "I believe it goes back a long time. Actually, I suspect that Father Dominic knows what it is."

"Dominic?" he said sharply, then, glancing at the door, lowered his voice. "What makes you think that?"

"First tell me what you think of him."

"He's very genuine. A natural jokester, but he has a serious side, too. He tends to follow his own version of things, but I like that about him. Now. What makes you think he knows anything about this?"

"Mother implied as much," I said. "And a while ago in the kitchen, I heard Dominic ask her if she was ever going to forgive them. 'Us,' he said. 'Aren't you ever going to forgive *us?*'"

Whit shook his head, plainly bewildered. "Forgiveness? For what?"

I shrugged. "I wish I knew. I tried to talk to Dominic about it earlier, but he was very secretive. And Mother . . . well, she's not going to tell me anything."

He looked again at the clock. "I'm sorry, but I should've left five minutes ago."

"Yes, go. I'll wait here a few minutes and then leave."

When he'd gone, I stood in the middle of Dominic's office, in all that brittle light, and my mind went back to the moment when Whit had opened the Bible and read the verse to me out loud, the harsh words about severing one's hand in order to save the whole body. Had that reading been entirely about my mother? Or had he been thinking about the way he'd caressed my breast, my hip, tugged me against him? Was he, in his way, telling me something? About us?

CHAPTER
Twenty-six

A brown pelican perched on the bow of the monastery's johnboat like a hood ornament, the S of its neck slumped onto its white breast. As I approached the rookery dock, the bird unfurled its wings—the span of them outlandish—and held them wide open, air-drying its feathers. Whit stood on the dock staring at the spectacle. He did not see me until I called his name, and as he turned, the pelican flapped her wings and took to the air.

I didn't know what to expect, whether we would get in the boat and go back to his hermitage, or remain on the dock. Whether he would pull me into his arms or sever me from his life. I'd sat up in bed the night before, jerked awake by a nightmare of amputated hands and fingers. There were piles of them in the rose garden at the monastery heaped around St. Senara's feet, all of them still wiggling, still alive.

"Can you believe how beautiful the day is?" he said in a carefree way.

Do not talk about the weather. If you talk about the weather, I'll start screaming.

"Yes, beautiful," I said. It was actually the most splendid day you could imagine. Brilliant, warm, that feeling of spring taking hold around us.

I'd worn my jeans with a long-sleeved white shirt, and I was already hot and perspiring. Strands of hair were spit-plastered, as Dee would say, to my neck. I reached into the side pocket of my purse, pulled out the garnet baseball cap, and yanked it low over my forehead, then dug out my sunglasses.

"How about a ride?" he asked, and when I nodded, he began untying the dock line. Climbing into the boat, I noticed he'd already tucked his canvas bag under the seat.

"Where's Max?" I asked.

He looked back at the walkway and shrugged. "I guess he's abandoned me today."

"Maybe he's miffed that I horned in last time."

"As I recall, it was *you* he was cuddling up to after—" He stopped abruptly, unable or unwilling to say the words, letting the sentence hang in the air.

He guided the boat slowly through the creek while I sat in the bow seat, gazing straight ahead, aware of the thin scum of guilt and hesitancy that had formed—and knowing that the mention of Hugh's name the day before had helped create it.

It had been two weeks since Hugh had walked away from me at the slave cemetery, and he hadn't called once during that time. He was bound to be hurt, and of course, angry. But I had a feeling he was also waiting me out. Hugh was the most patient person, always the champion of letting things settle, run their course, come slowly to a head—all pet phrases of his. I'm sure it was the psychiatrist in him, presiding as he did over the age-old mysteries of the human psyche. He'd told Dee a story once about a girl who'd found a cocoon and snipped off the end of it to let the butterfly out, how the poor creature had emerged with deformed wings. "You can't force things," he'd said to her.

I'd told Hugh I wanted time apart, and by God, he was giving it to me.

"We're separated, you know," I said, turning to Whit. "Hugh and I. We're taking time apart."

He looked down into the flat bottom of the boat, then back at me, his face very grave, but I think grateful as well. He slowed the boat to idle speed, and everything grew much quieter.

"How long have you been married?" he asked.

"Twenty years."

He was fingering his cross, unaware he was doing it. "Happily?"

"Yes, happily at first. But then—oh, I don't know. It's not that we were unhappy. People looking at us would've said it was a good marriage—'Hugh and Jessie, they're so compatible.' It wouldn't be untrue."

I pulled off my sunglasses, wanting him to see my face, my eyes, wanting nothing between us. I listened a moment to the water gently slapping the boat. When he didn't comment, I went on. "You know how couples always say, 'We just grew apart'? That's what I wanted to say at first. To believe that my discontent came from the distance between us. It's logical to think that after twenty years. But I don't believe that was it. We didn't grow apart, we grew too much together. Too enmeshed and dependent on each other. I guess I needed—" I stopped. I didn't know what to call it. "What comes to my mind are ridiculous things like 'my own space,' 'my independence,' but they sound so shallow. They don't capture it."

"I know, it's hard to explain an impulse like that. The day I told my law partners I was coming here, they laughed like I was joking." He shook his head and smiled a little, as if the memory amused him. "I never could make them understand that what I needed was somehow to be alone with myself. In a spiritual way, I mean."

As he'd talked, his gaze had been on the twists and turns in the creek, but now he leveled it on me. "Around here they call it 'a solitude of being.' "

My eyes slowly began to fill up. Because I *did* understand what he meant, because he was offering these words to me—*a solitude of being*—and they were perfect.

Sliding my sunglasses onto my face, I turned back to face the creek, the bulging in-rush of tide.

Ten minutes later Whit angled the boat off the creek into the tributary that led to the marsh island where we'd made love. I recognized it right away and looked over at him. He smiled in that way I'd come to love, the corners of his lips barely lifting. It seemed to me then that something had changed in him, something had broken. I felt it in the air around our heads.

When the tributary opened upon the pool of water hedged perfectly by the marsh grass, Whit steered the boat into the very center of it and cut off the engine. The sound died around us as he dropped the anchor line.

"Let's go swimming," he said, and began unbuttoning his shirt. I sat speechless as he stood in the boat and stripped completely naked, the most disarming boyishness taking over his face. Then he jumped cannon-ball style over the side, rocking the boat so hard I grabbed on to the gunnels.

He came up, laughing, shaking his head, the droplets flying off his hair like fracturing glass. "Why are you still sitting there?" he cried, and broke into an accomplished crawl.

I peeled off every stitch I had on and jumped.

The creek was absolutely freezing. Like smacking into a glacier. For a moment all I could do was tread water, my body shocked wide open. There had been a December a few years earlier when Hugh had looked up from the television set and proposed that we go to Lake Lanier on New Year's Day and take part in a Polar Bear Plunge. It involved otherwise-normal people throwing themselves into a body of shivering water. I'd looked at him with complete incredulity, unwilling even to consider it. And now here I was in this bright, cold water.

I finally began swimming, not Whit's controlled, athletic movement but playfully diving, just splashing around. The water was turgid, like milk coffee, and deeper than I'd thought, fifteen or twenty feet perhaps. It was exhilarating, as if my body were emphatically awake and singing after a long silence.

I caught sight of Whit in the boat, with a ragged white towel around his waist. I hadn't realized he'd climbed back in. I dog-paddled over to him, and he pulled me up and draped me in a towel that was only slightly less frayed than his own. "Is monastery linen always so austere?" I joked.

"It's part of our overall Body Negation Program," he said.

He maneuvered the boat to the edge of the island, and we made our way to the hermitage still wearing our towels, clutching our clothes. He spread a brown blanket in the sun, next to the little hut. Peering inside it, I saw Hepzibah's turtle skull sitting on the crab trap, exactly as I'd left it.

As we stretched out on the blanket, side by side, the sky rose over us, marbled with remnants of clouds. I felt woozy for a moment, that sensation you get as a child when you turn in circles and fall over in sweet dizziness. I lay there with wet hair, with mud caked on my feet, and said to him, "All I want is for us to be honest with each other, brutally honest."

He said, "Brutally?"

I smiled. "Yes, *brutally*."

"All right," he said, his tone still teasing. "But I'm generally against brutality in any form."

I fixed my eyes on a fleck of glinting cloud.

"I've fallen in love with you," I said. "I wouldn't be out here otherwise."

His hands had been tucked behind his head in the most casual way, and he moved them slowly to his sides. He said, "I know we should be honest about what's going on, but—I felt like it would open a door we couldn't close."

"Why would we have to close it?"

He sat up, staring ahead with the curve of his back to me. "But, Jessie, what if you walk away from your marriage because of me and then—" He stopped.

"And then *you* can't walk away from the abbey? Is that what you're saying?"

"That's not what I'm saying." He pushed a breath through his mouth. "Okay, you want to know how I feel?" He sounded provoked, as if he'd been forced out onto a little ledge and seen how far he would have to jump.

My throat burned, down in the notch where my collarbones came together.

"I love you, too," he said. "And it scares me to death."

The air around us stilled. I could only look at him. His body was shingled with bits of shadow coming from the hermitage behind us.

"But we both know it isn't that simple," he said. "What I meant before was, what if you left your marriage and then later you regretted it? I know you said you're separated from Hugh, but how are you going to live with ending your marriage completely? My God, Jessie, how am *I* going to live with it?" He sighed, and his breath fell across my face.

I pulled him back down beside me. We lay there and listened to the small, searching sounds of the world. "If we do this, there will be suffering," he said. "We'll be damned and saved *both*."

"I know," I told him. *"I know."*

He rose up on one elbow and drew me hard against him. I knew he was giving himself over. To me, to us, to whatever would happen. He clutched me, holding the back of my head with his hand. His fingers pressed into my scalp, and his heart pounded, filling my body.

We made love in the sun, and afterward, lying on the blanket, I began to cry. A shuddering cry that alarmed Whit at first, but I kept smiling at him with my wet face, saying, "No, no, it's all right, it's because I feel so happy." I hadn't said, *so complete,* though I'd wanted to.

We got dressed, and he arranged the blanket beneath the hermitage roof, out of the sun. As we settled on top of it, he handed me an old-fashioned metal thermos filled with water, then rummaged deeper in his canvas bag.

"There's something I want to show you," he said, pulling out two books: *Legenda Aurea: Readings on the Saints* by Jacobus de Voragine; the other title I couldn't see.

"I looked up some of the saints—the ones who took Jesus too seriously when it came to cutting off the 'offending member.'"

It pleased me that he wanted to be involved, to help me with Mother. It was only later that I remembered how thoroughly I'd been against Hugh's involvement, and I couldn't account for the difference.

"I found a St. Eudoria in the twelfth century who cut off her finger," he said. "She was a prostitute until she was converted by a Franciscan friar."

"A prostitute?"

"Yeah, but that's not the interesting part," he said, though to be honest, I wasn't so sure.

"Supposedly after she cut off her finger, she planted it in a field, and it sprouted into a sheaf of wheat. Nelle could've been *planting* her finger, not burying it."

The thought jolted me a little.

"You think Mother was copying her?"

"In Ireland there used to be something called 'white martyrdom,' " Whit said. "Our abbot is always preaching sermons about it—I'm sure Nelle must've heard some of them. It means following in the footsteps of one of the saints, imitating what he or she did."

"That sounds like Mother—cutting off her finger and planting it because some saint did it six hundred years ago."

Legenda Aurea had a worn, outdated jacket with a hideous picture of Jesus wearing what looked like a British crown. He lifted a scepter over a throng of kneeling, haloed men.

"When I first started looking for this book," Whit said, "I couldn't find it on the shelf, so I went and asked Dominic. He opened his desk drawer, and it was in there along with this book." He held it out to me: *Indigenous Religious Traditions.*

"Dominic told me Brother Timothy had found both books in the kitchen right after Nelle cut off her finger. Apparently she'd taken them out of the library. She marked a page in each of them—the one on St. Eudoria and then this." He flipped open the second book to a dog-eared page and laid it across my lap.

I stared at an illustration of a mermaid whose fingers were depicted as dolphins, seals, fish, whales.

"What *is* this?"

"Her name's Sedna. She's an Inuit sea goddess. *All* of her fingers were severed. All ten."

I read the text under the picture, a magical if slightly horrifying story. A young woman sends word to her father to come rescue her from a cruel husband. They are fleeing in his boat when her husband pursues them. Fearing for his life, the father throws his daughter overboard, but she grabs on to the side of the boat and refuses to let go. Panicked, her father cuts off each of her fingers. One by one.

I read the last couple of sentences out loud. " 'Sinking into the ocean, Sedna became a powerful female deity with the head and torso of a woman and the tail of a fish or a seal. She came to be known as "Mother of the Ocean," her severed fingers becoming the sea creatures that filled the waters.' "

There was a sidebar accompanying the story, about the number ten, I supposed because she'd lost ten fingers. I skimmed it. "'Ten was considered the holiest number. Pythagoreans deemed it the number of regeneration and fulfillment. Everything sprang from ten.'"

I stared at Sedna's image, her hair in long braids, her strong Inuit face. "She's not exactly a Catholic saint."

"But she could've reminded Nelle of St. Senara," Whit said. "Before she was converted, when she was still Asenora, the mermaid."

I shuddered, and he slid over and drew me against him. We sat in silence for a while. I couldn't talk about it anymore, this martyring side of my mother.

A breeze had come up and was flapping the sides of the blanket. I noticed that the light had dissolved a little.

Whit said, "I hate to say this, but I need to go."

He tucked the books back into his bag, screwed the top onto the thermos, folded the blanket that I was sure had come off his bed. He did this without speaking, and I watched his hands, how they scissored through the air, the skin tanned like parchment, the fingers long and roughened with small calluses.

I put my hand on his arm. "Will it be hard going to choir now and praying after . . . after this?"

"Yes," he said, not looking at me.

When we got to the water's edge, I saw that it was slack tide, those few suspended moments between ebb and flow. My father had called it "the turn'bout." He'd beckoned me and Mike out of the yard one day and marched us down to Caw Caw Creek so we could see it. We'd stared at the rising tidewater, utterly bored, Mike throwing mud snails across the surface, making them skip. When the current finally reached the end of its striving, the whole creek grew perfectly still—not one floating blade of spartina grass moved, and then, minutes later, as if some maestro had gestured, all the water began to roll in the opposite direction, moving back out.

Whit steered the boat into the tributary that crooked left into the creek. Overhead, gulls wheeled through the sky, and behind us the small marsh island tilted away. I could feel him slipping again into his monk's life, the ocean turning around us. The ruthless ebb and flow.

CHAPTER
Twenty-seven

Whit

Whit stood outside the abbot's office on the first day of spring, clutching a note that had been placed in his hands by Brother Bede, the abbot's diminutive secretary. He'd passed it to Whit just before the office of terce, whispering, "The abbot wishes to see you immediately after choir."

Whit had folded it up with a hot, tremulous feeling in his stomach. After prayers were over, he'd followed Bede through the transept of the church to Dom Anthony's office. Though he'd tried to read Bede's face when they reached the door, scanning the impossibly small forehead and the pea-size green eyes, he could see nothing telling in them.

"The abbot will call for you in a moment," Bede told him, and ambled away, the hem of his robe dragging on the hall carpet.

Now he waited, the kind of waiting that is crusted over with false calm but underneath tosses around violently.

He heard a sharp, serrated buzzing and walked to the window in the corridor. One of the monks was taking down a dead crepe myrtle with a chain saw. Had he been summoned because of Jessie? Because Father Sebastian had read his notebook that night he'd come to his cottage?

When Dom Anthony opened the door, he nodded once, his Irish face stern and chafed cherry pink across his cheeks. Whit gave him a little bow before stepping inside.

There was a painting behind the abbot's desk that Whit loved—an annunciation in which Mary is so shocked by Gabriel's news of her impending motherhood that she drops the book she's reading. It spills from her hand, which hangs suspended in the air. Her lips are parted, her eyes shocked and deer-

like. Whit glanced up at the picture, seeing
for the first time the look of complete dread
on her face. He felt sorry for her suddenly.
Bearing God. It was too much to ask.

Dom Anthony sat down behind the ma-
hogany desk, but Whit went on standing.
Waiting. He felt regretful, sorry it would
end like this. He wondered how he could
go back out there. To Rambo movies and
Boy George on the radio. To Tammy Faye
Bakker's streaked face on television. How
could he go back to all that greed and con-
sumption? The stock market had crashed
last October, plunged five hundred points—
he'd read it in the papers—and it hadn't even
fazed him. If he returned to the world, he'd
have to think about the economy, about
starting up his law practice again.

Through the window on his right, he
glimpsed a wedge of sapphire sky, and it
made him think of the rookery, the egrets filling the trees, and the white flames their
feathers made on the branches. He thought
how much he would miss that.

"It is not too soon," Dom Anthony was saying, "to schedule your ceremony for solemn
vows." The old man began riffling the pages
of a desk calendar. "I was thinking of the Na-

tivity of St. John the Baptist on June twenty-fourth, or there's St. Barnabas on the eleventh."

"Solemn vows?" Whit repeated. He'd been so sure he was about to be asked to leave. He'd braced himself for the humiliation of that. He said it a second time. "Solemn vows?"

Dom Anthony squinted up at him. "Yes, Brother Thomas. It's time to be thinking about making your petition." Exasperation tugged on his voice, the tone of a teacher with an absentminded pupil. He picked up a pencil, holding it loosely, letting it rap on the desk like a drumstick. "Now. As for the ceremony. You're allowed to invite whomever you want. Are your parents living?"

"I don't know," said Whit.

Dom Anthony laid down the pencil and folded his hands together. "*You don't know? You don't know if your parents are dead or alive?*"

"Yes, of course I know that," Whit said. "My mother is alive. What I meant is that—" He looked at the annunciation, aware of the abbot watching him.

He'd been on the verge of saying he didn't know if he could take the vows, then stopped himself. He thought of Thomas Merton's prayer that he'd printed on a little blue card and kept taped to the mirror over his sink: *"My Lord God, I have no idea where I am going. I do not see the road ahead of me. I cannot know for certain where it will end. Nor do I really know myself, and the fact that I think I am following your will does not mean that I am actually doing so."*

"Reverend Father," he began, "I don't know about solemn vows. I'm not sure anymore about taking them."

Dom Anthony pushed back his chair and stood with painful slowness. He stared a moment at the junior monk, sighing. "Have you been reading Dietrich Bonhoeffer again?" he asked.

"No, Reverend Father."

The abbot had forbidden him to read any more of the Protestant theologian's writing after he'd found a certain unresolvable quotation of Bonhoeffer's copied into Whit's notebook: *"Before and with God we live without God."* Whit had liked the searing honesty of that. It had seemed to capture the paradox he was always carrying around inside.

Dom Anthony walked around the desk and laid his hand on Whit's shoulder. "I'm glad to hear you've set him aside. You're particularly sensitive to doubt, so it's best not to feed it. Especially now that you've come to the point of taking vows. It's a dark night of testing that we've all gone through—you're not alone in that. You will be vowing to spend the rest of your life here, to die here, to own nothing at all, to be perfectly celibate, and to give yourself over to obedience. No one does this lightly, but we do it just the same. We do it because the desire of our heart is God." The abbot smiled at him. "You will come through your dark night, Brother Thomas. Think of the disciple for whom you're named. Why do you think I chose that name for you? He doubted, didn't he? But in the end he overcame it with his faith, and you will, too."

Dom Anthony returned to his chair as if it were all settled—the dark night, doubt, faith—all of it properly dissected, reassembled, and put in its proper place. Whit wanted to tell him that he should've taken the name Jonah, that he'd been swallowed into the abbey, that he'd been traveling in the dark, luminous belly of this place from the moment he'd arrived, but now he would be spit back into that other life. Phil, Oprah,

Sally. Madonna's fishnet hose. *Revenge of the Nerds* movies. Out there where normal people, even bank tellers, used the words "totally awesome" to describe the most banal things.

He heard the chain saw again, more distantly this time. He felt it in his chest. Dom Anthony was brooding over the calendar. Whit noticed the tufts of pale hair on his knuckles. Over his head Mary's book was perpetually tumbling.

What had he *really* been doing here?

What if his being here wasn't about making peace with a God who was both here and not here but more about finding some kind of immunity from life? What if he'd mixed up enlightenment with asylum?

What if holiness had more to do with seizing his life *out there?*

The abbot had said he should take his vows because the desire of his heart was for God, and he did want God, but—he knew now—he wanted Jessie more.

He couldn't dismiss that. Neither his body nor his heart would let him, but neither would his *soul.* It was trying to tell him something. He was certain of it. One thing he'd learned from being here was how incessantly the soul tried to speak up, and usually in maddeningly cryptic ways—in his dreams, in the jumble of impressions and feelings he got when alone in the marsh, and occasionally in the symptoms in his body, that way he'd broken out in hives the time he was taken off rookery duty and made to help in the Net House. Nowhere, though, did the soul speak more insistently than through desire. Sometimes the heart wanted what the soul demanded.

"I think the Nativity of John the Baptist would be best," Dom Anthony said.

"I'm sorry, Reverend Father. I can't set the date now." Whit lifted his chin. He crossed his arms over his chest and planted his feet in that wide, commanding stance he'd always used in court during his closing summations. A court reporter had compared him once to Napoleon standing on a ship bow, dug in for battle. "I can't because I don't know if I'll ever be able to take my vows. I don't know if the desire of my heart is God."

The room filled with silence, a perfect silence. It pressed heavily in his ears, popping on his drums as if he were descending from the clouds in an airplane. Dom Anthony walked to the window and stood with his back to Whit.

Minutes passed before he finally turned around. "You are to give yourself over to the dark night, then. You are to stay there as long as it takes you to find your faith and come to your decision. May God be with you." He raised his hand in dismissal.

Walking to his cottage, Whit thought of the countless small things on the island he would miss. The alligators cruising the creeks submerged except for the great humps of their eyes. The oysters in their shells at night, how they opened when no one was looking. But mostly the egrets lifting out of the marsh carrying the light on their backs.

CHAPTER
Twenty-eight

I began to go alone to the marsh island in
the rookery, paddling there in Hepzibah's old
canoe, arriving well before Whit appeared
on his rounds. I created a place for myself, a
place where I felt hidden away with the blue
crabs and the wading egrets. All through the
rest of March and the first two weeks of
April, I went to the island nearly every day,
hungry for Whit but driven, too, by an insa-
tiable need to be alone.

I told Mother the truth, at least partially—
that I was paddling around in the creeks,
needing time to think through some things.
She immediately leaped to the conclusion

that I was thinking about my marriage. She had noticed my wedding rings on the pincushion in my room and asked repeatedly why Hugh had left the island so quickly, why he didn't call anymore. It was only Dee I spoke with now, weekly on the phone, and if *she* was suspicious about my sustained absence from Atlanta, she didn't mention it.

"Your marriage is in trouble, isn't it?" Mother prodded, and before I could form an answer, she said, "Don't deny it. It's written all over you, and I don't see how you expect to fix things if all you're going to do is stay here and loaf around in the creeks." She had carried on about this for days.

Even when Kat and Hepzibah dropped by one day, Mother brought it up, launching into the details of my daily absences. "Really," she said to them, "how much piddling around can a person actually do out there all by herself? It's like she's reverted to her childhood, back when she and Mike stayed out there the better part of the day."

Hepzibah and Kat exchanged glances.

"I've been going out there to think and be *alone*," I rushed to say.

When the two of them left, I followed them onto the porch. "I do meet him," I said. "Every afternoon for a couple of hours. But most of the time that I'm out there, I'm alone; I don't know why—I just need to be by myself."

"Sounds like you're *traveling*," Hepzibah said.

I stared a moment, wondering what she meant before remembering what she'd said on the tour that day about the Gullah people going off to the woods.

I'm sure my solitary visitations to the rookery represented some kind of migration, but I doubt they were as lofty as the visits the Gullah people made. Mine were decidedly sensual, a kind of affair with myself and with the island. And, of course, with Whit.

I do know this: They obscured everything else—all my concerns about Mother, why she'd been reading the books from the monastery library, the notion that she'd been involved in some kind of white martyrdom. It was easy to overlook now because of how much better she seemed. Cooking for the monks, busy, industrious, *normal.*

It was *I* who began to indulge in strange behavior—outrageous, extravagant acts that would've been unthinkable two months earlier.

One afternoon right after the spring equinox, I sat beside Whit's hermitage watching a willet build a nest in the marsh and listening to David Bowie sing "Let's Dance" on a Walkman I'd found at Caw Caw General. The day was almost sultry, and the periwinkle snails sat along the cordgrass in their little stupors. Egrets, oystercatchers, and herons were crowded into the shallows, so thickly it looked like an Audubon parking lot. Noticing a small diamondback terrapin nearby—what Mike used to call a "cooter"—I got up and followed it.

The creature reminded me of the turtle skull permanently installed now on top of the crab trap in the hermitage, which in turn reminded me of Kat, Hepzibah, and Mother dancing at the All-Girls Picnics. Picturing them, I began to sway a little. I'd never danced at the picnics; it had been *their* thing. Later, as an adult, I'd felt self-conscious dancing, too inhibited even to do it alone, but that day, with David Bowie insisting in my ear—"Let's dance, let's dance"—I began to do so with complete abandon, the skirt on my white muslin sundress flaring out like Isadora Duncan's. I loved the feel of my body moving like that, doing what it wanted.

Each day I took the Walkman to the island

and danced to whatever cassettes I could find in Caw Caw: Julio Iglesias and Willie Nelson singing "To All the Girls I've Loved Before," Stevie Wonder's "Woman in Love," the soundtrack to *Dirty Dancing.* I even bought Pink Floyd.

Afterward, breathless and spent, I would lie down beside the pluff mud and pat the shining black muck along my arms and legs—as if I were having a skin treatment at the spa. The goo smelled warm, alive, chlorophyll green, and rotten as the paper mills near Savannah, but I needed it. I cannot even tell you why; it was, I suppose, an irrational act. I would actually lie there with mud caked and drying on my skin and luxuriate in it for an hour or more, watching the sky reflected in the water and feeling the enduring breath of the earth moving around me.

One afternoon when Whit failed to show up because of a flooded toilet in the Monastery Reception Center, I watched the sun set and the water's surface bleed into carnelian and topaz. I heard dolphins pass, spewing their breath, and when the quiet became overbearing, I listened to the crackling advance of fiddler crabs on the mudflats and the tiny pops of pistol shrimp snapping their claws together.

During those times I sank into the compost of the island and became inseparable from it. It was only when my skin began to tighten and itch to the point I wanted to claw it that I would plunge into the water and swim away the mud. With my skin pink and vibrating, I would recline on the tides and let myself float. Once they carried me across the circular pool, along the tributary back into Caw Caw Creek, and I had to vie with a deceptively strong ebb to get back to the island.

More than the dancing or the mud bathing, it was the water I reveled in. Traveling water. It was filled with decay and death, and at the same time with plankton and eggs and burgeoning life. It would recede, stripping everything in its path, then turn into a brimming, amniotic estuary. I needed it like air.

I never told Whit about these things, though he had to know I'd been swimming, and maybe he guessed at the rest. Every afternoon he would find me waiting for him with soggy hair and telltale traces of marsh mud in the creases of my elbows.

I look back now at my Dionysian tangent

and understand it only a little better, how I was opening to the most rhapsodic thing in myself. To some extent those days were governed by instinct and flesh. When I was hungry, I ate what I'd brought from home, typically gorging myself on apples, and when I was sleepy, I simply lay down on one of Mother's discarded bedspreads and napped. But at the heart of it all, I believe that Hepzibah was right. I was *traveling.*

I took over Whit's crab trap, draped it with a cast net and gradually gathered a little assemblage of things to go with the turtle skull. Osprey feathers, clusters of blossoming trumpet flowers, oyster and bivalve shells, a crab claw I'd found at the water's edge. On a whim I added the so-called Mermaid Tears to the mix—the small pebbles I'd picked up in Kat's shop the first time I'd visited it. There were half a dozen apple peelings on top of the trap, too, my pathetic attempts at making whirly girls, which had ended up as a mass of broken red tendrils. One day while rummaging in my bag for a comb, I took out my father's pipe and added that to the collection as well.

Each day when I left the island, I stored everything in a plastic bag, which I tucked inside the trap, then faithfully reassembled when I returned. At first I thought I was following Hepzibah's example and making my own tiny show-and-tell table. Then it occurred to me that maybe I was trying to domesticate the hermitage, decorate it, make it *ours.* Was I playing house?

I caught Whit staring at the arrangement once, the way it sat beneath the palmetto-leaf cross he'd nailed on the wall. "Is it an altar?" he asked, startling me.

I would often set up my palette and canvas inside the hermitage and paint one diving woman after another. I painted her from different angles, capturing her in progressive stages of the dive. The water around her changed colors with each canvas, going through a succession of violet-blues, greens, yellow-oranges, and finally, fiery Pompeiian reds. Sometimes the diving woman—always nude—was done with Pre-Raphaelite realism and attention to detail, and other times she was a black shape rimmed in gold, primitive and stylized, but always, to me at least, radiant in her descent. Some paintings showed her letting go of an odd stream of paraphernalia that floated back to the surface as she plunged deeper. Spatulas, refrigerator magnets, kitchen bric-a-brac, wedding rings, crucifixes, charred wood, apple peels, a tiny pair of plastic kissing geese.

Yes, of course I realized that the paintings were a series of self-portraits—how could I not?—yet I didn't control them. They came like eruptions, like geysers. I didn't know when the diving would stop, what spectrum of the rainbow the water would turn next, where the bottom was or what might happen when the woman reached it.

Around midafternoon each day, I would begin to watch for Whit. By the time he arrived on the island, I would be in a frenzy of desire. We would twine ourselves together in the hermitage and make love, growing more and more fluent with each other's bodies, muttering our love over and over. I felt drunk with happiness and passion during those meetings, with the sense of having come home, but at the same time of making an exodus, of flying away to an eternal place.

After making love, we talked until he had to leave. Lying in his arms, I told him once about Chagall's *Lovers in the Red Sky,* how the pair—some thought Chagall and his wife, Bella—were wrapped in a glorious knot, how they floated above the world.

"But they can't stay up there forever," Whit had said, and I'd felt a slight deflation, an unease.

Only now and then did we talk about any kind of future. We both assumed there would be one, but we weren't ready to act on it. That seemed precipitous to both of us. Part of him, a quiet, concealed part that I loved and feared at the same time, was saying a grievous good-bye to the monastery, to his life there. And somewhere inside of me, I suppose I was saying good-bye, too, to twenty years of marriage, though in all honesty I consciously tried not to think about it.

What I *did* think about relentlessly during those hours on the island was my father. He seemed like a ghost hovering over the hermitage roof and everywhere in the needle rush. Again and again I would go back in my mind to the day the monks came to the door bearing the burned remains of his boat, the stoic way Mother had built the fire in the fireplace and tossed the boards on the flames. Watching them burn had been the first time I'd felt the deep crevice his dying was to make in my life.

During Easter week I saw Whit only once.

His work in the rookery was suspended while he assisted Brother Bede with Passiontide, all the high and holy preparations that had to be carried out between Palm Sunday and the Easter vigil. The matter of Easter lilies, holy oil, Paschal candles, the basin and pitcher for the foot washing, black vestments, white vestments. He did not get there until Thursday, Maundy Thursday, or as Mother had said that morning, reverting to her Catholic Latin, *"Feria Quinta in Coena Domini,"* the Thursday of the Lord's Supper.

Wearing the aqua shirt he loved, I met him at the edge of the water and waited while he anchored the johnboat. I'd fixed a picnic on a red-and-white floral tablecloth that I'd spread nearby: Mother's Wadmalaw tomato pie, strawberries, Market Street pralines, a bottle of red wine. Clusters of wild white azaleas that I'd picked in Kat's front yard filled the center of the cloth.

When Whit saw what I'd done, he bent over and kissed my forehead. "This is a surprise. What's the occasion?"

"Well, let me see." I pretended to be racking my brain. "It *is* Maundy Thursday. Plus, it happens to be our six-week-and-one-day anniversary."

"We have an anniversary?"

"Of course we do. February seventeenth, the day we met. It was Ash Wednesday. Remember? It hasn't always been the most cheerful day of the year for me, so I thought I'd turn it into an anniversary."

"I see."

We sat down on the tablecloth, and he reached for the wine. I'd forgotten cups, so we each took a swig straight from the bottle, laughing when it dribbled down my chin. As I sliced the tomato pie and placed the thick wedges on paper plates, I went on talking, caught up in my delirious chatter. "The first year we'll celebrate our anniversary monthly on the seventeenth, and then we'll mark it annually. Every Ash Wednesday."

When I looked up, he was no longer smiling. I set the plate down. I had the terrible feeling he was going to tell me we would not be having annual anniversaries, that he'd decided to stay at the abbey. What if Easter had gotten to him? God resurrecting. I went cold.

He reached for me, holding me almost painfully close. "We could live near Asheville," he said. "At the end of some dirt road in the middle of nowhere. And hike on weekends.

Or go to Malaprop's Bookstore and sit in the café." I realized then that he was simply affected by the thought of having a life in which there would be small domestic details and a flow of days, of anniversaries. It was as if it had all somehow just become real to him.

"I would love that," I told him. But in truth it made me uncomfortable. Hiking is what Hugh and I had done. Weekends in the mountains north of Atlanta, in a little place called Mineral Bluff.

Later, after we'd eaten, bees flitted in the azalea blossoms, and Whit told an outlandish story about a three-foot alligator that had gotten into the church the second year he was at the monastery and how, upon seeing it, the abbot had leaped up onto the altar.

I leaned back on my elbows and placed my bare feet in his lap. I fed myself the last of the strawberries while he rubbed my feet. He said something about brides having their feet washed before the wedding, that it was an old custom. I don't remember now if he said it was biblical or Asian, just that it was the kind of obscure, antediluvian trivia only Whit would know.

He slid closer to the edge of the water,

tugging me with him. Scooping handfuls of water from the creek, he poured it over my feet, sliding his hands across my wet skin. He moved them slowly over my ankles, stroked the arches of my feet with his thumbs, then let his fingers slide in and out between my toes. I watched him without speaking. I didn't know what covenant we were making, but I felt it in his hands and saw it in his face.

I closed my eyes and felt myself going down with the diving woman. Somewhere in my paintings, there was a place of no return.

CHAPTER
Twenty-nine

On the evening of the All-Girls Picnic, Mother balked. She stood on the front porch holding a bag of benne wafers, wearing a navy cotton shirt with the collar all wrinkled and baggy beige pants stretched out at the elastic waist, and informed Kat, Hepzibah, Benne, and me that she would not be going. She had washed her hair earlier and let it dry naturally, which had caused a wild white wave to rise straight up from her forehead and splash down on top of her head, flipping out erratically.

"Oh, for the love of God," said Kat. "How pigheaded can one woman be? Am I going to have to go get the damn hibiscus scarf again?"

Mother jabbed her fists onto her hips. "I'm not worried about my hand, Kat Bowers."

"Well, what is it? It is because of your hair?"

"What's wrong with my hair?" Mother practically shouted.

"Catfight," said Benne.

Hepzibah stepped between them. "What is wrong with you two? *Lord.*"

"Mother, look, I understand your reluctance," I said. "But we've fixed all this food. The golf carts are loaded, and Hepzibah has already gathered the wood for a fire down on the beach. We've got our hearts set on this."

"Then by all means, go without me."

"We're not going without you," said Kat. "It's all of us or none of us—that's the deal."

There was the reason my father had called them the Three Egreteers. The unspoken *deal,* that tiny, cemented knot they'd tied in their threads and tossed into the ocean.

We went on coaxing, making good use of guilt, ignoring her excuses until she finally climbed into one of the carts.

I wish now I'd listened to her, that one of us had had the decent foresight to listen. Not even Benne caught the quiet, dire quality echoing inside her resistance.

It was the first Saturday after Easter, April 16, 6:00 P.M. We'd decided not to wait until May Day eve, when the All-Girls Picnics had traditionally been held in the past. Mother needed this *now,* we'd reasoned.

The day was warm, with bright, sparkly afternoon light gleaming off the edges of things. I drove behind Kat, following her through the dunes and sea oats right down onto Bone Yard Beach. The wind was hitting the waves and breaking open the tops of them, releasing sudden belches of spray. Max, who'd ridden over in the backseat of my cart, jumped out while we were still moving, tearing for the water.

Hepzibah had piled the driftwood in a heap far up on the beach, anticipating high tide. "Watch where you park," I heard her tell Kat as we braked—a loaded comment referring to the time Kat had left her golf cart on the beach and the tide took it. She'd come back hours later to see it bobbing off toward England.

We spread out a blanket on the sand, and Mother sat down, huddling on the corner farthest from the water, gathering an old alpaca sweater around her shoulders. She positioned her back to the water and stared at the dunes. There was a weirdness about that, like someone on an elevator facing the back wall instead of the doors. I could feel her retreating, being sucked back into the old darkness.

Two weeks ago, when I'd taken her to Mount Pleasant for her follow-up appointment with the doctor, she'd sat inside the ferry and stared carefully at the floor, as if she didn't want to be reminded of what had happened out on the water thirty-three years ago. Her behavior now reminded me of that. Had she had this aversion to the island waters ever since Dad died, and somehow I'd just not noticed? It struck me as the same unaccountable antagonism she'd harbored for the mermaid chair. That, too, had started after he died. I had seen her leave the room at the mere mention of it.

I kept on observing her as I unpacked the food. We'd gone out of our way to bring the same dishes as before: crab cakes, hoppin' John, pimento cheese, raisin-bread pudding, wine—Chianti for Kat, Chardonnay for the rest of us. Looking at the spread, I thought of Whit and the picnic I'd made for us a little over a week before on the opposite side of the island, the way he'd bathed my feet, the unspoken ceremony it had become, full of faint connubial undertones.

Max had settled into his favorite sport—catching sand crabs, trotting up to us with legs and claws hanging out of his mouth. I watched him bring one to Mother, dropping it proudly at her feet, and the limp, distracted way she placed her hand on his head. She had not said three words. Kat handed her the Saran wrap, asking her to find the end of it, and Mother simply laid it down on the sand without trying. If the point was to cheer Mother up, it wasn't working. Something was deeply wrong.

Kat, however, would not relent. Her attempts to draw Mother into the evening, to consummate the vision we all had of her reverting miraculously to her All-Girls Picnic self, became increasingly forced. "Nelle, who do you think should be our first female president—Geraldine Ferraro or Patricia Schroeder?" Kat asked.

This barely got a shrug out of her.

"Come on, you *have* to answer. Jessie and Hepzibah say Patricia; I say Geraldine."

"Nancy Reagan," Mother muttered. We all

perked up, thinking she was going to join in, the salvation of Nelle Dubois at hand.

"Well, if Nancy runs, I for one will . . . *just say no!*" Kat said. It was the kind of goading usually guaranteed to get Mother going, but there was no comeback, nothing but the sinking of her shoulders into their former slump.

She ate only a little—half a crab cake and a spoonful of bread pudding. The rest of us loaded our plates, still determined.

As darkness materialized out over the ocean, Hepzibah lit the fire. The wind-dried wood flamed up quickly. Within moments it was raging, spattering the air with sparks that trailed off into the blackness. We sat in a globe of light, the smell of burning everywhere, and no one considered how a fire blazing right there beside the water might affect a woman for whom fire and water meant nothing but tragedy and death, a woman who could not look seawater in the face, who'd boarded up her fireplace. We were blinded by nostalgia for the woman she'd been before all of that. It makes me weep now to think how hard Mother must have been trying that night. How she came only to please us and went on sitting there as her agony grew.

Throughout the evening she remained at the edge of the blanket, back where the light didn't reach. Hepzibah beat her Gullah drum. The sound came out lamenting and slow. Benne laid her head in Kat's lap, and Max fell asleep with the gloss of firelight on his back. The wood crackled. The ocean heaved, slamming down on the beach. No one talked. We had given up.

Sometime around 3:00 A.M., hours after our bonfire had turned to embers and we'd packed up our failed experiment and left the beach, I was wakened in my bed by someone calling my name. I recall it as a shrill, urgent whisper.

"Jessie!"

I sat up. Confused, surfacing, my head gummed with sleep. I could see a shape, *a person,* shadowed in the doorway. My heart began a wild, adrenaline-soaked pounding. I fumbled for the lamp switch beside the bed, tipping over a glass of water that spilled across the table, onto the floor.

"I'm sorry. I *had* to," a voice said.

"Mother?"

The shock of lamplight cut through the room, blinding me for a moment. Squinting, I swept my hand through the air as if I could wipe the glare out of it. Her face appeared dazed. Her hand lifted as if she were a student asking permission to speak. Blood was everywhere. Soaked across the front of her pale nylon gown. Winding in streams down her forearm. Pelting the floor.

"I had to," she said again, repeating it I don't know how many times—a hysterical whisper that seemed to incapacitate me.

For several seconds I didn't move, speak, blink. I stared hypnotically at the blood coursing from her hand, the dazzling brightness of it, the way it flowed in small, measured spurts. I was blunted with awe—floating in the moment of blessed disconnection that comes before panic, before the full tonnage of the moment drops.

But even then I did not leap from bed in a frenzy. I rose slowly and moved toward her as if weightless, one foot and then the other, transfixed with horror.

The little finger on her right hand was missing.

I lashed Mother's forearm with a belt, creating a tourniquet. She lay on the floor while I compressed a towel tightly against the gaping place where her little finger had been, aware all of a sudden that she could die. My mother could bleed to death on the floor of my bedroom, on the spot near the window where I'd strung whirly girls.

There was no emergency service on the island, no doctor. When the towel ran red, I got another. Mother became still. The color was sliding out of her face.

As the hemorrhage finally began to stop, I dialed Kat's number with one hand, bearing down on her wound with the other one.

Kat arrived with Shem, who despite his age grasped Mother in his burly arms and carried her outside to the golf cart. I walked beside them, keeping steady pressure on Mother's hand. At the ferry dock, he lifted her once again and bore her onto the pontoon. He was breathing hard but talking to her the whole way: "Stay with us, now, Nelle. Stay with us."

Inside the boat he laid her on the passenger bench, instructing us to keep her feet elevated. Kat held them aloft for the entire trip. And Mother, still conscious but drifting somewhere far away from us, gazed at the roof of the boat for a while before finally closing her eyes.

Kat and I did not exchange a word. We

crossed the rolling black water while the wind moved like smoke and the blood on Mother's gown dried, turning to a stiff, brown crust.

A waning three-quarter moon loomed over us. I watched its light, soft as mohair, collect around Mother's head and wondered if she'd used a meat cleaver. Had there been one hidden somewhere in the kitchen that I'd missed? After Kat had arrived, I'd looked for Mother's finger, thinking the doctor might be able to reattach it. I'd expected to find it lying on the cutting board like a discarded vegetable peel, but it had been nowhere in sight. Just puddles of blood everywhere.

That trip across the bay was like being jerked out of the sea on a barbed hook and hauled back into reality. Back to where you know all over again there is no immunity, no storm tent, no illusion. Mother's ruthless, mutilating compulsion had been there all along, consuming her like cancer, and I . . . I had been engrossed elsewhere.

Until tonight I'd actually thought we were making progress—that three-steps-forward, two-steps-backward kind of advance—slow and frustrating but still *progress*. The mind is so good at revising reality to suit our needs. I had seen what I wanted. I had reinvented the objectionable, the most indigestible pieces of my life into something just palatable enough to bear. I had taken Mother's craziness and normalized it.

How do I describe how flattened I felt by the depth of her madness? By my own passivity and denial and guilt?

I turned my face to the plastic window on the boat. Behind us the island was swallowed in darkness. The water seemed immense, glowing as if lit from underneath. I stared at a short beam of light coming from the bow of the boat, sliding needlelike in and out of the waves, and thought suddenly of the sea goddess, the mermaid Sedna whom Mother had read about in Dominic's library book. She had ten severed fingers. *Ten.*

The whole horrible thing fell into place then.

My mother was not going to stop until she'd cut every single finger from her hands.

She had emulated Eudoria, the prostitute-turned-saint, by cutting off one finger and planting it, and then, getting no relief, she had moved on to Sedna, whose fingers had turned into sea creatures—frolicking dolphins and seals, singing whales—forming the entire harmonic ocean world out of her pain and sacrifice. Ten fingers to create a new world. Ten. The day Whit had shown me the book on Sedna, I'd read about the number, the same words Mother must have read: *"Ten was considered the holiest number. Pythagoreans deemed it the number of regeneration and fulfillment. Everything sprang from ten."*

How had I not seen it? The way Mother had taken a simple story, a myth, a number, things meant to be symbolic, and contorted it into something dangerous and literal? How had I underestimated the desperation in her to grow the world back the way it had been before my father died? That singing world in which we had lived by the sea.

CHAPTER Thirty

As Hugh crossed the parking lot in front of East Cooper Hospital, I watched him from a window in the third-floor waiting room where Kat and I had been ensconced since dawn. Even from up here, I could see that his face was tanned, and I knew he'd been tilling up the backyard again. When confronted with loss, Hugh got out the old hand tiller that had belonged to his father and exhausted himself with physical labor, plowing up huge stretches of the yard. Sometimes he wouldn't even get around to planting anything; the point seemed to be just ripping up the ground. After his father died, I'd watched him plow with such sorrow and drivenness, stoically propelling himself into the early-summer darkness, that I could not bear to watch. He had rendered much of the two acres around the house a bare, exposed ground of fresh wounds. I'd once seen him pick up a handful of the upturned dirt and, closing his eyes, smell it.

I'd called him at six this morning. It had been dawn by then, but the forbidding dark-ness and quiet that had floated through the hospital all night had not yet lifted. Dialing the number, I'd felt overwhelmed by the shrouded, deft way Mother had been laying siege to herself. I was defeated, to tell the truth. I knew that Hugh would understand how I felt, the exact contours of every feel-ing. I would not have to explain anything. When I heard his voice, I started to cry—the tears I squashed on the ferry.

"I have to commit her," I'd said, struggling for composure. The surgeon on call, who'd repaired Mother's hand, had made that clear enough. "I suggest *this time* you get a psy-chiatrist in to see her and start commitment papers," he'd said, kindly enough, but with emphasis on *"this time."*

"Do you want me to come?" Hugh asked.

"I can't do this alone," I told him. "Kat's here, but—yes, please, could you come?"

He'd gotten there in record time. I looked at the clock on the wall. It was just past 1:00 P.M.

He was wearing a knit sport shirt, the terra-cotta one I liked so much, and crisp khaki pants with his tasseled loafers. He looked well, the same handsome, golden look about him, and his hair was cut shorter than I'd seen it in years. I, on the other hand, looked like one of those people you see on the television news who shuffle around in the aftermath of some natural disaster.

My hair needed washing, my teeth needed brushing, and my eyes had puffy, bruised-looking smudges underneath from lack of sleep. I wore the gray warm-up pants and white T-shirt I'd slept in. I'd had to scrub Mother's blood off them in the visitors' bathroom. Most embarrassing of all, I had no shoes. How could I have left without shoes? I'd been startled on the ferry when I saw that my feet were bare. One of the nurses had given me a cheap pair of terry-cloth slippers sealed in a plastic bag.

The worst part of the night had been waiting to hear if Mother would be okay—*physically,* I should say; at that point I don't think either Kat or I had a lot of hope for her men- tally. They'd let us in to see her while she was still in the recovery room. We'd held on to the bed rail, staring down at her face, which was the color of oatmeal. A pale green oxygen tube had gurgled under her nose and blood was dripping, thick as resin, into her arm from a plastic bag over her head. Reaching down under the sheet, I'd picked up her good hand and squeezed it. "It's me, Mother. It's Jessie."

After several attempts she'd cracked open her eyes and tried to focus on me, parting and closing her lips repeatedly without mak- ing a sound, priming the words from what I imagined to be a contaminated well deep in- side her.

"Don't throw it away," she mumbled, her tone barely audible.

I bent over her. "What are you saying? Throw *what* away?"

A nurse making marks on a clipboard nearby looked up. "She's been saying that since she started waking."

I bent down where I could smell the nox- ious odor of the anesthetic from her mouth. "Throw *what* away?" I repeated.

"My finger," she said, and the nurse

stopped writing and stared at me with her mouth formed into a small, pinched circle.

"Where *is* your finger?" I asked. "I looked for it."

"In a bowl, in the refrigerator," she said, her eyes already closed.

I'd called Mike at 10:00 A.M.—7:00 in California. Waiting for him to pick up, I'd felt like his little sister again, needing him, needing him to come and take care of things. Once, as children, we'd run the bateau aground on a mudflat and, trying to help push us off, I'd fallen over the side, up to my waist in mud. In places the mud could suck you down like jungle quicksand, and I'd flailed around hysterically as he'd hauled me out. That's what I wanted now. Mike to reach down and lift me out of this.

When he answered, I told him everything, and that I was going to have to commit Mother. He responded that I should keep him informed. Not "I'll get the next plane," the way Hugh had said, only that impotent token of concern.

I felt for a moment like I was going under. "Oh," I said.

"I'm sorry I'm not there to help, Jess. I'll

come when I can, it's just that now is not good."

"When is it ever good?"

"Not ever," he responded. "I wish I were more like you, able to face . . . *things* better. You always dealt with it better than I did."

We never talked about the bedroom drawer we'd rummaged through as children, reading the clipping about our father's death, the strange, sad spiral Mother's life had taken, the mounting religious obsessions we'd witnessed with confusion. We both knew he'd run away from the island the same as I had, but he'd gone farther, and not just in miles. He'd washed his hands of it.

"I found his pipe," I said abruptly, feeling furious at his desertion.

He was silent. I pictured the news poised over his head, guillotine style, waiting to drop the way it had with me—the sudden slice of recognition that a crucial piece of one's past has been a lie.

"But . . ." he said, and, bogging down, started again. "But that's what caused the fire."

"Apparently not." I was suddenly fatigued in the tiniest creases of my body—between my fingers, behind my ears, in the corners of my mouth.

"God, it never ends, does it?"

He sounded so damaged saying it that my anger began to dissolve. I knew then he would never come back and face all of this. He wasn't able.

"Do you remember Father Dominic?" I asked. "The monk who always wore the straw hat?"

"How could I forget?"

"Do you think there could've been something between him and Mother?"

He actually laughed. "You can't be serious! You mean, an *affair?* You think that's the reason she's cut off her fingers? To pay her pound of flesh for it?"

"I don't know, but there's some kind of history between them."

"Jess, come *on.*"

"Don't laugh at this, Mike. I don't think I can take that right now." My voice rose. "You're not here, you don't see what I see. Believe me, there are more outrageous things than *that* in her life."

"You're right, sorry," he said. He let go of his breath, let it melt into the phone. "I only saw them together once. I went over to the monastery to ask Mom if she'd let me go out with Shem on the trawler—I was around fifteen, I think—and I found her and Father Dominic in the kitchen, fighting."

"About what, you remember?"

"It was about the mermaid chair. Father Dominic was trying to get her to go sit in it, and she was furious for some reason. He told her twice, 'You have to make your peace with it.' It didn't make sense to me. But for a long time after that, I wondered about it. All I can tell you is that if the two of them had an affair, which honestly I can't begin to conceive, they didn't seem remotely amicable at that point."

When we hung up, I felt more confused than when I'd called, but at least he knew now about Mother. And I knew about him—that part of him would always be lost to me. I felt comforted, though, that we were at least linked the way we'd been as children—not partners in conquering the island, which had been our carefree alliance before Father died, but partners in survival. Surviving Mother.

Outside in the parking lot, Hugh was approaching the hospital entrance. I watched him pause on the sidewalk, looking down as if studying the spidery cracks in the cement. He seemed to be preparing himself. For me, no doubt. It was a moment of such private vulnerability that I stepped back from the window.

I darted a glance toward Kat, who sat across the room squeezing the bridge of her nose. Mother's behavior seemed to have had a sobering effect on her; I'd never seen her so quiet. Earlier, beside the bed in the recovery room, I'd watched Kat close her eyes and tighten both her fists, as if swearing a private oath to herself, or at least that's how I read it.

"He's here," I said to her, trying to sound casual. I had a skittish feeling in my stomach.

This would be the first time I'd seen him since making love with Whit. I had the irrational feeling that the knowledge was somehow posted all over me for him to read, little scarlet *A*'s popping out like freckles in the sun. Crossing the bay last night, jerked out of my illusory storm tent and acutely aware of my ability to twist things to my liking, I'd kept my shock confined to Mother. But now, seeing Hugh, it was like coming upon my world of deceit, seeing it diagrammed like a map with a pointing arrow: YOU ARE HERE.

Here. A place where the heart and its crav-
ings obliterate everything: conscience, the
will of the mind, the careful plaiting together
of lives.

The ache in my stomach was the knot of
blame, I know that. Hugh had staked his life
on me and lost. But there was defiance coiled
in the feeling as well. What I'd felt, what I'd
done—it wasn't only some unstoppable erotic
urge pent up too long, not just lust and libido
and overactive sex organs. That wouldn't be
fair. The heart was an organ, too, wasn't it? It
had been so easy to dismiss the heart before.
A little feeling factory you could shut down
if necessary. How unfair. The feelings that
ripped through it had power and force, perhaps at times the consent of the soul. I'd felt it
myself, the way my soul had raised its hand to
consecrate what was happening to me.

"Do you have a comb?" I asked Kat. "And
lipstick?" I'd not brought a purse either.

She handed me a tube and a small brush,
lifting her eyebrows.

"I look like shit," I told her. "I don't want him
to think I'm so lost without him I've gone to
pot."

"Good luck with *that*," she said, but smiling at me.

When he stepped into the waiting room, he looked at me, then away. I thought suddenly of Whit and felt my stomach turn over, the need to breathe, to paddle to the island in the marsh, a million miles from the world, and go down into the cool, dark water.

All three of us, even Kat, struggled as we waded through the initial greetings, the how-have-you-beens. Part of me didn't *want* to know how he'd been, for fear my knees would buckle, and part of me felt that if he described every ounce of pain and trauma I'd inflicted on him, it was the least I deserved.

For a good three or four minutes, Hugh and I seemed to be calibrating an emotional thermostat. Tapping it up and down, acting too friendly, then too reserved. It wasn't until the focus turned to Mother that we began to get comfortable in the room together, which is saying a lot, considering how wretched that situation was.

We sat in padded wooden chairs near the window, around a coffee table covered in old magazines, some going back to 1982. I was freshly knowledgeable about everything from Sandra Day O'Connor's appointment to the Supreme Court to Michael Jackson's glove.

Hugh was wearing a thin bracelet of what looked like braided embroidery thread around his right wrist—blue, tan, and black—which floored me because Hugh hated to wear any sort of jewelry except his wedding ring. That, I noticed, was still on his left hand.

He saw me staring at the bracelet. "It's from Dee," he said. "She made it herself. I believe she called it a friendship bracelet." He lifted it up with abashed amusement, shrugging at the oddity of such a thing's being there, his daughter's wanting to seal their friendship. "I'm under orders not to take it off. I'm told there will be terrible consequences if—"

The absurdity of worrying about terrible consequences, given the fact they'd already happened, caused him to stop midsentence and lower his arm.

What he didn't know was that Dee had made one of these bracelets for her high-school friend Heather Morgan, as a way to comfort her after she'd been dumped. It had been an act of sisterly solidarity. Dee would never have made one of these for Hugh unless she knew about us. Had he told her?

"How nice that she made it for you," I said. "What was the occasion?"

He looked uncomfortable. "April tenth."

His birthday. I'd forgotten. But even if I'd remembered, I doubted I would've called. Considering. "Happy birthday," I offered.

"I missed our Follies this year," he said. "Maybe next year." He settled the full force of his gaze on me. It was laden with the unspoken question of *"next year."*

"Follies?" Kat said. "Now, that sounds fascinating."

"We need to talk about Mother," I said with obvious discomfort, such a transparent evasion tactic that he smiled slightly.

I glanced at the blank commitment papers lying in the empty chair next to mine. They carried the presence of a full-blooded person sitting there, a dismal, menacing person needing attention.

Hugh reached over and picked them up. There were small Band-Aids on the insides of both his thumbs. Tiller blisters. Proof he'd been trying to plow through. I watched as he skimmed the pages, staring at his hands. For a strange second, it seemed my whole marriage was visible in them. In the tufts of hair near his wrists, the lines on his palms, his fingers filled with memories of touching me. The mystery of what held people together was right there.

"Okay," he said, lowering the papers to his lap. "Let's talk about her."

I started at the beginning. "The night I arrived on the island, I found Mother burying her finger beside St. Senara's statue—you remember me telling you about that."

Hugh nodded.

"I asked her why she'd cut it off, and she started to tell me—you know, the way you say something before you remember it's a secret. She mentioned Dad's name and Father Dominic's and then, realizing what she'd said, stopped and wouldn't go on. So obviously Dominic is involved somehow." I glanced at Kat. "Of course, Kat disagrees with me."

She didn't defend herself; in part I'd said it just to see if she might. She merely stared back at me, crossing and uncrossing her legs.

"Did you ask this Father Dominic about it?" Hugh said.

"Yes, and he suggested to me that some things are better off left secret."

Hugh was leaning forward, his hands clasped between his knees. "Okay, forget Dominic for the moment. Why do *you* think she's cutting off her fingers? You've been with her for over two months. What's your gut say?"

My gut? I was momentarily speechless. Hugh was asking *me* for a gut feeling, and on something about which he was the expert. Before, he'd always brusquely given me his clinical opinion—very textbook, right out of the *DSM III*—and dismissed what I'd thought.

"I have a feeling it goes back to something she thinks she's done," I said, measuring my words, wanting so much to say it right. "Something having to do with my father, and it's so awful it has driven her crazy, literally. I believe that her insane need to butcher herself is a way of doing penance. She's trying to atone."

I remember how Kat looked away and shook her head slightly, like people do when they're disbelieving.

I was determined to convince her, as much as Hugh. I quoted the Scripture that says if your right hand offends you, it's better to cut it off than to have your whole body cast into hell.

"Do you have any idea what sin Nelle is trying to expunge?" Hugh asked.

Kat brought her hand to her forehead and

rubbed a patch of redness into her skin. I saw that her eyes looked wide and, yes, scared.

I started to answer that it had occurred to me more than once that Mother and Dominic might have had an affair, but I caught myself. There was no way I could say that. It was too close to my own truth. And what evidence did I have anyway? How Dominic had asked my mother if she would ever forgive them? That he'd written an unmonklike paragraph in his little booklet, suggesting that erotic love was every bit as spiritual as divine love? That St. Eudoria, whom Mother may have been emulating, was a prostitute?

I shrugged. "I don't know. But penance is only part of it. I think she believes she can bring about some kind of redemption by doing this."

"What do you mean, 'redemption'?" Kat asked.

I told them about the two books Mother had gotten out of the monastery library. The stories of St. Eudoria, who cut off her finger and planted it in a field, and Sedna, whose ten severed fingers fell into the ocean and turned into the first sea creatures.

As I talked, I kept looking at Hugh to see if

he was taking what I said with a grain of salt or whether he thought it really had merit. I didn't want to care what he thought, but I did. I wanted him to say, *Yes, yes, you have seen through to the truth. You have done this for your mother.*

"That's what I mean about redemption," I said. "I think all this dismembering she's doing is really about her need to grow something, or make a new world, to re-member herself back in a new way."

Dismembering and re-membering. The idea had only just occurred to me that moment.

"Interesting," Hugh said, and when I rolled my eyes, thinking he'd dismissed me, he shook his head. "No, I mean it *is* interesting, more than interesting."

He offered me a sad, disappointed smile. "I used to say that, didn't I, as a way of glossing over what you said?"

Kat got up and wandered to the other side of the room, where she rummaged purposelessly through her purse.

"We both did things," I told him.

"I'm sorry," he said.

I didn't know what to say. He wanted me to reach out to him, to say, *Yes, next year we'll have the Follies. . . . I've made a vast mistake. I want to come home.* And I couldn't.

I had thought our life together was vouchsafed. It was one of those unpremeditated facts I'd lived with every single day. Like the sun going through its motions—coming and going, an automaton. Like the stars fixed in the Milky Way. Who questions these things? They just are. I'd thought we would be buried together. Side by side in a nice cemetery in Atlanta. Or that our cremated remains would sit in matching urns in Dee's house until she found it in herself to go out and scatter them. Once I'd imagined her hauling the urns all the way to Egret Island and tossing handfuls of us in the air on Bone Yard Beach. I'd pictured the wind whipping us together in a blizzard of indistinguishable particles—Hugh and me flying to the sky, returning to the earth, together. And Dee walking away with bits of us in her hair. What was the mysterious and enduring thing that had made me so certain of us for so long? Where had it gone?

I looked at his hands. The silence was terrible.

He ended it himself.

"If you're right about Nelle, Jessie—and you really could be—then maybe the key is simply remembering, recalling the past in a way that allows her to face it. That can be very healing sometimes."

He placed the commitment papers back on the empty chair. "Are you going to sign?"

When I scrawled my name, Kat held her head in her hands and didn't look at me.

Hugh came back to Egret Island with me that evening, taking his suitcase into Mike's old room while I went straight to the bathroom and filled the tub with steaming water. Kat had insisted on staying overnight at the hospital, that I be the one to go home. Tomorrow Mother would be transported to the psychiatric unit at the Medical University of South Carolina in Charleston, and Hugh had agreed to be there when I checked her in and met with the psychiatrist. I felt grateful to him.

I slid down into the water, going all the way under, and lay as still as I could, so motionless I began to hear my heart resounding through the water. I held my breath and thought of those World War II movies where the submarine hides on the bottom of the ocean, shut down except for the *ping, ping* of the sonar, everyone holding his breath, waiting to see if the Japanese would hear it. I felt like that, as if my heart might give me away.

Maybe next year, Hugh had said. The words made my chest start to hurt.

The Follies—the "Psychiatric Follies," as we facetiously called them—were Hugh's favorite birthday present. In some ways I think they were the highlight of his year.

I'd overheard Dee trying to describe the Follies once to Heather: "See, Mom and I put on a show for my dad. We make up a song about his work, about hypnotizing somebody and not being able to wake them up, or having an Oedipus complex, something like that."

Heather had screwed up her nose. "Your family is weird."

"I *know,*" Dee had said, as if this were a great big compliment.

Surfacing, I lay in the tub with the water just under my nostrils and felt the wrench of knowing that even though Dee was away at college this year, she'd probably remembered the Follies but hadn't mentioned them to me when we'd talked, for reasons I was afraid to know. Hugh had told her about us, I was sure of it. And yet she'd said nothing.

Dee had been the one who'd started the Follies, though I'd been her inspiration, I guess you'd say. It began when I'd gotten my hair cut at a salon over in Buckhead. There had been a bowl of Godiva chocolates at the entrance, and, standing beside it, I'd fidgeted with my watch, an inexpensive Timex with an expandable band. I did that sometimes, sliding it on and off my wrist the way someone twirls her hair or taps a pencil. Later, when I left, I'd reached for a chocolate, and there it was: My watch was in the candy bowl.

"Isn't that odd?" I'd said at dinner that night, relating the incident to Hugh and Dee, only making conversation, but Hugh had perked right up.

"It's a Freudian slip," he said.

"What's that?" asked Dee, only thirteen then.

"It's when you say or do something without being aware of it," Hugh told her. "Something that's got a hidden meaning."

He leaned forward, and I saw it coming—the god-awful Freudian-slip joke. "Like when you say one thing and mean *a-mother*," he said.

"That's funny," Dee said. "But what did it mean when Mom took off her watch like that?"

He looked at me, and I felt momentarily like a lab rat. Pointing his fork in my direction, he said, "She wanted to remove herself from the constraints of time. It's a classic fear of death."

"Oh, *please*," I said.

"You know what I think?" said Dee, and Hugh and I sat up, expecting something precocious. "I think Mom just left her watch in the candy bowl."

Dee and I burst into conspiratorial laughter.

It had escalated from there. Fear of Death became FOD, and we teased him without mercy. That year Dee wrote a farcical song about FOD and enlisted me to sing it with her on his birthday, to the tune of "Pop Goes the Weasel," and so began the Psychiatric Follies. No one loved them more than Hugh.

Around March he would start bugging the hell out of us to reveal the theme. Last year Dee had written an opus to her own original tune, called "Penis Envy: The Musical."

Dear Dr. Freud,
We are overjoyed
To declare null and void
Your penis envy fraud.
Do you really think we peg
Our hope between your legs?
Must your beloved male part
Be the desire of our heart?
A penis—are you serious?
A woman would be delirious.
Just between us—
There's more to life than a penis.
I say with no trace of mirth
Has Dr. Freud given birth?
Could we just assume
You're pining for a womb?

We performed it in the living room, pregnant with sofa pillows that were stuffed under our shirts, doing choreographed steps
and gestures worthy of the Supremes. An
hour later Hugh was still laughing. I'd felt
then there was so much glue between us
that nothing could splinter it.

Now, in the little bathroom, I rubbed the
bar of soap over my arms and studied the
square pink tiles on the wall. Mike had hated
sharing what he'd called "the girly bath-

room." The same pale pink organdy curtains hung in the small window, dingy now to the point of appearing orange. I shampooed my hair, scrubbed my skin.

When I'd signed the commitment papers, I'd had to write the date. April 17. It had made me think of Whit. *The first year we'll celebrate our anniversary monthly on the seventeenth,* I'd told him.

I wished I could call him. I knew that earlier today, even though it was Sunday, he would've been at the rookery. I pictured him arriving at the dock, spotting the red canoe, and glancing around for me. I wondered if he'd waited awhile for me to show up before setting out, whether he'd sat on the bank where he'd washed my feet and listened for the quiet sound of my paddle. Perhaps by vespers, before the rule had folded them all back into wordless silence till the morning, the news about Nelle had spread across the island and spilled over the brick abbey wall. Maybe he knew why I hadn't come to him.

I heard Hugh's footsteps pacing the hallway, back and forth. When they stopped, I could tell he was just outside the door. I looked around to see if I'd locked it, though I was sure Hugh would never come in without knocking. The latch, an old-fashioned hook and eye, was unfastened. I waited. Held my breath. *Ping, ping, ping.* Finally he moved away.

What had caused him to tread up and down the hallway like that?

When I came out of the bathroom, I wore Mother's blue bathrobe, my hair wet, combed back and slicked down like enamel. It was when the cool air hit my face that I remembered. I'd propped my canvases across the bed, the dresser, and the floor in Mike's room, ostensibly for storage, but I would go in there at times and stare at my work. It was like standing in a gallery inside myself, gazing at the deep, dark marvels. My thirteen diving women, their wild, sensual bodies grandly nude.

I thought of Hugh in there studying them, examining the cast-off pieces of their lives that I'd painted floating to the surface. The kitchen spatulas, the apple peels, the wedding rings, the geese . . . oh, God, the kissing geese. *Our* kissing geese.

Frozen in place outside the bathroom door, I realized that even the colored-pencil sketch I'd made back in February was in there, the one I'd hidden for weeks behind the lighthouse picture over the mantel. He would see my enraptured couple clinging to each other's bodies, encircled by the woman's exceedingly long hair. Sometimes when I'd looked at the picture, all I could see was her hair, and I'd remembered Dee teasing me, calling my attic studio Rapunzel's tower, wanting to know when I was going to let my hair down.

Hugh had always grimaced at that, even defended me to her, sometimes snappishly. "Your mother isn't locked in a tower, Dee," he said. "Now, stop it." Maybe he'd thought it was a reflection on him, or maybe somewhere inside he'd known it was true and was afraid of it. None of us ever mentioned the rest of the tale—how Rapunzel did finally let down her hair for the prince and escaped.

Hugh Sullivan was the most astute man on earth. I began to feel a dilating pressure in my chest. I walked to Mike's room and paused in the doorway. Inside, it was dim, lit by one small table lamp with a low-wattage bulb.

Hugh was staring at my underwater couple—*Lovers in the Blue Sea,* I called them, after Chagall's *Lovers in the Red Sky.* His back was to me. His hands were in his pockets. He turned around, parting this night from all other nights, letting his eyes, bruised and disbelieving, come slowly to my face, and I could feel the air around us blaze up with the terrible thing that was about to happen.

"Who is he?" he asked.

CHAPTER
Thirty-one

Whit

He sat in the music-listening room on a ladder-back chair, staring at the television set, which was perched on a table conspicuously covered with an old altar cloth. It was the top of the seventh of a Braves doubleheader on TBS. Tom Glavine had just struck out. Whit took his pencil and traced a small *K* on the scorecard he'd drawn in the back of his journal.

There was something about watching baseball that took him completely out of himself. It worked on him better than meditation. He could never meditate more than two minutes without chasing one thought after another or becoming so self-conscious it defeated the whole purpose, but he could sit in front of a game with absolute absorption. He lost himself in the tension of the play, the strategy, the intricacies of scoring—all the diagrams, symbols, and numbers. He would never have been able to explain to Father Sebastian or any of the others why it was a refuge for him; he just knew he felt exempt sitting here. From the monastery. From himself.

Before vespers the abbot had announced Nelle's latest "tragedy," as he now delicately referred to her amputations, asking the monks to pray for her, their beloved cook and friend. Whit had stood in choir staring stoically ahead, aware of Dominic turning to look at him. He'd thought then how he'd spent all afternoon waiting for Jessie in the rookery to no avail, only to come back and find Dominic pacing the porch of the cottage. He'd been the one to give Whit the news, even the part about Jessie's husband coming from Atlanta to be with her. He'd delivered that portion with scrupulous concern.

Whit had not had the presence of mind to

ask Dominic until later how he'd come to know all this, when he discovered that Hepzibah Postell, the Gullah woman, had come to the monastery and explained everything to Dominic. Why would Hepzibah come to Dominic, of all people?

All through vespers Whit had yearned to come here and turn on the doubleheader and disappear into the game. He'd burst out of his choir stall like a racehorse so he could get the game on before the other monks came herding in for community time.

They inevitably spent it watching the evening news. It mostly boiled down to watching Tom Brokaw announcing Reagan's latest social cutbacks. The last time he'd come in here, they had been watching a segment on how to "dress for success"—something about designer suits by Perry Ellis and Calvin Klein—and the monks had sat there with such rapt attention he'd wanted to stand up and shout, *But you're wearing* robes! The point of their robes was the exact opposite of dressing for success. Surely they saw that. He'd gotten up and left. On weekends Brother Fabian would put one of the monastery's scratchy old 33⅓ rpm records on the stereo, usually Wagner's *The Ring of the Nibelung.* He would turn the volume so loud the air would tremble with the bass.

Tonight, when the monks had arrived to find that Whit had commandeered the TV set and filled it with the announcers' play-by-play, they'd complained to Father Sebastian, who had sovereign jurisdiction over the room. Sebastian had scrutinized Whit before telling the men to stop whining, it wouldn't kill them to miss the news once in a blue moon. They had all left and gone back to their rooms to wait for compline, except for Dominic and Sebastian.

He wanted to be angry at them, to use this as just more justification for leaving, but the sight of the monks shuffling off in various degrees of huff was no different, really, from his own arrogant refusal to be in here when they watched Brokaw or listened to Siegfried and Brünnhilde.

It reminded him suddenly of the whole point of existing here with these curmudgeonly old men—that somewhere on the face of the earth, there needed to be people bound together with irrevocable stamina, figuring out a way to live with one another. He'd come here with such idiotic notions, expecting a slight variation on utopia—everybody loving everybody else, returning good for evil, turning the other cheek left and right. Monks, it'd turned out, were no more perfect than any other group of people. He'd gradually realized with a kind of wonder that they'd been picked for a hidden but noble experiment—to see if people might actually be able to live in genuine relatedness, to see if perhaps God had made a mistake by creating the human species.

He seemed to think constantly these days about what it meant to be at the monastery, to be part of it—the whole outrageous thing. He thought equally about Jessie, what it meant to love her, to be part of her. *That* was outrageous, too. What he'd not thought about was her husband. A real person, a man who'd rushed here to be with his wife at a moment of crisis. What was his name? He forced himself to remember. *Hugh.* Yes, Hugh. It repeated in his mind with the drone of the stadium noise, with Skip Caray and the baseball trivia question.

Hugh was the ruptured place in Whit's conscience, one that had—in a self-protective act—gotten walled off. Even now, after two walks and the bases loaded, when he should have been completely immersed in the game,

Whit could not stop thinking of the man. He could see how Hugh, the very reality of him, had been inside all along, quietly turning to an abscess. The poisonous mess starting to leak.

After the third out, everyone in the stadium stood for the seventh-inning stretch, and he stood up and put his journal down on the chair. He thought of the day he'd told Jessie he loved her. They'd been in the rookery, lying on the blanket.

We'll be damned and saved both, he'd told her. And already it was happening.

He closed his eyes and tried to listen to the song the fans on TV were singing. He'd thought he could blot everything out, calm the anxiety that had begun on the porch with Dominic, but all he wanted now was to bolt and go to her. He felt consumed with the need to pull her into his arms. To claim her again. *Jessie,* he thought. He could barely stand still.

Across the room Dominic sat in an old lounge chair with his hat in his lap. After Whit had confessed to Dominic all those weeks ago that he'd fallen in love, they hadn't spoken of it again. Of course the old monk had to know it was Jessie. Why else would he have pulled Whit aside like that and given him this extra bit of information about her husband's being on the island, staying in Nelle's house with her?

He wanted to concentrate his distress on how upset Jessie must be over her mother, and yet he stood before the television and could not keep himself from imagining her with Hugh. In the kitchen with a glass of wine, the solacing embrace, telling small jokes to break the agony—the myriad ways Hugh might comfort her. He felt frightened by the lifetime of small, secret rituals they must've shared at moments like this, the magnitude of such things.

The man is her husband, he told himself. *For the love of God, he's her* husband.

CHAPTER
Thirty-two

Hugh

His wife stood in her mother's island home in South Carolina and calmly told him the name of her lover. "His name is Brother Thomas," she said.

For a moment Hugh stared at the drops of bathwater sliding along her neck toward the opening of her robe. Her hair was wet and plastered back from her face. He watched how she took a sharp breath with her mouth open and let her gaze drop.

They were in the doorway of her brother's old room, and he reached out and placed his hands on the doorjamb. He watched her without any pain at all, stood protected and benumbed in the last seconds of a dying illusion, the truth flying toward him with the speed of an arrow, but not yet there. It allowed him to see her one last time before the tip gashed into him and everything changed. What he thought standing there was how beautiful she looked with the bathwater still netted on her skin, running in drops between her breasts. *How beautiful.*

His name is Brother Thomas.

She had said it with complete candor and matter-of-factness as if she were telling him the name of her dentist.

Then it slammed into him—more pain than he'd known in his life. It rocked him backward on his heels, as if there had been a blast of wind. He went on holding the sides of the door, wondering if he might be having an attack of angina. The power of the feeling was crushing.

He stepped back, engulfed suddenly with fury. He wanted to smash his fist into the wall. Instead he waited for her to raise her eyes to his face again. "Brother Thomas," he said with lacerating calm. "Is that what you call him when you're fucking him?"

"Hugh," she said. It came out broken and splintered. It sounded pleading in a way that enraged him even more.

He could tell she had shocked herself with the admission; her eyes seemed dazed and frantic. Stumbling toward him, reaching out to grab his arm, she looked like a scalded animal trying to understand what had happened to it.

When her hand found his arm, he wrenched it out of her grasp.

"Get away," he said through his teeth.

He watched her back out of the room, her lips moving with no words coming out and her eyes wide. He slammed the door and locked it. She stood outside.

"Hugh, open the door. Please, Hugh."

There was scarcely any light in the room, and he'd stared at the back of the door, at the shadows running across it like pieces of wire and black vines. He wanted to wound her with his silence. Later, though, it occurred to him that he may have wanted to protect her, too, from the pulverizing things he could have said.

She went on calling him for an unbearable amount of time. When she finally left, tears shot up behind his eyes. He sat on one of the twin beds, trying to choke down the urge to cry. He wouldn't have Jessie hearing him cry. He needed to get hold of himself. The force of his anger had started to frighten him. He had an overwhelming need to go to the monastery and find the man. He wanted to take him by the throat and pin him to the wall of the church.

He stayed in the dark little room like that for hours. In the beginning he was gripped by repeated convulsions of anguish, by an actual trembling in his limbs. After that subsided, he was able to think.

When he'd asked Jessie the question— *Who is he?*—he hadn't really believed there was anyone else. Not really.

The possibility that there could be another man had come to him in a flash of intuition as he'd looked at her paintings. He'd been shocked by them, by their highly charged eroticism, by the depth of the plunge the woman in them was taking. It had been like looking at a death—Jessie's death. Her previous life, all the old adaptations and roles, were breaking away and rising to the surface while the woman kept going deeper and deeper. He'd stood there confused, puzzled by what she might be plunging toward. And then he'd seen the sketch of the two lovers embracing at the bottom of the ocean. The flash had come instantly. It had struck him to the heart.

The couple at the bottom of the ocean. That place where you have gone as far as you can go. When he'd first seen the image and the crazy idea had seized him, he'd stood there for several minutes, then thought, *No.* It was preposterous to think Jessie capable of that. *Preposterous.* He'd always trusted her. Without question.

But it explained so much. Her uncommunicative behavior almost from the moment she'd gotten to Egret Island. The strange abruptness of her wanting time apart from him, her inability to articulate any real reason for it. She'd been aloof even before departing Atlanta, depressed about Dee's leaving for college, questioning herself, her life.

And so he'd asked the question. It had just come out. *Who is he?*

It occurred to him that Jessie had answered him truthfully, not only because she wanted to end her deceit but because she wanted to force something to happen. Realizing this, he felt a vibration of panic in his chest. *Could it be this was not a casual affair? Did she actually love this man?* He spread his hand across his chest and pressed hard against the sick, betrayed feeling.

He began to feel emptied out. A deep-boned sadness. On and off during the night, he lay down and tried to sleep, but it was useless to try, and each time he would get up again and pace beside Jessie's paintings, which sat on the floor leaning against the opposite twin bed.

Through the small window, he could see the sky lightening slightly, black turning to gray, that smoked look that comes before dawn, and for the hundredth time he looked at his watch. There was no way off the island until the first ferry run at nine, but he knew that the moment it was light enough, he would leave the house.

When he stepped into the hallway, it was not yet six. He carried his suitcase to the living room and set it down, then wandered back to Jessie's room.

Her door was closed, and he simply opened it and walked in. She was sleeping the way he'd seen her sleep for twenty years, on her right side with her hair spread behind her on the pillow and her hand tucked under her cheek. The windowpanes were silver. Daylight had just begun to seep in. He stood there and watched her, studying the gray in her hair, the saliva gathered in the corners of her open mouth, the soft grating breath that was almost but not quite a snore, and all these things had made him want to lie down beside her.

Her wedding rings were gone from her finger. He found them on a velvet pincushion on top of the dresser, circled around a straight pin. He touched them with his finger, thinking of the geese in her painting, how she'd jettisoned them to the surface.

He twisted his gold band off his finger and placed it on top of the diamond engagement ring and platinum band he'd given her so long ago.

Nine days later, back home in Atlanta, he still felt the same hopelessness that had come over him that night.

For the last twenty minutes, the patient seated in his office had been talking about the death of her eighteen-year-old dachshund, Abercrombie, alternately recounting stories of his life and crying. He'd let her go on and on about the dog because today it was just easier, and he suspected she wasn't crying for the dog anyway but for her brother who'd died three months earlier after years of estrangement and for whom she'd cried not a tear.

The woman pulled the last tissue from the box beside her and held out the empty carton to him like a child needing her glass refilled. He got up from his leather armchair and pulled more tissues from the louvered cabinet beneath the bookshelf, then sat down again, forcing his mind off Jessie and onto his patient's dissociated feelings.

It had been like this since he'd returned, this painful inability to concentrate. One moment he would be listening to his patient and the next he was back at that moment—Jessie announcing the name Brother Thomas.

"I don't know what else I could've done," his patient said, sitting on the sofa with her legs tucked under her. "Abercrombie's arthritis was getting so bad he couldn't walk, and he was on so many steroids already. I mean, really, what else could I have done?"

"I'm sure you did the right thing by putting him down," Hugh told her, which prompted her to begin crying again.

He watched her bent head bobbing up and down in her hands, and castigated himself for sitting in the room with her and not being present, for hearing everything she said and not listening to any of it.

His mind wandered, and he was standing once more before the picture Jessie had made with colored pencils. The man was a monk. This was not as shocking as the thought of Jessie, his Jessie, having an affair, but it was still stunning to him. She had wanted him to know; otherwise she would've simply answered by saying "Thomas." He couldn't imagine why she'd added "Brother" unless there was an unconscious message in it somewhere. What? Did she want him to know how much this man would have to give up to be with her?

Since returning, he'd felt his life continually imploding, the emptiness welling up like the immense reaches of space. Two nights ago he'd dreamed he was an astronaut making a space walk, tethered to the space shuttle by a cord that had suddenly snapped. He had simply drifted off into an abyss of darkness, watching his craft grow smaller and smaller until it was a speck of white in the silence.

His hatred for the man Jessie had been

with would come over him with torrential suddenness. He would picture the two of them—how the man would touch her in places that had belonged only to him, breathing into her hair. How many times had they done it? Where? He had wakened once in a drenching sweat, wondering if they were having sex right then, at that very moment.

It had been humbling to discover his capacity for violence and revenge. He'd acknowledged this, like all good analysts, in a theoretical way while studying Jung's concept of the personal and collective shadow, but he knew it now as a living reality. He had stopped envisioning himself going to the monastery and taking the man by the throat, but he did not deny there were moments he wanted the monk to choke and bleed.

He would never act on it, of course, but even the wanting to, the needing to, expelled cherished notions he'd held about himself. He was not special. He was not entitled. His goodness, his enlightenment, did not set him apart. He was like all the rest, carrying around the same huge quantities of darkness.

The knowledge of this had driven him down into his own humanity. Once in a while, when he was capable of seeing himself as more than the pain he felt, he'd hoped his suffering was not being squandered, that somewhere inside it was making him pliant and tender.

The woman across the room from him, he realized, was explaining the details of her dog's death.

"He was in such pain—just to pick him up made him yelp—so the vet came to the car to give him the shot. Abercrombie was lying on the backseat, and when he saw Dr. Yarborough, do you know what he did?"

Hugh shook his head.

"He looked up at him and wagged his tail. Can you *believe* that?"

Yes, Hugh thought. He could believe that.

When Jessie had called him that Sunday and asked him to come, he'd gone just like the damn stupid dog—wagging his tail. He'd thought he was going to a reconciliation. He'd thought whatever had come over her had run its course.

It had been easy to see how much she'd changed. She'd looked tired and frazzled from the ordeal with Nelle, but underneath he'd sensed aliveness. There was an unmistakable independence taking hold, a self-containment that hadn't been there before. He'd seen how her paintings had changed, too, exploding out of their little boxes, becoming bold excerpts of the mystifying process she was in.

In the past so much of her had been invisible to him. Looking at her in the hospital waiting room, after being apart from her for so long, he'd been able to see her again.

How often did we do that, he wondered— look at someone and fail to see what's really there? Why had it been so hard to look at his wife and understand his need for her, the way his life was held in the accumulation of moments they'd shared?

He looked at the woman in front of him and tried for a second to see her. She was telling him now about the pet cemetery.

He touched the odd little bracelet on his wrist.

The last time Dee had phoned had been his birthday. "When is Mom coming home?" she'd asked.

He'd paused. Too long.

"Something's wrong, isn't it? She's been there forever."

"I won't lie to you, honey. We're having a few problems," he'd told his daughter. "But nothing that serious, okay? Every marriage has them. We'll work it out."

Five days later the bracelet had arrived. She'd made it herself.

He didn't know what to tell Dee now. He didn't know what to tell himself.

He looked at the clock in the office, just over the woman's head. He dreaded the end of the day. At night Jessie's paintings haunted him, waking him up. He would sit on the side of the bed remembering how the colors had grown fiercer the farther the woman went.

Last night, desperate to alleviate his anguish, he'd tried to look at what Jessie had done not as a husband but as a psychiatrist. The impulse was ludicrous, but the analytical thinking had given him a hallowed hour or two of distance from his torment. It had aerated his emotions, generated a measure of perspective. He was grateful for every small mercy.

What he'd done was go to his study and flip around in various books, reading and jotting notes. Over and over he'd come across the same idea—not the least bit unfamiliar to him—that when a person was in need of cataclysmic change, of a whole new center in the personality, for instance, his or her psyche would induce an infatuation, an erotic attachment, an intense falling-in-love.

He knew this. Every analyst knew it. Falling in love was the oldest, most ruthless catalyst on earth.

But typically you fell in love with something missing in yourself that you recognized in the other person, yet he couldn't grasp what Jessie had seen in this supposedly spiritual man that could capture her so profoundly.

After almost an hour of this kind of thing, he'd shoved his notes back in the drawer and returned to bed. It had suddenly felt like a lot of abstract drivel. He didn't want to apply any of it to Jessie. He didn't want to bring the grace of understanding into it. Her reasons were unforgivable, no matter how powerful they were.

His wife had been with another man. She had betrayed him, and even if she came to him begging, he didn't know if he could ever take her back.

"Dr. Sullivan?" his patient said.

He had pivoted away from her toward the window, his elbow on the chair arm, his chin on his fist, and was staring at the outline of the Bradford pear tree flowering profusely against the pane. His eyes were burning with tears.

Turning toward the woman, he felt intense embarrassment. She handed him the tissue box she'd been cradling, and he took one and awkwardly dabbed at his eyes. "I'm sorry," he said. He shook his head, astonished at himself.

"No, please," she said, crossing her hands one on top of the other at her neck. "Don't apologize. I'm . . . I'm touched."

She thought his tears were for her. For her dachshund. She was smiling at him, awestruck by his godlike heart. He didn't know how to tell her his emotion had nothing to do with her, that in fact he was being the worst possible psychiatrist at the moment.

"We all fail one another," he said.

The woman's eyes widened as she cast around for his meaning.

"I have failed my wife," he added.

Jessie had failed him, yes, horribly, but he'd failed her, too. He had carelessly glossed over her. He had not given her the small kindness of letting her grow into herself.

"I have failed . . . people," the woman said,

as if he were trying out an innovative new approach, and she was joining in.

"You mean your brother?" he said gently, and heard the sob break loose in her and fill the room.

CHAPTER
Thirty-three

I brought Mother home from the hospital on St. Senara's Day, Saturday, April 30, a day flooded with brightness.

After thirteen days in the hospital, Mother had made enough progress to come home, which seemed to mean she was medicated enough not to hurt herself again. According to the nurse, she'd been pleasant without exhibiting aberrant behavior but had refused to open up. "These things take time," the nurse had explained, then given me a slightly patronizing talk on the importance of Mother's coming back weekly to see her psychiatrist and faithfully swallowing her pills.

As I boarded the ferry early that morning, preparations for St. Senara's Day were already under way. One of the monks was on all fours at the edge of the dock laying out a rectangle of coral-colored carpet on which the mermaid chair would sit after its winding procession from the abbey. When I was a girl, the carpet had invariably been red, though one year it had turned up pink and fringed, with the suspicious look of a bath mat, which set off a small controversy.

A folding table had been set up, and Shem's wife, Mary Eva, was setting out boxes of Mermaid Tears, which would be thrown into the sea during the ceremony.

Crossing the bay, I thought of the Mermaid Tears I'd kept on top of the crab trap in Whit's hermitage. I hadn't been out there since Mother had gone to the hospital, nor had I seen Whit—not once in two weeks. I'd sent him a note, passed along by Kat, explaining I would be spending my days at the hospital with Mother and wouldn't be able to see him for a while.

He had not sent a note back. He had not walked to the edge of Mother's backyard and looked over the brick wall and called me out of the house. I was there alone each night, and he didn't come. Maybe he suspected that my note didn't tell the whole story. Perhaps he'd detected the sadness beneath my words.

The morning after I'd confessed my affair to Hugh, I'd found his wedding ring on the pincushion along with mine, and no trace of him in the house. I'd rushed out, wanting to catch him at the ferry dock before he left the island, but by the time I reached the slave cemetery, I thought better of it. I remembered the way he'd recoiled, almost violently, when I'd reached for him, the rage in his voice when he'd told me to get away. He had said it with his teeth clenched. His eyes had looked so pained, so shocked, I did not recognize him. It seemed now I could at least spare him the fresh sight of me. I could do that much for him. Depression had descended then like a great fatigue, and I'd sat down beside the graves and watched a dove scratch the dirt, making small, neglected sounds that were heartbreaking to me. It was as if someone had suddenly handed me a huge stone, the weight of all the suffering I'd caused, and said, *Here, you must carry this now.*

So I had. These thirteen days.

It is still hard for me to understand, much less explain, the descent that comes with necessary loss, how requisite it is. It came to me like the darkening of the day.

It wasn't that I rued what I'd done, that I wanted a reversal of some kind; I would not have taken back the way my loving Whit had impregnated me with life, with myself, the hundred ways I'd been broken and made larger. It's that I *saw* the effect of it. I saw it in the immortal hurt in Hugh's eyes, in the bracelet Dee had woven for him, in the unbearable ceremony our rings were performing on the pincushion.

Each morning I'd left the island and returned in the late afternoon. I'd sat with Mother in what they called the dayroom. With its television and sofas and strange, shuffling people, it had reminded me of Dante's *Purgatorio,* which I'd read in school. The only part of the story I remembered was the inhabitants lugging huge stones around a mountain.

I'd watched the medicines make Mother docile, watched everything from a place of fallowness and grief, always going back to the moment when Hugh saw through it all and posed his question. It stupefied me daily that I'd answered him without hesitation, using Whit's monk name. As if underscoring his spiritual credentials. As if that somehow made what we were doing loftier.

Mother had sat each day with her body slackened on the chair, moving her fingers around the Rubik's Cube that I'd brought her from home. She'd asked me so many times about her finger I'd finally brought that, too. I'd washed it under the faucet one night, forcing myself to hold the lost piece of her in my palm and scrub the bloodstains. I'd brought it to her in a mason jar, submerged in rubbing alcohol so it wouldn't putrefy. I'd gotten permission for her to keep it in her room, but just in case, I'd written DO NOT THROW AWAY on the side of the jar.

In the evenings I'd given progress reports to Kat and Hepzibah on the phone, warmed soup from the cans in the pantry, and listened to the endless soliloquy of sadness and blame that went on and on inside me. Whenever I thought of Whit, I'd longed to be with him, but I didn't know anymore whether my wanting came from love or the simple need to be comforted.

Despite that, I couldn't let myself be with him yet. It seemed perverse to make love with him given the freshness of the pain Hugh was in, that we were both in. No doubt it was illogical, but I felt I was abstaining out of respect for the death of my marriage.

Mother seemed excited as we left the hospital that afternoon. Inside the rental car, she pulled down the sun visor and dragged a comb through her white hair, then astonished me by dabbing on her old fire-engine red lipstick. She blotted her lips on a gas receipt she found on the seat. It was a gesture of such normalcy that I smiled at her. "You look nice," I said, worried for a moment that she might respond by wiping the color off her lips, but she'd smiled back.

The ferry was crammed with tourists; not even standing room was left. Mother clutched the jar that held her finger like a child bringing a goldfish home from the store. I had wrapped it in a paper towel fastened with a rubber band, but she still got a few curious looks from the passengers.

As we got closer, I could see the line of shrimp trawlers already forming on the southeast side of the island, out on the Atlantic. "It's St. Senara's Day," I said to Mother.

"You think I don't know that?" she snapped.

She had not gone to the festivities since Dad died. As she had with the All-Girls Picnics, she'd simply eradicated them from her life. Her abolishing this one, however, had genuinely puzzled me. Senara was, after all, *her* saint.

Kat met us at the dock, smelling like the lavender lotion she used. Not Benne, just Kat. She kissed Mother on the cheek.

I hadn't expected her.

Mother inspected the dock, the boxes of Mermaid Tears, as well as a small table from the monastery with a silver cruet on top—the one used year after year to splash seawater across the mermaid chair. I watched her eyes search for the coral carpet at the dock's edge. Max was stretched out on it as if the rug had been put there specifically for him.

She stared at the wedge of carpet with something like revulsion in her face, and I imagined she was picturing the mermaid chair sitting on top of it.

"Let's take a walk," Kat said, grasping Mother by the arm. "You, too, Jessie."

She whisked Mother across the dock, down to the sidewalk where I'd left the golf cart. I was about to slide behind the wheel, but Kat guided Mother on past it. I set her suitcase down on the seat and followed.

I remember being aware of a small passing dread and pushing it aside. I didn't ask where we were going; I think I was under the impression Kat wanted to distract Mother from the moment on the dock when she'd seen the rug. I trailed behind them, along the row of shops, past Caw Caw General and the Island Dog B&B, listening to Kat ply Mother with harmless questions. The smell of fried shrimp coming from Max's Café was so thick the air felt oily.

I checked my watch. It was five in the afternoon, the light slumping, the clouds veined with red. The day was taking on the first bloodshot look of sunset. The festivities would begin at six, when every monk and islander who could walk would come pouring onto the dock behind the mermaid chair. Leading the parade, the abbot would be decked out in chasuble and stole and carrying his crosier. And somewhere in all that hoopla would be Whit.

Beneath the striped awning of the Mermaid's Tale, Kat paused and, using her key, opened the door. The sign in the window said CLOSED. Absurd as this sounds, not even then did it cross my mind that our stroll might have some purpose other than diverting Mother from whatever horrible old memory had settled over her back on the dock.

Stepping inside the shop behind them, listening to the sounds on the street seep away, I noticed Hepzibah, Shem, and Father Dominic standing at the rear of the store near the cash register. Back there with the boat-wreck picture I'd painted when I was eleven—the flames beneath the water, all the happy sea creatures. Dominic was not wearing his robe or his hat, but instead a suit with his priest's collar. Shem, flushed and constrained looking, had his arms folded across his barrel of a chest and his hands stuck under his armpits, as if someone had forced him here at gunpoint.

Apparently catching sight of them at the same moment as I, Mother stopped in the middle of the store. She stood paralyzed, surrounded by Kat's great convocation of mermaids. They hung over her from the ceiling in the form of aluminum wind chimes and flanked her on all sides in an array of ceramic sculptures, necklaces, soap carvings, candles, and beach towels. I watched her begin to take small steps backward across the floor.

Hepzibah hurried toward her with a funny mixture of determination and reluctance in her face, that look of moving toward what *must* be done. She lassoed Mother with both her arms, stopping her in her tracks. "It's going to be all right, Nelle. I promise you. We're just going to have a talk, okay?"

Even now that image never leaves me— Mother standing in the dark circle of Hepzibah's arms not moving a muscle, clasping her jar with excruciating stillness.

There were two sharp clicks, and I realized Kat had locked the door behind us. I swung around to her then. "For heaven's sake. What's all this *about?*"

Groping for my hands, Kat held them tightly in front of her. "I'm sorry, Jessie," she said. "I haven't been honest with you. I'm an obstinate, know-it-all, damn idiot of a woman who thought I was doing the right thing, and I guess what I've done is to make it worse."

I drew my head back slightly, taking in her face. It had the look of ice about to break. Her eyes were tightened, her mouth hitched to the side to keep from crying, and I knew what it must've taken for her to say these

words. I felt myself bracing for what lay behind them.

"It's just . . . I swear to you, I didn't think
Nelle was as bad off as she was."

"But why are we *here?*"

"The day we were up there in the hospital
waiting room, I realized if I didn't at least try
to get everything out in the open, Nelle was
going to end up bleeding to death one night.
If re-membering is what she needs, like you
and Hugh said, then okay, by God, we're going to sit here and remember."

My mind spun. It was slowly dawning on
me: Kat, Hepzibah, Dominic, Shem—all of
them knew. They knew the reason Mother
had mutilated herself, why my father's death
had more or less ended my mother's life,
too. Even why his pipe was buried in her
drawer and not in the ocean. These things
had been like hibernating cicadas that live in
the ground for seventeen years and then
one day, when the circadian wheel turns, all
come crawling up into the light of day.

I glanced back at Dominic, who met my
gaze, lifting the sides of his mouth in a tem-
pered smile, trying to reassure me.

They'd known for thirty-three years. When
I was a little girl and had painted the boat

wreck, when I'd gathered roses in the monastery garden and scattered them like my father's ashes across the island. Every time I'd come back to visit, they had known.

Hepzibah had settled Mother into one of the folding chairs near the counter. The jar, I noticed, had been tugged away from her and stood between the cash register and a display of sugarless gum. Mother sat with what struck me as remarkable resignation.

Hepzibah had not worn any kind of headdress today, but had done her hair in cornrows. I stared at her a moment as she worked a finger along the little hedges, her other hand patting Mother's arm. The last time I'd sat over there, Kat, Hepzibah, and Benne had been eating butter pecan ice cream.

Standing at the door next to Kat, I considered for the first time that what they were doing—this so-called *remembering,* as Kat had put it—might not be good for Mother. I couldn't believe that I, of all people, was thinking this, after everything I'd had to say, but what if the truth overwhelmed her, caused her to break down again, to curl up in a ball on the floor?

I leaned over to Kat, keeping my voice

low. "I want Mother to confront things as much as anyone does, but is *this* the right way to go about it? I mean, she just got out of the hospital."

"I called Hugh this morning," Kat said.

"Hugh?" I said his name and felt it magnify in the room, the way it sucked up the air.

"I wouldn't be doing this if he hadn't said it was okay," she assured me. "Actually, he seemed to think it was a fairly brilliant idea."

"Really?" I acted surprised, but I could easily see how he would rally behind this: loving friends gathering around Mother, helping her confront the thing that was slowly destroying her.

Kat said, "Hugh suggested we just talk with her like friends, not push her too much. She has to be the one to say it."

It. "And did you explain to him what 'it' was?" I asked.

She looked away from me. "I told him everything."

"Oh. But you couldn't tell *me?*" My voice was filled with exasperation and anger. "You have to ambush me along with Mother?"

She shook her head, making the wisps of her hair float around her face. I could hear the others across the room murmuring in the quiet.

"I don't blame you for being angry," Kat said, her testiness back. "Okay, I deserve it. I do believe we've settled that. But do me a favor and do *not* call this an ambush. Whether you want to believe it or not, it comes out of love for Nelle and nothing else." She stood there gesticulating, small and tough, and I did not doubt she loved my mother, that she had carried around my mother's misery these last thirty-three years as if it somehow belonged to her, too.

"It was *you* who convinced me we all needed to talk about this," she railed. "Plus Nelle up there in a hospital bed with one more finger chopped off. I would've told you about it sooner, but it took me until last night to work it all out in my head. I didn't know if I could go through with it till this morning."

I took a breath, feeling myself give way, annoyed she had turned to Hugh, but relieved at the same time.

Kat began to unruffle herself. "Hugh said Nelle was stabilized on medicine now and that even her doctor thinks she's ready to go back and look at what started everything."

So, I thought, Hugh had stayed in touch with Nelle's doctor.

Kat and I went over and sat down—me next to Mother, while Shem and Dominic took the last two chairs.

"I didn't know anything about this," I told Mother.

"If you don't hate me already, you will," she responded.

"Nobody is going to hate anybody," Kat said. "I realize getting you here wasn't the most straightforward thing in the world, but the fact is, we need to do this."

Mother stared into her palms, cupped like small basins on each of her knees.

"Look. I stopped at your house and got your rosary," Kat said. She reached in her pocket, drew out the red beads, and coiled them into Mother's good hand.

She closed her fingers around them. "What do you want me to do?"

"Just try to put what happened with Joe into words," Dominic told her.

We waited.

My heart began to beat convulsively. I didn't want to know. I'd more or less pushed everyone into this, and now I felt undone at the thought of what "it" might be.

If you don't hate me already, you will.

Mother turned her head and looked at me, and it was like staring into a dark hatchway, so much black sorrow below.

"I'm not going to hate you," I said. "You need to talk about it. Whatever it is."

I could see the chinks in her resistance. We all could. We sat there avoiding one another's eyes. The silence turned oceanic. Outside, the St. Senara crowd that had come over on the ferry was beginning to line the sidewalk to wait for the mermaid chair. I could see a cluster of them through the plate-glass window at the front. Imagining them out there doing the ordinary things people did—window-shopping, licking snow cones, lifting their children onto their shoulders, these acts of daily grace—filled me with the ache one has for such seeming insignificance only when it goes missing. I wanted everything to be ordinary again. To walk around with the glorious nonchalance reserved for oblivious people.

"Your father, he was ill," Mother said, the words spit into the middle of us like the hard bitter pit of some fruit she'd been eating.

She paused and looked toward the door.

"Nelle," Dominic said. "Go ahead and say

it. We'll all be the better for it. Do it for your-self. And for Jessie. Do it for our blessed St. Senara."

Immediately the room filled with brilliance. It was only the sun dropping through fath-oms of sky, hitting the window and bombard-ing us with light beams, but in that way of magical thinking, it seemed as if Senara had lifted her hand to bless Dominic's words, causing light to rise and scatter. Mother crossed herself.

"It was the same disease *his* father had," she said. She was resolved now; it was hard-ened in her eyes. "It's called Pick's disease."

She stared at the hardwood planks on the floor as if directing her story to them, but clearly she was talking to me. "When he was a little boy, Joe watched his own father—your grandfather—grow senile and die with it. Back then, though, they just called it de-mentia. It wasn't till Joe got diagnosed with it that they realized what kind of dementia his father probably had."

I shut my eyes. *Pick's disease.* I'd never even heard of it. I could feel the groundswell, the whirling up of grief. In my mind I saw Bone Yard Beach with gale winds surging off the water and ripping into the dunes, knowing that it would rearrange the island into new contours.

"When we first met, Joe told me about his father, how the disease destroyed his brain." She spoke in a halting, heavy way, each word laid down like a brick she was trying to lift and place just right. "But I don't think it ever entered his mind that he could get it; there's just the smallest tendency for it to run in families. He just talked about how there wasn't a cure, that kind of thing."

She crossed herself again. Tears were beading up in the gray floss of her lashes. She said, "One time his father got him mixed up with a boy he'd known growing up. It nearly killed Joe. Later his father couldn't place him at all. The disease completely ate his memory. That's how Joe always put it, like it was devouring his father from the inside out. It got where he couldn't talk right, and the spit would run out of his mouth. At the end Joe's mother was always mopping his chin, and finally she put a bib on him."

She was leaning forward in her chair, her words suddenly pouring out in a turbulent stream. It seemed that finding a crack, the force of the story had thrown the door wide open.

"In the beginning he said it was mostly his father's personality that started changing. He did things, real odd things. He'd shout at people on the street for no good reason or blurt out something crazy. A lot of times, it would be something lewd. Like he'd lost all his inhibitions. But the part that got stuck the worst in Joe's head was the day his father knocked him onto the floor. When he saw what he'd done, he started crying, 'I'm sorry, little boy, I'm sorry.' Like he didn't know who he was. Joe broke down every time he remembered it. I think it was a relief when his father finally died. He was ten years old. And his father just forty-eight."

Her eyes looked shrunken, tiny almonds in her face. The big crucifix on the end of the rosary hung off the edge of her lap, swaying slightly as she worked the beads with her fingers in the accomplished way of old nuns.

Hepzibah reached over and patted her arm, her hands, the lumps and dough of her skin, wanting, it seemed, to mold her back together. "Go on, tell the rest, Nelle."

Mother wiped at her eyes. "Joe came to me one day and said he was sure he had his father's disease. He'd been out in the boat, and when he'd tried to throw out the anchor line, he couldn't remember where he kept it or even how to say the words *anchor line* in his head. He was so confused he came straight back to the dock afraid he'd forget where *that* was. I can still see his face when he walked through the kitchen door, how pale and scared it was. He said, 'God help me, Nelle, I have the disease.' He knew it, and I think I did, too. There'd been other signs—little things slipping his mind, plus he'd been losing his temper over nothing and just not thinking straight. A few months later the doctors in Charleston told us what we already knew."

She did not look at us. She made a little altar of the floor, of the light shafts, of the granules of dust illuminated inside them, and concentrated her eyes upon it.

"Your father did not want to forget your name," she said, and I could hear the desperation in her voice, the ragged way it sounded in her throat. "He did not want to forget Mike's name either, but it was *your* name, Jessie, that he would wake up shouting. Sometimes he would bolt out of his sleep crying, 'I'm sorry, little girl! I'm sorry!' " She rocked her body back and forth, and I knew in my bones that's what she must've done when he woke like that—taken him in her arms and rocked back and forth with him.

I couldn't bear watching her. My mind went to the time I found my mother and father in the kitchen dancing without music. They had poured so much love on each other.

"I told him a thousand times, 'You *won't* forget your children's names; I won't let you. God will cure you.'" She had begun twisting the rosary in her hands. I slid forward and reached out to touch her. I wanted my mother. I wanted to bend over and kiss her the way a mother kisses her injured child. My love for her was such a rubble.

The rosary fell onto the floor. She began talking to my father as if he were sitting in the room with us. "Don't ask me to do this, Joe. Please, don't ask me. I'll walk on my knees across the island if I have to. I won't eat. I'll sleep on the floor, on the dirty ground. I'll *make* God hear me. *Jesus and Mary.* Don't ask me to do this. It would be damnation for us."

Her face was blazing.

The light on the floor had disappeared as if it had boiled away. Mother stared at the darkness rising around our feet, the quiet way the shadows pooled out from under the chairs.

Kat reached down and picked up the rosary. None of us said a word. I had the blurred, disoriented feeling of floating, waving like an eel in the ocean. I could grasp nothing. What was she trying to say?

I believe, though, part of me knew. I began pulling air down the chute of my throat, into my lungs, like stuffing cotton batting into a pillow that would soon absorb an unthinkable blow.

Mother turned slowly to face me. "He wouldn't listen to me. Every time I refused to do it, he smiled and said, 'Nelle, it'll be okay. God won't blame you. Why, it's God's tender mercy you'll be dispensing. Let me have my dignity. Let me go the way I need to.' "

I understood then.

I think I must have made a sound, a moan. It caused them all to turn and stare at me. Even Mother. I felt awe at the sight of her.

"I shouldn't have listened to him," Mother said. "Why did I listen to him?"

Dominic's eyelids were opening and closing repeatedly, and all I could think was how thin they seemed, two bluish white films.

I sat in amazement, the translucence that

comes when life hardens into a bead of such cruel perfection you see it with the purest clarity. Everything suddenly there—life as it truly is, enormous, appalling, devastating. You see the great sinkholes it makes in people and the harrowing lengths to which love will go to fill them.

Mother had started to sob. Her head drooped toward her chest, heaving up and down with her shoulders. I reached for her hand, because it was there and it had to be taken. Because I both loved and hated her for what she'd done, but mostly I pitied her.

Her hand was leaden and damp. I touched the veins twisting toward her knuckles. "You did the only thing you could," I said. It was all I could manage—this concession, this forbearance.

I wasn't sure if she would tell me how she did it, whether I wanted to know.

I began to feel the first traces of relief. I looked at Dominic silently moving his lips and thought it was a prayer of thanksgiving that Mother's surrender to the past was finally over. I believed that as ghastly as the truth was, it was at least *out.* I believed it could not get worse. These were my mistakes.

Hepzibah brought Mother a glass of water. We watched solemnly as she found her composure and drank it, the sound of her swallowing exaggerated in the silence. A picture came into my mind: rummaging through her dresser drawer, finding the pipe.

"It wasn't the pipe that caused it," I said to her. "It was never the pipe."

"No," she said. The skin on her face was rubbery and pouched, like small, deflated balloons beneath her eyes. There was an expression in her eyes, though—the empty calm that follows catharsis.

"Do you know what dead finger is, Jessie?" said Kat.

I turned to her, startled. *"What?"* I sat there stupidly thinking she must be referring to Mother's finger in the jar on the counter. The room was utterly still.

"Dead finger," she repeated. She said it with softness, with kindness. "It's a plant. It's from the nightshade family." She looked at me quizzically to see if I grasped her meaning. "It's very poisonous," she added.

I understood instantly—my father had died from ingesting some kind of toxic plant.

I stood up, shaking my head. How do you

suddenly revise images and understandings you've carried in the cells of your body for thirty-three years?

I walked to the counter and leaned on the worn wood, lowering my head into my hands. "Dead finger," I said, realizing the name had started all Mother's warped reasons for mutilating herself.

Hepzibah came and stood beside me. She touched my shoulder. "It used to grow around the slave cemetery. It still crops up sometimes if I'm not careful. It's a shrub with fuzzy leaves and grayish white blossoms shaped like fingers, and it has a terrible rotting odor. You've probably seen it on the island."

"No," I said, still cradling my head, not wanting to picture it.

"It's more merciful than other nightshades. Back in the forties and fifties, people here used it to put their pets out of their misery. Your father died peacefully, Jessie. He fell asleep, and he didn't wake up."

I turned around to Mother, who appeared tranquil but spent. "How did you know what to do? I didn't think you knew anything about plants."

She didn't answer. What she did was to look at Kat and then at Hepzibah.

They had been part of it, too.

"You helped her," I said, looking from one to the other.

Kat glanced at the floor, then back at me. "We did it because your father asked us. He came to each one of us—to Shem and Dominic, too—begging our help the same way he did your mother's. We loved Joe. We would've done anything for him, but none of us arrived at this easily."

I looked at Dominic, confused. Why would my father make *him* part of this? Kat and Hepzibah, I understood. They were devoted to Mother, and Dad would've known how much she would need them afterward. Shem had been his best friend. But Dominic . . .

He read my expression. "Come, sit down," Dominic told me, and waited while I went and lowered myself into the chair. "Joe came to me one day and said he was going to die, that it would be a long, horrible death and he couldn't put himself through it, much less his family. He said he would like to leave this life sitting in the mermaid chair. He wanted to sit in the holiest spot on the island, surrounded by his wife and his friends."

Dominic couldn't have said anything in the world that would've surprised me more—or at the same time seemed more natural, truer to my father.

"Your father was a charming man," he said. "He had what I would call an imaginative sense of humor, and he used it even then. He told me with a grin that God once sent real live mermaids to his boat, which, he pointed out, was surely a sign that when he died, he should be sitting in the chair holding on to them. But mostly what he wanted was—" Dominic looked at Mother. "He wanted to sit in the chair because it needed to be a holy place for Nelle's sake. I was supposed to be the officiant—you know, preside over his dying, give him last rites, then absolve Nelle and the rest of us. I told him no at first. I was the last holdout."

I was still trying to reconfigure my father's dying—change the pictures, the accompanying feelings. I tried to imagine him sitting in the mermaid chair, staring into Mother's face, slowly slipping into a coma. Had I been asleep in my bed while all of this happened? Had he come to my room to say good-bye? A fragment of memory hung in my head like a little green fruit that had never ripened: opening my eyes, seeing him standing by my bed. The whirly girl he'd peeled for me

earlier that evening sat browning on my bedside table, and I watched him reach out and
touch it with his fingers.

"Daddy?" My voice was woozy with sleep.

"Shhh," he said. "It's okay."

He knelt on the floor and sliding his arm
under my shoulders, held me against his
chest, my cheek crushed against the rough
nap of his corduroy shirt. He smelled of pipe
tobacco and apples.

"Jessie," he said. "My little Whirly Girl."

I was sure I heard the soft sound of his
crying. He sang my name over and over, soft
against my ear, before lowering me back to
my pillow, back into the fuzzy world of my
dreams.

I'd always known these things had taken
place. As a child, every time I'd sung my
name across the empty marsh I'd known. I'd
just never understood until now that they'd
happened on the night he died.

I was holding the sides of my chair. I was
trying to keep myself there.

"Why did you change your mind?" I asked
Dominic.

"Joe was determined," he said. "And not
just charming but shrewd. He let me know
he was going to take his life whether I

helped or not, but that it would be so much better for Nelle if I did. I realized I could either stand on dogma and turn my back or I could take something terrible and inevitable and bestow a little mercy on it. I decided to try to help the situation."

I started to say the obvious, that gathering around a holy relic, and Dominic's absolution of Mother, hadn't helped her much in the end, but how did I know? Maybe it had kept her saner than she would've been otherwise.

"The boat," I said. "Was he even on it?"

Shem, who'd not said a word since we'd sat down, looked up at me with red-rimmed eyes. "He was on it. I took him to his boat myself—that old Chris-Craft of his—and laid him inside it. It was tied up at my dock."

The *Jes-Sea.*

It occurred to me suddenly that Shem had been involved not because he was a close friend but because he knew how to make the boat explode, to make it seem like an accident.

Shem looked at Mother, as if asking whether he should go on. The last few minutes, she'd been quiet and drawn into herself, sagged down into the chair. "Nelle?" Shem said, and she nodded at him.

I watched him take a breath. As he exhaled, his chin quivered. "Joe had already filled the bilge with gasoline and tied the steering wheel so it would take him straight out into the bay. That night after I laid him down inside it, I cranked the boat and left it in neutral while I disconnected the battery cable. Then I throttled it up to ten miles an hour and untied the boat cleat. When it hit choppy water, the loose cable began to bounce around and threw a spark. The boat exploded before it got two hundred yards."

"But why go to all those lengths just to make it look like an accident? That's crazy."

Mother glared at me like her old combative self. "That was the most important thing to your father. He wanted it that way for you, so don't you dare say it was crazy."

I walked over and squatted beside her chair.

It was a relief to me that she could be angry, that there was something left inside her.

"What do you mean, he wanted it that way for *me?*"

She tilted her face down to mine and I saw her eyes filling up again. "He said his dying would be hard on you, but living with his suicide would be a thousand times worse. He couldn't bear your thinking he'd abandoned you."

The room grew quiet.

Somewhere in the mangled remnants of childhood that were left inside me, I knew that what my father had done had been for *me,* for his Whirly Girl, and I didn't know how to bear the weight of that—the merciless blame of his sacrifice.

I closed my eyes and heard my father singing my name soft against my ear. Singing his good-bye.

Jessie Jessie Jessie.

As long as he lived, he did not forget my name.

I dropped my head straight down onto my mother's lap and sobbed my grief into her thin cotton skirt. I could feel the hard, lacy border of her slip press against my forehead. This was supposed to be about Mother emptying out all the dark pockets inside and sorting the contents. It was supposed to be about her remembering things and maybe somehow putting her broken self back together. And it had come to this. To me bent over her lap, her maimed hand coming up to rest on my head.

*   *   *

When we stepped outside onto the sidewalk, the dark blue haze of dusk was everywhere. The mermaid chair's procession had already coursed along the street onto the dock. Climbing into the golf cart, I could see the crowd massed along the rails. I imagined the shrimp boats passing by out on the water with colored lights wound along the raised nets. I pictured the mermaid chair perched on its scrap of coral rug in all that soft, glittering light, freshly splashed and blessed.

Mother sat beside me in the golf cart as we drove through the falling darkness and did not remember she had left her finger on the counter in the store.

CHAPTER
Thirty-four

In May the tides went to work hauling away the dead marsh grass. It drifted along the salt creeks like a constant flotilla of rotting, hay-brown rafts. Early in the mornings, when I knew I would be alone, I stole out to the dock in the rookery. I would stand there with the light soaring across the marsh, filling my nostrils with the egg and sperm smell, and watch the great floating exodus, the immaculate, scouring way nature renews herself.

After I'd learned how my father had died, there was a lifting away of sorrow. I can't explain that, except to say there's release in knowing the truth no matter how anguishing it is. You come finally to the irreducible thing, and there's nothing left to do but pick it up and hold it. Then, at least, you can enter the severe mercy of acceptance.

Mother seemed relieved to have the truth come out of its long hibernation. She went on confessing pieces of it to me, usually in the evenings when the day turned dark and grainy and sifted past the windows. She told me that Kat and Hepzibah had boiled batches of the plant leaves and chunks of the root, cooking them down to the consistency of pea soup. My father had insisted on drinking the brew from one of the chalices used during mass. I'm sure he was trying to help my mother understand that dying is a sacrament, too, that there was holiness in the sacrifice he was making, though I'm sure she never understood it.

I'm not at all sure *I* understood it completely. I didn't know if my father had horned in on God's territory and cut the thread that belonged to the Fates . . . if he'd usurped what wasn't rightly his—the terrifying power to say *when.* Or did he only usurp God's deep heart, laying his life down as a sacrifice, wanting only to take away our suffering? I didn't know if it was hubris or fear or courage or love or all of them.

In the night I dreamed of whales thrusting their sickly bodies onto the shore to die willful deaths. At first I stood there bewildered, screaming for them to go back to the ocean, but in the end I simply walked among them, running my hands along their mountainous backs, easing them toward the mystery they'd chosen.

Mother said my father had held the chalice with both hands and gulped quickly. Later Dominic had sent the cup with Shem to be placed on the boat, fearing that the poison might never be washed out of it. She told me that as he drank, she started to sob, but he'd gone on swallowing until there was no more, and then, looking at her, said, "I didn't just drink my death, Nelle. Try to remember that for me. I drank my life."

What I most wished was that my mother could somehow have remembered that, as he'd wanted her to.

Hepzibah showed up at the door one day with the jar containing Mother's finger. Mother placed it on a lace handkerchief atop her dresser, between the Mary statue and the photograph of Dad on his boat. Gradually other objects appeared around it—three scallop shells, an old starfish, a sand dollar. It began to look like a small shrine.

I didn't ask her what it meant—it seemed wrong, somehow, to intrude—but I felt she was, in some obscure way, offering her finger to the ocean, hoping it might be transformed into something else, the way Sedna's fingers were.

One night, as the breezes off Bone Yard pulled the scent of the sea through the open windows, I went to Mother's room to say good night. She sat at the dresser, gazing at the finger jar. I let my hand brush across her thumb, touching the scar on her index finger. "I wish you'd tell me why you felt you had to do this to yourself," I said.

When she looked at me, her eyes were as clear as I'd ever seen them. She said, "Last February, right before Ash Wednesday, I found dead finger growing on the side of the house by the water spigot. I smelled it from the porch. Two little plants. The next day there were three of them. I'd *never* had it grow in my yard once since Joe died, and then there it was. I couldn't stop thinking about it, Jessie. I dreamed the leaves were growing through the windows into the house.

I had to do something to make it stop. To make everything stop."

She lifted her hand to Dad's face in the photograph, and her eyes welled up. "I wanted to make up for what I did. To undo it. I just wanted him back again."

That was all she said about it. All she would ever say.

She wanted to undo it. She wanted him back.

I don't know if I'll ever understand it. Whatever it was she was trying to do by planting her finger in the rose garden and adorning the jar with sea trinkets, it was more than a sad gesture of atonement. It was a last, desperate reach for him. I believe that what she wanted was to regrow him from all the cleaved, tortured places inside, to re-member him the way he'd been, the way *they'd* been, before everything happened. She wanted to make the guilt and longing stop.

During those days I compulsively painted my father as I imagined he looked that night sitting in the mermaid chair having just drunk his death and his life. Using the photograph on Mother's dresser as a model for his face, I painted him with squinting eyes, his face engraved with weather lines, browned and tough as boot leather—that "old salt" look visible on so many island faces. He sat very tall and regal, as if on a throne, holding the winged mermaids on the chair arms and gazing out at me.

Directly beneath the chair, at the bottom of the canvas, as if down in a subterranean realm under the floor, I painted a rectangular chamber, a secret, magical room. Inside it I painted a little girl.

I worked in the living room and occasionally on the porch, unwilling to hide what I was doing from Mother, who would sit for hours and watch with squeamish wonder as his image came forth, as if observing the birth of a baby.

I felt that way, too, but for different reasons. What I realized was the amazing degree to which my life had been shaped around my father, around his living and dying, the apple peels and the pipe. I saw it clearly as he streamed out from my brushes: Joe Dubois, the hidden, pulsing nucleus around which my life had taken form.

"Who's that in the box under the chair?" Mother asked, peering over my shoulder at the painting.

"I suppose it's me," I told her, slightly irritated at her use of the word "box." I hadn't thought of it quite like that, but I saw how true it was. *The little girl was not in a magic room, a lovely room. She was in a box. The same girl who would grow up to express herself through diminutive art boxes.*

When I was finished with the portrait, I hung it in my bedroom, where it became almost iconic in its presence, in its ability to speak to me of invisible things. It had never been a secret that I'd idealized my father, that I would've done anything to please him—to be the apple of his eye (to use the worst and most obvious cliché)—but what I didn't quite get until the painting was the sadness of all that trying. I hadn't understood the small, powerless places it had taken me. But even more than this, I had never completely realized how this same thing had gone on with Hugh. I'd accommodated myself to him for twenty years without any real idea of what it was to have possession of my own self. To *own* myself, so to speak.

I felt as if I'd found the fairy-tale pea hidden under the mattress, the thing that had kept the princess tossing all those nights, that had quietly made her black and blue.

I would sit cross-legged on the bed staring at the painting and listening to my tapes on the Walkman, thinking what an ideal father Hugh had been, not just to Dee but to me. *God,* to me, too.

I couldn't imagine what it would be like if I took that away. If I tried to relate to more than his fatherly side. Let him be Hugh. Just Hugh.

On Mother's Day, Dee called. I stood in the kitchen holding the wall phone, leaning against the refrigerator. At first the conversation was all about happy Mother's Day and summer plans. She told me she would not be taking classes but going home to be with her father.

At the mention of Hugh, there was a pause, and then her voice rushed at me, full of anger and incomprehension. "Why are you doing this?"

"Doing what?" It was such a stupid thing to say.

"You know what I mean!" she shouted. "You left him. And you didn't even tell me." I could hear her crying, these horrible muffled sounds far away.

"Oh, Dee, I'm sorry." It became one of

those songs you sing in rounds. *I'm sorry, I'm sorry, I'm sorry.*

"Why?" she pleaded. "Why?"

"I don't know how to explain any of this to you."

In my head I could hear Whit in the boat that day, the precise words he'd used. *I never could make them understand that what I needed was somehow to be alone with myself. In a spiritual way, I mean.* He'd called that aloneness *a solitude of being.*

"Try," she said.

There was only so much I could say to her. I drew a breath. "This will sound ridiculous, I guess, but my life had started to feel so stagnant, like it was atrophied. Everything shrunk down to the roles I played. I had loved doing them, Dee, I really had, but they were drying up, and they weren't really me. Do you understand? I felt there had to be some other life beneath the one I had, like an underground river or something, and that I would die if I didn't dig down to it."

Her silence after I'd spoken was a relief to me. I let myself slide down the refrigerator until I was sitting on the floor.

Back there, somewhere, I'd lost the solitude of being that told me who I was. The whole mystery of myself. I'd been incapable of wearing the earth on my arms and legs, of diving and surfacing in my own erotic depths.

"Don't you love Dad anymore?" Dee asked.

"Of course I do. Of course. How could I not love him?" I didn't know why I was saying this to her. How much of it was placation, how much true.

Hugh and I had gone through our days with such good intentions, but with the imagination leaking out of our togetherness. We'd become exceptionally functional partners in the business of making a life. Even in the hidden business of being what the other one needed: good father, good daughter, little girl in a box. All those ghosts that hide in the cracks of a relationship.

It seemed right to have destroyed all that. Not to have hurt Hugh; I would always be sorry for that.

"Are you staying there all summer?" Dee asked.

"I don't know," I told her. "I just know that I—" I didn't know whether to say it, whether she wanted to hear it.

"That you love me," she said, which was exactly the thing I was going to say.

* * *

I showed up at the monastery in the middle of May. The heat had descended in typical fashion—all at once, an oppressive, woolen canopy pitched across the island overnight. It would not be lifted until October.

Approaching the Reception Center, I saw a dozen monks sitting on the wide lawn in the abbey quadrangle hand-tying cast nets. They were spread out in orderly exactitude like chess pieces on a great green board, each with a heap of cotton twine in his lap. I paused, taken back momentarily to my childhood, those days when the monks fled the scourging heat of the Net House for the breezes coming off the marsh.

"The air conditioner quit on them," a voice said, and I turned to find the bald monk I'd met that day in the gift shop when I'd bought Dominic's book. He frowned at me from his huge Jack Benny glasses. It took me a moment to remember his name. Father Sebastian. The humorless one. The one who kept the monastery on the straight and narrow.

"I don't know how you get through the summer in these robes," I replied.

"It's a small sacrifice we make," he said. "People don't want to make sacrifices anymore." The steady way he gazed at me, emphasizing the word "sacrifices," gave me an odd feeling, and I thought suddenly of my father.

I turned to stare again at the monks on the grass.

"Are you looking for Brother Thomas?" he asked.

I whirled around. "No, why would I?" I was stunned by his question, and I'm sure it showed on my face.

"You don't really want me to answer that, do you?" he said.

How could he possibly know about Whit and me? I couldn't believe Whit would have confided in him. In Dominic maybe, but not Sebastian.

"No," I said, and it was barely a whisper. "I don't." I drew back my shoulders and walked away, out into the cloister square toward the abbey church.

The wind had blown snipped-off bits of twine all over the place. It looked as if the Fates had come through on a binge of cutting. One of the monks was chasing a strand, repeatedly reaching for it just as the wind snatched it away. Something about this filled me with sorrow and longing. I began picking up pieces of thread as I walked, whatever little scraps were in my path, tucking them into my pocket. I could feel Sebastian still there, watching me.

I hadn't lied to him. I had not come to see Whit. I was here because no matter how hard I tried, I couldn't resist the morbid fascination of seeing the mermaid chair again in light of what I now knew about my father's dying. But it was also true that I'd come in the morning when I knew that Whit would be on the abbey grounds and not in the rookery. I had washed my hair. I had worn the aqua shirt.

I hadn't seen him in almost a month, not since Mother's hospitalization. The absence had created a strangeness, an incipient, self-fulfilling distance between us that I didn't know how to confront. Much of our time apart had been necessary, dictated by circumstances. But some of it—a lot of it, really—had not. I couldn't account for the part of me that remained removed from him.

The church was empty. I slipped back into the ambulatory, pausing at the entrance to the tiny chapel. The mermaid chair sat alone, the clerestory window behind it siphoning in a frail, trimmed light. My eyes went instantly to the mermaids on the chair arms. Their greens, reds, and golds were the only brightness in the room.

As I'd painted my father, I'd imagined the chair as maternal—the pietà, the immense lap of dying. I'd envisioned the mermaids like exotic midwives on either side of him, their wings conjuring up images of angels carrying him to heaven, their fish tails making me think of night-sea psychopomps bearing him into the dark mother of the ocean. I'd imagined them singing eerie, plaintive songs, crying—not the fake pebbles in the boxes in Kat's shop but real tears. I'd thought that when I actually saw the chair, I would be weighed under by all this, but what I felt was the most extraordinary lightness.

I went and sat down. Leaning my head against the twisting Celtic knot, I let my hands hold on to the mermaids' backs. What came first to my mind was the time I'd spent as a child scattering rose petals around the island as if they were my father's ashes, how I'd especially heaped them *here* on the seat of the mermaid chair. I wondered if I could possibly have recognized the residue his death left behind, the concentration of good-byes.

Sitting there, I understood so little, and yet much more than I had before. My father had died here, but in a way I had, too. When I'd sat in the chair all those weeks ago, I'd given myself over to loving Whit, abandoning my old life. I had begun then to die away.

I sensed that Whit had come into the chapel even before I saw him. He called my name. "Jessie."

He was wearing his robe and his cross.

As he walked toward me, I stood up. The knocking started inside my chest.

"How's Nelle?" he asked.

"Much better. She's out of the hospital."

His face was pinched, and I knew in a way I can't explain that he possessed the same removed piece inside that I did.

"I'm glad," he said.

"Yes, me, too."

I felt the moat widening and thought how like detachment the sounds between us were. He seemed to be waiting for me to say something.

"Father Sebastian told me you wanted to see me," he said, the formality in his voice unmistakable.

My mouth opened in surprise. "But I didn't." Realizing how that must sound, I added, "I mean, I'm happy to see you, but I didn't tell him that."

Whit frowned.

"A while ago when I bumped into him, he made it perfectly clear to me that he knew about us. He was very pointed about it." I felt awkward saying the word "us."

"I'm afraid Sebastian has a nasty habit of reading my journal."

"But that's inexcusable."

The light flickered in the room. I remembered how it had played on his face when he slept. How he'd washed my feet in creek water. I did not understand the mystifying place where our intimacy had flowed back into reserve.

"You know, I wasn't sure until now that he'd actually read it," he said. "I only suspected."

"I had the feeling when Sebastian was talking to me that he was really asking me to leave you alone—without really saying it. I can only imagine how hard he's made it for *you*."

"You would think so, but the truth is, he's been kinder to me since then. Like he wanted me to really do what's best. He told me I should ask myself why I came here, what it means to me to be hidden here with

God. I guess he got tired of waiting for me to figure it out." He shrugged. "Sebastian is a great believer in facing things head-on."

People don't want to make sacrifices anymore.

I think beginnings must have their own endings hidden inside them. Gazing at Whit, I knew that the end had been there the first night we met, back when he'd stood on one side of the monastery wall and I on the other. The sturdy bricks.

Whit knew it. I could tell by the way he'd slid his hands inside the sleeves of his robe, the sadness caked in his eyes. I could see he'd *already* made the sacrifice.

We stood there staring at each other. I wondered if I would've fallen in love with him if he'd been a shoe salesman in Atlanta. It was a bizarre thought, but it seemed somehow the most sensible thought of my life. I doubted I would have, and it was disillusioning to me in the sense of stripping away the last remaining illusions. My falling in love with him had had everything to do with his monkness, his loyalty to what lay deep within him, the self-containment of his solitude, that desire to be transformed. What I'd loved in him most was my own aliveness, his ability to give me back to myself.

It felt cruel and astonishing to realize that our relationship had never belonged out there in the world, in a real house where you wash socks and slice onions. It belonged in the shadowed linings of the soul.

I had come to the irreducible thing, just as I had with my father, and there was nothing to do but accept, to learn to accept, to lie down every night and accept.

I closed my eyes, and it was Hugh I saw. His hands, the hair on his fingers, the Band-Aids on his thumbs. How real all of that was. How ordinary. How achingly beautiful. I wanted him back. Not like before but new, all new. I wanted what came after the passion had blown through: flawed, married love.

Whit said, "I honestly thought I could go through with this, I wanted to." He shook his head and looked down at a fraying place on the dark, carpeted dais.

"I know. Me, too."

I didn't want him to say anything more. I wanted the letting go to be silent, to go quickly.

Whit nodded. A deep, emphatic nod at

something I could not see or hear. He said, "I will miss you."

"I'm sorry." My words cracked as I spoke. I felt I'd been the seducer. I'd sat on the sea rocks like one of Homer's sirens and lured him. Even though he was ending it as much as I, I felt *I* was really the betrayer. That I'd betrayed my confessions of love to him, my promise of anniversaries.

"I don't want you to be sorry," he said. "The thing is, I needed"—he reached out and touched my face, a place near my jaw—"I *needed* to love you."

He could have meant a million things, but what I wanted to believe was that his grief over his wife had deadened his heart and falling in love with me had resurrected it. I wanted to believe that now he would give his heart back to the monastery. He would go on foraging in the rookery, waking to the sound of frogs in the bent island oaks, to the smell of Brother Timothy's bread, catching these little bits of God showing through.

"It's true of both of us, then. I needed to love you, too." It came out with so much awkwardness, so much ineptness, I felt as if I should go on explaining, but he smiled at me and stepped closer.

He said, "I told you we'd be damned and saved both. Remember?"

I tried to smile back at him, but it moved painfully on my lips for only a second before evaporating. I reached for him. We held each other without the slightest worry of someone's wandering by. I did not cry, not then. I held him and felt the tides sweep out from the marsh island where we'd made love. I felt a place inside open up, the secret place where I would carry him. And when he'd left, and I was there alone, I felt the pull that must happen inside the egrets when the moon rises in the early dark—that unbearable tug home.

I walked to Bone Yard Beach and sat on a piece of driftwood that arched out over the sand. I stared at the ocean, where shrimp boats were roosting in thick, green waves. The tide was coming in instead of going out, which seemed backward and ironic to me. It seemed everything should be leaving. That there should be stretches and stretches of emptiness.

I had lost both of them.

Long ago, at the All-Girls Picnic when Mother, Kat, and Hepzibah had walked into the ocean up to their waists, I'd watched them from nearly this same spot. I began to picture them out there, the way they'd giggled as they'd tied their three threads together and thrown them into the waves. Benne and I had wanted to go with them, had *begged* to go.

No, this is just for us. Y'all stay back there.

Who would've imagined what would come out of the knots they'd made that night?

I tugged off my sandals and rolled my pants as high as I could. Despite the heat, the ocean was still chilled from the winter. I had to go in slowly.

When the water swelled above my knees, I stopped and dug in my pocket for the bits of twine I'd gathered off the lawn at the monastery. I wanted to tie a knot that would go on forever. But not with anyone else. With myself.

All my life, in nameless, indeterminate ways, I'd tried to complete myself with someone else—first my father, then Hugh, even Whit, and I didn't want that anymore. I wanted to belong to myself.

I sorted through the cotton strands, wondering if something in me had known what must be done even as I'd collected them.

I stood still with the waves cascading against my thighs, elongating as they flowed beyond me toward the shore.

Jessie. I take you, Jessie . . .

The wind moved sideways past my ears, and I could smell the aloneness in it.

For better or for worse.

The words rose from my chest and recited themselves in my mind.

To love and to cherish.

I took the longest string and tied a knot in the center of it. I gazed at it for a minute, then flung it into the ocean at roughly one o'clock in the afternoon, May 17, 1988, and every day of my life since, I return to that insoluble moment with veneration and homage, as if it possesses the weight and ceremony of marriage.

CHAPTER
Thirty-five

On the last Saturday of May, I stood on the ferry dock with Mother, Kat, Hepzibah, and Benne, all of us lined up at the railing, staring at the wind-chopped bay. White ibis were everywhere. We watched them flying in boomerangs across the bay.

My suitcase sat near the gangplank. Kat had brought a basket of purple beach phlox, Carolina jessamine, and pink oleander blossoms, which she intended to toss at the pontoon when it pulled away, like it was the *Queen Mary*. She poured lemonade from a thermos into little paper cups and handed out benne wafers. She had been adamant about its being a bon voyage party.

Having little appetite, I fed most of my wafers to Max.

"Where will you live now?" Benne asked.

I thought of my big, drafty house, the turret and the stained glass over the doorways, my studio tucked beneath the roof. *Home,* I wanted to tell her, *I'll live at home,* but I wasn't sure I could claim it now.

"I don't know," I said.

"You can always live here," said Mother.

I looked at the faded orange buoys bobbling on the water, marking the crab traps, and felt the twisted tie deep inside that tethered me to her, to this place. For a moment I almost believed I could stay.

"I'll come back," I said, and abruptly broke down crying, setting off a whole chain reaction: Hepzibah, then Benne, Mother, and finally Kat.

"Well, isn't this *fun?*" said Kat, doling out paper napkins. "I always said there's nothing like a lot of bawling women to liven up a party."

Having the opportunity, we fled into laughter.

I was the last one on the ferry. I stood at the rail, as Kat had instructed, so I could see the flower toss. It rained oleander, jessamine, and phlox for all of thirty seconds, but I have wrapped and contained the sight very carefully in my mind. I am still able to close my eyes and see the blossoms light on the water like tiny firebirds.

I stood there watching after the dock disappeared from sight, and I knew they had all climbed into Kat's golf cart by then. As the island slid into the distance, I stored everything away—the bright expanse of water, the crushing scent of the marsh, the wind soaring in canticles across the bay—and tried not to think what waited for me.

Hugh was asleep in his leather chair in the den, wearing black socks worn down at the heels, a book open across his chest— *The Portable Jung.* He'd forgotten to close the curtains, and the windows behind him blazed with darkness and lamplight.

I stood unmoving, startled by the sight of him, a kind of fluttering in my stomach.

My flight had been delayed from Charleston to Atlanta because of thunderstorms, and it was late, close to midnight. I had not told him I was coming. Part of it was pure, cowardly fear, but it was also the hope that I might catch him off guard, and in those one or two moments he would forget what I'd done, and his heart would fill with so much love it would override every justified reason to send me away. That was my foolish, un-reasoned hope.

I'd let myself in with the key we kept hidden under the flagstone at the rear of the house, leaving my suitcase in the foyer beside the front door. Noticing the light in the den, I'd thought only that Hugh had forgotten to turn it out when he went to bed. And here he was.

For whole minutes I stood there listening to the puffing noise he made with his mouth when he slept—rhythmic, sonorous, filled with the rush of years.

His arm dangled over the side of the chair. The little bracelet Dee had made was still on his wrist. Outside, there was thunder far away.

Hugh.

I thought of a time long ago, the year before Dee was born. We'd gone hiking in the Pisgah National Forest up in the Blue Ridge Mountains and come upon a waterfall. It dropped twenty or thirty feet from an overhang of rocks, and we'd stood a moment staring up at the plunging water, the way it flashed and held the sun, hundreds of tiny, iridescent rainbows fluttering out of it like a swarm of dragonflies.

We'd yanked off our clothes, tossing them on rocks and lady ferns. It was hot, the deep of August, and the water still had the memory of snow in it. Holding hands, we picked our way over mossy stones until we stood beneath the overhang with the water crashing down in front of us. The spray was like a driving rain, the sound deafening. Hugh smoothed my wet hair behind my ears and kissed my shoulders and breasts. We made love pressed against the cliff face. For weeks I felt the water hitting the earth inside my body.

Watching him sleep now, I wanted to pull him back into that niche of wild rock. I would have been happy just to pull him into the ordinary niche we'd carved out together with little domestic tools for all these years, but I didn't know how to return to either one of those places. How to make them the same place.

I felt amazed at the choosing one had to do, over and over, a million times daily—

choosing love, then choosing it again, how loving and being in love could be so different.

Rolling his head to the side, he shifted in the chair. Sometimes I think it was my remembering that woke him, that the waterfall spilled out of my mind and caused him to open his eyes.

He gazed at me with sleep and confusion. "You're here," he said. Not to me, I realized, but to himself.

I smiled at him, but I didn't say anything, unable to scrape my voice up out of my throat.

He stood. He lifted his shoulders. I don't think he knew what to feel any more than what to say. He stood in his stocking feet and stared at me, a private, unreadable expression on his face. A car went by out on the street, the motor gunning and falling away.

When he spoke, the words sounded curled up and wounded. "What are you doing here?"

I think now of the ten thousand things I could have said to him, whether it would have made any difference if I'd gone down on my knees and canted all my transgressions.

"I . . . I brought you something," I answered, and, raising my hand as if motioning him to wait, I went to the foyer for my pocket-book. I returned, digging through it. Unzipping my coin purse, I took out his wedding ring.

"You left this on Egret Island," I said, and held the ring out to him, grasping it between my right thumb and forefinger, lifting my left hand so he could see I was wearing my ring, too. "Oh, Hugh, I want to come home," I said. "I want to be here, with *you.*"

He didn't move, didn't reach for the ring.

"I'm so sorry," I said. "I'm so sorry I hurt you."

He still didn't move, and it began to feel as if I were holding the ring across a chasm, that if I dropped it, it would fall through the earth. But I couldn't draw back my hand. It was held by that mysterious quality that appears in cats when they've climbed to the top of the tree, to the end of the limb, and then, seeing with horror where they are, simply refuse to come down. I went on holding the ring out to him. *Take it, please take it—* hoping so hard I pinched the imprint of the ring into the pads of my fingers.

He stepped backward before turning and left the room.

When he'd gone, I set the ring on the

table beside his chair. I set it beneath the lamp, which I could not bear to switch off.

I slept in the guest room, or, to be accurate—I *lay awake* in the guest room. As atonement I kept forcing myself to see him in that moment as he'd turned to leave, his profile against the gleaming windows. The hardness he felt toward me had risen to his face and tensed in his cheek.

Forgiveness was so much harder than being remorseful. I couldn't imagine the terrible surrender it would take.

It rained much of the night, coming down in great black wheels and shaking the trees. I saw dawn push at the window before I finally fell asleep and woke not long afterward to the aroma of sausage and eggs, to the overwhelming smell of Hugh cooking.

There are things without explanation, moments when life will become arranged in such odd ways that you imagine a whole vocabulary of meaning inside them. The breakfast smell struck me like that.

That was where our marriage had left off, that day back in February—February 17, Ash Wednesday, the day of ashes and endings. Hugh had cooked breakfast, sausage and eggs. It had been the final thing before I'd left. The benediction.

I went downstairs. Hugh stood at the stove, holding a spatula. The frying pan was crackling furiously. He'd set two plates on the breakfast bar.

"Hungry?" he said.

I wasn't at all, but knowing his abiding faith in the power of such breakfasts, I nodded and smiled at him, sensing the tremor of some quiet new rhythm wanting to establish itself.

I climbed onto the bar chair. He spooned half of a vegetable omelette onto my plate, sausage links, a buttered English muffin. "There you go," he said.

He paused, and I felt him just behind me, breathing in an uneven way. I stared into my plate, wanting to look around at him but afraid I would ruin whatever was about to happen.

The moment seemed to hang in the air, revolving, deliberate, like a bit of glass lifted to the sun and turned slowly to refract the light.

Suddenly he laid his hand on my arm. I sat still as he slid it slowly up to my shoulder and back down.

"I missed you," he said, leaning close to my ear.

I clutched his hand almost fiercely, pulling his fingers to my face, touching them with my lips. After a moment he gently pulled them away and put the other half of the omelette on his plate.

We sat in our kitchen and ate. Through the windows I could see the washed world, the trees and the grass and the shrubs silvered with raindrops.

There would be no grand absolution, only forgiveness meted out in these precious sips. It would well up from Hugh's heart in spoonfuls, and he would feed it to me. And it would be enough.

Epilogue

As the ferry nudges against the dock on Egret Island, the captain blows his horn a second time, and I go out to the railing. I remember the flowers spilling into the water as the boat pulled away last May. The sad little bon voyage party. It seems now like a piece of history starting to sift into dust and, at the same time, as if I have only just been here. As if the petals will still be floating on the water.

It is February now. The marshlands are floods of golden yellow. The color settles on me like the heat and light of the sun. The island will always be the fixed point of the migrating world.

Out there on the dock, Max is barking. I think of the mermaids hanging from the ceiling in Kat's shop, the egrets flying above Caw Caw Creek, the bare rosebushes in the monastery garden. I picture the mermaid chair alone in the chapel. The whole island rises up to me, and I have a moment when I honestly don't know if I can step off the boat. I stand there and let it pass, *knowing* it will pass. All things do.

When I told Hugh I needed to come and see Mother, to be here on Ash Wednesday, he said, "Of course." Then a moment later, "Is it just your mother you're going to see?"

Not that often, but once in a while, the sorrow and mistrust will form across his eyes. His face will close in. And he will be gone. His mind and body will still be there, of course, but his heart—his spirit, even—will go to the outer banks of our marriage and camp. A day or two later, he will be back. I will find him cooking breakfast, whistling, bearing more forgiveness.

Each day we pick our way through unfamiliar terrain. Hugh and I did not resume our old marriage—that was never what I wanted, and it was not what Hugh wanted either—rather we laid it aside and began a whole new one. Our love is not the same. It feels both young and old to me. It feels wise, as an old woman is wise after a long life, but also fresh and tender, something we must cradle and protect. We have become closer in some ways, the pain we experienced weaving tenacious knots of intimacy, but there is a separateness as well, the necessary distances.

I have not told him yet about the knot I tied in my thread that day in the ocean. I talk to him instead about the mermaids. They belong to themselves, I told him once, and he frowned in that way he does when weighing something he's unsure of. I know at times he's afraid of the separateness, my independence, this abiding new loyalty I have to myself now, but I believe he will come to love this part of me, just as I do.

I tell him, smiling, that it was the mermaids who brought me home. I mean, to the water and the mud and the pull of the tides in my own body. To the solitary island submerged so long in myself, which I desperately needed to find. But I also try to explain they brought me home to *him.* I'm not sure he understands any more than I do how belonging to myself allows me to belong more truly to him. I just know it's true.

"No, no, I'm not planning to see him," I said to Hugh that day. "You can come with me if you want. We'll both go."

"It's okay. You should go by yourself," he said. "You need to go back and face the island and be done with it."

Now, stepping onto the island, I feel myself bracing, feel my need to gather everything up so I can finally lay it down.

Mother's house has been repainted cobalt blue. It is practically radiating when I arrive, chauffeured by Kat in the golf cart. She lays on the air horn in the front yard, and the rest of them come out onto the porch. Mother, Hepzibah, Benne.

Inside, sitting at the kitchen table, I look at them and see how everything continues and equally how it changes.

Mother tells me how Kat takes her across the bay every month to see the doctor, that she is on much less medication now. Her finger is still in the jar of alcohol on her dresser. Last August she went back to her passion for feeding the monks, abandoning Julia Child for James Beard. "The monks miss Julia's food," she tells me. "But they'll get over it."

When I ask Hepzibah about the Grand Gullah Tour, she sits straighter in her African print dress and tells me it's listed these days in all the tourist magazines in Charleston, that she may have to offer it every single day by the time summer comes around.

Kat surprises me most. She has written up her own booklet to sell along with Dominic's in the Mermaid's Tale. Called *Island Dog,* it's the legendary story of Max meeting the ferry every day with unfailing precision. Shaking her head and causing her precarious hairdo to slide out of its combs, she announces that she and Max will be on the television news next week.

Benne adds that Max is excited and not at all nervous.

They want to talk about my paintings, so I let them. I've lost my shyness about all that. Kat chirps about my "Diving Women" show at the Phoebe Pember Gallery in Charleston last October. I had *her* to thank for it. She was the one who packed all the paintings I'd left behind and took them to the gallery owner herself. "I knew she would want them," she said.

I hadn't come for the opening—I wasn't ready to come back then—but the Egreteers had gone and stood in for me. I am working now on a series of island landscapes. Once in a while, though, I stop and paint one of my quirky mermaids for Kat, just to make her happy. The last one was of a real mermaid, working as a saleswoman inside Kat's own shop. She stands behind the counter selling mermaid trinkets to the tourists, wearing a T-shirt that says THE MERMAID'S TALE.

When Mother asks about Dee, I don't know how much to say. The truth is that Dee was shaken by what happened between Hugh and me. There was a brief period at the end of last summer when she talked about withdrawing from school, taking a semester off. I think she only wanted to be near us, to protect us somehow, as if she bore some responsibility in it all. We had to sit her down and tell her we would be okay, better than okay, that our problems had had nothing to do with her, only with ourselves. In the end she'd gone back to Vanderbilt, more serious, more grown up. Despite that, she called before I left home to say she was writing Hugh's birthday song: "If Sofas Could Talk."

What I tell Mother is that Dee has

switched her major from English to premed, that she has decided to be a psychiatrist like Hugh. Mother wants to know if Dee's decision has anything to do with what she did to her fingers. "No," I say. "I think it has more to do with what *I* did." I laugh, but there's truth in it.

The five of us talk all afternoon. Till the sky darkens and the palmettos make pronged shadows at the window.

As they are leaving, Kat tugs me aside, over to a private place in the yard beside the bathtub Mary. She hands me a tan canvas bag, which I recognize instantly. It is the one Whit carried in the johnboat on rookery rounds.

"Dominic brought this to the shop a couple of weeks ago," she says. "He asked me to give it to you."

I do not open it then, but wait until Mother is asleep and I am alone in my room.

I take everything out and lay it across the bed. Four dried brown apple peels tucked inside a plastic bag. A battered box of Mermaid Tears. White egret feathers. The turtle skull. My father's pipe.

All the things I'd left inside the crab trap in Whit's hermitage are here. During the past year, not a week had gone by that I didn't think about them, wishing I could've managed to go back for them.

Whit's letter is at the bottom of the bag.

Dear Jessie,

I am returning your things. I have kept them all this time in my cottage, thinking I would give them to you myself when you returned to the island. I didn't want to intrude on your life in Atlanta by sending them in the mail. I felt when you were ready, you would return for them.

I am not here, however, to give them to you in person. I will leave the monastery February 1. I took solemn vows last August, but, ironically enough, decided at Christmas that I would not stay after all.

I want to be in the world again. I understand now that a large part of me is not so much hidden here with God but hiding. I have decided to take back the hazard of life. I came here wanting God, but truthfully I was also looking for some kind of immunity from life. There is none.

And, of course, I may find that God is out there, too. Dominic reminded me that "God is the one whose center is everywhere and

circumference is nowhere." I'll go see if he's right.

At first it was difficult for me to go back to the hermitage, to remember you there, to realize I would know you only as a memory or a longing. But finally I'm able to think of our time together without regret. You brought me deeper into life—how could I regret that?

I want you to be well. Please be happy.

Your Whit

I sit in my Mother's blue house and cry into my hands. When that is done, I close the long year of my life, knowing it will stay with me like the turtle skull worn down by the sea, shining and white-boned.

The last thing Hugh said to me when I left was this: "You *are* coming back this time, right?" He was smiling, teasing, wanting to lighten the tension we both felt at my returning.

I look toward the window. I want to tell him, *Yes, I'm coming back, Hugh. When I die, it will be your face I see hovering over me, whether in flesh or in memory. Don't you know? What I want is you. What I want is the enduring. The beautiful enduring.*

Author's Note

The Mermaid Chair is a work of fiction. The story, the characters, and the setting come purely from my imagination.

I've imagined Egret Island as part of the beautiful necklace of barrier islands along the coast of South Carolina, but you will not find the island on a map. It's not a real place. Nevertheless, it's similar to existing South Carolina islands when it comes to its beach, maritime forest, tidal marshes, estuaries, creeks, birds, and animals. I drew on numerous natural history and nature guidebooks; Todd Ballantine's *Tideland Treasure* was particularly useful. All the plants, trees, and flora referred to in the book are real, though I took the liberty of inventing one fictitious plant that you will be able to distinguish in retrospect.

I've explored numerous barrier islands in South Carolina, but it was Bull Island—an uninhabited and pristine place—that was often in the back of my mind as I wrote. Not only did I position Egret Island geographically where Bull Island is located on South Carolina's coastline, I also borrowed the name of Bull Island's magnificent beach: Bone Yard.

St. Eudoria is not a real saint in the Catholic Church, as far as I know, though I based her story on accounts of saints who mutilated their bodies in the pursuit of holiness.

The legend of Sedna is a genuine Native American tale from the Inuit people, which has several variations. In recounting the story in the novel, I've attempted to be true to its source.

The monastery of St. Senara is nonexistent. In writing about it I've relied on a list of books too long to enumerate and on my years of study of contemplative spirituality and the monastic life.

The Gullah culture, which is referred to in

the novel, is a distinct heritage belonging to African-American descendants of slaves who settled along the southeast coast. The culture contains its own customs, food, art, and language, some of which appear in the novel. The Gullah phrases that I've used are part of the Gullah language still spoken in parts of South Carolina. I'm indebted to the wonderful book *Gullah Cultural Legacies* by Emory S. Campbell.

This novel began one summer day in 2001 when my friend Cheri Tyree mentioned that she'd seen a "mermaid chair" during a visit to England. I'm deeply grateful to her for this chance comment, which led me to the chair that sits in St. Senara Church in the ancient village of Zennor, in the beautiful and magical land of Cornwall. The chair is made from two fifteenth-century bench ends, one of which is carved with a mysterious mermaid. The carving is associated with the fabled Mermaid of Zennor, who fell in love with one of the church's choristers, then lured him into the sea.

Little historical information is available about St. Senara, the saint for whom the Cornish church is named, but I was intrigued by a legend suggesting that before Senara's conversion, she was a Celtic princess named Asenora.

Armed with these two morsels of inspiration—the historical mermaid chair and the bit of lore about Senara and Asenora—I began to weave my own story. I created a distinctly different mermaid chair for the novel—different in appearance, in history, and in the mythology that surrounds it—though I did use some fragments from the Mermaid of Zennor myth. I am indebted and grateful to St. Senara Church in Cornwall, for without its famous chair, this novel could not have been written.

Finally, I would like to acknowledge two books that became my companions as I immersed myself in the symbolism, mythology, art, and history of mermaids: *Sirens* by Meri Lao and *Mermaids,* compiled by Elizabeth Ratisseau.